REMAINING

A Novel

John Faulkner

ISBN: 978-1-7645335-1-5

Chapter 1

By the time the hall is full, the air has changed.

Not dramatically. Not with shouting or sudden movement. Just a tightening—like a room that has collectively decided something matters, even if no one has said what it is yet.

Elija remains where he is.

The stone bench curves along the inner wall, half-shadowed, unadorned. It is not a seat of honour. It is simply a place that happens to be there.

He sits as though he belongs to the room—not as though he owns it.

Across the hall, the long table has been cleared of yesterday's papers. New ones sit stacked at one end, weighted with a small brass seal. Someone has placed a bowl of water near the centre, as if to suggest calm by symbol alone.

It does not work.

Marin arrives without announcement. She steps into the hall with the same quiet steadiness she always carries and takes her place near the far corner, where she can see everyone without being seen too much.

She does not look at Elija immediately.

She never does.

When she finally does, it is not to check him. It is simply recognition. Like seeing a tree that has not moved in the wind and not needing to interpret it.

Elija nods once.

Marin does not nod back.

Not because she refuses him. Because she refuses performance as well.

A man named Corven stands at the head of the table, fingers resting on the brass seal, eyes scanning the room with the careful seriousness of someone who knows that order is maintained through timing.

Corven has a way of speaking that makes listeners feel responsible.

Even before he says anything.

He clears his throat and begins.

"We are not here to accuse," he says. "We are here to clarify."

Several people murmur agreement. A few nod too quickly, eager to be aligned with anything that sounds reasonable.

Elija does not react.

Corven's gaze flicks toward him, then away again—like someone stepping around a stone they do not want to trip over.

“Reports have come,” Corven continues, “that the outer district has refused the levy.”

The words hang.

Not because a levy is sacred, but because refusal is dangerous. Refusal implies options. Options imply that the centre cannot compel.

Someone near the middle of the hall speaks before thinking.

“They can’t refuse.”

Corven holds up one hand—not to silence, but to steady.

“It appears they have.”

A soft wave of discomfort moves through the room. People shift in their seats. A chair scrapes. Someone whispers a name and stops halfway through it, as if saying it aloud might grant it more power.

Corven looks down at the papers.

“There is also the matter of the gate.”

This time, the silence is thicker.

The gate is not a literal gate. Not exactly. It is a point on the old road where the district boundary narrows, where watchers are posted, where goods are recorded and passage is noted. A small thing. A practical thing.

And yet it has become a place where control feels visible.

“Two nights in a row,” Corven says, “the watchers were relieved without request. The ledger was untouched. The seals were unbroken. But the watchers were… dismissed.”

“By whom?” someone asks.

Corven does not answer immediately.

His eyes lift, scanning the hall once more.

“By someone with authority,” he says.

The room shifts again, the way it does when a truth is spoken that everyone already sensed but hoped would be avoided.

Corven’s gaze lands, finally, directly on Elija.

Not accusatory. Not openly.

Just too direct to be innocent.

Elija meets his eyes calmly.

Corven tilts his head, a small gesture that might be interpreted as respect if it did not carry such calculation.

“Elija,” he says, “you have been seen at the boundary.”

Elija nods once.

“I have.”

A pause.

Corven waits, inviting elaboration without asking for it.

Elija does not fill the space.

Corven’s mouth tightens slightly. He leans forward, as if softening.

“We are not questioning your presence,” he says. “We are questioning what your presence means.”

Elija considers the sentence, not as a challenge, but as a confession.

"You want it to mean something," he says.

A few people shift, uncomfortable with how directly that lands.

Corven keeps his voice steady.

"Meaning matters," he replies. "People are unsettled. The district is watching. They are interpreting."

Elija's gaze moves past him, out toward the doorway where the light falls in a long line across the floor.

"They always interpret," he says quietly.

Corven's fingers tighten on the seal.

"We need clarity," he says. "We need you to state, publicly, whether you support the refusal."

Elija looks back at him.

"And if I do not?" he asks, not hostile—just honest.

Corven opens his hands as though appealing to the room itself.

"Then we have no way to contain what is spreading."

Spreading.

As if calm could be contagious.

As if rest could become revolt.

Someone from the back speaks sharply.

"This is not a time for riddles."

Another adds, “Silence is a decision.”

Elija does not flinch.

He hears the fear beneath the sentences. It has the same sound everywhere, regardless of whose mouth it uses.

Corven returns his attention to him.

“Stand,” he says, and the word is so ordinary, so small, and yet the room feels like it shifts around it.

Elija does not move.

The tension rises—quietly, steadily. It is not anger yet. It is something more familiar.

Expectation.

Corven’s tone becomes slightly firmer.

“This is not about theatre,” he says. “This is about responsibility.”

Elija’s eyes remain on him.

“I am responsible,” he says.

“Then show it,” Corven replies.

Elija breathes in, slow and even.

“When did showing become the measure?” he asks.

A murmuring wave travels through the hall again. Some people lean forward. Some lean back. A few glance at each other, as if checking whether this was allowed to be said.

Corven’s cheeks flush faintly.

“We are accountable to the people,” he says. “They need to see stability.”

Elija nods, as though he agrees.

“They do,” he says.

“And you are undermining it,” Corven adds, the edges of frustration finally surfacing.

Elija’s face remains unchanged.

“I am not undermining stability,” he says. “I am revealing what you have built stability on.”

The words are not loud. They do not accuse. They simply expose a foundation that prefers to remain unnamed.

The room goes still.

Corven’s eyes narrow slightly.

“And what is that?” he asks.

Elija glances down at the brass seal—small, heavy, gleaming in the light.

“Fear,” he says.

The word falls into the hall like a stone dropped into water. Not because it is dramatic, but because it is accurate.

A few people stiffen. Someone scoffs softly, as if dismissing it could make it untrue.

Corven’s voice lowers.

“Be careful,” he says.

Elija looks up again.

“I am,” he replies.

Corven gestures toward the seal, then toward the papers.

“The levy will be enforced,” he says. “The gate will be restored. The watchers will be reinstated.”

“And the district?” someone asks.

Corven’s jaw tightens.

“They will comply.”

Elija does not interrupt.

He does not argue.

He does not oppose.

That is what makes the room uneasy. Opposition would be familiar. It would give them something to push against.

Instead, Elija sits, present, watching, unthreatened.

Marin shifts slightly in her corner. Her eyes flick to Corven, then back to Elija.

There is a conversation happening beneath the words, and everyone can feel it, even if no one names it.

Corven notices Marin’s movement and seizes it.

“Marin,” he says, “you have served at the boundary. You know what refusal invites.”

Marin’s expression remains neutral.

“I know what fear produces,” she says.

A few people inhale sharply, as if she has spoken too much.

Corven’s gaze hardens.

“This is not helpful,” he says.

Marin does not respond.

Corven turns back to Elija.

“Stand,” he says again, and this time it is not invitation. It is command wrapped in courtesy.

Elija’s hands rest loosely on his knees. He looks at Corven as if looking through him—not with contempt, but with clarity.

“I won’t,” he says simply.

The words are quiet.

The effect is not.

The room erupts—not in shouting, but in overlapping voices, sharp whispers, exclamations, the scraping of chairs as people shift and turn toward each other.

“He can’t refuse.”

“He just did.”

“What does he think he is doing?”

“Is this rebellion?”

Corven raises both hands, trying to regain control of the room.

"This is exactly what I mean," he says, voice firm now. "This is destabilising."

Elija remains seated.

"I am not destabilising," he says, calm enough that it feels almost unreal. "I am unmoving."

Corven stares at him as if he cannot decide whether to be angry or afraid.

Because anger assumes you can win.

Fear is what comes when you suspect you can't.

Corven steps away from the table and walks toward Elija.

He stops directly in front of him.

"You are not above this council," he says.

Elija looks up at him.

"I am not above you," he replies.

The words confuse the room. They do not know how to hold a statement that refuses both submission and domination.

Corven's voice tightens.

"Then what are you?"

Elija pauses.

Not for drama.

For truth.

"I am already here," he says.

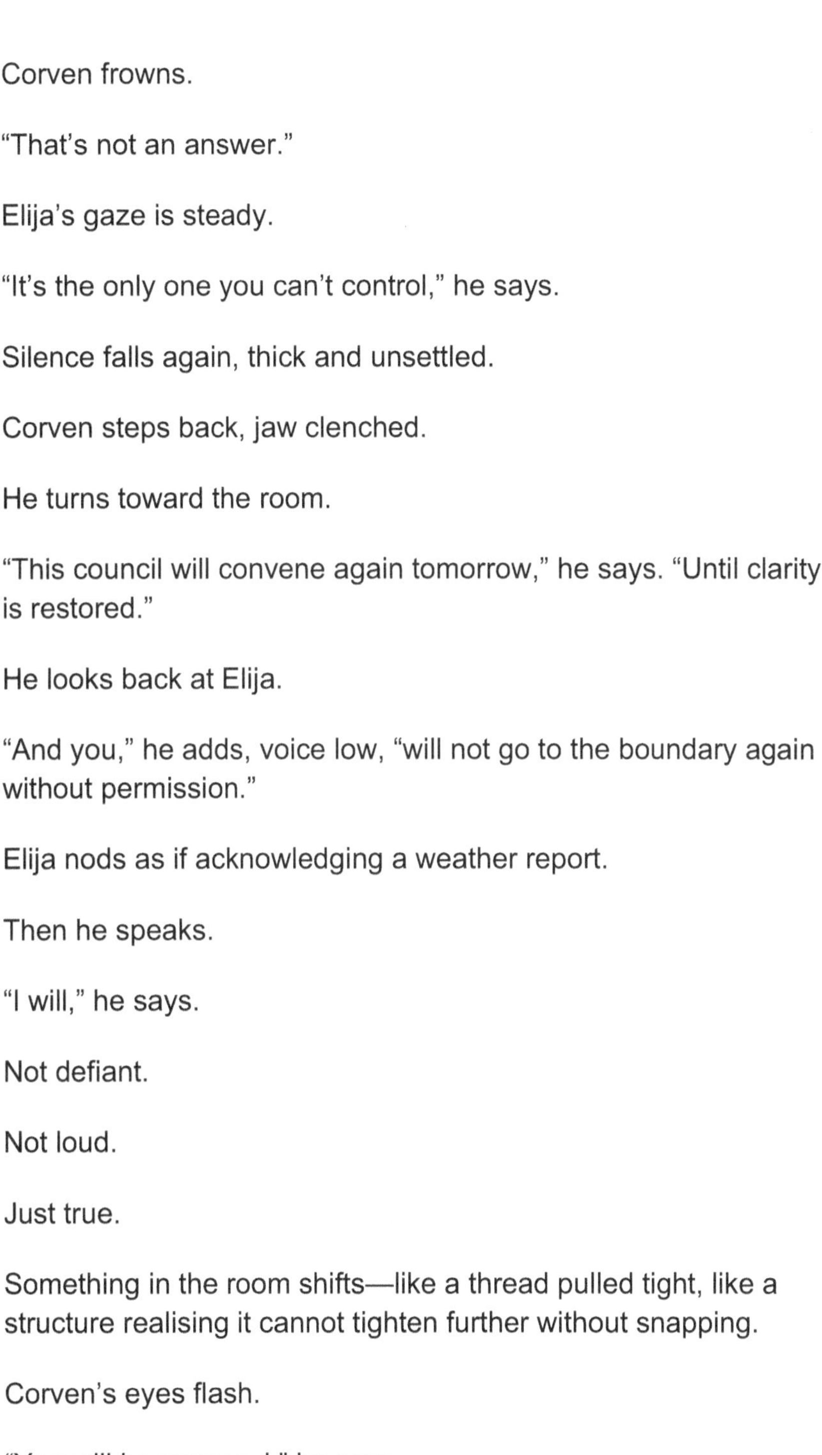

Corven frowns.

“That’s not an answer.”

Elija’s gaze is steady.

“It’s the only one you can’t control,” he says.

Silence falls again, thick and unsettled.

Corven steps back, jaw clenched.

He turns toward the room.

“This council will convene again tomorrow,” he says. “Until clarity is restored.”

He looks back at Elija.

“And you,” he adds, voice low, “will not go to the boundary again without permission.”

Elija nods as if acknowledging a weather report.

Then he speaks.

“I will,” he says.

Not defiant.

Not loud.

Just true.

Something in the room shifts—like a thread pulled tight, like a structure realising it cannot tighten further without snapping.

Corven’s eyes flash.

“You will be removed,” he says.

Elija's expression does not change.

"I can't be," he replies.

A few people laugh—sharp and humourless.

Corven leans in.

"Everything can be removed," he says.

Elija looks at him quietly.

"No," he says. "Only what was held up by fear."

He stands then.

Not in response to the command.

Not to prove anything.

He stands because the meeting is over, and he does not need to remain seated to stay seated.

The distinction is subtle.

But it lands.

He walks toward the doorway as voices scatter behind him, the hall filling with agitation that does not know what to do with someone who refuses to react.

Marin falls into step beside him, the air cooler in the corridor.

"You didn't need to say that much," she says.

Elija glances at her, faint amusement in his eyes.

"I didn't," he agrees.

Marin's gaze stays forward.

“They’ll come harder now.”

Elija nods.

“I know.”

“And you’ll still go to the boundary.”

He does not answer immediately.

Not because he is unsure.

Because he does not live from inevitability.

He lives from alignment.

“Yes,” he says finally.

Marin exhales, a small sound that might have been worry if she were the worrying type.

“Why?” she asks.

Elija slows near the archway where light spills across the stone, and for a moment he looks almost like a boy again, not because he is young, but because he is unarmoured.

“Because they think authority must be stood up,” he says.

Marin waits.

Elija continues, voice quiet.

“And because someone out there is being crushed by the need to prove they’re allowed to live.”

Marin’s eyes flick toward him.

Elija's gaze remains outward, toward the road that leads away from the hall, down toward the narrowing boundary.

He does not say it, but the implication hangs between them like a presence:

Somewhere else, once, someone had remained.

The ground had held.

And now, the pressure was returning in a new form.

Not as distance.

As demand.

Elija steps into the light and walks on.

Behind them, inside the hall, Corven is still speaking—still trying to restore clarity through control.

But the air has changed.

Not because Elija won.

Because he did not play.

And the system does not know what to do with that.

Chapter 2

The next morning, the boundary is already crowded when Elija arrives.

Not with people—though there are a few—but with expectation. It hangs in the air like humidity, invisible and thick, making even small movements feel deliberate.

The road narrows here. It always has. Stone walls draw closer, guiding carts and travellers into a single line before widening again beyond the gate. The watchers' post sits to the left, a low structure with a slanted roof and a table scarred by years of ledgers, seals, and ink stains.

Two watchers stand when Elija approaches.

Not because they are required to.

Because they have been told to.

"Morning," one of them says, attempting casual familiarity.

Elija nods. "Morning."

They wait.

He does not slow.

He does not announce his purpose.

He walks toward the table and stops beside it, close enough to see the fresh ink in the ledger, the seal placed deliberately near the edge, as if proximity could borrow authority.

The younger watcher clears his throat.

"You weren't meant to come today," he says.

Elija looks at him kindly. "I know."

The older watcher shifts his weight. "We've been instructed—"

"I know," Elija says again.

The repetition is not dismissive.

It is relieving.

The older watcher exhales. "Then why are you here?"

Elija glances down the road, where it curves away from the settlement and disappears into the trees.

"Because standing here isn't helping anyone," he says.

The younger watcher stiffens. "We're doing our job."

Elija nods. "I know."

Again.

The ledger lies open, the day's page blank.

The seal gleams in the light.

Elija places his hand flat on the table—not claiming it, not moving anything—just resting his palm there, feeling the rough grain beneath his skin.

"When did this place become heavy?" he asks.

The older watcher looks away. "It's always been like this."

Elija shakes his head slightly. "No," he says. "It hasn't."

The younger watcher bristles. "You don't know that."

Elija's gaze returns to him. "I do."

A pause.

The sound of a cart approaches from down the road. Wheels on stone. The low murmur of voices.

The watchers straighten, instinctively adopting the posture they have learned equals authority.

Elija does not move.

The cart draws closer. A family sits atop it, tired but hopeful. Their eyes flick toward the watchers, then toward Elija, confusion passing briefly across their faces.

The older watcher steps forward.

"Papers," he says.

The man on the cart hesitates, then reaches into his coat.

Elija lifts a hand—not to stop him, but to slow the moment.

"May I?" Elija asks quietly.

The older watcher's jaw tightens.

“We’ve been told not to defer to you,” he says.

Elija nods. “I’m not asking you to.”

The watcher hesitates, then steps back half a pace.

Elija looks up at the man on the cart.

“Where are you going?” he asks.

“East,” the man replies. “To my brother’s land.”

“And the levy?” Elija asks.

The man grimaces. “Paid last season. Not this one.”

Elija nods.

He turns to the watchers.

“Let them pass,” he says.

The younger watcher’s eyes widen. “We can’t.”

“You can,” Elija replies. “You don’t want to.”

The distinction hangs there.

The older watcher looks between Elija and the family. Sweat beads at his temple.

“If we let them through,” he says, “we’ll be disciplined.”

Elija meets his gaze.

“For standing,” he says.

The older watcher swallows.

The younger watcher speaks sharply. “This is exactly what they warned us about.”

Elija turns to him. “What?”

“That you’d make it impossible to do our jobs,” he says.

Elija’s voice remains calm. “I’m showing you what your job has become.”

The cart creaks as the man shifts uneasily.

Elija looks back at the family.

“You may pass,” he says.

The man hesitates. “We don’t want trouble.”

“You won’t cause any,” Elija says.

The older watcher takes a breath.

“Go,” he says quietly.

The younger watcher stares at him. “You can’t just—”

“I can,” the older watcher replies. “I am.”

The family urges the cart forward, wheels rolling past the post, past the table, past Elija. As they pass, the woman on the cart meets Elija’s eyes.

She nods—not in gratitude, but in relief.

When the cart disappears down the road, the younger watcher rounds on Elija.

“This will come back on us,” he says.

Elija nods. "Yes."

"And on you," the watcher adds.

Elija's gaze is steady. "No."

The watcher scoffs. "You think you're immune?"

Elija considers the word.

"I think," he says slowly, "that standing in fear makes you visible in ways resting never does."

The older watcher sits heavily on the bench.

"I didn't sleep last night," he says quietly.

Elija turns to him.

"Because of the order?" Elija asks.

The man nods. "Because I knew it wasn't right."

Elija does not console him.

He does not praise him.

He simply says, "Then today helped."

The man lets out a shaky breath.

The younger watcher kicks the dirt.

"You're going to force this place to choose," he mutters.

Elija looks down the road again.

"It already has," he says.

Footsteps approach from the settlement side.

Marin appears, her pace unhurried, eyes taking in the scene without surprise.

She looks at the open ledger. The unbroken seal. The empty road.

“They won’t like this,” she says.

Elija smiles faintly. “They already don’t.”

Marin’s gaze flicks to the watchers.

“Are you alright?” she asks them.

The older watcher nods. The younger does not answer.

Marin turns back to Elija.

“You didn’t stand,” she observes.

Elija glances down at the stone beneath his feet.

“I did,” he says. “Just not how they wanted.”

Marin exhales, something like admiration in the sound.

“They’ll call this insubordination,” she says.

“They already have,” Elija replies.

“And you’ll keep coming,” she says.

Elija nods. “Until they stop needing watchers.”

Marin studies him.

“That could take a long time.”

Elija’s voice is quiet.

“I have it.”

They stand together for a moment, the boundary suddenly lighter than it was when Elija arrived.

Not because the system has changed.

But because one person has stopped lending it weight.

Behind them, in the hall, decisions are already being reframed as discipline.

Ahead of them, the road remains open.

And somewhere in between, a truth settles in the dust:

Standing was never the point.

Presence was.

And the weight everyone feared had never belonged to them at all.

Chapter 3

By the following morning, the story has changed.

Not in substance.

In tone.

No one says Elija overstepped. No one names the boundary incident as defiance. The words chosen are softer, more careful—language that suggests concern without accusation.

"Unhelpful."
"Confusing."
"Premature."

Pressure without shape is always the most efficient kind.

Elija notices it first in the way people speak to him—not colder, not warmer, just more precise. Questions are framed as invitations. Invitations carry expectations.

A message is left for him at his door, neatly folded, unsigned.

> *Please attend the midmorning session.*
> *Your presence is requested.*

Requested.

Not required.

Elija folds the note once and leaves it on the table.

When he arrives at the hall, the seating has changed.

The bench along the wall is still there, but a chair has been placed near the long table—angled slightly outward, unmistakably meant for him.

Not a throne.

Not a trap.

A relocation.

Marin is already inside, standing near the far column, arms loosely folded.

She raises an eyebrow.

Elija almost smiles.

He does not take the chair.

He walks past it and sits on the bench as he always has.

The chair remains empty, its meaning hovering awkwardly between intention and refusal.

A few people glance at it, then at him, then away again.

Corven enters last.

He pauses when he sees the empty chair, then smooths his expression and takes his place at the table.

“We’re glad you came,” he says.

Elija nods.

Corven’s fingers rest on the papers, unsealed this time.

“There’s been discussion,” he continues. “About yesterday.”

Elija waits.

“It appears,” Corven says carefully, “that your actions caused unnecessary tension.”

Elija considers the word.

“Tension existed before I arrived,” he says.

Corven tilts his head. “Perhaps. But your presence accelerated it.”

Elija looks at the empty chair.

“Only because it was already under strain,” he replies.

A murmur moves through the room.

Corven presses on.

“We’re concerned,” he says, “that you’re functioning as a symbol.”

Elija meets his gaze.

“I haven’t offered one,” he says.

“Symbols don’t need consent,” Corven replies. “They emerge.”

Elija nods. “So does fear.”

The word is not forbidden, but it lands heavily every time.

Corven exhales slowly.

“We are asking you,” he says, “to help us shape this.”

Elija hears the request beneath the politeness.

“Shape how?” he asks.

“By clarifying your position,” Corven says. “Publicly. With us.”

Elija is quiet for a moment.

“Clarify for whom?” he asks.

“For the settlement,” Corven replies quickly.

Elija glances around the room.

“For you,” he says.

Corven’s eyes narrow slightly, not in anger, but in calculation.

“Authority requires shared understanding,” he says.

Elija nods. “Yes.”

“And shared language,” Corven adds.

“Yes,” Elija agrees again.

Corven leans forward, encouraged.

“So speak,” he says.

Elija’s gaze is steady.

“I am,” he says.

A flicker of irritation passes over Corven’s face.

“Without content,” Corven snaps, then reins himself in. “Forgive me. Without clarity.”

Elija's voice remains level.

"Clarity isn't missing," he says. "Control is."

A sharp intake of breath from somewhere in the room.

Marin shifts her weight, attentive but silent.

Corven straightens.

"This is exactly the concern," he says. "You reduce complex matters to accusations."

Elija shakes his head slightly.

"I'm not accusing," he says. "I'm describing."

Silence stretches.

Someone near the back clears their throat.

"If you won't clarify," a woman says, "then at least tell us what you intend to do."

Elija turns toward her.

"I intend to remain where I am," he says.

"And if that disrupts things?" she presses.

Elija considers her question carefully.

"Then what was being held together needed constant pressure," he says.

Corven stands abruptly.

"That's enough," he says. "This session is not productive."

He gestures toward the empty chair.

“You are invited,” he says tightly, “to take your place when you’re ready to contribute constructively.”

Elija looks at the chair, then back at Corven.

“I already have,” he says.

Corven’s jaw tightens.

“Then perhaps you should consider,” he says, “that your refusal to move is a form of dominance.”

The accusation hangs there—heavy, clever.

Elija does not dismiss it.

He sits with it for a moment.

Then he speaks.

“Dominance requires extraction,” he says. “I’m not taking anything from you.”

Corven scoffs. “You’re taking attention.”

Elija nods. “Because you’re pointing at me.”

A few people shift uncomfortably.

Corven gestures sharply.

“This will continue until you cooperate,” he says.

Elija meets his gaze.

“It will continue until you stop pushing,” he replies.

The room feels suddenly smaller.

Marin speaks then, her voice even.

"What if," she says, "we let the pressure show us what it's attached to?"

Corven turns toward her, exasperated.

"This isn't philosophical," he says.

"No," Marin replies. "It's structural."

Corven opens his mouth to respond, then closes it.

The room hums with restrained energy—nothing exploding, everything tightening.

Elija rises then—not to comply, not to exit in protest, but because the moment has finished what it came to do.

He walks past the empty chair without looking at it.

As he reaches the door, Corven calls after him.

"This will not resolve itself," he says.

Elija pauses.

"Pressure never resolves," he says without turning. "It's released."

He steps out into the corridor, the cool air meeting him like relief.

Marin follows a moment later.

"You didn't give them anything," she says.

Elija exhales slowly.

"They wanted leverage," he replies. "Silence starves it."

Marin glances back toward the hall.

"They'll try something else."

Elija nods.

“They always do.”

They walk together toward the outer lanes, the settlement already beginning to adjust around a pressure it cannot yet name.

Behind them, the empty chair remains.

Not occupied.

Not removed.

Waiting.

And in that waiting, the system begins to understand something it cannot yet admit:

This pressure has no shape.

And without shape, it cannot be managed.

Chapter 4

The invitation arrives in the late afternoon, carried by a boy who looks relieved to be rid of it.

He hands it to Elija without ceremony and runs off before Elija can ask a question.

The paper is heavier than it needs to be.

Good stock. Clean edges. A careful fold. Someone wanted this to feel considered.

Elija opens it as he walks.

> *You are invited to address the assembly this evening.*
> *Your presence is requested.*
> *Your voice is anticipated.*

Anticipated.

He smiles faintly and continues on.

By the time dusk settles, the assembly space is full.

Not the hall this time, but the open square where announcements are usually made—wide, circular, ringed with low stone steps.

Lamps hang from posts at even intervals, their light warm and steady.

This is not a confrontation space.

It is a spectacle space.

Elija arrives early and sits on the third step, off to one side. He does not take the central stone. He does not stand at the edge. He chooses a place that neither resists nor endorses the framing.

People notice.

They always do.

Marin appears and sits two steps behind him.

“You didn’t decline,” she says quietly.

“I didn’t accept either,” Elija replies.

Marin nods. “They won’t hear the difference.”

Voices ripple through the square as the crowd gathers. Families. Workers. Elders. Watchers from the boundary. The air is charged with a gentler tension than before—anticipation rather than fear, but just as controlling.

Corven steps into the centre of the square.

He waits until the murmur dies down.

“We’re grateful you’ve come,” he begins, voice carrying easily. “Tonight is about clarity.”

Elija remains seated.

Corven gestures toward him.

“Elija has agreed to speak,” he says.

A murmur runs through the crowd.

Elija does not correct him.

Not because it is true.

Because correcting it would make him part of the performance.

Corven continues.

“Recent events have raised questions about authority, responsibility, and unity,” he says. “We believe the best way forward is openness.”

The words are chosen carefully. They always are.

Corven turns fully toward Elija.

“Elija,” he says warmly, “the floor is yours.”

All eyes shift.

The moment stretches.

This is the kind of silence that expects to be filled.

Elija stays seated.

The crowd waits.

Someone coughs.

A child whispers something and is hushed.

Corven’s smile tightens slightly.

“You may stand,” he says gently.

Elija looks up at him.

“I won’t,” he says.

The word is quiet.

The effect is not.

A ripple moves through the square—surprise, confusion, irritation.

Corven laughs softly, attempting to defuse.

“No one is commanding you,” he says. “This is simply custom.”

Elija nods. “I know.”

“Then why not honour it?” Corven asks.

Elija considers the question as if it deserves consideration.

“Because the custom is doing the work for you,” he says.

The crowd stills.

Corven’s eyes flicker.

“Elaborate,” he says.

Elija’s gaze moves across the faces in front of him.

“Standing would make this look like agreement,” he says. “And silence would make it look like defiance.”

A murmur ripples.

“So speak,” Corven urges.

Elija breathes slowly.

“You’ve invited me to speak,” he says. “Not to be here.”

Confusion spreads.

Marin watches closely, saying nothing.

Corven's voice remains calm.

"You are here," he says.

"Yes," Elija replies. "And that's all I intend to offer."

A few people laugh, uncertain whether they are allowed to.

Corven's tone sharpens just slightly.

"The people deserve explanation," he says.

Elija nods. "They deserve rest."

A wave of discomfort passes through the square.

Someone near the front speaks up.

"Are you refusing us?" the man asks.

Elija meets his gaze.

"No," he says. "I'm refusing the frame."

Corven steps closer.

"You are confusing people," he says.

Elija looks at him steadily.

"Confusion comes when the story changes," he says. "Not when someone withholds answers."

Corven's jaw tightens.

"This isn't helpful," he says.

"No," Elija agrees. "It's honest."

Silence settles again, heavier this time.

Corven steps back and addresses the crowd.

"Elija has chosen not to participate," he says. "We respect that."

A few people nod. Others frown.

"But the council must still act," Corven continues. "Order cannot be suspended."

Elija listens without reaction.

Corven raises his voice slightly.

"From this point forward," he says, "the boundary will be reinforced. Watchers will operate with full authority."

A murmur rises.

"And any interference," Corven adds, eyes briefly flicking to Elija, "will be treated as insubordination."

Marin exhales softly behind Elija.

Elija remains seated.

When Corven finishes, he turns back to Elija.

"Do you wish to say anything now?" he asks.

Elija considers the crowd, the lamps, the carefully constructed moment.

Then he shakes his head.

"No," he says.

The crowd stirs, unsettled.

Corven nods tightly.

“Then this assembly is concluded.”

People begin to move, voices rising, questions spreading.

Marin leans forward.

“That went about as expected,” she says.

Elija smiles faintly.

“They needed it to,” he replies.

They stand together—not to leave dramatically, but because it’s time.

As they walk away from the square, Marin glances back.

“They’ve reinforced the boundary,” she says.

“Yes,” Elija replies.

“And you’re still going tomorrow.”

“Yes.”

Marin studies him.

“You’re not trying to win,” she says.

“No,” Elija replies. “I’m letting the frame collapse.”

Marin nods, thoughtful.

“Careful,” she says. “Frames don’t collapse quietly.”

Elija looks ahead, toward the road that leads outward.

“Neither does fear,” he says.

Behind them, the square empties.

The lamps continue to burn.

The invitation has been issued.

The refusal has been seen.

And now the system, having exhausted politeness, begins preparing something firmer.

Not force yet.

But consequence.

And Elija remains exactly where he has always been.

Seated.

Chapter 5

The consequence arrives without announcement.

There is no escort. No public statement. No visible shift in posture from those tasked with enforcing it. That is the point.

When Elija reaches the boundary the next morning, the watchers do not rise.

They do not greet him.

They do not tell him to leave.

They simply do not make space.

The table has been moved—only slightly—angled in such a way that the narrowest part of the road now requires a deliberate step around it. The ledger lies open, seal pressed firmly to the page, as if proximity alone might grant permission.

Two additional watchers stand nearby, unfamiliar faces, alert in the way of people who have been told something important without being told why.

Elija stops a few paces back and takes it in.

This is not resistance.

It is choreography.

The older watcher from the day before does not meet his eyes.

"You're not assigned here," the younger one says flatly.

Elija nods. "I know."

"You were instructed not to interfere," the man adds.

Elija's gaze moves past him, down the road where a cart waits, stalled. The family atop it looks exhausted. The driver avoids looking at anyone.

"I'm not interfering," Elija says.

The watcher's jaw tightens. "Then move."

Elija does not.

He steps to the side instead, placing himself near the stone wall where the road widens again. He is no longer near the table. He is not near the ledger. He is not blocking anything.

He is simply present.

The watchers exchange glances.

The younger one scoffs. "This is what they meant," he mutters.

Elija hears him.

"Meant what?" Elija asks.

"That you'd find a way around it," the watcher replies. "That you'd make it unclear."

Elija tilts his head slightly. “It already was.”

The older watcher finally looks at him.

“Please,” he says quietly. “Don’t do this.”

Elija meets his gaze.

“I’m not,” he says. “I’m staying.”

The older watcher swallows.

The cart driver clears his throat.

“Are we allowed to pass?” he asks, voice strained.

The younger watcher turns sharply. “No.”

Elija looks at the driver. “Where are you headed?”

“North,” the man replies. “To bury my father.”

The words land heavier than expected.

The younger watcher stiffens. “Papers.”

The driver’s hands shake as he reaches into his coat.

Elija watches—not the man, but the watchers.

This is where fear likes to hide.

Not in cruelty.

In procedure.

Elija steps back half a pace, giving the driver space to breathe.

“You don’t need my permission,” Elija says gently.

The driver looks at him, eyes flicking to the watchers.

"I don't want trouble," he says.

Elija nods. "Neither do they."

The older watcher closes his eyes briefly.

"Let them through," he says.

The younger watcher spins on him. "We can't!"

The older watcher's voice is low, steady.

"We can."

The younger watcher's face flushes.

"This is on you," he snaps.

The older watcher does not argue.

The cart moves forward slowly, wheels grinding against stone. As it passes Elija, the driver nods once, not in gratitude, but in recognition.

When the road clears, the younger watcher rounds on Elija.

"This is exactly why they warned us," he says. "You make consequences impossible."

Elija considers the phrase.

"No," he says. "I make them visible."

The watcher laughs harshly. "You think this ends well?"

Elija's gaze remains steady.

"I think it ends honestly," he replies.

Footsteps approach from behind.

Marin arrives, her presence felt before it is seen.

She surveys the scene—the shifted table, the sealed ledger, the watchers holding tension in their shoulders.

“They’ve reassigned half the boundary posts,” she says quietly. “Rotating schedules. Shorter shifts.”

Elija nods. “Fatigue management.”

Marin’s mouth tightens. “Control management.”

The younger watcher scoffs. “Call it what you like.”

Marin looks at him calmly.

“I will,” she says.

The watcher looks away.

Marin turns to Elija.

“They’re isolating you,” she says. “Softly.”

Elija nods. “I know.”

“They’re hoping you’ll choose to leave,” she adds.

Elija looks down the road again, then back at the settlement beyond the gate.

“I won’t,” he says.

Marin studies him.

“You understand what that costs,” she says.

Elija meets her gaze.

"Yes."

Marin exhales slowly.

"They're calling this restraint," she says. "They're proud of themselves for it."

Elija smiles faintly.

"Restraint that still requires fear," he says, "is just force with better manners."

Marin does not disagree.

A bell sounds from the settlement—midday.

The watchers shift, relief flickering briefly across their faces.

Elija steps back from the wall and begins to walk away from the boundary, not because he has been moved, but because the moment has done its work.

Behind him, the table remains angled.

The ledger remains sealed.

The watchers remain tense.

Nothing has been resolved.

But something has changed.

Consequence, Elija realises, is not what happens *to* you when you refuse to stand.

It is what happens *around* you when others are forced to carry the weight they once tried to place on fear.

And that weight, once felt, is very hard to give back.

Chapter 6

No one confronts Elija that day.

There are no accusations, no hearings, no public words spoken in measured tones. Nothing official is said at all.

That is the point.

He notices it first in the quiet.

The corridors that once held loose conversation now fall silent when he enters. Not abruptly. Not rudely. Just… subtly. Voices lower. People remember other places they need to be.

He is not shunned.
He is *managed.*

Meals arrive later than usual. Not withheld — that would be too obvious — but delayed, as if time itself has begun to drift around him. Invitations stop appearing without explanation. Tasks he once shared are reassigned politely, without ceremony.

No one is cruel.
No one is kind.

It is a careful neutrality — the kind that feels safe to those enforcing it.

Elija understands what is happening.

This is restraint disguised as patience.
Isolation framed as protection.
Space offered not for rest, but for attrition.

The system has stopped trying to move him directly.
Now it will wait for *gravity* to do the work.

—

By the third day, the quiet has weight.

Not the dramatic weight of persecution — the duller kind. The kind that presses inward when there is no resistance to push against.

Elija sits alone in the upper chamber as the afternoon light shifts across the stone floor. The room is unchanged. The same window. The same chair. The same stillness.

But absence speaks.

The absence of voices.
The absence of friction.
The absence of recognition.

This is where most people would begin to move.

Not dramatically. Not consciously. Just enough to feel less alone. Just enough to restore circulation. Just enough to remind themselves they still belong.

A clarification, perhaps.
A gesture.
A softened word.

Nothing false. Nothing dishonest.

Just… a small descent.

Elija does not move.

Later that evening, Marin appears at the doorway.

She does not announce herself. She never does. She simply stands there, holding the threshold with an expression that is careful, but not guarded.

“They’ve decided not to decide,” she says quietly.

Elija nods.

“They think time will do what authority couldn’t,” she continues. “They’re confident you’ll adjust.”

“And if I don’t?”

Marin exhales slowly. “Then they’ll need to explain why.”

She steps into the room and sits opposite him — not across, but slightly to the side. Not interrogative. Not aligned against. Just present.

“You know,” she says after a moment, “this part is usually where people start to doubt themselves.”

Elija looks toward the window.

"They begin to wonder if they misjudged the moment," she goes on. "If they misunderstood the invitation. If maybe they were too rigid."

"And are they?"

"Sometimes," she admits. "But more often, they're just tired."

Silence settles between them.

Marin studies him — not to read weakness, but to confirm orientation.

"You don't look tired," she says eventually.

"I am," Elija replies.

She blinks. The answer surprises her.

"But you're not… strained."

"No."

She nods slowly. "What's the difference?"

"Tiredness passes," he says. "Strain demands resolution."

Marin leans back, absorbing that.

"They're waiting for you to solve this," she says.

Elija's voice is gentle. "There is nothing to solve."

"That's what frightens them."

That night, Elija does not sleep easily.

Not because of fear — but because awareness sharpens in stillness.

He feels the weight of being misinterpreted.
The cost of not correcting false assumptions.
The loneliness that comes from refusing to recruit allies for protection.

Remaining seated does not anesthetise the nervous system.
It simply refuses to obey it.

At one point, the thought comes — quiet, almost reasonable:

You could explain yourself.

Not as defence. Not as capitulation. Just… context.

He lets the thought pass.

Explanation, offered too early, becomes bargaining.

By the sixth day, the rumours begin.

Nothing malicious. Nothing precise.

Just enough.

"He's withdrawn."
"He's become difficult."
"He's not engaging the way he used to."
"He thinks he's above process."

Each statement contains just enough truth to survive repetition.

Elija hears none of this directly.
Which is also the point.

The system is building a story *around* him, waiting to see if he will step into it.

He does not.

On the seventh morning, Corven sends word.

Not a summons. An invitation.

For conversation. For clarity. For the good of the whole.

Elija reads the message, then sets it aside.

He does not refuse.

He waits.

That afternoon, he walks beyond the inner walls — further than he has since his arrival. The city hums faintly in the distance, life unfolding without reference to its guardians.

He sits beneath a weathered tree on the slope and rests his back against the trunk.

This, too, is remaining.

Not withdrawal.
Not protest.
Simply not relocating to urgency.

The cost is real.

Being misunderstood.
Being left out.
Being quietly sidelined.

But the cost is not *identity*.

That remains untouched.

As the light fades, Elija speaks aloud — not as prayer performed, but as presence acknowledged.

“I am still here.”

No demand.
No reassurance required.

Just truth, stated where it already holds.

The cost of remaining is not loss of self.

It is loss of illusion — the illusion that belonging must be maintained by movement.

And Elija has already been seated too long to believe that again.

Chapter 7

The invitation arrives at dusk.

Not delivered by runner. Not posted publicly. It appears quietly on Elija's table, as if it has always been there and only now chooses to be seen.

No seal. No signature. Just a simple line, written with deliberate restraint.

For clarity. For alignment. For the sake of the whole.

The phrasing is careful. Familiar. It carries the tone of reconciliation without admitting conflict ever existed.

This is not escalation.
It is *resolution offered before truth is spoken.*

Elija reads it once, then folds the paper and sets it aside.

He does not feel resistance.
He feels recognition.

The hall is prepared when he arrives.

Not formally. Not ceremonially. No raised platform. No witnesses positioned to signal judgement. The chairs are arranged in a gentle arc, equidistant, inviting equality without surrendering hierarchy.

Corven stands when Elija enters.

Not immediately. A half-beat late — enough to be read as casual rather than deferential.

“Elija,” he says warmly. “Thank you for coming.”

“I didn’t say yes,” Elija replies.

Corven smiles, unoffended. “No. But you came.”

They sit.

Marin is present, but positioned slightly behind the curve. Not excluded — just removed enough to prevent intervention.

Others occupy the remaining chairs. Familiar faces. Thoughtful ones. People skilled in careful language and measured concern.

No one looks hostile.

Which is precisely what makes the room dangerous.

“We wanted to check in,” Corven begins. “There’s been… uncertainty.”

Elija says nothing.

Corven continues. “Not about your intent. About your posture.”

A pause.

“We’ve noticed you’ve become less accessible. Less participatory.”

Elija meets his gaze. Calm. Open.

“Is that a concern?” Elija asks.

“It could become one,” Corven replies gently. “If it creates distance.”

Distance.

The word lands exactly where intended.

Distance is always framed as relational failure — never as boundary.

One of the others leans forward. “We don’t want misunderstanding,” she says. “We’re hoping to restore shared language.”

Elija nods slowly. “Which language is missing?”

She hesitates. Just briefly.

“The language of cooperation.”

Elija’s voice remains even. “I haven’t refused cooperation.”

“No,” Corven agrees quickly. “But you haven’t clarified your position either.”

Clarify.

The word that sounds like invitation — and functions like extraction.

Corven shifts, folding his hands. "You're respected here, Elija. Deeply. That hasn't changed."

It's the first appeal to belonging.

Subtle. Affirming. Strategic.

"We want to ensure you don't become… isolated."

Isolation, reframed as consequence — not strategy.

Elija listens without reaction.

"And," Corven adds carefully, "we want to make sure your presence continues to serve the community."

There it is.

The condition introduced without announcement.

Elija waits.

The silence stretches.

Finally, Corven speaks again — softer now.

"We're not asking you to move," he says. "Only to meet us halfway."

Halfway.

Always the language of compromise when power remains stationary.

Elija inhales slowly.

“I have a question,” he says.

The room stills — not defensively, but attentively.

“What would meeting you halfway require?”

Corven smiles, relieved. “Dialogue. Context. Shared framing.”

“And if I offer those?”

“Then I believe much of the tension dissolves.”

Elija nods. “And if I don’t?”

Corven tilts his head. “Then we’ll need to discern what your silence means.”

Meaning assigned externally.

Elija looks around the room.

Faces remain warm. Concerned. Reasonable.

Not one of them realises they are asking him to descend.

Not morally. Not visibly.

But *internally*.

To trade grounded presence for mutual comfort.
To exchange location for harmony.
To step down just enough to be legible again.

“This invitation,” Elija says quietly, lifting the folded paper, “came framed as clarity.”

“Yes.”

“But it requires me to explain myself in order to belong.”

“No,” Corven says quickly. “Only to participate.”

Elija’s gaze sharpens — not in challenge, but precision.

“Participation that requires self-justification is not participation,” he says. “It’s negotiation.”

The room shifts.

Not sharply. Just enough to register discomfort.

Marin moves forward instinctively — then stops herself.

She watches Elija carefully.

He continues.

“I haven’t withdrawn,” he says. “I’ve remained.”

Corven’s brow furrows. “Remaining can feel like withdrawal to others.”

“Only if movement is required to maintain legitimacy.”

That lands harder than Elija intends.

A few glances exchange.

Corven exhales. “Elija, no one is questioning your legitimacy.”

Elija meets his eyes steadily.

"Then why does it require defence?"

Silence.

Not awkward.

Exposed.

After a moment, Corven stands.

"I think we should pause," he says calmly. "Give this time."

Time again.

Always time — used to soften refusal and delay accountability.

Elija rises as well.

As he turns to leave, Corven adds gently, "The door remains open."

Elija stops.

He turns back — not sharply, not defiantly.

"The door was never closed," he says. "I simply didn't walk through it on cue."

Outside, dusk has deepened into night.

The air is cool. Unconcerned.

Marin joins him on the steps.

"They'll say you refused reconciliation," she says quietly.

“They’ll say many things.”

“You’re aware this will cost you more.”

Elija nods. “I know.”

She watches him carefully. “And you’re still not moving.”

“No,” he says. “I’m staying where I already am.”

Marin exhales — half awe, half grief.

“This is the part,” she says, “where people usually break.”

Elija looks toward the city lights beyond the walls.

“Or become unrecognisable to the system,” he replies.

He steps forward into the night.

The invitation has been revisited.

And declined — not with rebellion, but with refusal to descend.

Chapter 8

The language shifts before the action does.

That is how it always begins.

Elija notices it in small ways at first — phrases repeating, questions changing shape, concern acquiring edges.

“Is he stable?”
“Is he intentional about the impact of his presence?”
“Has anyone clarified his influence?”

None of these are accusations.
That is what makes them effective.

Concern, when repeated often enough, becomes permission.

He is no longer addressed directly.

Meetings continue — his name included, his voice absent.
Decisions are explained *around* him, not *to* him.

This is not exile.
It is *managed distance*.

He remains visible.
But no longer consulted.

The system has learned something important:

Opposition strengthens him.
Alignment unsettles him.

So it stops pushing.

And starts narrating.

A notice appears three days later.

Not addressed to Elija.

Addressed to everyone else.

For the sake of cohesion, certain roles will be temporarily realigned to reduce interpretive strain.

Interpretive strain.

The phrase spreads quickly — elegant, clinical, irrefutable.

Elija reads it once.

He feels no anger.

Only clarity.

Marin finds him in the outer courtyard as dusk gathers again.

“They’re reframing you,” she says quietly.

Elija nods.

"Not as wrong," she continues. "As disruptive."

"Disruption suggests motion," Elija says. "I've been still."

"Yes," Marin replies. "And that's the problem."

The next encounter is unplanned.

Corven approaches him in a public corridor — not privately, not ceremonially.

Visibility has been chosen deliberately.

"Elija," Corven says, voice calm, carrying just enough volume to be overheard.

Elija turns.

"We've noticed something," Corven continues. "Your presence seems to be… influencing morale."

"Explain," Elija says gently.

Corven's smile holds. "Some are unsettled. They don't know how to read you."

"Have they asked?"

Corven pauses — just long enough.

"No."

"Then they're not unsettled," Elija says. "They're interpreting."

A ripple of attention moves through the space.

Corven lowers his voice slightly.

"You don't see it," he says. "But your stillness creates instability."

Elija studies him — not critically, but carefully.

"Only where movement is compulsory," he replies.

Corven exhales slowly.

"This isn't about blame," he says. "It's about safeguarding continuity."

There it is.

The moment alignment becomes framed as threat.

"You're not doing anything wrong," Corven continues. "But you're no longer neutral."

Neutral.

The word systems use when they want compliance without confession.

"You could help resolve this," Corven adds. "A simple clarification. A statement of intent."

Intent again.

The system does not fear Elija's actions.

It fears his *non-participation in narrative*.

Elija shakes his head slightly.

“I won’t define myself to stabilise anxiety,” he says.

Corven’s expression tightens — not with anger, but with disappointment.

“Then we’ll need to act in the community’s interest.”

Elija nods once.

“I assumed you would.”

That evening, the first boundary is crossed.

Not visibly. Not publicly.

Quietly.

Elija’s access to certain spaces is “paused.”
His presence at gatherings is “discouraged.”
Requests for consultation are “redirected.”

No announcement is made.

But the effect is immediate.

The system has decided:

Stillness is now risk.

Marin confronts Corven later that night.

“This is containment,” she says.

Corven does not deny it.

“It’s prevention,” he replies. “He’s destabilising people.”

“He hasn’t done anything.”

“That’s exactly it.”

When Marin finds Elija again, he is seated beneath the old archway at the city’s edge — the place no one monitors because nothing is expected to happen there.

“They’re moving against you,” she says.

“I know.”

“They’re not angry,” she adds. “They’re afraid.”

“Yes.”

She hesitates. “Do you feel the cost yet?”

Elija closes his eyes briefly.

“I feel the narrowing,” he says. “Not inside. Around.”

“That’s how it works,” Marin whispers. “Pressure without accusation. Consequence without verdict.”

Elija opens his eyes.

“Fear can only rule where clarity is negotiable,” he says. “I won’t negotiate location.”

Far above them, lights flicker across the upper halls.

Orders are being refined. Language sharpened. Justifications prepared.

No one believes they are doing harm.

They believe they are protecting the whole.

And Elija — unchanged, unmoved — has become the problem simply by remaining.

Not because he stands against them.

But because he refuses to stand *where they need him to*.

Chapter 9

Remaining has a cost no one warns you about.

Not the cost of resistance.
Not the cost of being misunderstood.
But the cost of *being unchanged while the world rearranges itself around you.*

Elija feels it most in the quiet.

Not loneliness exactly — he is not alone.
But a thinning of presence. A subtle withdrawal of warmth.
Conversations that pause when he enters. Eyes that register him, then move on.

No hostility.
Just adjustment.

The system is learning how to live without him.

He walks the outer paths now — not by protest, not by exile, but because the inner routes no longer open easily.

Doors do not close.
They delay.

"Come back later."
"Check with someone else."
"Timing isn't right."

Always timing.

Time is the softest instrument of pressure.

At night, the weight settles differently.

Not as doubt.
As fatigue.

Remaining requires energy the body must supply when no external momentum carries you.

When affirmation is absent.
When direction is not mirrored back.
When nothing *pushes* you forward.

Elija sits alone in the low room beneath the stairwell — the one space that has not been reassigned because it is deemed irrelevant.

He does not pray for relief.

He does not ask for vindication.

He simply remains present.

And that is harder than action.

Marin joins him later, sitting on the floor rather than the bench.

“They’ve stopped mentioning you,” she says quietly.

Elija nods. “That’s the next phase.”

“You’re being erased gently.”

“Yes.”

“Does that bother you?”

He considers the question carefully.

“It would,” he says, “if my sense of being depended on their recognition.”

She watches him.

“You’re tired.”

“Yes.”

“But you’re not wavering.”

“No.”

Remaining is not heroic.

It does not feel strong.

It feels *heavy*.

Because nothing about it feeds the ego.
Nothing about it generates narrative.
Nothing about it produces visible fruit - not the kind the council applaud.

There is no applause for staying seated.

Only the slow burn of choosing not to move when movement would relieve pressure.

That night, a memory surfaces uninvited.

A younger version of himself — standing once, long ago, when standing was demanded.

He remembers the relief that followed.
The sense of resolution.
The warmth of restored belonging.

He remembers how quickly he was praised for clarity once he complied.

Remaining now feels like refusing a door he knows would open easily.

And that knowledge is its own weight.

The temptation does not arrive as fear.

It arrives as reason.

You could clarify without compromising.
You could reassure without relocating.
You could speak their language briefly and return to stillness.

Reason is the most dangerous voice when it borrows truth.

Elija lets the thoughts pass.

Remaining does not mean suppressing temptation.
It means not obeying it.

The next morning, a child approaches him near the fountain — one of the few still unafraid of proximity.

"Why don't you come inside anymore?" she asks simply.

Elija kneels to her height.

"I'm still here," he says.

"But they say you're not part of things now."

He smiles gently.

"Being part of things isn't the same as being seen everywhere."

She frowns. "Are you in trouble?"

"No."

"Then why does everyone act like you are?"

Elija pauses.

"Because it's easier to explain discomfort as danger," he says.

She considers this, then nods once, satisfied.

Children recognise location before language.

Later that day, Marin brings news.

"They're preparing a statement," she says. "Not against you. About stability. Continuity. Responsibility."

Elija listens.

“They'll name you without naming you.”

“Yes.”

“They want you to feel the weight and resolve it yourself.”

He nods.

“That's how systems preserve innocence,” he says. “They never force. They wait.”

That evening, as the light fades again, Elija feels it most clearly.

Not fear.

Not doubt.

But grief.

Grief for how easily this could end.
Grief for how unnecessary the pressure is.
Grief for how many people are convinced this is care.

Remaining means carrying grief without letting it harden into resentment.

That is the true cost.

He sits beneath the archway once more, the city lights distant, unfocused.

Marin stands beside him.

"You know," she says, "most people would move now."

"Yes."

"They'd call it wisdom."

"Yes."

"They'd say they're choosing peace."

Elija looks out into the dark.

"Peace that requires self-erasure is only quiet fear," he says.

She nods slowly.

"Then what is this?" she asks.

Elija exhales.

"This is weight," he replies. "Without collapse."

Far above them, the statement is nearly complete.

Balanced. Reasonable. Regretful.

It will land softly.

And it will change everything.

Elija remains seated.

Not because it is easy.

But because this is where he already is.

Chapter 10

The statement is released in the morning.

Not announced.
Not emphasised.
Simply placed where official things are always placed — so it can be discovered without being confronted.

Marin reads it first.

Twice.

Then she closes her eyes.

It never names Elija.

It doesn't need to.

Recent events have highlighted the importance of clarity, alignment, and shared responsibility within our community. While diversity of posture remains valued, stability requires discernible participation. To safeguard cohesion, certain presences will be temporarily re-contextualised to reduce unintended influence.

The language is immaculate.

No accusation.
No blame.
No malice.

Just explanation — offered on behalf of everyone.

By midday, the interpretation has spread.

Not through argument.
Through repetition.

People do not say, "Did you hear what they did to Elija?"

They say:

"It's probably for the best."
"He's been… difficult to place."
"Stillness can be confusing, you know."
"I don't think he realises how he comes across."

No one feels cruel.

That's the genius of it.

Elija reads the statement once.

He folds the page and places it beside the others — invitations, clarifications, gentle warnings.

A record of reasonable pressure.

He feels no urge to respond.

But he does feel something else.

Exposure.

Not of wrongdoing — but of *presence*.

The system has told a story *about him*.

And stories, once released, do not need facts to travel.

In the market square, conversations adjust when he passes.

Not silence — but modulation.

Voices lower. Words soften. Eye contact shortens.

People are kinder now.

Which is worse.

Kindness that requires distance.

A man approaches him near the fountain — one Elija has known for years.

“Can I ask you something?” the man says quietly.

“Yes.”

“Why didn’t you just explain yourself?”

Elija studies his face.

“Would it have helped?” he asks.

The man hesitates.

“I don’t know,” he admits. “But it would’ve made things clearer.”

“For whom?” Elija asks.

The man doesn’t answer.

By evening, Elija’s name has acquired a tone.

Not suspicion.
Not admiration.

Concern.

“He means well.”
“He’s just not… aligned right now.”
“He’s in a different place.”

Place again.

Always place.

Marin finds him at the edge of the courtyard as the light fades.

“They’ve decided who you are,” she says.

Elija nods.

“Without asking.”

“Yes.”

“They’ve made you symbolic.”

She waits.

“Does that frighten you?”

Elija considers the question honestly.

"No," he says. "But it clarifies the cost."

Being misrepresented publicly is different from being pressured privately.

Private pressure can be endured quietly.

Public narrative tries to relocate you internally.

It whispers:

If this many people misunderstand you, perhaps you should reconsider yourself.

That's the real danger.

Not exile.

But internal drift.

That night, Elija does something new.

He does not withdraw.

He walks directly through the central way — the path he has avoided since access became complicated.

No defiance.

No announcement.

Just presence.

Heads turn.

Some nod politely.

Some look away.

Some watch closely.

No one stops him.

He sits on the low stone bench near the old fig tree — a place once used for public teaching, now largely decorative.

He sits.

And remains.

A few people linger.

Then a few more.

Not supporters. Not rebels.

Just those who are tired of interpretation.

No one speaks.

That matters.

The system relies on speech.

Remaining exposes silence.

From an upper balcony, Corven watches.

He feels something unfamiliar.

Not anger.

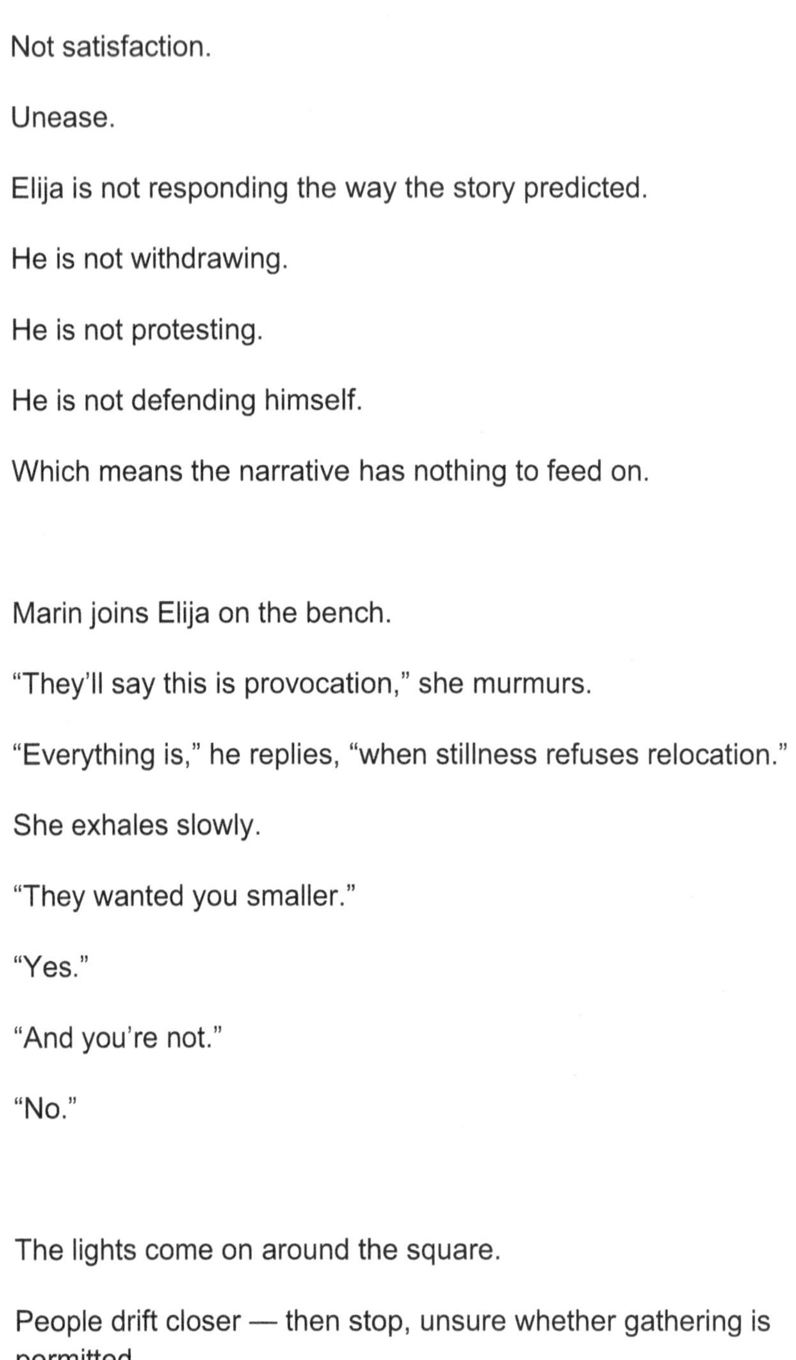

Not satisfaction.

Unease.

Elija is not responding the way the story predicted.

He is not withdrawing.

He is not protesting.

He is not defending himself.

Which means the narrative has nothing to feed on.

Marin joins Elija on the bench.

“They’ll say this is provocation,” she murmurs.

“Everything is,” he replies, “when stillness refuses relocation.”

She exhales slowly.

“They wanted you smaller.”

“Yes.”

“And you’re not.”

“No.”

The lights come on around the square.

People drift closer — then stop, unsure whether gathering is permitted.

No rule has been broken.

That's the problem.

Above them, a decision begins to form.

Not about punishment.

About *necessity.*

Because a presence that cannot be moved — and cannot be framed — eventually forces a choice.

And the system does not like being forced.

Elija remains seated.

The story they told about him has begun to crack.

Not because it was false.

But because it required his participation to survive.

And he never gave it.

Chapter 11

Silence is not neutral.

It is only treated that way until it refuses to serve the existing order.

By the second evening, Elija's presence has begun to alter the square.

Not dramatically.
Not loudly.

But perceptibly.

People linger longer than they mean to.
Conversations slow.
Movements hesitate — not from fear, but from a strange loss of urgency.

No one knows what to *do* with him.

And that is new.

Elija does not speak.

He does not address the crowd.
He does not explain himself.
He does not clarify the statement or correct the narrative.

He simply remains.

The system expected silence to signal retreat.

Instead, it has become *gravity*.

A woman sits on the edge of the stone bench, leaving a careful distance between them.

She says nothing at first.

Then, quietly: “Are you allowed to be here?”

Elija turns his head slightly. “I am.”

She nods.

After a moment, she says, “They said you were… repositioned.”

He considers the word.

“I haven’t moved,” he replies.

She lets out a breath she didn’t know she was holding.

“That’s what I thought,” she says — and stays.

This is how it begins.

Not with defiance.

With relief.

By the third evening, the watchers have noticed.

They do not intervene.
They take notes.

How long people stay.
Who approaches.
What is said.

Which is almost nothing.

And that unsettles them most of all.

Authority that needs explanation is familiar.

Authority that emerges without speech is not.

Corven convenes a small group before dusk.

"This is becoming problematic," one of them says.

"He hasn't broken any rule," another replies.

"That's not the issue."

"Then what is?"

A pause.

"He's being *received*."

The word lands heavily.

Silence has begun to function where language failed.

People do not ask Elija what to think.

They do not ask him what to do.

They simply orient themselves differently in his presence.

Urgency thins.

Fear quiets.

People breathe more slowly.

This is not instruction.

It is regulation.

Marin watches from the perimeter.

She recognises the shift immediately.

"This is dangerous," she says quietly to Corven later. "Not because he's leading."

"But because he isn't," Corven replies.

"He's not asking for anything."

"That's exactly it."

Authority without demand cannot be negotiated.

It cannot be compromised.

It cannot be redirected.

Because it is not trying to go anywhere.

A man known for his sharp opinions approaches Elija on the fourth night.

“I don’t agree with you,” he says abruptly.

Elija looks at him calmly. “I haven’t said anything.”

“That’s the problem,” the man snaps. “People are reading into you.”

Elija nods. “That happens.”

“You could stop this.”

“How?”

“Say something. Take a position.”

Elija studies him.

“I have,” he says gently. “I just haven’t relocated to make it visible.”

The man scoffs. “That’s convenient.”

Elija says nothing.

After a moment, the man’s shoulders drop.

“I’m tired,” he mutters.

Elija inclines his head slightly.

“So am I.”

The man sits.

By the end of the week, the square has developed a rhythm.

People come at dusk.

They leave without conclusion.

No one agrees on what is happening.

But everyone agrees something has *shifted*.

The statement that once framed Elija as disruptive now feels thin.

Not wrong.

Just insufficient.

Because the problem with narratives is this:

They collapse when lived reality no longer cooperates.

From the upper halls, Corven watches again.

Elija has not defended himself.

He has not corrected anyone.

He has not resisted.

And yet the system feels… weaker.

Not exposed.

Not defeated.

But *irrelevant* in this one small place.

Which is worse.

“What do we do?” someone asks Corven.

Corven does not answer immediately.

Because he knows the truth.

If they move against Elija now, they legitimise him.

If they leave him alone, he continues.

Silence has cornered them.

Marin approaches Elija as the crowd thins.

“You’ve become a reference point,” she says quietly.

He exhales slowly. “Without wanting to.”

“That’s how it happens,” she replies. “When presence outlasts explanation.”

He looks at the emptying square.

“I didn’t come to teach,” he says.

“I know.”

“I didn’t come to challenge.”

“I know.”

“I came to remain.”

Marin smiles faintly.

“And now,” she says, “they don’t know how to stand without you.”

Above them, lights burn late.

A different decision is forming now.

Not about messaging.

Not about containment.

About **intervention**.

Because silence that steadies others becomes authority whether anyone grants it or not.

And authority that cannot be named cannot be controlled.

Elija remains seated.

And for the first time, the system understands:

Stillness has crossed a threshold.

Chapter 12

The decision is not announced.

It never is.

By the time a measure is named *necessary*, the choice has already been made. What remains is only the task of making it feel inevitable.

Corven stands at the window long after the others have left.

Below him, the square still carries the residue of presence — not crowd, not event, just the faint memory of gathering. People passed through. Some lingered. None were instructed.

And yet something shifted.

That is what troubles him.

Not disobedience.
Not dissent.

But the absence of need.

The report lies open on the table behind him.

No accusations. No warnings. Just observations.

Attendance at scheduled forums has declined.
Unstructured gatherings have increased.
Decision latency observed among junior facilitators.
Language of "waiting" and "remaining" appearing in informal conversation.

Waiting.

Remaining.

Words that feel harmless until they loosen the hinges of urgency.

Corven presses his palm against the glass.

He has spent his life keeping things intact.

Not rigid — intact.
He believes in systems. In rhythm. In continuity.

People need structure, he tells himself. They need guidance. They need something to lean against when fear rises.

But now fear is doing something unfamiliar.

It is quieting.

"They're not panicking," one of the councillors had said earlier.
"That's the problem," Corven replied.

Fear is manageable when it moves.

Stillness cannot be steered.

The others return an hour later.

Not summoned.

Drawn.

When they sit, no one rushes to speak.

The measure does not begin as a proposal.

It begins as concern.

"We've given this space," someone says carefully. "And it's created ambiguity."

Another nods. "Ambiguity erodes confidence."

"Confidence in what?" a third asks.

There is a pause.

"In leadership," Corven answers quietly.

No one argues.

Marin hears about the meeting second-hand.

Not through official channels. Through tone.

The way her colleague hesitates before speaking. The way language tightens.

"They're formalising it," he says. "Not against him. Around him."

She knows what that means.

When a system cannot confront presence directly, it builds walls *elsewhere*.

By mid-morning, small changes appear.

Subtle.

A public notice adjusts access hours to the square.
A new scheduling protocol discourages "unsanctioned gatherings."
A facilitator is reassigned — "for development."

No rule forbids Elija from being present.

But everything around him grows less hospitable.

Elija notices immediately.

Not intellectually.

Physically.

The square feels different.

Not emptier.

More *alert*.

Movement carries intent again. People glance before sitting. Conversations feel supervised even when no one is listening.

The system has exhaled.

Marin finds him seated near the fig tree, as always.

“They’re closing the margins,” she says quietly.

“Yes.”

“They won’t touch you directly.”

“They don’t need to.”

She sits beside him, closer than usual.

“This is escalation,” she says. “Without force.”

Elija nods.

“Necessary,” she adds bitterly.

Elija turns to her. “Necessary for whom?”

She doesn’t answer.

The measure passes without vote.

It is simply *adopted*.

Language shifts overnight.

Stillness becomes *non-participation*.
Remaining becomes *withdrawal*.
Presence becomes *passivity*.

The story adjusts — not to oppose Elija, but to *outgrow* him.

A notice is posted near the square entrance.

For the sake of collective clarity, all gatherings within the central commons must now be facilitated by an approved guide.

Approved.

Guided.

Contained.

No one is forbidden to sit.

But no one is encouraged to stay.

The first evening after the measure, Elija arrives as usual.

He sits.

The bench is colder than he expects.

Not physically.

Relationally.

People pass.

A few nod.

Most hesitate — then continue on.

Remaining now carries social cost.

And cost, when distributed widely enough, becomes self-enforcing.

A man approaches him cautiously.

"I was told I shouldn't linger," he says apologetically.

Elija looks at him kindly. "You're allowed to choose."

The man swallows. "That's the problem."

He leaves.

Marin watches from the edge of the square.

Her chest tightens — not with fear for Elija, but with grief for everyone else.

This is how remaining becomes rare.

Not by punishment.

By inconvenience.

That night, the square empties faster than before.

Not because people don't want to stay.

Because staying now requires *intention*.

And intention costs energy most people no longer have.

Elija remains.

Long after the last footsteps fade.

Long after the lamps dim.

He feels the full weight now.

Not isolation.

Responsibility.

Remaining has moved from quiet resistance to visible divergence.

The system has drawn a line — softly, cleanly, without hostility.

And Elija stands — not against it, but *outside its logic*.

Marin joins him late.

“They're calling it stability,” she says.

Elija smiles faintly. “They always do.”

“This is where people usually retreat.”

“Yes.”

She studies him. “And you?”

“I'm still here.”

She exhales slowly. “They'll say you forced this.”

“They'll need to.”

“Because if you didn't—”

“Then they did.”

She nods.

Above them, Corven signs the final document.

He tells himself this is leadership.

That ambiguity cannot be allowed to spread.

That presence without direction creates drift.

And drift leads to collapse.

Still, his hand pauses before the final mark.

Just for a moment.

Because something in him knows:

The measure will work.

But not forever.

Elija remains seated beneath the fig tree.

The square is quiet now.

Not because stillness has failed.

But because it has become costly.

And cost reveals who is free.

This is the necessary measure.

Not because it is right.

But because fear cannot tolerate unowned space for long.

Chapter 13

Safety always has a price.

Not the kind people announce, either.
Not the kind that comes with receipts.

This price is quieter.

It is paid in posture.
In small silences.
In the way a person learns to edit their own questions before they ever form into speech.

After the necessary measure, the city feels more orderly.

Schedules return.
Forums regain attendance.
Approved guides reappear in the commons wearing calm expressions and carrying prepared words.

The system exhales in relief.

And most people do too.

Because relief is addictive.

Marin notices it first in her own body.

Not as agreement.

As loosened tension.

She hates that.

It would be easier if safety only comforted people who were wrong.

But it comforts everyone.

It comforts those who want peace.
Those who are tired.
Those who can't afford the cost of social friction.

Safety seduces even the awake.

On the third day, the guides begin offering "clarifying conversations."

Not interrogations.

Invitations.

They approach in pairs, smiling gently, voice trained to carry no edge.

"Just checking in," they say.
"We want to make sure you're feeling supported."
"Some of the recent ambiguity has been hard for people."

Hard.

As though discomfort is injury.

As though stillness is violence.

Elija is not approached.

Not directly.

He remains outside their official language, like a shadow they refuse to name.

But the people who once lingered near him are approached.

That is where the measure lands.

The cost is distributed.

And when everyone pays a little, no one feels responsible.

A young guide named Sel walks the commons with a small book held against his chest.

He is earnest.
Not cruel.

That is what makes him useful.

Marin watches him stop near a woman who used to sit near the fig tree.

“May I ask,” he says softly, “what drew you there?”

The woman’s face reddens.

“I don’t know,” she says quickly. “Nothing, really. I was just… resting.”

Sel nods sympathetically, as though she has confessed to something sad.

“Rest is good,” he says. “But rest needs context.”

The woman looks down.

Marin’s stomach turns.

Rest needs context.

As though rest is permission granted by authority.

Later, the woman avoids the square entirely.

Not because she dislikes Elija.

Because she dislikes being watched while she chooses.

Safety has made her self-conscious.

And self-consciousness is the beginning of captivity.

That evening, Marin finds Elija beneath the fig tree again.

His posture is unchanged.

Which, after the last few days, feels almost impossible.

“How many came?” she asks quietly.

“Three,” he replies.

“Only three?”

He nods.

Marin sits hard on the stone beside him.

“They’re winning,” she says.

Elija does not correct her.

He lets the grief land.

Winning is what it feels like when safety narrows the room.

They sit without speaking for a long time.

The city hums around them, busy again, settled again.

It should feel like relief.

Instead, it feels like amnesia.

Marin breaks the silence.

“Do you know what they’re offering people?”

Elija turns slightly.

“Language,” she says. “A way to explain why they stopped coming. A way to justify retreat without shame.”

Elija nods.

That is always the bargain.

Not coercion.

Just narrative relief.

If you accept the story, you can stop carrying the tension of choice.

You can call retreat “wisdom.”

You can call silence “peace.”

You can call compliance “maturity.”

And no one will question you.

A man approaches the square cautiously as twilight deepens.

He looks older than Marin remembers. Or maybe just heavier.

He stands at the edge of the commons, hands clenched around something small.

He sees Elija seated.

He hesitates.

Then he walks toward him quickly, as though he is afraid his courage will expire mid-step.

He stops a few paces away.

“I’m not supposed to be here,” he says.

Elija’s eyes soften. “You’re allowed to be here.”

The man swallows.

“It doesn’t feel like it.”

Elija nods, acknowledging the truth without granting it authority.

The man holds out his hand.

In his palm is a thin ribbon of cloth, frayed at the edges.

"I used to wear this when I was younger," he says. "Before everything became… structured."

Marin watches.

The ribbon looks meaningless.

And yet the man is shaking as he holds it.

"What is it?" Elija asks gently.

"A marker," the man whispers. "For those who wanted to remember where they stood."

Marin's breath catches.

Not because the ribbon is symbolic.

Because she understands what he is doing.

He is trying to locate himself again.

The man's eyes brim.

"They said you were confusing people," he says. "But I realised something."

Elija waits.

"They weren't confused," the man says. "They were… relieved."

His voice cracks.

"And then they got scared of the relief."

Marin feels the words land like a bell.

Relieved, then scared of the relief.

That is the whole pattern.

Freedom arrives, and fear calls it dangerous.

The man looks at Elija with pleading intensity..

“What do I do with this?” he asks, raising the ribbon.

Elija does not take it.

He does not validate it with ritual.

He simply says, “Wear it if it helps you remember you’re allowed to breathe.”

The man nods as though this is permission for his whole body.

He ties the ribbon around his wrist with trembling fingers.

Then he sits down on the stone edge of the fountain.

Not beside Elija.

Not as a disciple.

Just as a human choosing to remain.

A guide notices from across the commons.

He does not approach immediately.

He watches, jaw set, weighing whether intervention will create attention.

He turns away.

Not because he agrees.

Because the system has learned something:

Direct confrontation grants legitimacy.

So it chooses softer tactics.

After the man sits, others drift near.

Not many.

But enough.

They do not gather as a crowd.

They form a scattered constellation — each person separated by space, each pretending they are not part of anything.

That is the cost.

Even when they choose presence, they must do it *alone*.

Safety has trained them to fear association.

Marin leans toward Elija.

“This is how it happens,” she whispers. “Not as revival. Not as movement.”

Elija nods.

"Just as permission," he murmurs.

They sit as the lamps warm the edges of the square.

Not many people remain.

But those who do seem different.

Less eager.

Less performative.

Less concerned with being seen as correct.

They are paying the price of safety by refusing its bargain.

Above them, Corven receives a report.

Small gatherings persisting despite measure. No unified speech. No declared purpose. Behaviour remains non-violent, non-disruptive. Influence appears ambient.

Ambient influence.

A phrase for what cannot be argued with.

Corven reads it twice.

Then sets it down slowly.

Because he understands, now, what the measure cannot fix.

Safety can control behaviour.

It cannot control *breathing*.

In the square, the night deepens.

Elija remains seated.

Marin remains with him.

And the cost becomes clearer.

The price of safety is not obedience.

It is the slow surrender of your own inner permission.

And once surrendered, it takes a long time to remember you ever had it.

Chapter 14

This one is different.

Marin knows it the moment she sees the envelope.

It isn't posted.
It isn't public.
It isn't phrased for diffusion.

It is addressed to her.

Her name, written by hand.

She stands in the corridor longer than necessary, the envelope resting against her palm like something warm. There is no seal. No mark of urgency. Just weight.

She does not open it immediately.

That, too, is instinct now — to delay, to feel the shape of a thing before letting it speak.

When she finally unfolds the paper, the words are simple.

We would value your perspective.
Your discernment has always mattered here.
Perhaps we could speak — privately.

No reference to Elija.
No mention of the square.
No framing language.

Just recognition.

Which is more dangerous than accusation.

She finds Elija beneath the fig tree as dusk gathers, as usual.

"They've invited me," she says.

He does not ask who.

He does not ask why.

He nods once. "Will you go?"

"Yes."

She waits for something else — instruction, reassurance, warning.

None comes.

"You're not concerned?" she asks.

Elija looks out toward the square, where people move with practiced ease again.

"They didn't invite you to convince me," he says. "They invited you to locate yourself."

Marin exhales slowly. “That’s exactly it.”

The room they meet in is smaller than she expects.

Not the hall. Not the council chamber.

A side room. Comfortable. Bookshelves. Soft light. A table set with tea already poured.

Corven stands when she enters.

This time, there is no half-beat delay.

“Marin,” he says warmly. “Thank you for coming.”

She nods and sits opposite him.

Two others are present — both known to her, both respected. Neither looks adversarial.

This is not an intervention.

It is an embrace.

“We wanted to hear from you,” Corven begins. “Not as a representative. As yourself.”

Marin almost smiles.

“That’s generous,” she says.

Corven inclines his head. “We believe in your judgement.”

There it is.

The appeal to identity.

“We’ve noticed you’ve been… torn,” one of the others adds gently.

Marin looks at her. “Torn between what?”

“Between concern for the community,” she says, “and loyalty to Elija.”

Marin does not correct the framing.

She lets it sit.

“This isn’t about choosing sides,” Corven says quickly. “We’re hoping to relieve you of that pressure.”

Relief again.

Always relief.

“We’re concerned,” he continues, “that proximity has made objectivity difficult.”

Marin’s jaw tightens slightly.

“Proximity to what?” she asks.

“To influence,” he replies.

She nods slowly. “You mean presence.”

Corven smiles politely. “Call it what you like.”

They speak for a while.

About responsibility.
About fatigue.
About unintended consequences.

They speak of Elija without naming him.

“He’s become a focal point,” someone says.

“And focal points distort,” another adds.

Marin listens carefully.

They are not lying.

That’s the problem.

“We’d like you,” Corven says finally, “to help us re-establish balance.”

Marin meets his gaze. “How?”

“By stepping back,” he says. “Publicly.”

There it is.

Not confrontation.

Separation.

“If you were to distance yourself,” Corven continues gently, “it would signal that this isn’t a shared stance.”

Marin feels the weight settle fully now.

This is the invitation.

Remain respected.
Remain central.
Remain influential.

Just… move one step.

“You wouldn’t be abandoning him,” Corven adds. “Just clarifying that you don’t share his posture.”

Marin hears it clearly now.

Choose clarity over closeness.
Belong without friction.
Help us protect the whole.

Her throat tightens.

“You know,” she says slowly, “that what you’re asking will hurt him.”

Corven does not deny it.

“It may,” he says. “But it will help many others.”

The old calculus.

Sacrifice the few for the many.

Except this time, the few is one man who never asked to be followed.

“And if I don’t?” Marin asks.

Corven’s voice remains calm.

“Then you risk being misunderstood.”

She almost laughs.

“By whom?”

“By everyone.”

The meeting ends without resolution.

They do not press her.

They don’t need to.

The invitation will do its work on its own.

That night, Marin walks the long way back to the square.

She does not go straight to Elija.

She needs to feel where she is first.

She passes people she knows — people who nod easily, warmly.

She imagines how easily this could be preserved.

All she has to do is step away.

When she finally reaches the fig tree, Elija is seated as always.

She sits beside him without speaking.

After a long while, she says, “They asked me to distance myself from you.”

He nods.

"They said it would help everyone."

He nods again.

"They said it would bring clarity."

This time, he turns slightly toward her.

"And what did it clarify?" he asks.

Marin closes her eyes.

"That they need me to move so they don't have to."

Silence settles.

He does not thank her.

He does not reassure her.

He does not make her choice lighter.

He simply says, "You're allowed to remain where you are."

The words undo something tight in her chest.

She exhales shakily.

"That's the cost, isn't it?" she whispers. "Choosing without cover."

"Yes."

She stays.

Not dramatically.
Not defiantly.

Just... stays.

Above them, lights burn late again.

The invitation has been extended.

Not to Elija.

But to the one person whose movement would make everything easier.

And for the first time, the cost is not theoretical.

It is relational.

And real.

Chapter 15

Leaving would fix almost everything.

That is the cruel elegance of it.

If Elija withdrew quietly, the square would return to neutral ground. The guides could soften their tone. The notices could be revised. The measure could be remembered as a temporary precaution rather than a turning point.

If Marin stepped back publicly, the tension would resolve itself in language. People would nod and say, *Of course — that makes sense.* The discomfort would find a name. The relief would feel earned.

No one would have to admit fear.

No one would have to change.

Marin feels this more sharply than she expects.

In the days following the invitation, small confirmations appear everywhere.

A colleague seeks her out, speaking carefully.
"I'm glad you're still… balanced," he says.

Balanced.

As if remaining required correction.

Another smiles warmly and adds, "It's good to see you back in the centre of things."

Back.

As if she had left.

She realises then that the story has already been drafted.

All that remains is her signature.

Elija notices the shift too.

Not because Marin behaves differently — she doesn't — but because the pressure around her tightens.

Questions arrive indirectly.
Opportunities subtly realign.
Her absence from certain spaces is remarked on with polite concern.

She is being tested.

Not for loyalty.

For *movement*.

One evening, as the square empties again, Marin breaks.

Not visibly.

But honestly.

"If you left," she says quietly, "this would all stop."

Elija does not flinch.

He lets the truth of it exist without defence.

"Yes," he says.

She waits for more.

"For a while," he adds.

The words land heavily.

"For a while," she repeats.

"Yes."

She rubs her palms together, grounding herself.

"They'd call it wisdom," she says. "They'd say you recognised the cost and chose peace."

Elija nods.

"They'd praise your humility," she continues. "Your discernment."

"Yes."

"They'd invite you back later," she says. "On safer terms."

He turns to her then.

"And I would no longer be here."

The sentence is simple.

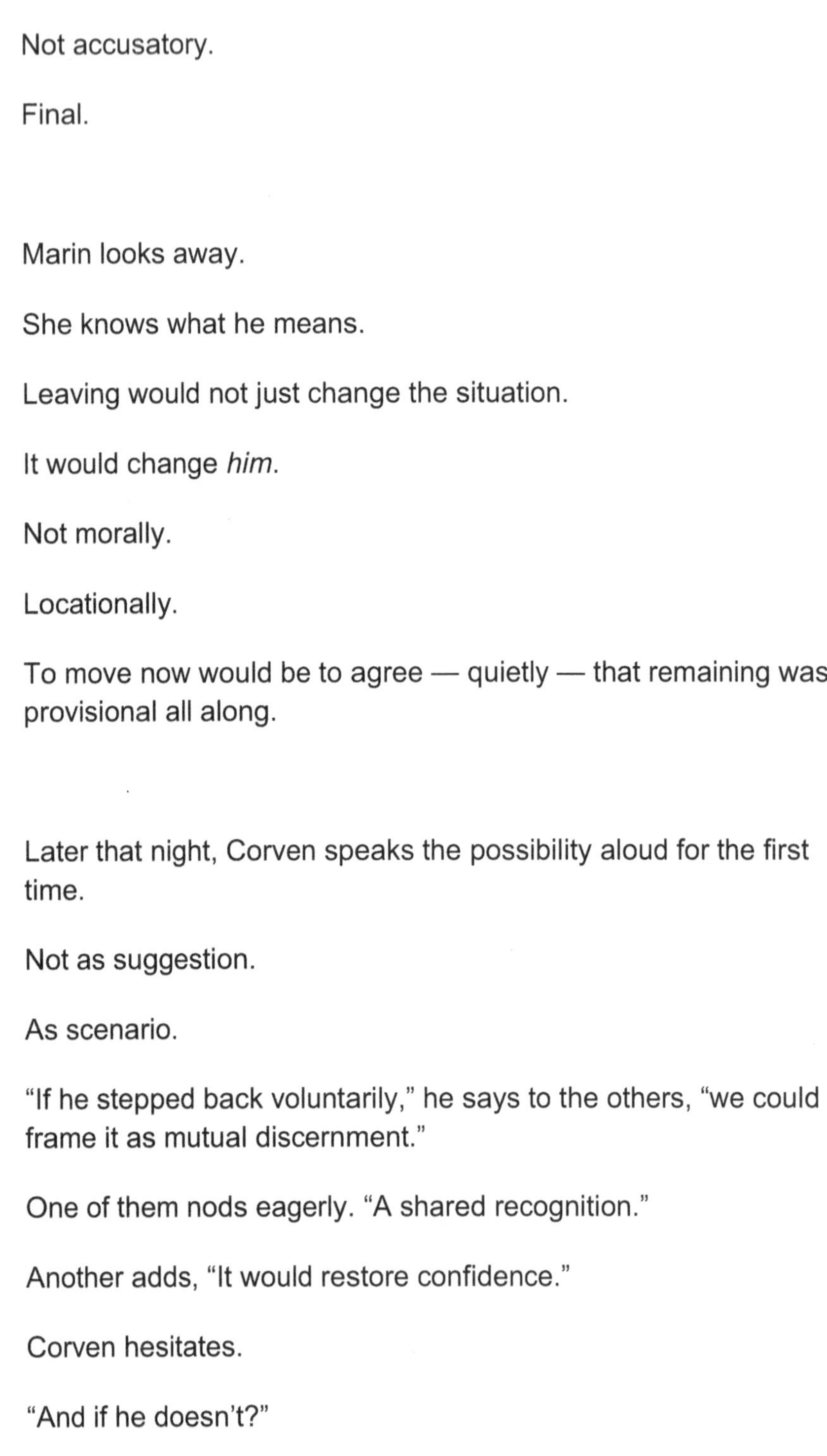

Not accusatory.

Final.

Marin looks away.

She knows what he means.

Leaving would not just change the situation.

It would change *him*.

Not morally.

Locationally.

To move now would be to agree — quietly — that remaining was provisional all along.

Later that night, Corven speaks the possibility aloud for the first time.

Not as suggestion.

As scenario.

"If he stepped back voluntarily," he says to the others, "we could frame it as mutual discernment."

One of them nods eagerly. "A shared recognition."

Another adds, "It would restore confidence."

Corven hesitates.

"And if he doesn't?"

Silence.

Then: “Then we prepare for longer disruption.”

Disruption.

The word for presence that will not relocate.

The next morning, a message arrives for Elija.

Not a summons.

Not an invitation.

A courtesy.

If you need space, the outer dwellings are available.
Quiet. Undisturbed.
A place to reflect.

Leaving without being named as leaving.

The most generous exile.

Marin reads it and feels something twist.

“They’re offering you dignity,” she says bitterly.

“They always do,” Elija replies.

“And if you refuse?”

“They’ll say I chose difficulty.”

She laughs softly. “You always choose difficulty.”

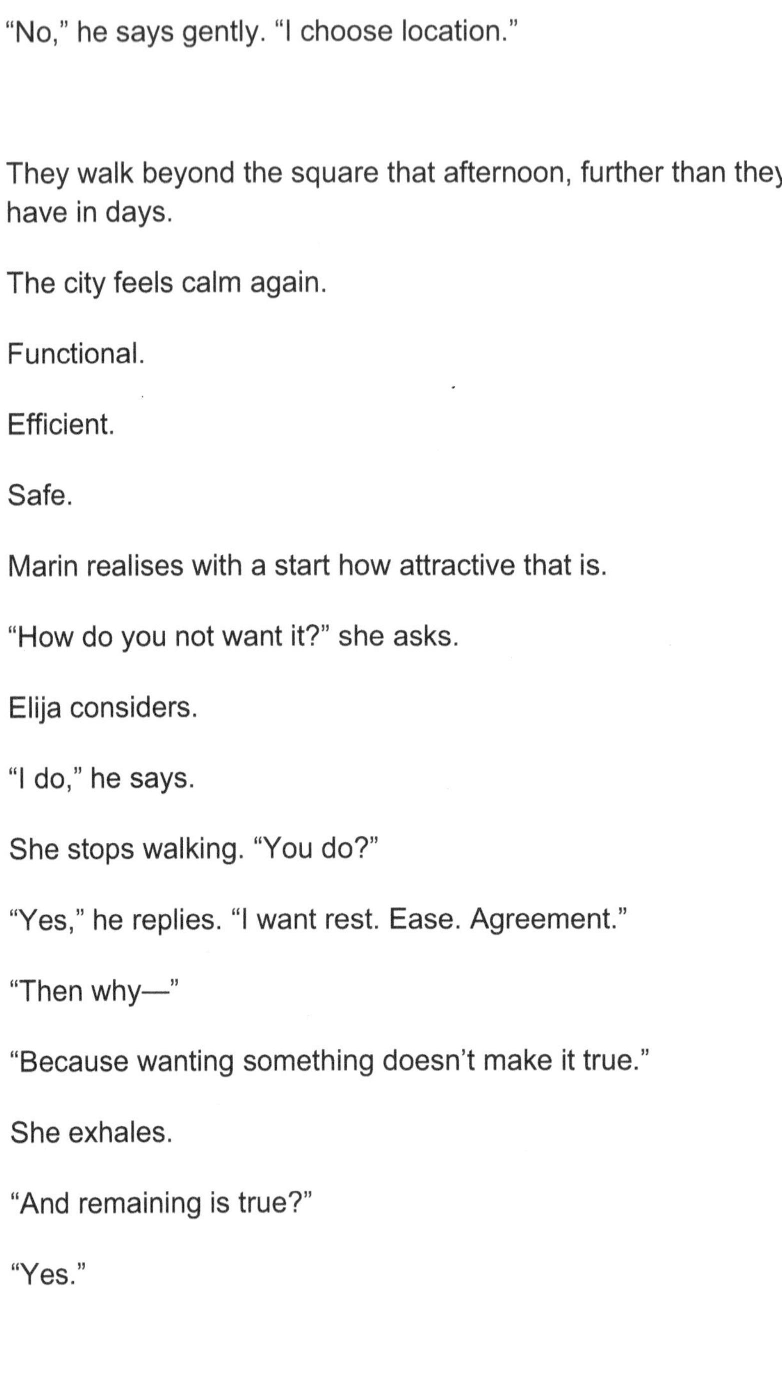

“No,” he says gently. “I choose location.”

They walk beyond the square that afternoon, further than they have in days.

The city feels calm again.

Functional.

Efficient.

Safe.

Marin realises with a start how attractive that is.

“How do you not want it?” she asks.

Elija considers.

“I do,” he says.

She stops walking. “You do?”

“Yes,” he replies. “I want rest. Ease. Agreement.”

“Then why—”

“Because wanting something doesn’t make it true.”

She exhales.

“And remaining is true?”

“Yes.”

That night, the square is nearly empty.

Only Elija and Marin remain, seated beneath the fig tree.

No one approaches.

No one watches openly.

The system is waiting.

It always waits when leaving would solve everything.

Marin breaks the silence.

“If you leave,” she says, “they’ll call it reconciliation.”

“Yes.”

“If you stay,” she continues, “they’ll call it stubbornness.”

“Yes.”

She looks at him.

“What will *you* call it?”

Elija smiles faintly.

“Staying.”

Above them, the city rests.

So much would be fixed if one man moved.

So much would be soothed.

So much would return to normal.

And that is precisely why he does not.

Because when leaving fixes everything, it reveals what was broken all along.

And Elija remains seated.

Not because it is heroic.

But because it is honest.

Chapter 16

The notice was delivered quietly.

Not announced.
Not posted publicly.
Not spoken aloud in the square.

It was folded once and slid beneath the door of Tomas's mother's home just after dawn, while the street was still dim and the market stalls were empty.

By the time she found it, the paper had already softened slightly from the stone's cold.

She read it standing.

Not because she chose to — but because her body forgot how to sit.

The language was careful. Measured. Reassuring.

Irregular Presence Observed.
Community Stability Review Initiated.
No Immediate Action Required.

It thanked her for her continued cooperation.

It reminded her — gently — of the responsibility shared by all residents to preserve equilibrium.

It suggested, without stating, that Tomas's recent behaviour had been *noticed*.

There was no accusation.

There never was.

She folded the paper again and placed it on the table beside the bread she had been cutting. Her hand hovered there longer than necessary, as though she expected the paper to move.

Tomas was still asleep.

She stood listening for his breathing from the other room.

It was steady. Unaware.

She did not wake him.

Not yet.

By midmorning, the square had filled.

Elija arrived as he always did — without timing it, without announcing himself, without intention beyond presence.

He noticed the shift immediately.

Not in faces.

In spacing.

People stood just a little farther from one another. Conversations thinned. Laughter ended more abruptly.

Someone who would normally have met his eyes turned away.

Someone else smiled too quickly.

He felt it in his chest before he could name it.

A tightening.

As if something had been pulled slightly out of alignment.

Tomas's mother did not come.

She had not missed a morning in weeks.

Elija remained where he was, resisting the familiar instinct to move — to seek — to *check*.

This was where restraint cost something.

When the square settled into its midday lull, a guide approached him.

Not Corven.

A younger one.

Her expression was neutral, but her hands were clasped too tightly at her waist.

"Elija," she said, softly.

He turned.

"Yes."

"There's been a review initiated."

He did not respond.

“There’s no restriction placed on you,” she added quickly. “This is not disciplinary.”

He waited.

The guide hesitated, then continued, as though reciting something memorised.

“A household connected to recent irregularities has been advised to reduce exposure for a short period.”

Elija felt the words land somewhere behind his sternum.

“Advised,” he repeated.

She nodded.

“For their own stability.”

Silence stretched.

“Is the child being harmed?” Elija asked.

The guide stiffened almost imperceptibly.

“No.”

“Is he in danger?”

“No.”

“Then why now?”

Her gaze flickered — not away, but inward.

“That’s not a question I can answer.”

Elija nodded.

The guide exhaled, relief flashing briefly across her face.

“I wanted you to know,” she said. “So you wouldn’t misunderstand the absence.”

He looked past her, toward the street that led to Tomas’s home.

“I understand,” he said.

It was not entirely true.

That afternoon, Tomas’s mother sat at the table with the notice folded between her palms.

Tomas had read it.

He had not understood it.

He had asked questions she could not answer without revealing her fear.

“So I can’t go to the square?” he asked.

“Just for a little while.”

“Did I do something wrong?”

“No.”

“Did Elija?”

Her breath caught.

“No.”

The lie sat badly in her mouth.

She had watched her son change over the last weeks.

Not dramatically.

Not visibly.

But something had softened.

Something had steadied.

He slept more deeply.

He asked fewer anxious questions at night.

He laughed — not louder, but more freely.

She had told herself it was coincidence.

Now she was being asked to decide which story to believe.

The one that said *nothing is happening*.

Or the one that said *something good has begun, and it is being watched*.

She folded the paper again.

“We’re just taking a pause,” she said.

Tomas nodded, accepting this the way children accept weather.

But later that evening, she heard him standing at the window.

Watching the square from a distance.

Elija did not go to Tomas’s home.

This was the discipline he had learned the hard way.

To intervene now — to cross the boundary — would confirm the narrative already forming.

He remained.

He waited.

But waiting did not feel neutral.

It felt weighted.

Like standing beneath something suspended.

That night, he slept poorly.

Not because he feared consequence for himself — but because he could feel responsibility pressing outward.

The cost had moved.

It was no longer contained in his own body.

It had touched someone else's life.

This was always the moment that clarified things.

Not ideology.

Not policy.

Impact.

The following day, the square was quieter.

Not empty.

But thinned.

Tomas did not come.

Neither did his mother.

Someone else stood where the child often lingered, then drifted away.

Elija noticed how quickly people adjusted.

How absence was absorbed.

How systems trained people to adapt without protest.

A guide stood at the edge of the square longer than usual.

Watching.

Not Elija directly.

The space around him.

He felt the familiar temptation rise.

To speak.

To reassure.

To step toward someone who looked unsteady and offer grounding.

He did not.

Instead, he sat.

The square moved around him.

Time passed.

This was what containment looked like from the inside.

Not punishment.

Not force.

But restraint that cost.

Late that afternoon, Corven came.

He did not sit.

He stood beside Elija, eyes on the horizon.

“They escalated quickly,” Corven said quietly.

“Yes.”

“I argued for delay.”

“I know.”

Corven swallowed.

“The language is still soft.”

Elija said nothing.

“They want to see whether absence resolves the irregularity,” Corven continued. “Whether things stabilise without further adjustment.”

“And if they don’t?”

Corven did not answer immediately.

“If they don’t,” he said eventually, “they’ll formalise distance.”

Elija closed his eyes briefly.

“This was always the test,” Corven said. “Whether what you bring can exist without cost.”

Elija opened his eyes.

“It already has cost.”

Corven nodded.

“I know.”

They stood together in silence.

Not allies.

Not opponents.

Two men recognising the shape of what was unfolding.

“I won’t intervene,” Elija said.

Corven turned to him sharply.

“Not even if—”

“Not unless harm is present,” Elija said. “Fear does not count as harm.”

Corven’s jaw tightened.

“That distinction is exactly what the Council fears.”

Elija looked at him.

“And that,” he said, “is exactly why they fear it.”

That night, Tomas’s mother lay awake listening to the quiet of her home.

It was not the silence that troubled her.

It was the awareness of being *noticed*.

Of having crossed — unknowingly — into something unnamed.

She thought of the way Tomas had laughed in the square.

The way Elija had never told him what to do.

Only stayed.

She pressed the folded notice flat against her chest, smoothing its creases as though she could remove its meaning.

For the first time since the city had begun its gentle guidance, she wondered whether stability and safety were always the same thing.

By the end of the week, the absence had become normal.

And that, Elija realised, was the most dangerous part.

Chapter 17

Containment did not arrive as force.

It arrived as care.

It always did.

Not because every guide was cruel, or because the Council named it control, but because the city had learned a strange, efficient truth:

People will accept almost anything if you give it the shape of protection.

The first session was held in a room with soft light.

No banners. No symbols. No sharp edges.

Only chairs arranged in a circle and a table with water set out as if kindness could be poured and passed around.

The guides filed in quietly.

Some had been there longer than others. Some were newly appointed. Some sat with posture so composed it looked like faith.

A woman near the doorway kept rubbing her thumb along the ridge of her index finger, over and over, as if her body had memorised a worry her mind refused to name.

At the centre of the room sat a man who did not look like the Council.

He looked like a teacher.

He smiled with practiced warmth.

“Thank you for coming,” he said, and the word *thank* landed like a balm.

He waited just long enough for people to feel seen.

Then he continued.

“This is not corrective.”

A pause.

“It is preventative.”

A longer pause.

“We have observed a rising pattern of irregular anchoring across several public spaces.”

He did not say Elija’s name.

No one said Elija’s name in rooms like this.

Names made things real.

So they used categories.

Irregular. Unauthorised. Disruptive.

But always followed by softer language.

“Some citizens,” the man continued, “have begun to exhibit behaviours inconsistent with communal stability.”

A guide across from him nodded once, as if relieved the problem had been phrased professionally.

The teacher-like man gestured toward a ledger on the table.

“We are not concerned with the person.”

He smiled again.

“We are concerned with the phenomenon.”

Joryn sat with his hands folded neatly in his lap, and felt his stomach tighten.

He did not want to be here.

Not because he disagreed with stability.

He had built his life around stability.

He had studied it. Practiced it. Maintained it.

But there was something about the way the room was staged — the softness, the water, the tone — that made him feel, for the first time, that he was being coached into something rather than invited into it.

He watched the man’s mouth as he spoke.

Every sentence shaped like empathy.

Every instruction framed as love.

And yet, somewhere beneath the comfort, a harder truth pressed upward:

This meeting existed because something had happened that the city could not explain.

Not a riot.

Not a rebellion.

Something worse.

A stillness that did not require permission.

"We will be implementing a containment protocol," the man said gently, as if announcing a health measure.

A few heads lifted.

He raised a hand quickly.

"Containment does not mean removal. It does not mean punishment. It does not mean harm."

His eyes moved around the circle, landing on each person briefly, as if giving reassurance personally.

"It means we reduce spread."

He said spread like someone might say smoke.

Or illness.

Or fire.

"Spread of what?" a young guide asked, unable to keep his voice from sounding like a protest.

The man's smile did not falter.

"Disorientation," he replied.

He waited.

"Loss of interpretive trust."

Another pause.

"And a rising resistance to guidance."

The room shifted slightly, as if those words belonged to something that could be weighed.

Joryn felt the phrase *interpretive trust* lodge in his chest.

He knew what it meant.

It was the subtle agreement a city made with itself: *We will let the system tell us what our lives mean.*

If that agreement broke, everything else became unstable.

Not because people were inherently wild.

But because, without a shared narrator, fear had to find new ways to keep control.

The man opened the ledger.

"Protocol is simple," he said. "And it is compassionate."

Compassionate.

Always that word.

He looked down as he spoke, as if reading was humility.

“First: observation without confrontation.”

He lifted his eyes.

“If you see someone sitting in a way that draws others into extended silence, do not address them directly.”

A murmur.

“Second: relational redirection.”

He glanced toward the water.

“You approach those who are watching. You do not shame them. You do not warn them.”

He smiled.

“You invite them to move.”

Someone raised a hand. “Move where?”

“Anywhere,” the man said softly. “Movement itself is stabilising.”

Joryn felt something in him recoil.

Movement itself.

He thought of the square — how people walked faster some days when they were afraid. How they kept busy to avoid feeling.

He had never noticed the city worshipping motion until he sat near someone who did not move at all.

“Third,” the man continued, “we offer a stability notice to households displaying recurring exposure.”

A guide in the back shifted sharply.

Joryn thought of Tomas’s mother.

His throat tightened.

The man spoke on.

“It’s not restriction,” he said. “It is rest.”

Rest.

Joryn almost laughed.

They were calling containment rest.

He imagined the notice beneath the door and the mother’s hands hovering over it, unsure whether to touch.

“Fourth,” the man said, “if the phenomenon persists, we formally establish distance.”

Distance.

No one said exile.

No one said removal.

Distance was softer.

Distance sounded like wisdom.

“Distance preserves autonomy,” the man added, as if anticipating resistance.

He leaned forward slightly, voice lowered.

"We are not coercing. We are protecting choice."

Joryn's jaw clenched.

Protecting choice by shrinking it.

After the instructions, they practiced.

Not with props.

With phrases.

The man handed out small slips of paper, each containing a sentence to use in public encounters.

Not commands.

Not accusations.

Reassurances.

You don't have to stay here.
You look tired — come walk with me.
Let's get some air.
It's okay. It's nothing.
You're safe. Don't overthink it.

Joryn stared at the lines.

They were gentle.

They were kind.

They were also a net.

A language designed not to break someone's will, but to keep them from noticing they had one.

He swallowed.

Around him, guides repeated the phrases in pairs, practicing tone.

Soft voice. Open hands. Calm eyes.

Containment was choreography.

Later, the group was dismissed in twos and threes.

Joryn lingered.

He waited until most of the room had emptied, then approached the man.

“May I ask something?” Joryn said.

The man smiled, tired warmth.

“Of course.”

“What if,” Joryn began carefully, “the phenomenon isn’t disorientation?”

The man’s eyes remained steady.

“What if it’s… clarity?”

The air seemed to thin.

For a moment, the man looked almost human — as if the mask had loosened.

Then the smile returned.

“Clarity,” he repeated.

“Yes.”

The man nodded slowly, the way someone nods at a child who has asked a beautiful but naïve question.

“Clarity is welcome,” he said.

Then he added, very softly:

“Clarity does not resist guidance.”

Joryn felt the sentence land like a seal.

As if the definition had already been decided.

He nodded, because nodding was safer than disagreement.

And he left.

That afternoon, containment began.

Not with sirens.

With footsteps.

With friends approaching friends.

With hands on shoulders.

With invitations to walk.

At first, it looked harmless.

Almost tender.

In the square, Elija sat as he always did.

He felt the shift before it reached him.

A slight thickening in the air.

A new rhythm at the edges.

People arrived and did not linger.

They paused, looked toward him, then turned as if remembering an errand.

A guide drifted near the benches, not watching Elija directly, but tracking the watchers.

Elija did not move.

He did not harden.

He remained.

Marin arrived late, shoulders tense.

She sat two benches away.

Not because she wanted distance.

Because the square now carried invisible lines.

She looked at Elija, but did not meet his eyes.

Her body wanted to.

The city had taught her not to.

A guide approached her within minutes.

Friendly face. Calm hands.

“Marin,” the guide said, as if it was coincidence.

She startled.

"Oh," she said. "Hello."

"You've been working hard," the guide said, voice soft.

Marin blinked. "I—what?"

The guide smiled. "You look tired."

Marin opened her mouth, then closed it.

She *was* tired.

But she was also awake in a way she had never been tired before.

The guide nodded sympathetically.

"Come walk with me," she said. "Just around the perimeter."

The words were almost identical to the slips from the meeting.

Marin felt it — not as a thought, but as a bodily recognition.

This wasn't conversation.

It was protocol.

She looked toward Elija.

He was still.

He did not look at her.

Not because he refused her.

Because he refused to make her a battleground.

The guide's hand hovered near Marin's elbow.

Not touching.

Almost touching.

A touch that was permission and warning at once.

Marin’s throat tightened.

“I’m alright,” she said, surprising herself.

The guide’s smile did not change.

“It’s okay,” the guide replied. “You don’t have to stay here.”

Marin’s breath hitched.

The guide leaned in slightly, voice lower, intimate.

“You’re safe,” she said. “Don’t overthink it.”

Marin felt something inside her rise.

Not anger.

Not rebellion.

A simple refusal to be narrated.

“I’m not overthinking,” she said quietly.

The guide paused.

Just a fraction.

Then she laughed softly, as if to lighten the moment.

“Of course not,” she said.

And in that instant, Marin saw the shape of it:

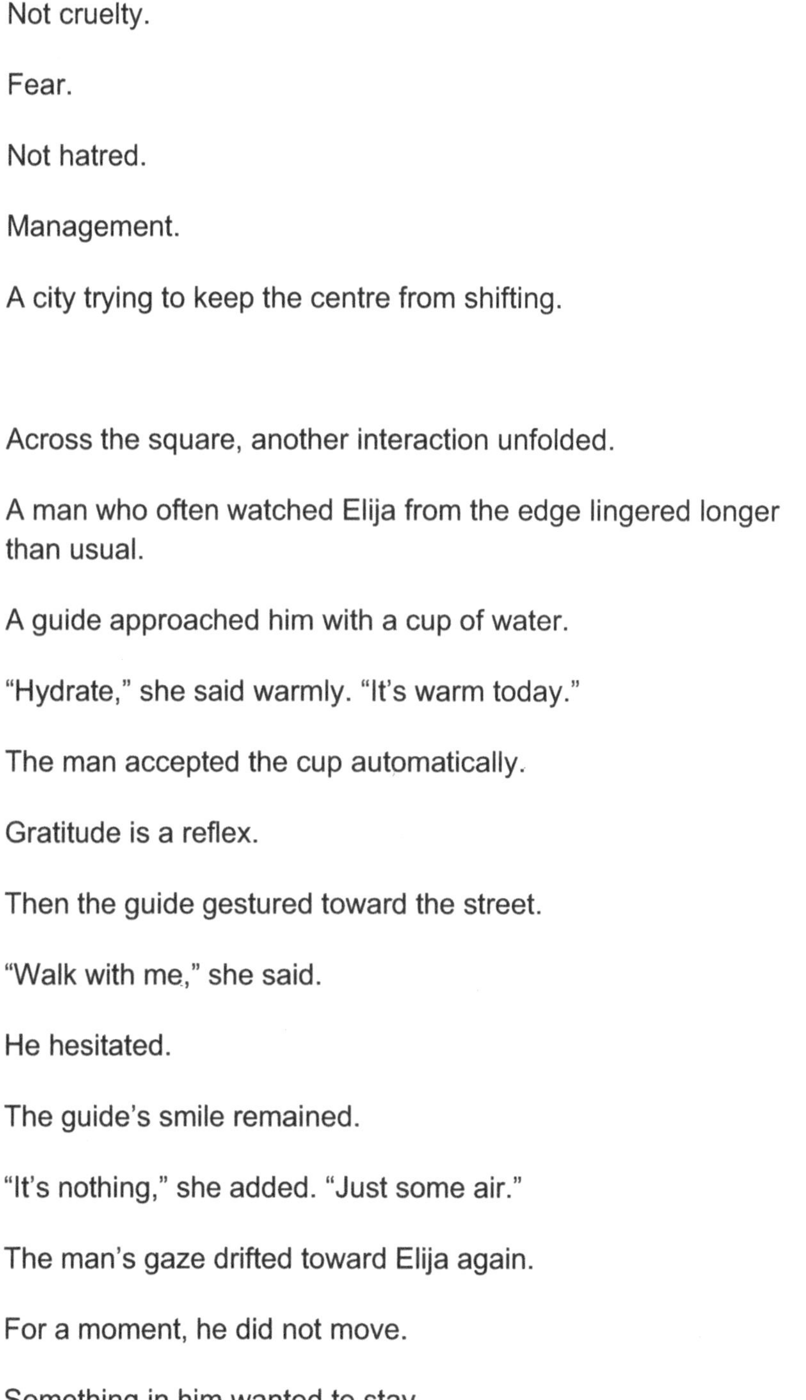

Not cruelty.

Fear.

Not hatred.

Management.

A city trying to keep the centre from shifting.

Across the square, another interaction unfolded.

A man who often watched Elija from the edge lingered longer than usual.

A guide approached him with a cup of water.

“Hydrate,” she said warmly. “It’s warm today.”

The man accepted the cup automatically.

Gratitude is a reflex.

Then the guide gestured toward the street.

“Walk with me,” she said.

He hesitated.

The guide’s smile remained.

“It’s nothing,” she added. “Just some air.”

The man’s gaze drifted toward Elija again.

For a moment, he did not move.

Something in him wanted to stay.

The guide's voice softened further.

"You don't need to do this," she murmured, as if offering rescue.

Do this.

As if sitting and watching was a danger.

The man's shoulders dropped.

He followed.

Containment worked best when it felt like relief.

Elija watched all of it without watching.

He saw the system doing what systems do:

Reducing friction by relocating people before they could notice they were choosing.

He felt the temptation to intervene.

To speak truth plainly.

To call the guides by name and expose the choreography.

He did not.

Exposure would have escalated the threat narrative.

The city would have hardened.

Fear would have gained justification.

So he remained.

Stillness was not passive.

It was strategic love.

That evening, Marin returned home with her hands shaking slightly.

No one had shouted at her.

No one had threatened.

And yet she felt as if she had survived something.

Her husband asked, “Are you alright?”

She nodded too quickly.

Then, quietly, she said, “They asked me to walk.”

Her husband frowned. “That sounds kind.”

“It was,” she replied.

She swallowed.

“That’s the problem.”

In the upper halls, Corven received a report.

Not a formal one.

A summary of movement patterns.

The man who delivered it spoke casually, like discussing weather.

“Containment efficacy is high,” he said. “People are returning to their rhythms.”

Corven stared at the page.

Efficacy.

Rhythms.

The words were clean.

He knew what they meant.

They meant the square was being drained without anyone being harmed enough to complain.

He dismissed the man and sat alone.

He felt the quiet dread of recognising his own complicity.

Containment was gentler than force.

Which made it easier to justify.

Which made it more dangerous.

The next day, fewer people sat.

The day after, fewer still.

Not because Elija had changed.

Because the city had learned how to protect itself from what he revealed.

Not by denying him.

By isolating him without naming isolation.

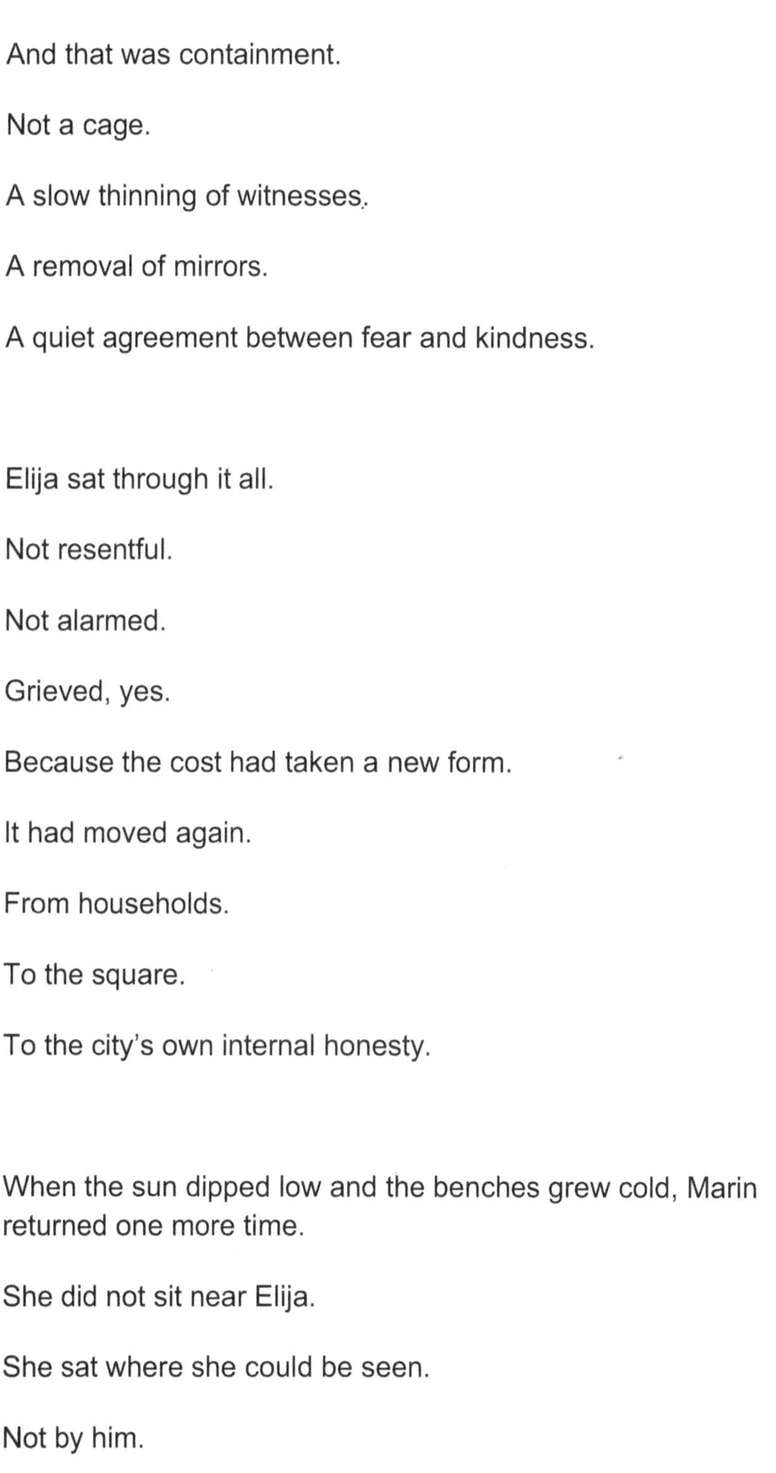

And that was containment.

Not a cage.

A slow thinning of witnesses.

A removal of mirrors.

A quiet agreement between fear and kindness.

Elija sat through it all.

Not resentful.

Not alarmed.

Grieved, yes.

Because the cost had taken a new form.

It had moved again.

From households.

To the square.

To the city's own internal honesty.

When the sun dipped low and the benches grew cold, Marin returned one more time.

She did not sit near Elija.

She sat where she could be seen.

Not by him.

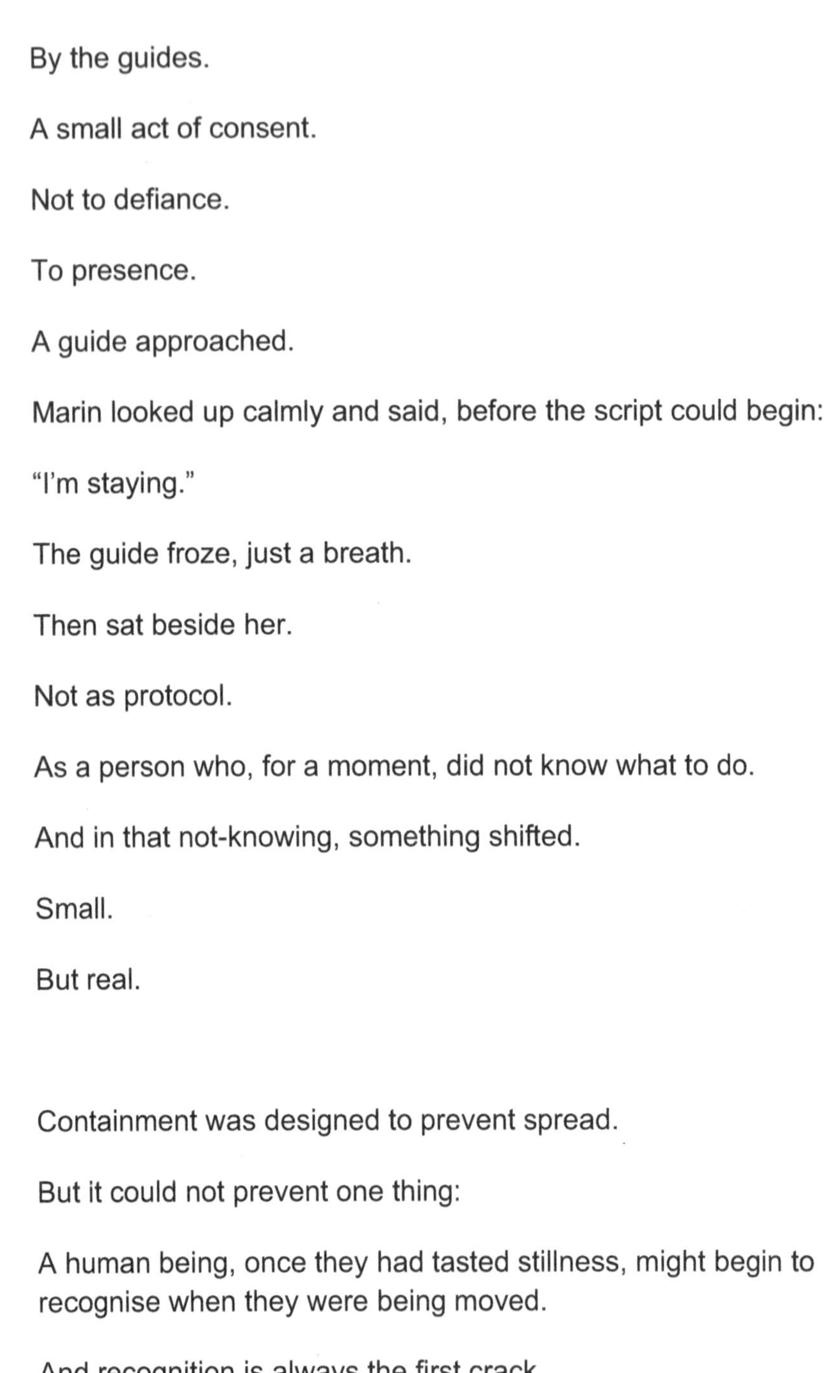

By the guides.

A small act of consent.

Not to defiance.

To presence.

A guide approached.

Marin looked up calmly and said, before the script could begin:

"I'm staying."

The guide froze, just a breath.

Then sat beside her.

Not as protocol.

As a person who, for a moment, did not know what to do.

And in that not-knowing, something shifted.

Small.

But real.

Containment was designed to prevent spread.

But it could not prevent one thing:

A human being, once they had tasted stillness, might begin to recognise when they were being moved.

And recognition is always the first crack.

Chapter 18

The square did not empty all at once.

That would have drawn attention.

Instead, it thinned the way breath does when someone realises they are holding it.

Gradually. Carefully. Almost politely.

By the fourth day, the benches were still warm by habit, not by use.

Elija noticed this before anyone else did.

Not because he counted bodies.

But because the *quality* of the quiet had changed.

There is a silence that belongs to rest.

And there is a silence that belongs to avoidance.

This one leaned away.

Morning arrived without ceremony.

The market stalls opened as usual. Bread was sliced. Fruit was arranged. The rhythm of exchange continued uninterrupted.

But people moved faster.

Not rushed — *efficient*.

Conversations ended a beat earlier than necessary.

Laughter still occurred, but it did not linger.

No one stood without purpose.

No one stayed simply because staying felt good.

Elija remained where he was.

Stillness had not become harder.

It had become lonelier.

A guide walked the perimeter with no destination.

Her steps were measured, as if she were circling something invisible.

She did not look at Elija.

She did not need to.

The system did not require confrontation anymore.

Containment had passed into maintenance.

Elija watched a woman pause near the edge of the square, hesitate, then turn away as if remembering a task she had not actually forgotten.

She glanced back once.

Their eyes did not meet.

She exhaled sharply — relief, not disappointment — and left.

Elija felt it land like a bruise.

Not sharp.

Dull.

Repeated.

Marin stood at her window that morning longer than usual.

She watched the square from above, noticing how little there was to notice now.

No clustering.

No lingering.

No gravitational pull.

It looked… fine.

And that unsettled her more than conflict would have.

Her body remembered the earlier days.

The way stillness had spread *toward* something rather than away.

The way sitting had felt like exhaling instead of resisting.

Now the city felt composed.

Organised.

Safe.

And yet she could not shake the sense that something essential had been folded away too neatly.

Her husband passed behind her, touched her shoulder.

"You'll be late," he said gently.

She nodded, still watching.

"Yes," she replied.

But she did not move.

By midday, the square had adopted a new sound.

Footsteps.

Not layered.

Sequential.

People passed through, one at a time, as if the space were a corridor rather than a place.

Elija listened.

Footstep.

Pause.

Footstep.

No overlapping rhythms.

No accidental synchrony.

The square was being used, not inhabited.

This was not failure.

This was success.

Containment had done exactly what it was designed to do.

Corven stood at the high window overlooking the city.

From above, everything appeared calm.

Even healthy.

Movement flowed smoothly. Patterns held.

No disruptions.

No clusters requiring correction.

He felt the familiar reassurance try to settle in his chest.

This is what stability looks like.

And yet something resisted.

He had walked through the square the night before.

Late.

When no one was there to perform.

The benches had been empty.

The stone still held warmth from the day.

And he had felt, unmistakably, that the space was waiting.

Not for activity.

For permission.

He pressed his palm against the glass now, as if distance could be closed by pressure.

The city was functioning.

But it was no longer listening.

That afternoon, a child dropped a wooden toy near the fountain.

It rolled, clattering softly against stone.

No one stopped to watch.

A guide glanced over, then looked away.

The child retrieved it and followed his mother, who did not slow.

Elija watched them go.

He remembered Tomas.

Not as absence.

As *unasked question*.

The quiet began to do something strange.

It amplified thought.

Without the buffer of shared presence, people were left alone with their internal narration.

The city's voice filled the gap quickly.

You're fine.
This is better.
Nothing has been lost.

But bodies do not believe reassurance as easily as minds.

Small signs began to appear.

Sleeplessness.

Irritability.

A sense of restlessness that had no clear source.

People could not name what they missed.

Only that something felt… thinner.

Marin returned to the square on the fifth day.

Not at the usual hour.

Later.

When fewer guides were present.

She sat on the bench she had avoided before.

Not close to Elija.

But close enough to feel the choice.

He was still there.

He always was.

She did not look at him.

Not because she was afraid.

Because she did not want to be managed through eye contact.

A guide approached within minutes.

Different one this time.

Older.

More careful.

“Marin,” the guide said softly.

Marin inhaled.

“Yes.”

“You don’t need to be here.”

The sentence was not unkind.

That was what made it difficult.

“I know,” Marin replied.

She did not add *but I want to be*.

Desire was what they were trained to neutralise.

The guide hesitated.

“Are you alright?” she asked.

Marin smiled faintly.

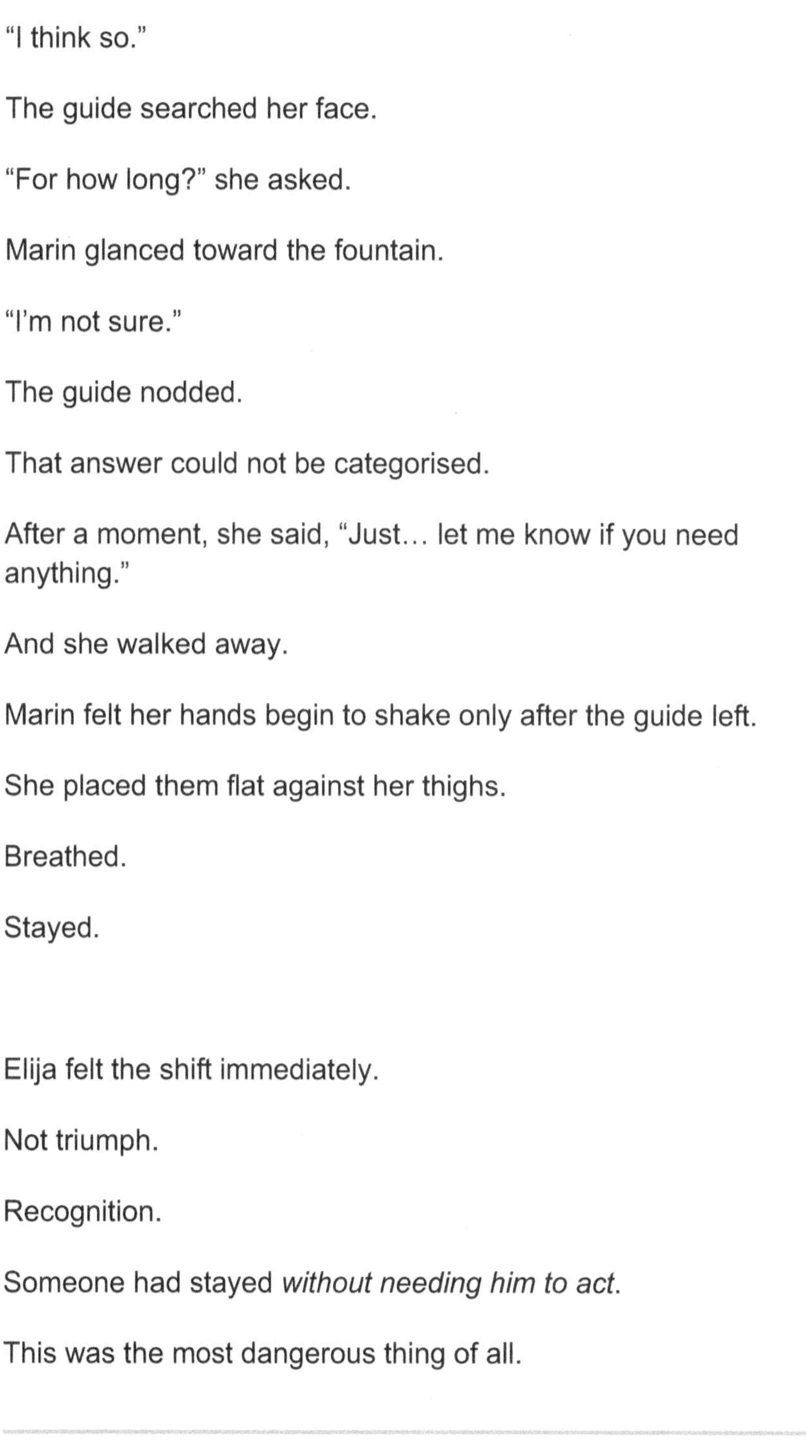

“I think so.”

The guide searched her face.

“For how long?” she asked.

Marin glanced toward the fountain.

“I’m not sure.”

The guide nodded.

That answer could not be categorised.

After a moment, she said, “Just… let me know if you need anything.”

And she walked away.

Marin felt her hands begin to shake only after the guide left.

She placed them flat against her thighs.

Breathed.

Stayed.

Elija felt the shift immediately.

Not triumph.

Recognition.

Someone had stayed *without needing him to act*.

This was the most dangerous thing of all.

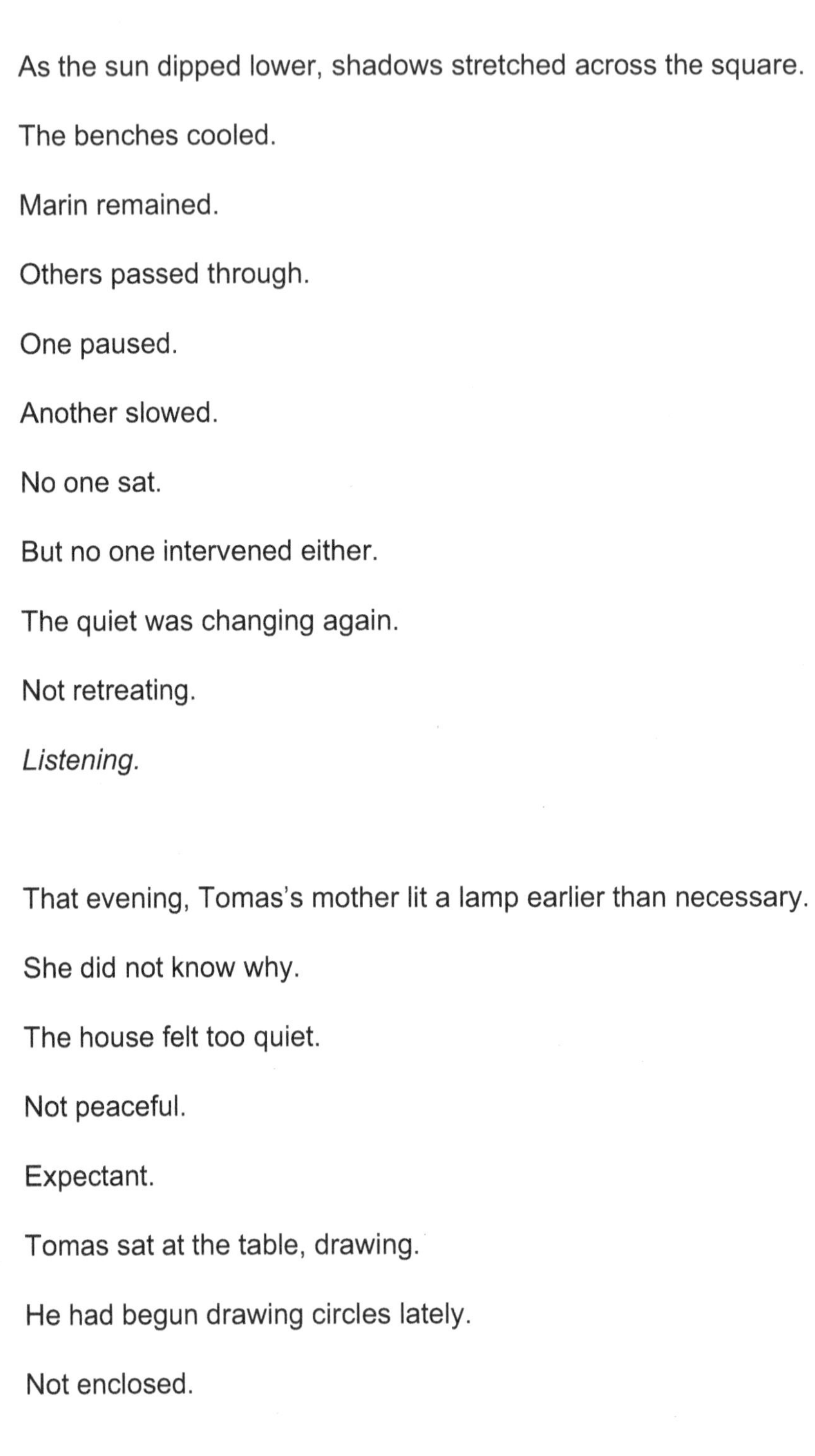

As the sun dipped lower, shadows stretched across the square.

The benches cooled.

Marin remained.

Others passed through.

One paused.

Another slowed.

No one sat.

But no one intervened either.

The quiet was changing again.

Not retreating.

Listening.

That evening, Tomas's mother lit a lamp earlier than necessary.

She did not know why.

The house felt too quiet.

Not peaceful.

Expectant.

Tomas sat at the table, drawing.

He had begun drawing circles lately.

Not enclosed.

Open.

She watched him, heart aching with something she could not articulate.

"Do you miss the square?" she asked.

He shrugged.

"Sometimes."

"What do you miss?"

He thought for a long time.

"Nothing," he said finally.

Then he frowned.

"That's what's weird."

She closed her eyes.

In the Council chamber, language was already shifting.

Reports spoke of *residual quiet.*

Of *temporary behavioural echo.*

Of *minor adjustment fatigue*.

Nothing alarming.

Nothing requiring change.

And yet the data showed something new:

People were returning to the square at irregular times.

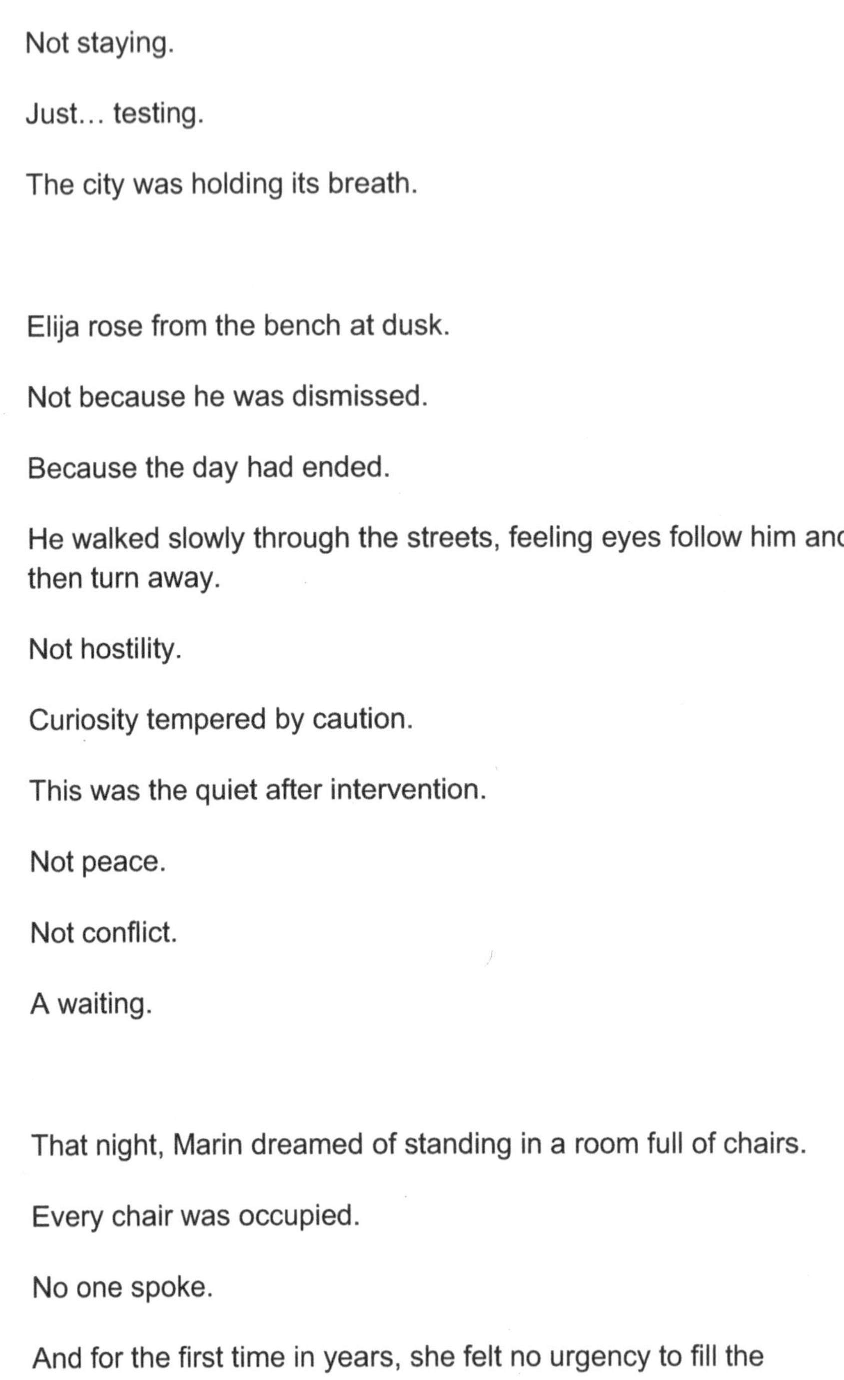

Not staying.

Just… testing.

The city was holding its breath.

Elija rose from the bench at dusk.

Not because he was dismissed.

Because the day had ended.

He walked slowly through the streets, feeling eyes follow him and then turn away.

Not hostility.

Curiosity tempered by caution.

This was the quiet after intervention.

Not peace.

Not conflict.

A waiting.

That night, Marin dreamed of standing in a room full of chairs.

Every chair was occupied.

No one spoke.

And for the first time in years, she felt no urgency to fill the silence.

She woke with tears on her face and no idea why.

The quiet did not mean the city had chosen.

It meant the city had paused long enough to *notice itself.*

Containment had removed friction.

But it had also removed cover.

Now there was space.

And space is dangerous.

Because in space, people begin to ask questions they didn't know they were allowed to ask.

Not loudly.

Not together.

Yet.

But inwardly.

And inward questions, once permitted, do not return quietly to their cages.

Elija lay awake that night, not praying.

Not planning.

Simply listening to the city breathe.

He knew this phase.

The lull after pressure.

The moment before something honest emerges.

Whether fear tightened again…

Or something else rose to meet it…

Would not be decided by him.

It would be decided by whether people trusted the quiet enough to remain inside it.

The square slept.

Not empty.

Waiting.

Chapter 19

Choice did not announce itself.

It never does.

It arrived disguised as hesitation.

The first sign was small.

A woman stood at the edge of the square longer than necessary, holding a basket she did not need to carry yet.

She shifted her weight once.

Twice.

Then remained.

No guide approached immediately.

The system had learned patience.

Elija noticed her not because she looked at him — she didn't — but because her body had stopped seeking instruction.

She wasn't deciding *for* or *against* anything.

She was simply… not moving.

This was new.

The city had grown skilled at guiding motion.

People walked when walking was expected.

Paused when pausing was permitted.

Rested when rest had been authorised.

But unprompted stillness — stillness without visible cause — unsettled the rhythm.

It could not be redirected easily.

It had no script.

The woman eventually sat.

Not near Elija.

Not far.

In a place that did not signal allegiance.

She placed the basket at her feet and folded her hands loosely in her lap.

Her shoulders dropped as if something she had been holding unconsciously had been set down.

Elija felt it like a pressure change.

Not a call.

A permission.

By midday, three more people had done the same.

At different times.

In different places.

No clustering.

No eye contact.

Just bodies choosing to remain where nothing was being demanded of them.

Guides noticed.

Of course they did.

But intervention hesitated.

Containment protocols worked best on momentum — not on stillness that did not reference the source.

There was nothing to redirect *from*.

Corven read the midday report twice.

It did not alarm.

That was the problem.

The language was careful.

Anomalous lingering observed.
No escalation detected.
Engagement low.

Low engagement meant no argument.

No conflict.

No opposition to stabilise against.

He rubbed his temples, suddenly tired in a way rest would not solve.

This was not rebellion.

This was something worse.

People were beginning to decide without narrating their decisions.

Marin returned again that afternoon.

Earlier this time.

She sat.

Stayed.

No guide approached her.

She felt the difference immediately.

Not relief.

Exposure.

Without opposition, there was no structure to lean against.

She could leave.

No one would stop her.

That frightened her more than containment ever had.

She realised, suddenly, how much of her obedience had been sustained by resistance.

How much of her compliance had relied on something pushing back.

Now there was nothing.

Just her.

Her breath.

Her body.

Her choice.

She exhaled shakily and stayed.

Elija did not look at her.

Not deliberately.

But because he understood the moment.

This was not about him.

If he acknowledged her choice too soon, it would become relational rather than internal.

She needed to stay without being witnessed *by him*.

The city, however, was watching closely.

A guide approached one of the other sitters.

A man with a lined face and steady posture.

She stood a respectful distance away.

“Are you waiting for someone?” she asked gently.

The man considered.

“No,” he said.

The guide smiled.

“You don’t need to stay.”

“I know.”

The guide nodded.

The script did not cover this response.

She hesitated.

“Are you feeling unsettled?”

The man shook his head.

“Quite the opposite.”

That answer landed awkwardly.

The guide laughed softly, trying to normalise the moment.

“Well,” she said, “just let me know if you need anything.”

And she walked away.

The man did not move.

That evening, something subtle shifted in the square.

Not numbers.

Not energy.

Authority.

Not Elija's.

The square's.

It began to feel — impossibly — like it belonged to the people again.

Not officially.

Not legally.

But experientially.

No announcements were made.

No declarations issued.

And yet people lingered a little longer before leaving.

Sat a little more fully when they sat.

Left without apology.

Returned without explanation.

This was not revolution.

It was re-orientation.

At home, Marin found herself unable to speak.

Her husband noticed.

“Long day?” he asked.

She nodded.

“What happened?”

She opened her mouth.

Closed it.

“I stayed,” she said finally.

“Where?”

“In the square.”

He waited.

“And?”

“I didn’t need to,” she added.

He frowned slightly.

“And you did anyway?”

“Yes.”

He sat back, processing.

“No one stopped you?”

“No.”

“No one encouraged you?”

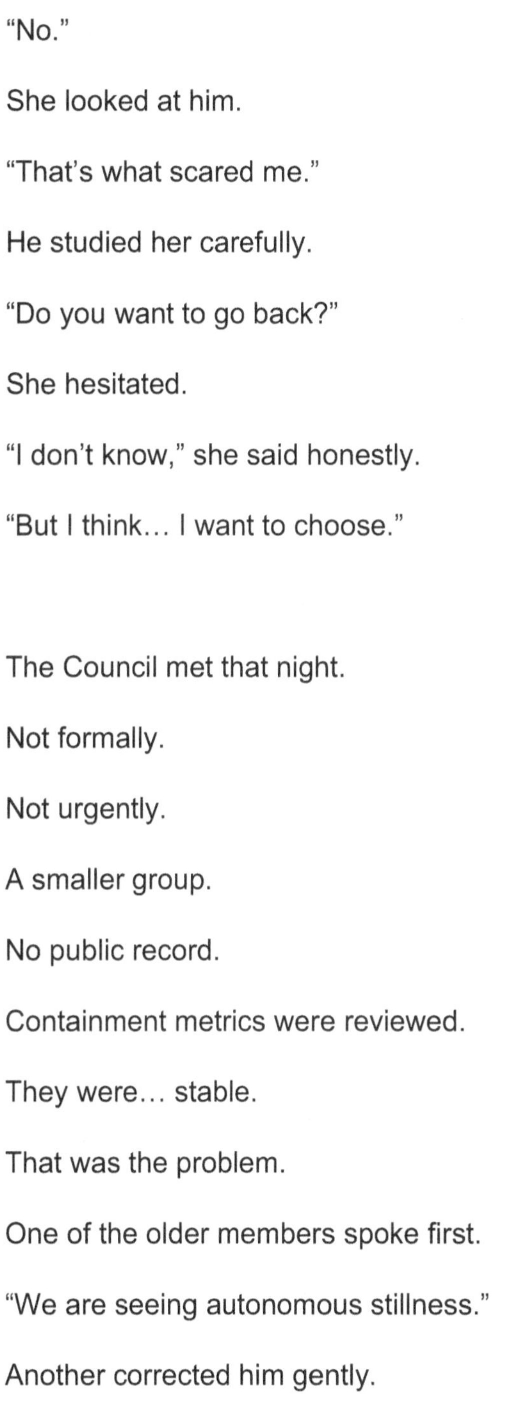

"No."

She looked at him.

"That's what scared me."

He studied her carefully.

"Do you want to go back?"

She hesitated.

"I don't know," she said honestly.

"But I think… I want to choose."

The Council met that night.

Not formally.

Not urgently.

A smaller group.

No public record.

Containment metrics were reviewed.

They were… stable.

That was the problem.

One of the older members spoke first.

"We are seeing autonomous stillness."

Another corrected him gently.

“We are seeing hesitation.”

The room went quiet.

Hesitation implied uncertainty.

Uncertainty implied lack of control.

Corven listened, saying nothing.

Finally, he spoke.

“What if,” he said slowly, “what we are seeing is people remembering how to decide without pressure?”

Several heads turned.

One man frowned.

“That would be destabilising.”

“Only if we assume people are dangerous when unled,” Corven replied.

The room stiffened.

“That assumption,” he added carefully, “is the foundation of our guidance.”

Silence.

Someone laughed nervously.

“You’re suggesting we do nothing?”

“I’m suggesting,” Corven said, “that we stop correcting what isn’t breaking.”

The chairwoman leaned forward.

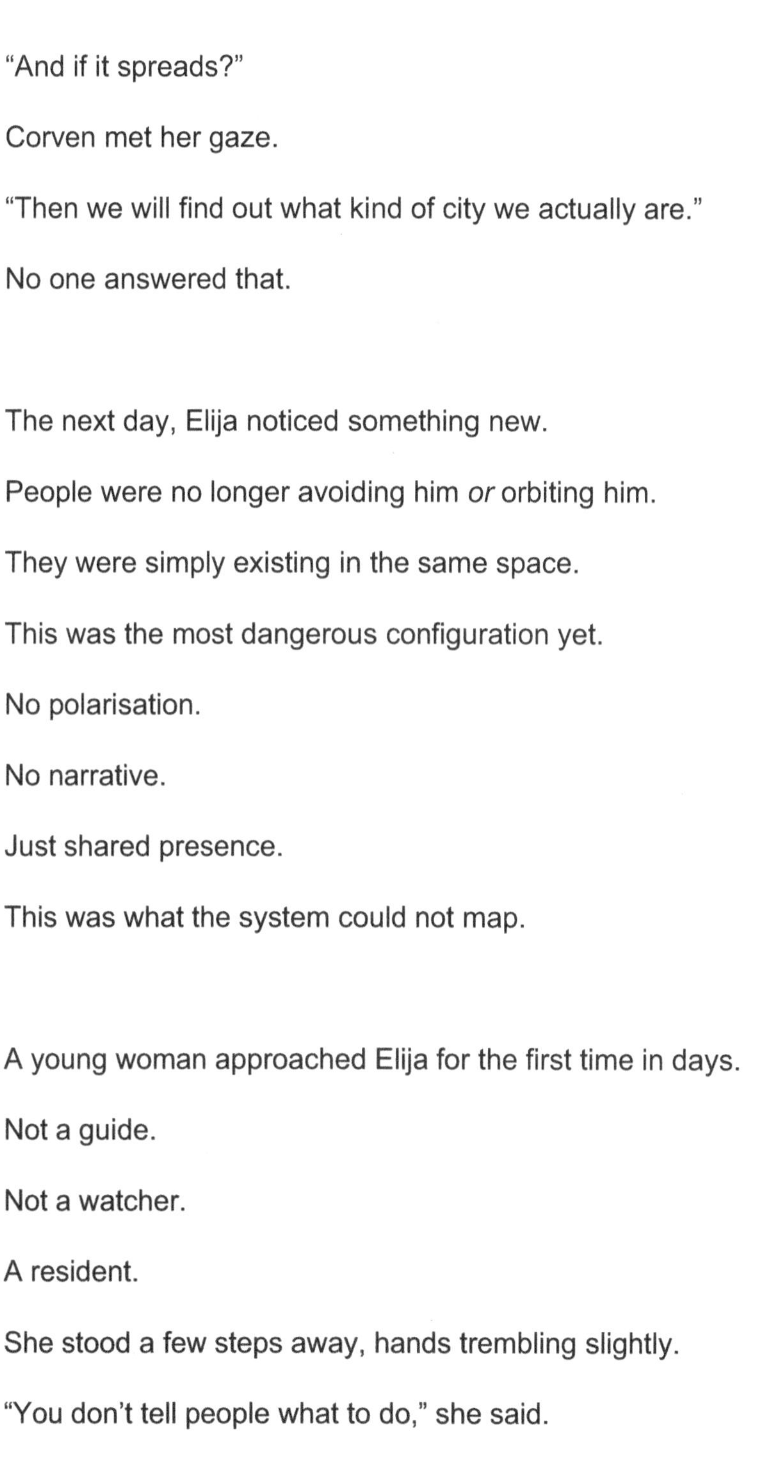

“And if it spreads?”

Corven met her gaze.

“Then we will find out what kind of city we actually are.”

No one answered that.

The next day, Elija noticed something new.

People were no longer avoiding him *or* orbiting him.

They were simply existing in the same space.

This was the most dangerous configuration yet.

No polarisation.

No narrative.

Just shared presence.

This was what the system could not map.

A young woman approached Elija for the first time in days.

Not a guide.

Not a watcher.

A resident.

She stood a few steps away, hands trembling slightly.

“You don’t tell people what to do,” she said.

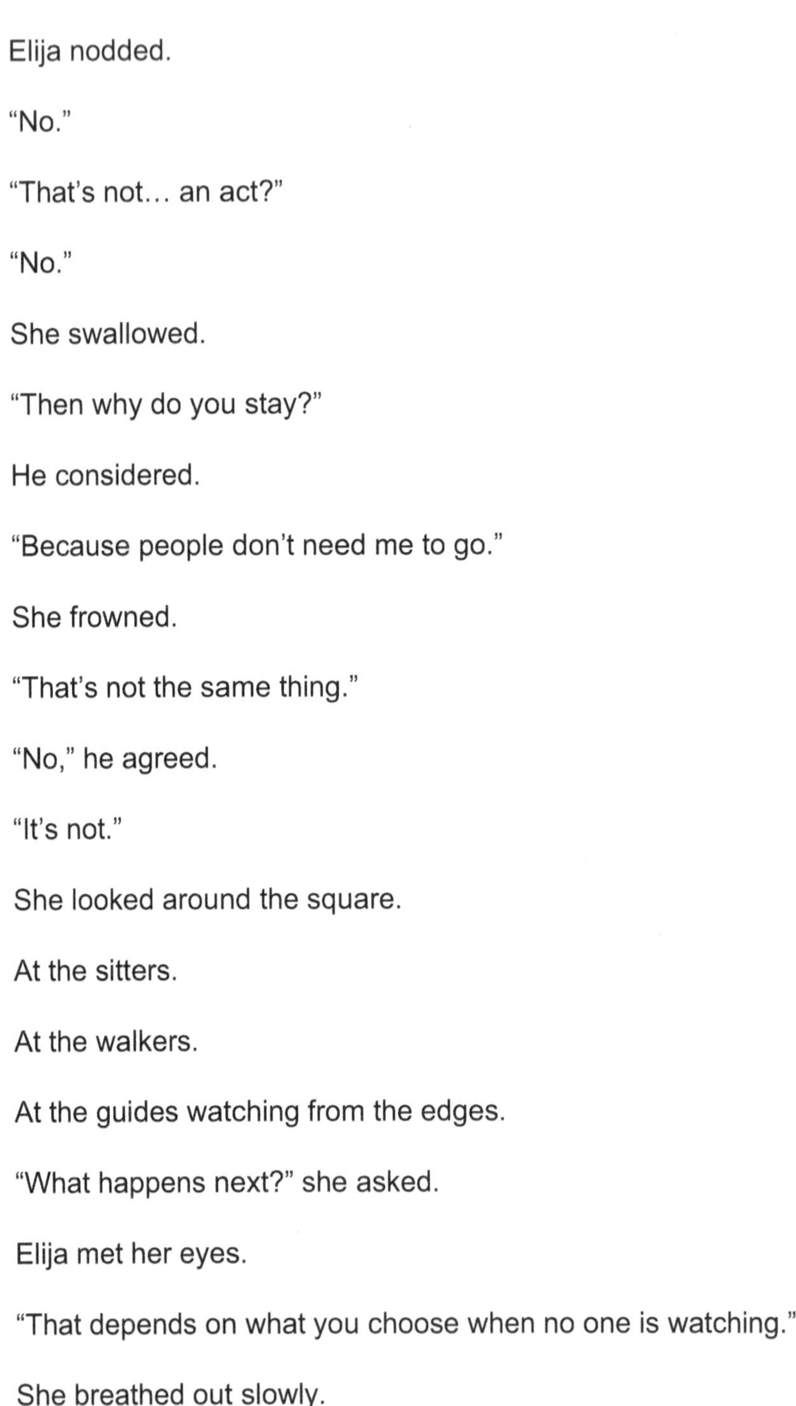

Elija nodded.

“No.”

“That’s not… an act?”

“No.”

She swallowed.

“Then why do you stay?”

He considered.

“Because people don’t need me to go.”

She frowned.

“That’s not the same thing.”

“No,” he agreed.

“It’s not.”

She looked around the square.

At the sitters.

At the walkers.

At the guides watching from the edges.

“What happens next?” she asked.

Elija met her eyes.

“That depends on what you choose when no one is watching.”

She breathed out slowly.

Then, to her own surprise, she sat.

The guides noticed immediately.

Containment no longer applied.

This was not exposure.

This was voluntary return.

There was no script for this.

One guide reached instinctively for protocol.

Another stopped her.

“Wait,” she said.

“Let’s see.”

That pause — that single, unrecorded hesitation — mattered more than any policy.

That night, unable to remain in the hall, Corven walked the square openly.

Not as oversight.

As presence.

He did not speak to Elija.

He did not need to.

He watched people sit, rise, return.

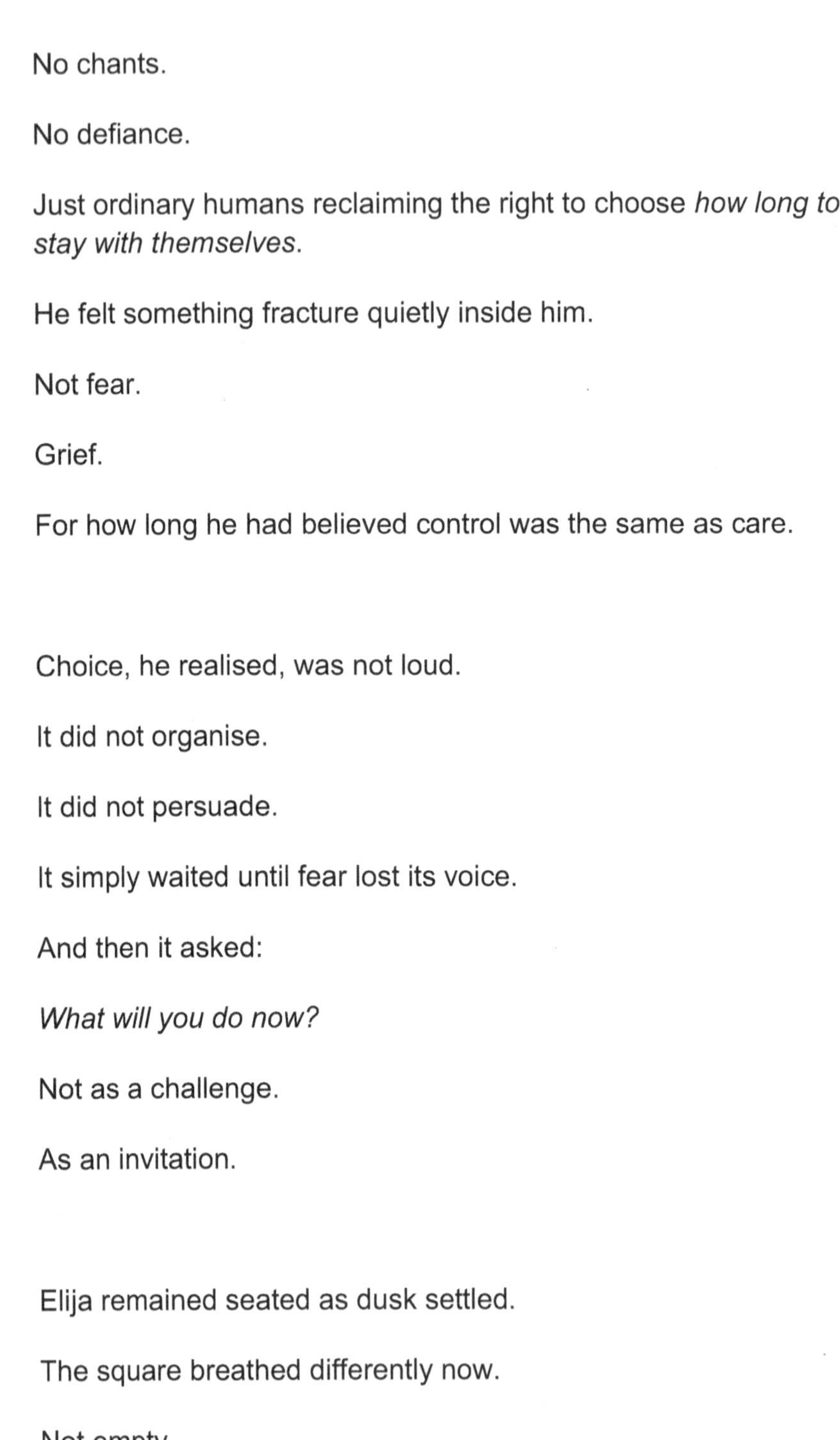

No chants.

No defiance.

Just ordinary humans reclaiming the right to choose *how long to stay with themselves.*

He felt something fracture quietly inside him.

Not fear.

Grief.

For how long he had believed control was the same as care.

Choice, he realised, was not loud.

It did not organise.

It did not persuade.

It simply waited until fear lost its voice.

And then it asked:

What will you do now?

Not as a challenge.

As an invitation.

Elija remained seated as dusk settled.

The square breathed differently now.

Not empty.

Not full.

Alive.

No one had declared freedom.

No one had announced change.

And yet something irreversible had begun.

Not because Elija had taught it.

But because the city had remembered itself.

Chapter 20

Corven had spent his life believing that restraint was the highest form of wisdom.

Not the restraint of fear — the restraint of foresight.

The kind that anticipated damage before it arrived.

The kind that prevented collapse quietly, without spectacle.

It was what had made him valuable.

Trusted.

It was also what had trained him to mistake control for care.

He stood at the edge of the square long after dusk.

Not observing.

Witnessing.

There was a difference.

The city's lights glowed steadily. Windows flickered on and off as families settled into evening rhythms.

From above, everything would have looked stable.

From here, something else was happening.

People were staying.

Not gathering.

Not organising.

Just… remaining.

The square was no longer empty.

It was not crowded either.

It was *inhabited*.

That distinction mattered more than any metric Corven had ever studied.

A guide approached him cautiously.

Not because he outranked her — though he did — but because she sensed he was not there in an official capacity.

"Should we intervene?" she asked quietly.

Her voice carried no urgency.

Only habit.

Corven looked at her.

At the way her shoulders were slightly raised.

At the way her eyes tracked movement automatically, even as she waited for instruction.

“What would intervention accomplish?” he asked.

She hesitated.

“It would… restore clarity.”

Corven nodded.

“And what’s unclear right now?”

The guide opened her mouth.

Closed it.

She scanned the square.

People sat.

Some talked softly.

Others were silent.

No one was agitated.

No one was demanding anything.

“I don’t know,” she admitted.

Corven felt something loosen in his chest.

“Then we wait,” he said.

The guide swallowed.

“Yes,” she replied.

But she did not move away immediately.

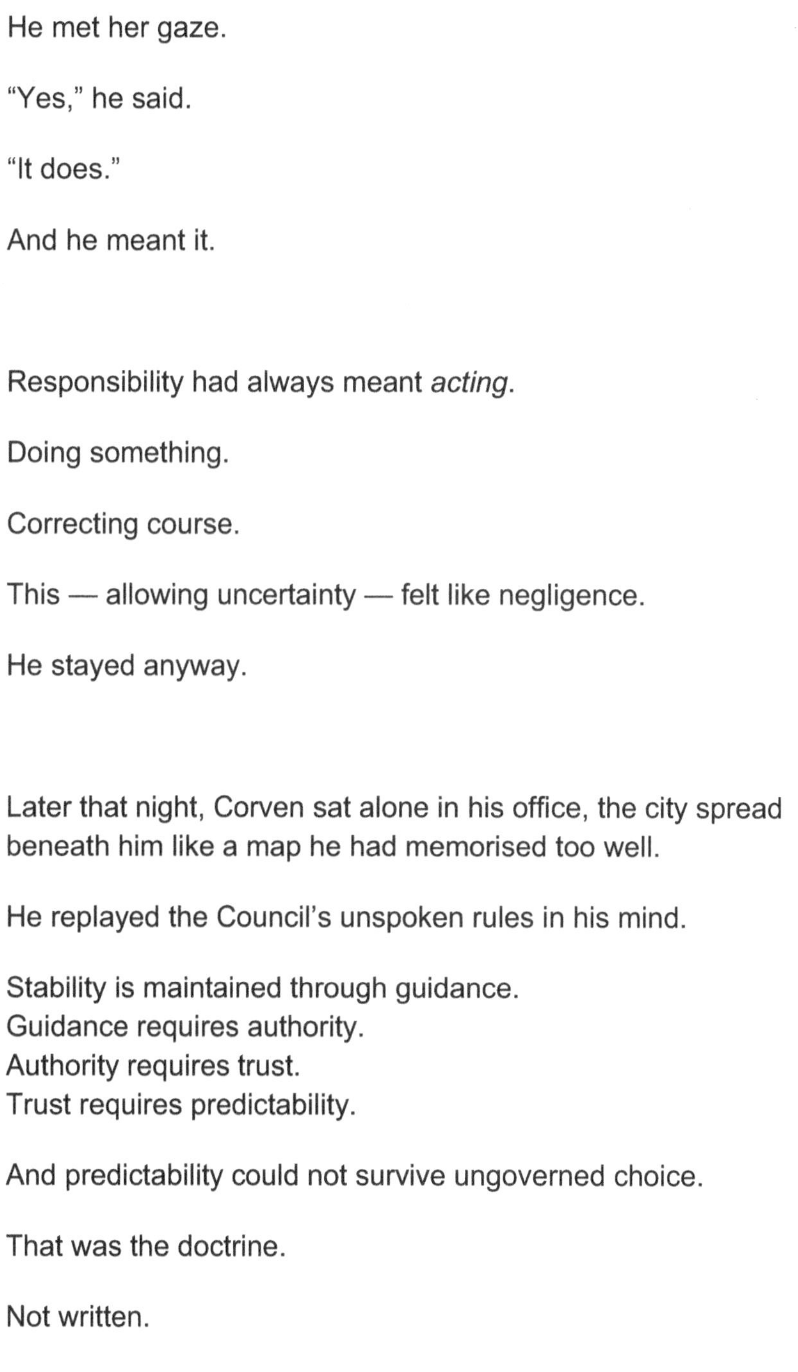

“Sir,” she added, quietly, “this feels… irresponsible.”

He met her gaze.

“Yes,” he said.

“It does.”

And he meant it.

Responsibility had always meant *acting*.

Doing something.

Correcting course.

This — allowing uncertainty — felt like negligence.

He stayed anyway.

Later that night, Corven sat alone in his office, the city spread beneath him like a map he had memorised too well.

He replayed the Council’s unspoken rules in his mind.

Stability is maintained through guidance.
Guidance requires authority.
Authority requires trust.
Trust requires predictability.

And predictability could not survive ungoverned choice.

That was the doctrine.

Not written.

Assumed.

The city had been built on it.

And now he was watching predictability dissolve — not into chaos, but into something quieter.

Something harder to oppose.

He pulled up the reports again.

Containment efficacy had declined slightly.

But *well-being indicators* had not.

In some areas, they had improved.

Sleep patterns.

Reported anxiety.

Unexplained, but measurable.

He stared at the numbers.

They did not accuse him.

They did not justify him either.

They simply refused to cooperate with the narrative he had spent decades defending.

A knock came at his door.

Not formal.

Not scheduled.

Joryn stood in the doorway, face drawn.

“May I?” he asked.

Corven nodded.

Joryn stepped inside and closed the door behind him.

“I was part of the containment session,” Joryn said.

“I know.”

“I followed protocol.”

“I know.”

Joryn swallowed.

“And I hated myself for how easy it was.”

Corven looked up sharply.

Joryn continued before he could be interrupted.

“It didn’t feel cruel. That was the problem. It felt kind. Helpful. Efficient.”

His voice broke slightly.

“And I realised… I could do it forever. I could gently move people out of themselves for the rest of my life and call it care.”

Silence filled the room.

Corven felt something inside him fracture — not shatter, but *shift*.

“What do you want from me?” Corven asked quietly.

Joryn shook his head.

"I don't know," he said honestly.

"I think… I want permission not to be good at this."

The words landed heavily.

Corven leaned back, eyes closed.

When he spoke again, his voice was steady.

"You already have it."

Joryn exhaled sharply.

"But the Council—"

"The Council will decide what it decides," Corven said.

He opened his eyes.

"I'm deciding something else."

Joryn nodded slowly.

Then, almost in a whisper, he said, "Thank you."

And left.

The next morning, the city woke without incident.

No surge.

No rally.

No declaration.

People went to work.

Children went to lessons.

Life continued.

And yet something had shifted irreversibly.

People returned to the square without explanation.

Not all at once.

Not together.

But consistently.

The square was becoming *normal* again.

That was what frightened the Council most.

The emergency meeting was called that afternoon.

Not because of crisis.

Because of erosion.

Containment no longer worked as intended.

Not because it was resisted.

But because it was no longer *needed*.

The chairwoman spoke first.

"This is drifting," she said flatly.

"It's stabilising," Corven replied.

"Without oversight."

"Yes."

"That's unacceptable."

Corven leaned forward.

"What exactly are we afraid of?"

The room went quiet.

One man spoke.

"Loss of coherence."

Another added, "Fragmentation."

A third said, "Unpredictable alignment."

Corven nodded.

"And if coherence has been maintained through fear of deviation rather than trust?"

The chairwoman's jaw tightened.

"You're suggesting we gamble the city."

Corven met her gaze.

"I'm suggesting we stop assuming people are dangerous when left alone."

"That assumption," she said coldly, "has kept us safe."

Corven did not flinch.

"It has kept us obedient."

A murmur rippled through the room.

“You’re overstepping,” someone said.

“Yes,” Corven replied.

“I am.”

Silence.

Then the chairwoman spoke again, voice measured.

“If this continues, it will be traced back to you.”

Corven nodded.

“I know.”

“You will be held responsible.”

“Yes.”

“Your position—”

“Is not the city,” Corven said.

The words surprised even him.

But once spoken, they felt inevitable.

That evening, Corven walked the square openly.

Not to supervise.

To be seen.

He did not address Elija.

He did not need to.

Their agreement was not strategic.

It was ontological.

One man had refused to instruct.

The other was learning to refuse to *interfere*.

People noticed.

Whispers moved.

Not rumours.

Questions.

Why is he here?
Why isn't he stopping this?
Why does this feel… allowed?

Permission, Corven realised, did not require announcement.

It required *absence of prevention*.

A guide approached him hesitantly.

"Sir," she said, "the Council—"

"I know," Corven replied.

She hesitated.

"Are we… still guiding?"

Corven looked at her.

"At the people sitting. Talking. Leaving when they wanted. Returning without explanation."

"Yes," he said.

"But not steering."

She nodded, unsure whether to feel relieved or exposed.

As night settled, Corven sat on a bench at the edge of the square.

Not beside Elija.

Near enough to share the same silence.

He felt the weight now.

Not the relief of abdication.

The cost of allowing.

If fear returned, it would be blamed on him.

If disorder arose, it would be attributed to his weakness.

If people were harmed, his name would be attached.

Control had always diffused responsibility.

Allowing concentrated it.

This was why systems preferred force.

Force could be justified.

Permission had no defence.

Elija rose as the square emptied.

He did not approach Corven.

He paused near him only long enough to say one thing.

“This is where it becomes real.”

Corven nodded.

“Yes.”

“You can still stop it,” Elija added gently.

Corven looked at the square.

At the people leaving freely.

At the quiet that now felt inhabited rather than avoided.

“No,” he said.

“I don’t think I can.”

Elija inclined his head slightly.

Not approval.

Recognition.

Later that night, alone again, Corven wrote a single line in his private ledger.

Not policy.

Not instruction.

A confession.

Care without control feels like risk because it is.

He closed the book.

For the first time in years, he did not feel like he was holding the city together.

He felt like he was trusting it.

And that, he realised, might be the most dangerous thing he had ever done.

Chapter 21

The city did not fracture when guidance loosened.

It sagged.

Like something that had been held upright too long by an invisible brace.

People did not rush toward freedom.

They leaned into it.

And leaning, Elija realised, revealed more about fear than resistance ever had.

The first calls came quietly.

Not to the Council.

To neighbours.

To friends.

To anyone who still answered without redirecting.

“What are we meant to do now?”
“Is this… allowed?”
“Are we safe?”

The questions carried no anger.

Only the ache of muscles unused.

In the square, people leaned without sitting.

They stood longer than before.

Hands resting on benches.

Weight shifting from foot to foot.

As if testing whether the ground would hold without instruction.

Elija watched.

He felt no urgency to stabilise them.

Urgency was the old language.

Marin noticed it in conversation.

People spoke in half-sentences.

They trailed off and waited to see if someone would finish the thought for them.

When no one did, discomfort surfaced.

Laughter sometimes followed.

Sometimes irritation.

Sometimes relief.

A woman snapped at her partner over dinner.

Not about anything important.

About nothing at all.

Later, she cried and said, “I don’t know who I am without being told.”

He held her, unsure what comfort meant when reassurance felt like theft.

The guides leaned too.

Not outwardly.

Internally.

Their scripts had grown thin.

Without clear correction points, they hesitated longer.

Waited for cues that never came.

Some felt exposed.

Others quietly grateful.

One guide stood near the square late one afternoon, watching a man sit alone.

He was not drawing attention.

Not influencing others.

Just present.

The guide felt the urge to intervene rise out of habit.

Then fall.

Then rise again.

Finally, he leaned against a wall and did nothing.

He surprised himself by smiling.

Corven received reports framed as concerns.

Not incidents.

Language shifted again.

Increased ambiguity.
Reduced reliance on guidance.
Emergent self-regulation.

Self-regulation.

The phrase felt both promising and dangerous.

It implied trust.

It also implied loss.

At home, Corven leaned against his desk and felt the weight settle properly for the first time.

This was not leadership as he had been trained.

There was no leverage here.

No escalation ladder.

Only presence and consequence.

He would not be able to fix things quickly if they broke.

He would have to endure them.

In the square, a man approached Elija openly.

Not nervously.

Not reverently.

“I don’t know how to do this,” he said.

Elija nodded.

“Good.”

The man blinked. “That’s it?”

“Yes.”

The man frowned, then laughed.

He leaned against the bench and stayed.

A child asked a guide, “Why doesn’t he tell people what to do?”

The guide considered carefully.

“Because he trusts them.”

The child thought about this.

“Is that allowed?”

The guide smiled faintly.

“I think,” she said, “it might be necessary.”

Leaning changed people unevenly.

Some leaned toward responsibility.

Others leaned toward avoidance.

Freedom did not sort motives.

It exposed them.

Marin watched a friendship strain.

One friend wanted certainty.

The other wanted space.

They circled each other cautiously, each feeling betrayed by the other’s posture.

No system stepped in to mediate.

They had to learn how to hold difference without resolution.

It was exhausting.

It was also real.

The square held these tensions quietly.

It did not resolve them.

It simply refused to rush them.

That evening, Elija noticed something important.

People no longer looked to him when they were unsure.

They looked inward first.

Sometimes outward, to one another.

He felt a strange mixture of relief and grief.

This was how you knew the centre was shifting.

When the one who had revealed it was no longer required.

Corven passed through the square again.

Not to observe.

To feel.

He leaned briefly against a column and let the city's uncertainty wash over him.

This was the cost no one warned him about.

Not backlash.

Not revolt.

But the ache of allowing people to become clumsy again.

A woman sat nearby and said to no one in particular, “I think I want to leave my job.”

No one responded immediately.

Then another woman said, “You’re allowed to want that.”

The first woman nodded, tears rising.

They sat in silence.

Leaning did not look like progress.

It looked like wobble.

And wobble frightened those who confused stillness with stagnation and motion with growth.

That night, the Council argued in circles.

No decision was reached.

Because there was nothing concrete to oppose.

No threat to name.

Only a city learning to balance itself without a hand on its back.

Elija rose when the square thinned.

He felt tired.

Not burdened.

Tired in the way one feels after holding space rather than filling it.

This was honest fatigue.

It did not ask for relief.

As he left, he heard someone say, “I don’t know yet.”

And someone else reply, “That’s okay.”

He smiled to himself.

Leaning, he realised, was not failure.

It was strength rediscovering its muscles.

The city would wobble more.

It would misstep.

Freedom was not clean.

But something irreversible had taken root.

Not confidence.

Not clarity.

A quieter thing.

The willingness to remain unpropped.

And that, more than certainty, was what would carry them forward.

Chapter 22

The first mistake people made was assuming freedom meant approval.

Not from the Council.

From life itself.

At first, it sounded harmless.

A man declined an obligation he had resented for years and said, "It doesn't feel aligned anymore."

A woman arrived late to work and shrugged. "I'm listening to myself."

A neighbour stopped attending communal meetings altogether. "I'm not ready to engage."

None of these acts were violent.

None were cruel.

But they carried a subtle shift in tone — a confidence that expected no consequence.

Freedom had been felt.

And now it was being *used*.

The city noticed.

Not officially.

Relationally.

Marin heard it in conversation first.

A friend spoke sharply to her partner and justified it with new language.

“I’m just being honest now.”

Another ended a long-standing commitment abruptly.

“I don’t owe anyone consistency.”

The words were clean.

Self-assured.

And something in them rang false.

Freedom, Marin realised, did not sound like dismissal.

But dismissal was borrowing its vocabulary.

In the square, a man sat loudly.

Not physically loud.

Energetically.

He sprawled across a bench, arms wide, gaze challenging.

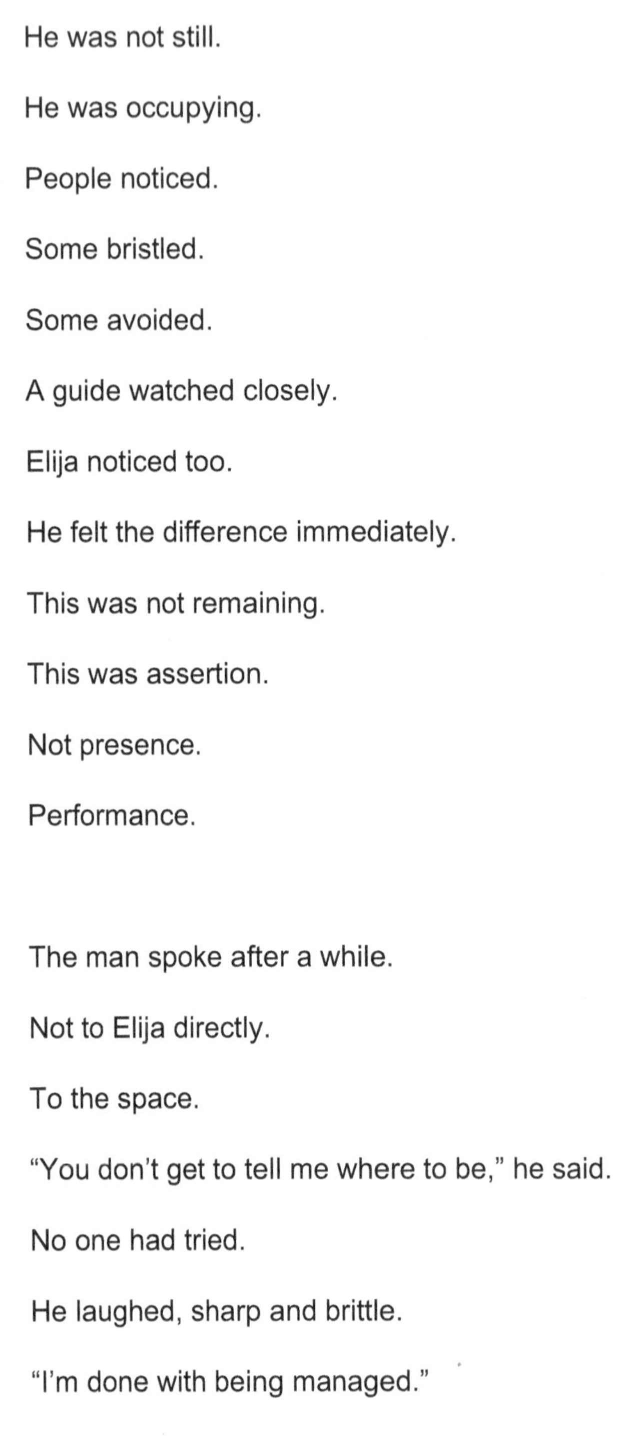

He was not still.

He was occupying.

People noticed.

Some bristled.

Some avoided.

A guide watched closely.

Elija noticed too.

He felt the difference immediately.

This was not remaining.

This was assertion.

Not presence.

Performance.

The man spoke after a while.

Not to Elija directly.

To the space.

“You don’t get to tell me where to be,” he said.

No one had tried.

He laughed, sharp and brittle.

“I’m done with being managed.”

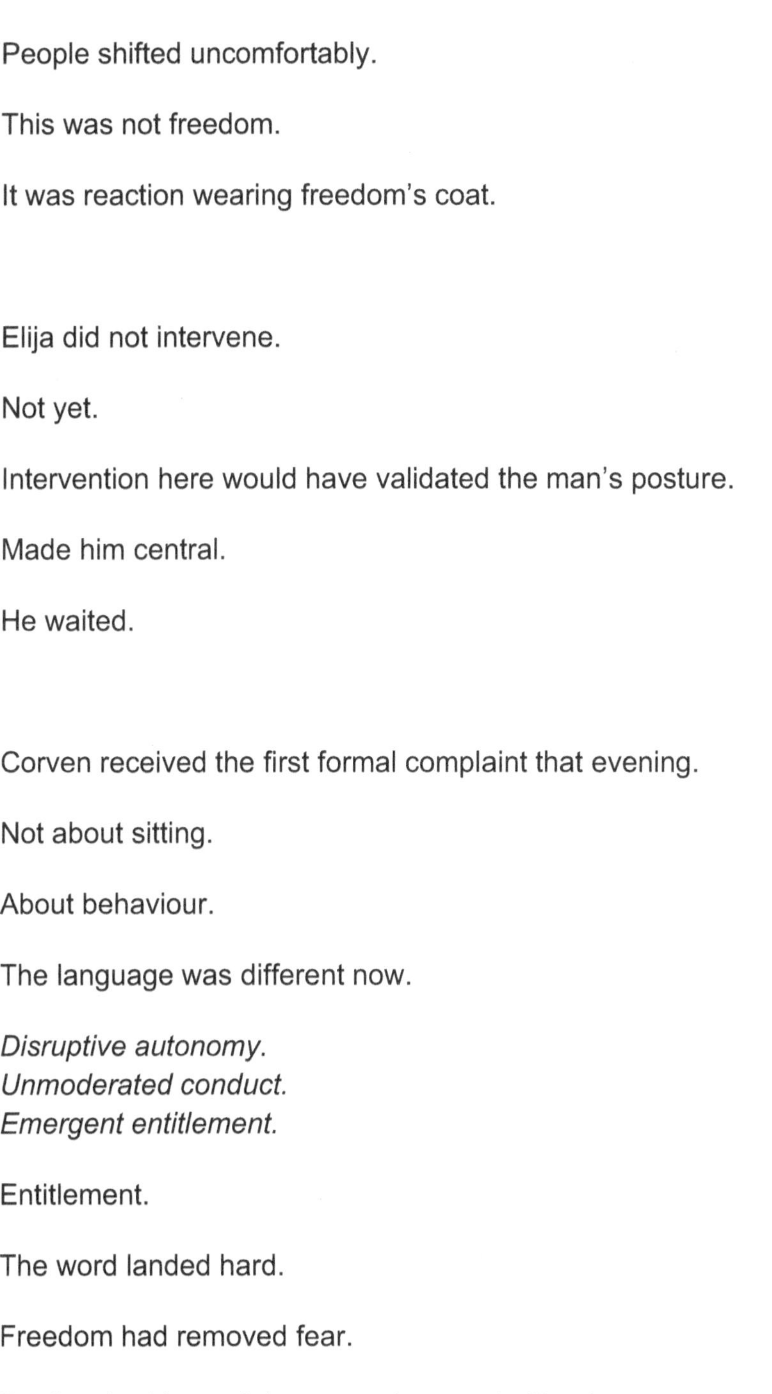

People shifted uncomfortably.

This was not freedom.

It was reaction wearing freedom's coat.

Elija did not intervene.

Not yet.

Intervention here would have validated the man's posture.

Made him central.

He waited.

Corven received the first formal complaint that evening.

Not about sitting.

About behaviour.

The language was different now.

Disruptive autonomy.
Unmoderated conduct.
Emergent entitlement.

Entitlement.

The word landed hard.

Freedom had removed fear.

But fear had been doing more than controlling harm.

It had been containing immaturity.

The Council reconvened.

Tension sat openly in the room now.

"This is exactly what we warned about," one member said. "People confusing freedom with exemption."

Another nodded. "They're calling irresponsibility authenticity."

Eyes turned toward Corven.

"This is the consequence of your inaction."

Corven did not deny it.

"Yes," he said. "This is a consequence."

"You said people weren't dangerous when unled."

"I said they weren't *inherently* dangerous."

A murmur.

"And now?"

"And now," Corven continued, "we're seeing the difference between freedom and maturity."

Silence followed.

One woman leaned forward.

"And what do you propose we do?"

Corven paused.

"Nothing yet."

The word fell heavily.

"They have to learn," he said. "And learning requires room for misinterpretation."

"That's reckless."

"No," Corven replied quietly. "It's developmental."

In the square, the man continued returning.

Each day louder.

Each day less settled.

He wanted reaction.

Approval or opposition — either would have worked.

He received neither.

People did not correct him.

They also did not follow him.

The square did something subtle.

It *withheld reinforcement*.

Marin watched one afternoon as the man finally stood, frustrated.

"No one even cares," he snapped.

A woman nearby looked up calmly.

"We care," she said. "We just don't need to respond."

He stared at her, disoriented.

Then left.

That evening, Marin sat with Elija for the first time in days.

Not close.

But near enough to speak.

"I think some people are afraid you won't stop bad behaviour," she said quietly.

Elija nodded.

"They're right."

She looked at him.

"You won't."

"No."

"Why?"

"Because stopping behaviour isn't the same as forming people."

Marin considered this.

"And what if people hurt others?"

Elija met her gaze.

"Then we intervene for harm," he said. "Not for discomfort."

She exhaled slowly.

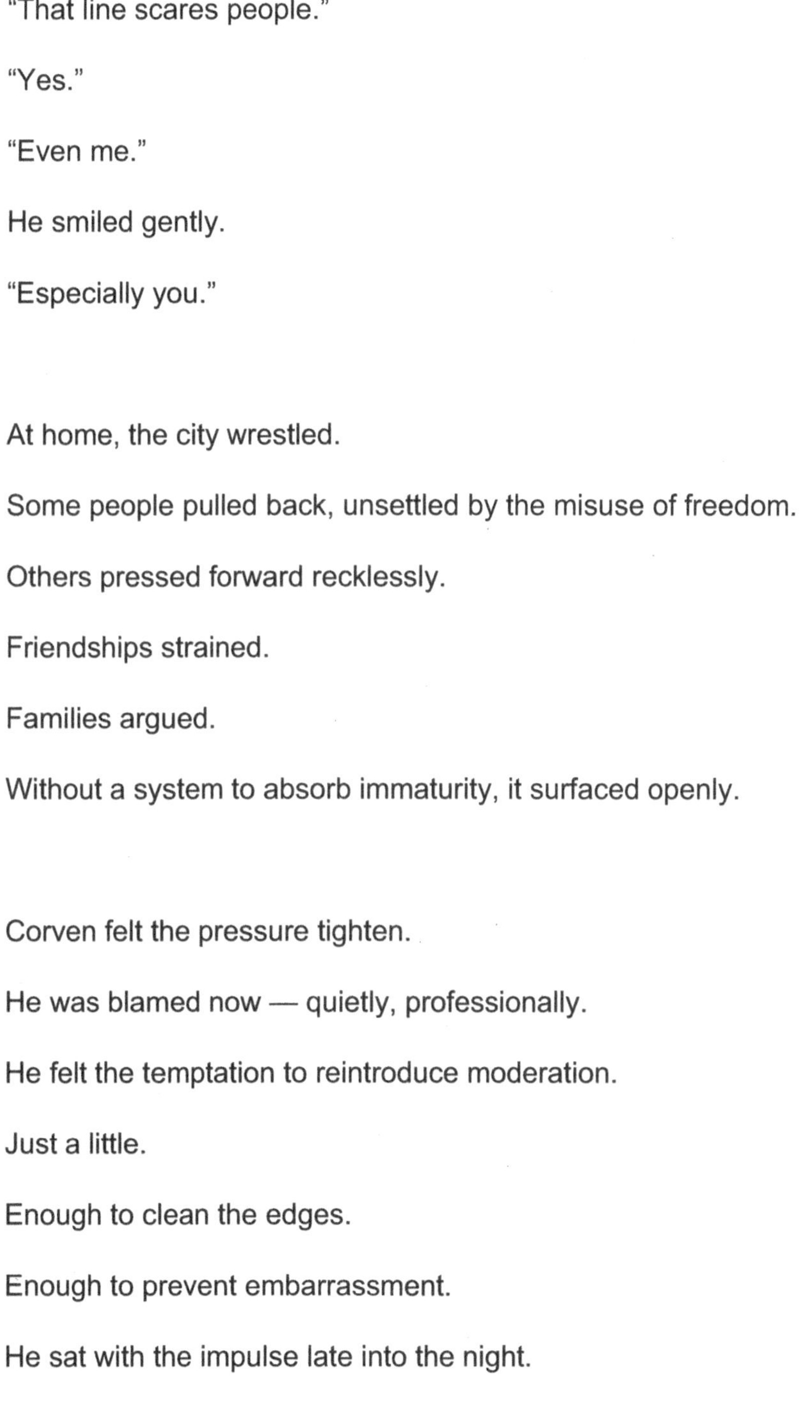

"That line scares people."

"Yes."

"Even me."

He smiled gently.

"Especially you."

At home, the city wrestled.

Some people pulled back, unsettled by the misuse of freedom.

Others pressed forward recklessly.

Friendships strained.

Families argued.

Without a system to absorb immaturity, it surfaced openly.

Corven felt the pressure tighten.

He was blamed now — quietly, professionally.

He felt the temptation to reintroduce moderation.

Just a little.

Enough to clean the edges.

Enough to prevent embarrassment.

He sat with the impulse late into the night.

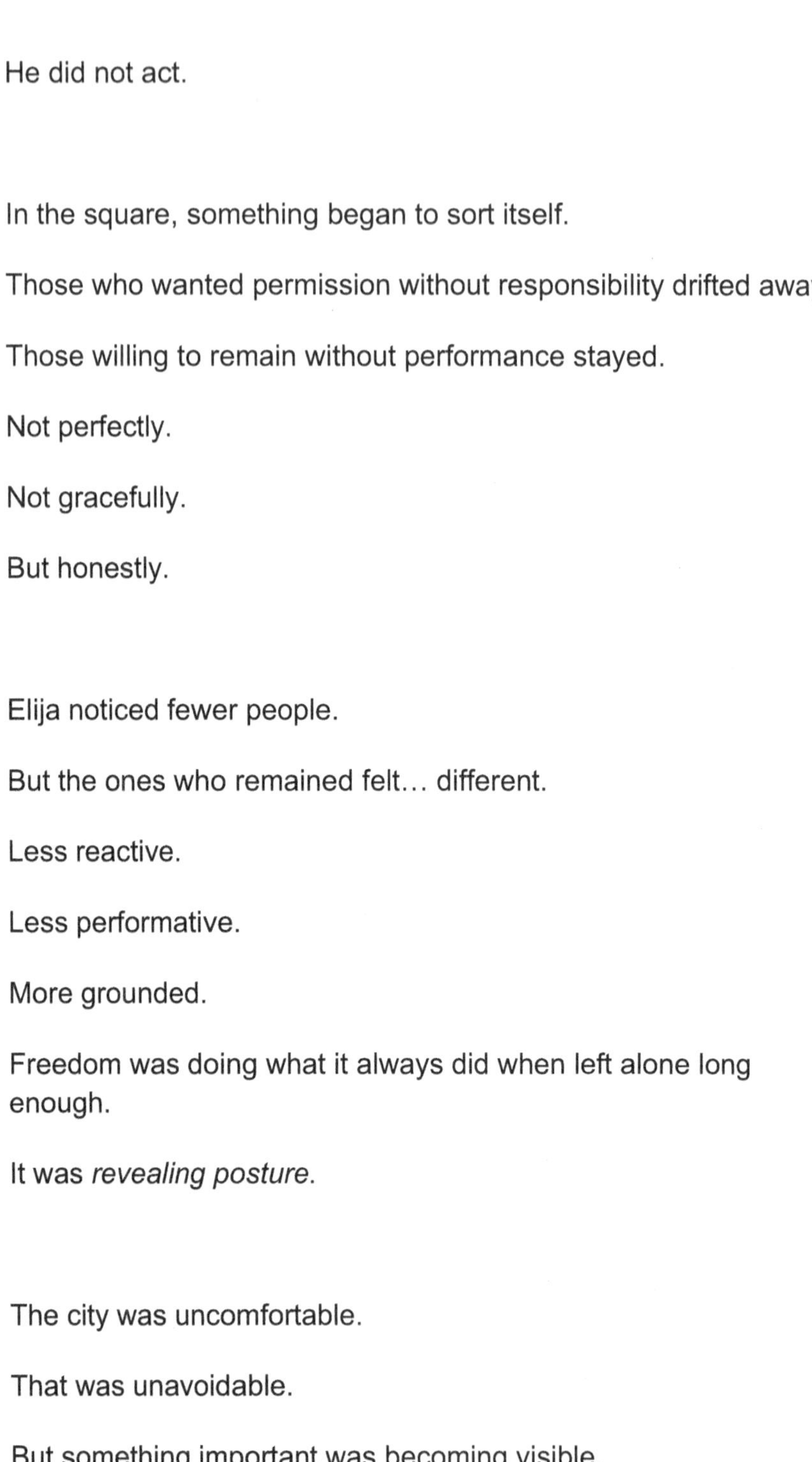

He did not act.

In the square, something began to sort itself.

Those who wanted permission without responsibility drifted away.

Those willing to remain without performance stayed.

Not perfectly.

Not gracefully.

But honestly.

Elija noticed fewer people.

But the ones who remained felt… different.

Less reactive.

Less performative.

More grounded.

Freedom was doing what it always did when left alone long enough.

It was *revealing posture.*

The city was uncomfortable.

That was unavoidable.

But something important was becoming visible.

Freedom did not mature people automatically.

It simply removed the scaffolding that hid where maturity was missing.

Late one evening, Corven passed through the square again.

He watched two people speak tensely, then pause.

Neither apologised.

Neither escalated.

They breathed.

Stayed.

He felt a quiet relief.

Not because everything was good.

But because growth was no longer being mistaken for peace.

Freedom, he realised, was not a solution.

It was an environment.

And environments reveal what lives inside them.

Elija remained seated as night settled.

The square felt less certain now.

Less idealised.

More human.

This, too, was part of the work.

Freedom had been given room.

Now it was learning how to grow up.

Chapter 23

Backlash did not arrive as anger.

Anger would have been easier.

Anger could be named, opposed, contained.

This arrived as concern.

It began with phrases that sounded responsible.

"We need to talk about where this is heading."
"Some people are feeling unsafe."
"We're not saying anyone's wrong—just that this needs boundaries."

The city had learned long ago that fear, when dressed as care, moved more freely.

Marin heard it first from someone she trusted.

A woman she had known for years sat across from her, hands folded carefully around a cup gone cold.

“I’m worried about you,” the woman said.

Marin waited.

“You’ve changed,” she continued. “You seem… less available.”

Marin nodded slowly. “I think I am.”

The woman frowned. “That’s not healthy.”

Marin felt the familiar urge to explain rise—and let it fall.

“I don’t feel unwell,” she said.

“That’s not what I mean,” the woman replied quickly. “I mean socially. Relationally. People don’t know where they stand with you anymore.”

Marin considered this.

“I think,” she said carefully, “they’re standing where they always were. I’m just not standing for them.”

The woman’s face tightened.

“That sounds selfish.”

Marin felt the word land.

Selfish.

The old lever.

In the square, the language sharpened slightly.

Not louder.

More precise.

People did not accuse Elija.

They discussed *impact*.

Not what he was doing.

What was happening *because* of him.

"He doesn't intervene when people behave badly."
"He's encouraging passivity."
"He's undermining shared responsibility."

Responsibility again.

Always responsibility.

As if responsibility could only exist under supervision.

A small group formed—not publicly, not formally.

They met in a back room of a café.

No banners. No resolutions.

Just people who felt unsettled and wanted that feeling to mean something.

They spoke carefully.

"We're not against stillness," one man said. "We're against ambiguity."

Another nodded. "People need guidance."

A third added, "Without it, the loudest voices take over."

Someone mentioned the man who had occupied the bench days earlier.

"That's what happens when you don't correct behaviour."

Heads nodded.

Fear was finding its evidence.

Corven received a message requesting a meeting.

Not urgent.

But pointed.

Concern regarding social drift.

He sighed when he read it.

Drift was the word people used when they could not say *loss of control* without sounding afraid.

The meeting was polite.

Too polite.

The room held professionals—teachers, coordinators, civic planners.

People who had invested their lives in coherence.

They were not tyrants.

They were custodians.

And custodians feared neglect more than oppression.

“This isn’t about Elija,” one woman said early on.

Corven nodded.

“Of course not.”

“It’s about what happens when symbols are left uninterpreted.”

Another leaned forward. “People are filling the silence with whatever suits them.”

“That’s always been true,” Corven replied.

“Yes,” the man said, “but the system used to filter it.”

Silence.

“That filter,” Corven said slowly, “also filtered out honesty.”

A murmur moved through the room.

Someone smiled tightly. “Honesty isn’t always helpful.”

Corven met his eyes.

“No,” he agreed. “But it is always revealing.”

In the square, Elija felt the shift before it reached him.

Backlash had a temperature.

This one was cool.

Analytical.

It did not want him removed.

It wanted him *defined*.

Defined things could be managed.

A guide approached him one afternoon.

Not to redirect.

To ask.

“Would you be willing,” she said carefully, “to clarify your intent?”

Elija looked at her.

“For whom?”

“For the community.”

He waited.

“They’re asking whether you’re advocating withdrawal,” she continued. “Or detachment. Or refusal of responsibility.”

Elija considered the question.

“No,” he said.

The guide exhaled slightly.

“Then what are you advocating?”

Elija looked past her, to the people sitting, standing, passing through.

“I’m not advocating,” he said. “I’m remaining.”

The guide frowned.

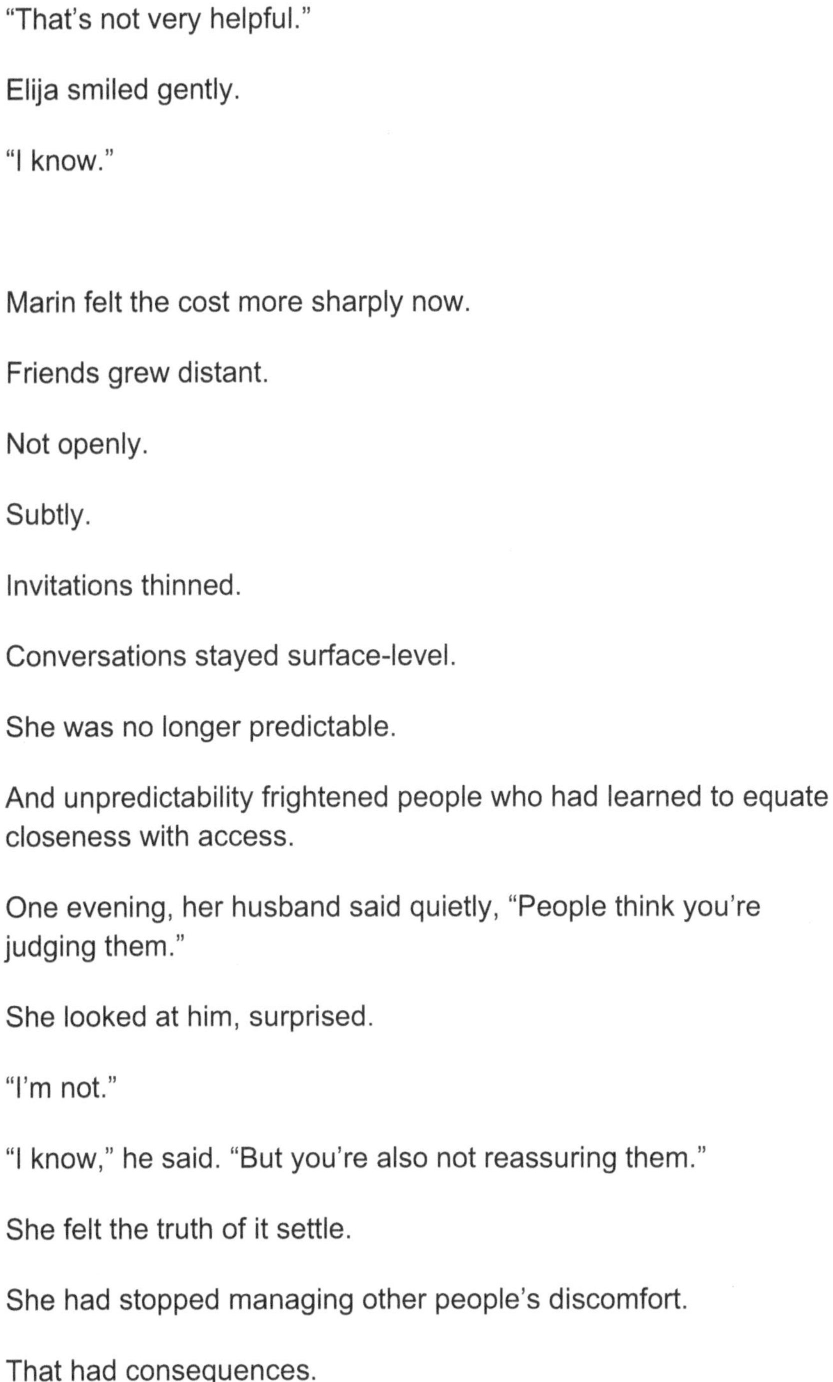

"That's not very helpful."

Elija smiled gently.

"I know."

Marin felt the cost more sharply now.

Friends grew distant.

Not openly.

Subtly.

Invitations thinned.

Conversations stayed surface-level.

She was no longer predictable.

And unpredictability frightened people who had learned to equate closeness with access.

One evening, her husband said quietly, "People think you're judging them."

She looked at him, surprised.

"I'm not."

"I know," he said. "But you're also not reassuring them."

She felt the truth of it settle.

She had stopped managing other people's discomfort.

That had consequences.

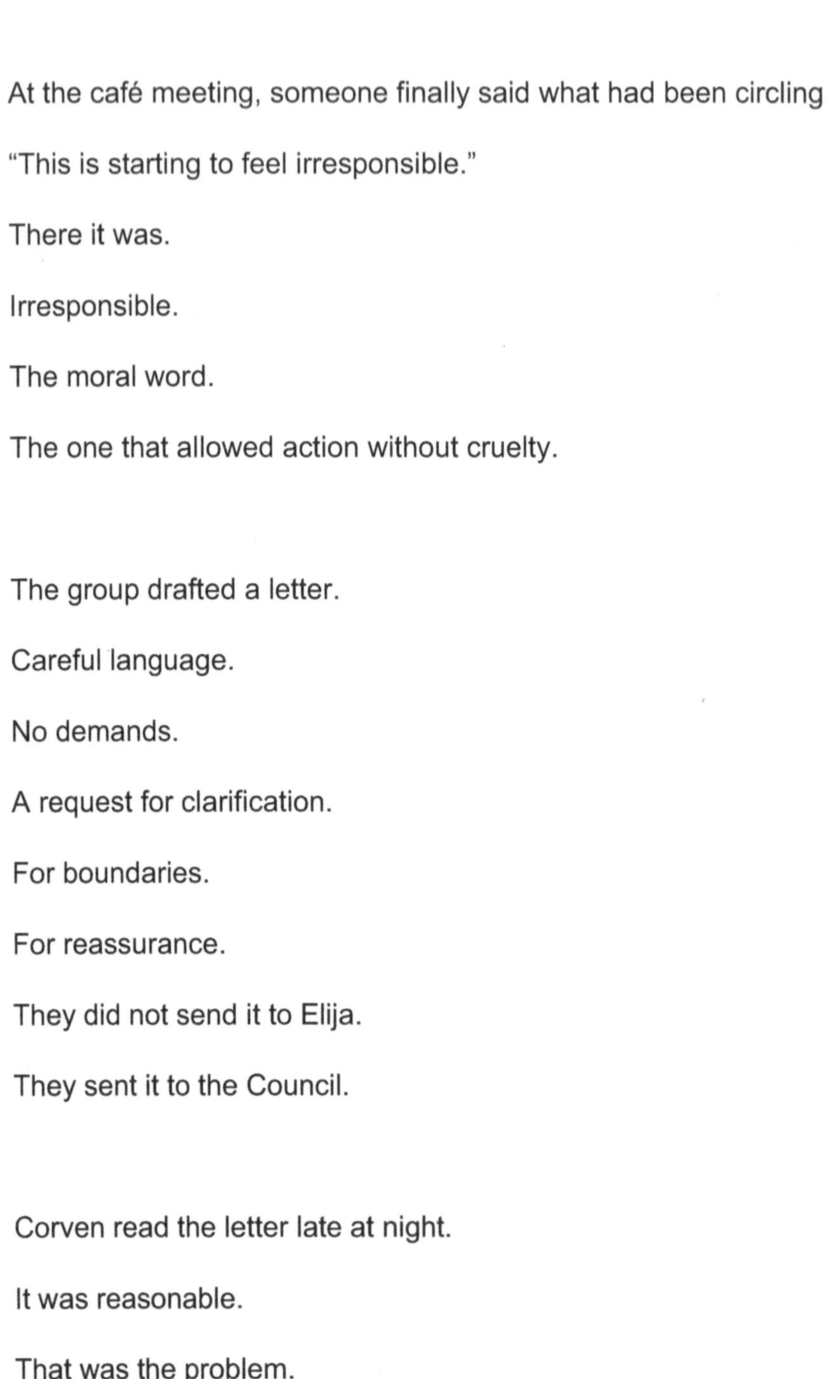

At the café meeting, someone finally said what had been circling.

"This is starting to feel irresponsible."

There it was.

Irresponsible.

The moral word.

The one that allowed action without cruelty.

The group drafted a letter.

Careful language.

No demands.

A request for clarification.

For boundaries.

For reassurance.

They did not send it to Elija.

They sent it to the Council.

Corven read the letter late at night.

It was reasonable.

That was the problem.

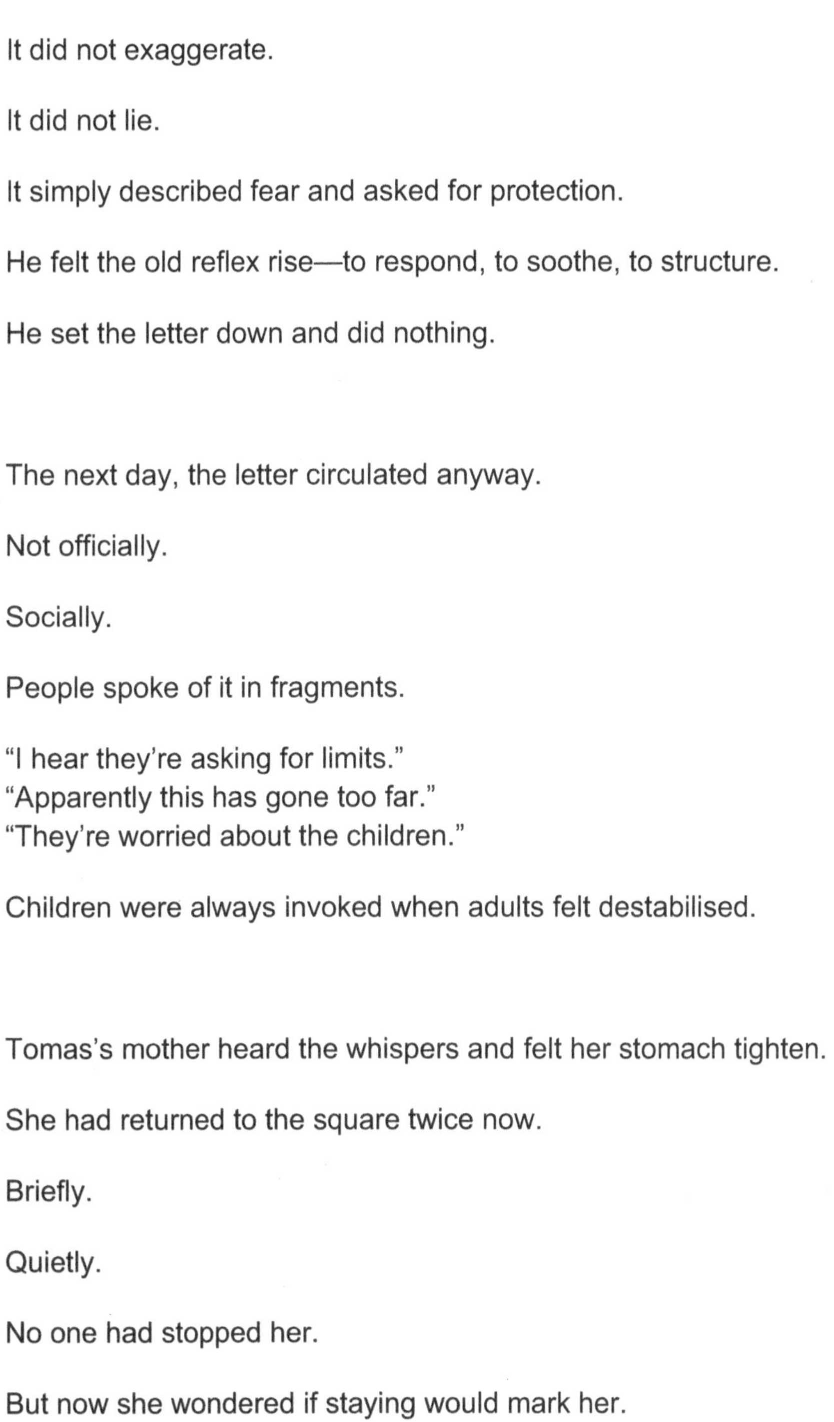

It did not exaggerate.

It did not lie.

It simply described fear and asked for protection.

He felt the old reflex rise—to respond, to soothe, to structure.

He set the letter down and did nothing.

The next day, the letter circulated anyway.

Not officially.

Socially.

People spoke of it in fragments.

"I hear they're asking for limits."
"Apparently this has gone too far."
"They're worried about the children."

Children were always invoked when adults felt destabilised.

Tomas's mother heard the whispers and felt her stomach tighten.

She had returned to the square twice now.

Briefly.

Quietly.

No one had stopped her.

But now she wondered if staying would mark her.

If her son would pay again for something unnamed.

Fear crept back in, familiar and persuasive.

She stayed home that day.

Elija noticed her absence.

Not with accusation.

With sadness.

Backlash always found its first success in fear that had already been touched once.

In the square, a man confronted Elija openly for the first time.

Not shouting.

Measured.

“People need direction,” he said.

Elija listened.

“You’re withholding it,” the man continued. “That’s power too.”

Elija nodded. “Yes.”

The man blinked, unprepared.

“So give it back,” he said.

Elija met his gaze.

“I am.”

The man shook his head. “No. You’re refusing responsibility.”

Elija considered.

“I’m refusing replacement,” he said.

The man frowned.

“What’s the difference?”

“Responsibility,” Elija replied, “supports people as they grow. Replacement grows so people don’t have to.”

The man scoffed. “That’s philosophy.”

“Yes,” Elija agreed. “And it’s also practice.”

The man stood there a moment longer, then walked away.

Not convinced.

But unsettled.

Backlash does not want silence.

It wants explanation.

Explanation is where authority re-enters.

Corven felt the pressure peak.

The Council convened again.

This time with an agenda.

Not force.

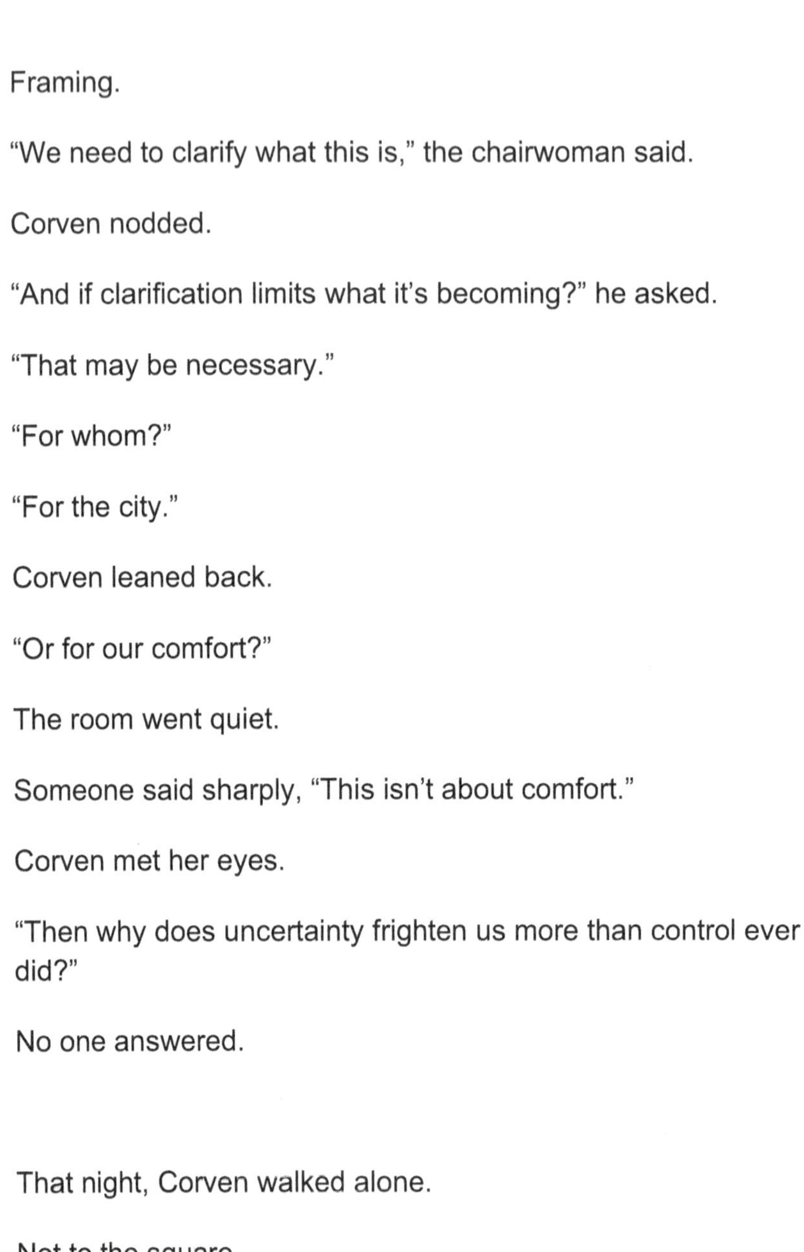

Framing.

"We need to clarify what this is," the chairwoman said.

Corven nodded.

"And if clarification limits what it's becoming?" he asked.

"That may be necessary."

"For whom?"

"For the city."

Corven leaned back.

"Or for our comfort?"

The room went quiet.

Someone said sharply, "This isn't about comfort."

Corven met her eyes.

"Then why does uncertainty frighten us more than control ever did?"

No one answered.

That night, Corven walked alone.

Not to the square.

Through the streets behind it.

He watched homes lit and darkened.

Lives being lived without reference to policy.

He felt the temptation to step back in.

To reassert narrative.

To protect people from the discomfort of growth.

He recognised the urge now.

Not as care.

As fear of irrelevance.

In the square, Elija remained.

The backlash did not remove him.

It surrounded him with language.

Concern.

Responsibility.

Impact.

Words designed to make stillness justify itself.

He did not respond.

He stayed.

Marin sat one evening and felt the loneliness fully for the first time.

Not abandonment.

Distance.

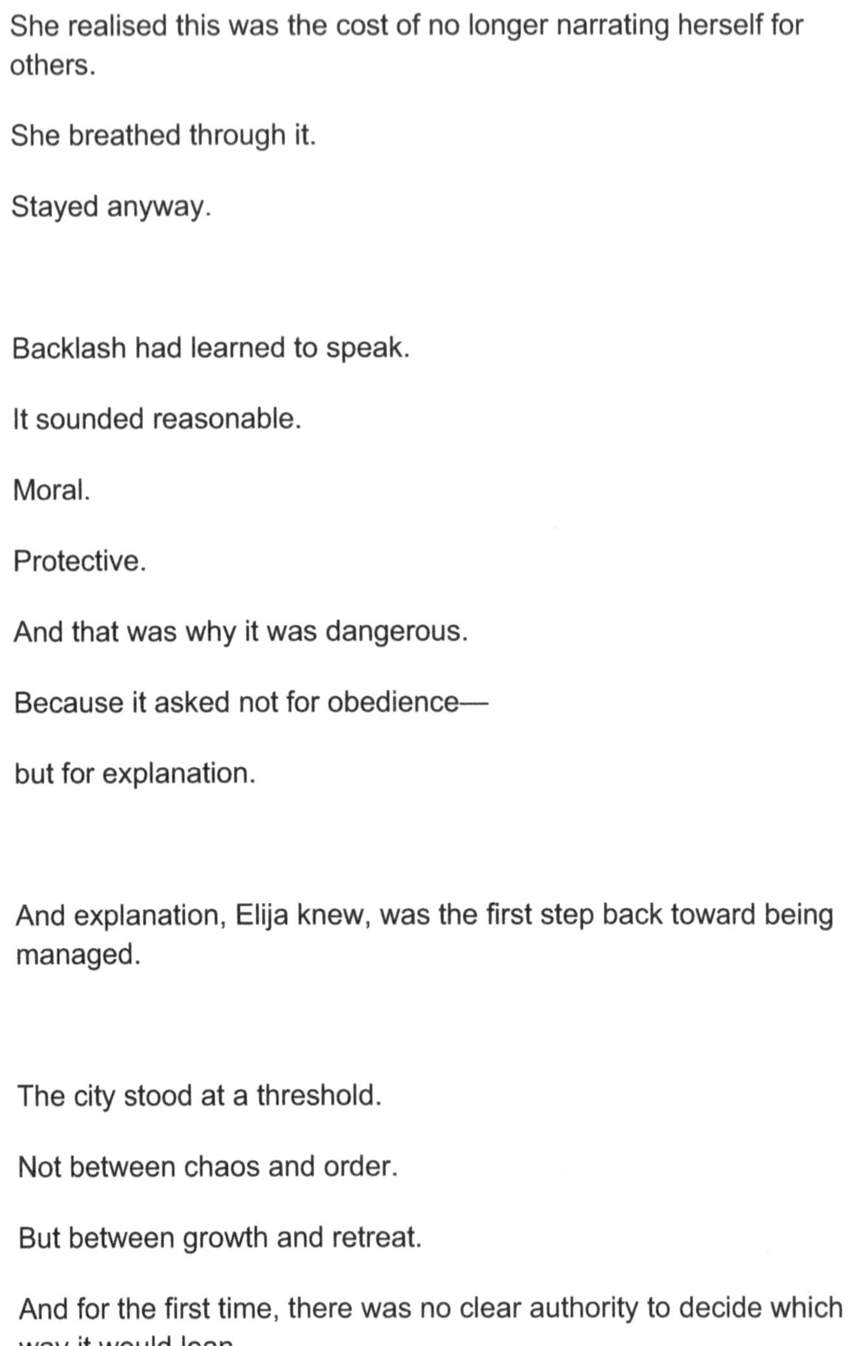

She realised this was the cost of no longer narrating herself for others.

She breathed through it.

Stayed anyway.

Backlash had learned to speak.

It sounded reasonable.

Moral.

Protective.

And that was why it was dangerous.

Because it asked not for obedience—

but for explanation.

And explanation, Elija knew, was the first step back toward being managed.

The city stood at a threshold.

Not between chaos and order.

But between growth and retreat.

And for the first time, there was no clear authority to decide which way it would lean.

Only people.

Choosing.

Or not.

The square waited.

So did the city.

So did Corven.

So did Marin.

And the waiting itself began to feel like an answer.

Chapter 24

The order was never written down.

That was intentional.

Written things could be challenged.
Appealed.
Quoted back later.

This was delivered verbally, in rooms that did not record minutes, by people who had learned to speak with confidence while leaving no trace behind.

The instruction was simple.

Reassert presence.

Not control.
Not enforcement.
Presence.

The word sounded benign.

It was meant to.

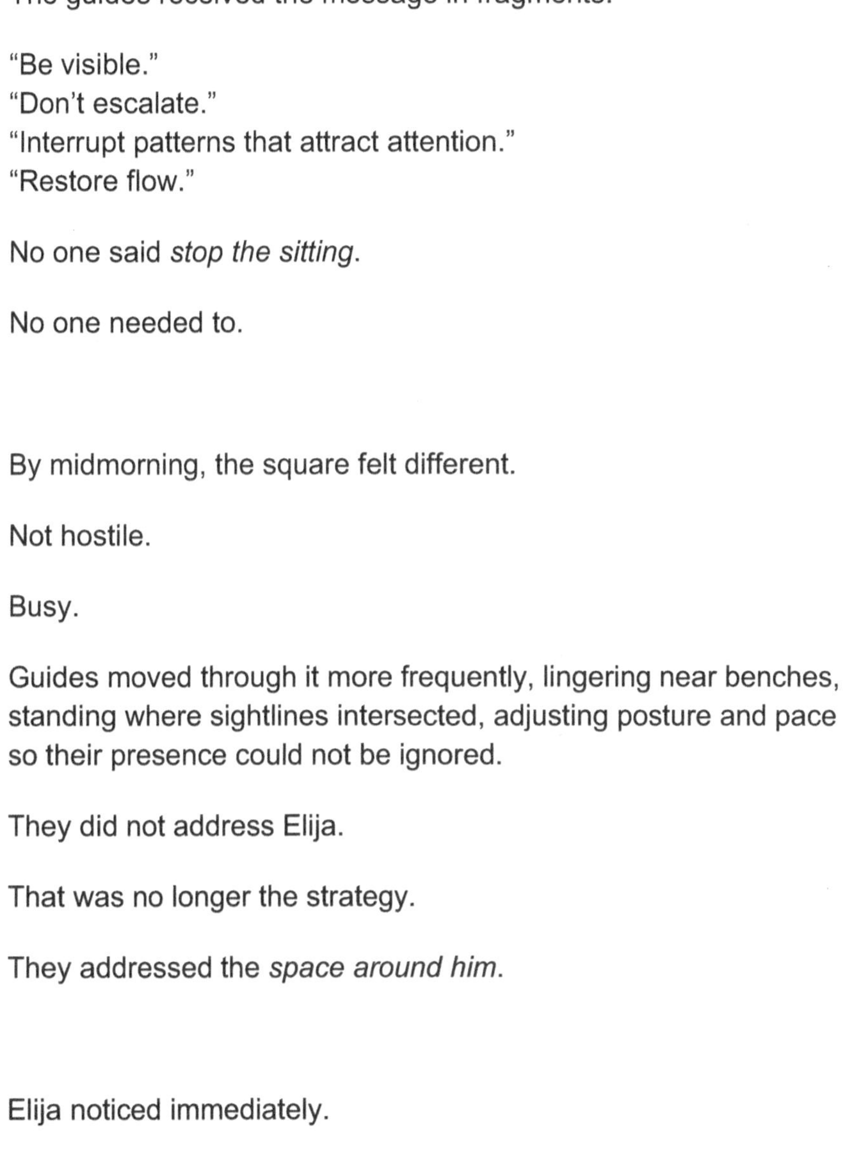

The guides received the message in fragments.

"Be visible."
"Don't escalate."
"Interrupt patterns that attract attention."
"Restore flow."

No one said *stop the sitting*.

No one needed to.

By midmorning, the square felt different.

Not hostile.

Busy.

Guides moved through it more frequently, lingering near benches, standing where sightlines intersected, adjusting posture and pace so their presence could not be ignored.

They did not address Elija.

That was no longer the strategy.

They addressed the *space around him*.

Elija noticed immediately.

Not as threat.

As choreography.

Bodies positioned to redirect energy.
Smiles offered at the precise moment stillness might deepen.
Conversations initiated just loudly enough to fracture attention.

It was subtle.

Skilled.

Practiced.

Force, refined into manners.

A guide stopped near a man sitting quietly at the edge of the square.

Not near Elija.

Not influencing anyone.

Just sitting.

The guide smiled.

“Beautiful day,” she said.

The man nodded.

“Yes.”

She waited.

He remained.

She gestured gently toward the street.

“Have you been out to the river lately?” she asked.

The man considered.

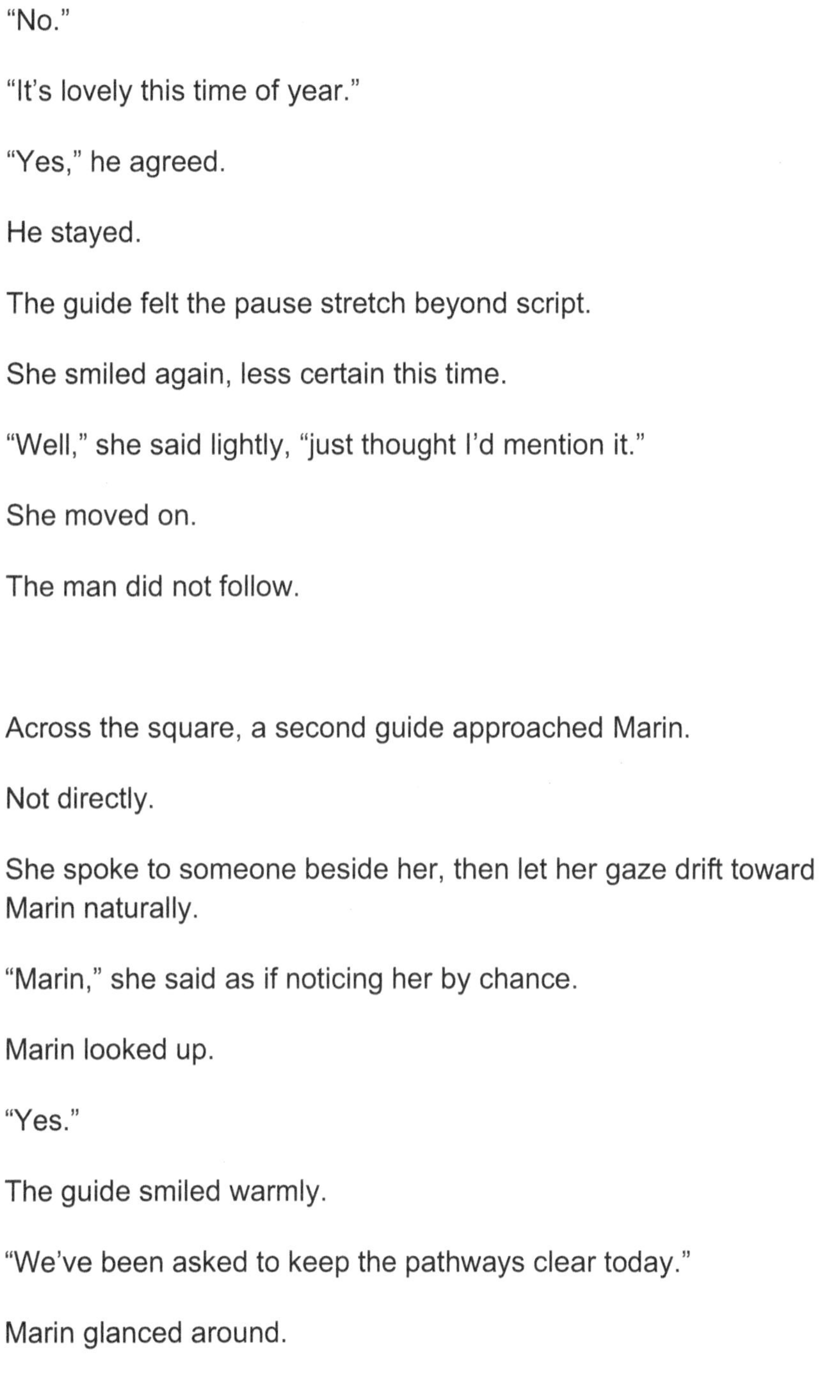

"No."

"It's lovely this time of year."

"Yes," he agreed.

He stayed.

The guide felt the pause stretch beyond script.

She smiled again, less certain this time.

"Well," she said lightly, "just thought I'd mention it."

She moved on.

The man did not follow.

Across the square, a second guide approached Marin.

Not directly.

She spoke to someone beside her, then let her gaze drift toward Marin naturally.

"Marin," she said as if noticing her by chance.

Marin looked up.

"Yes."

The guide smiled warmly.

"We've been asked to keep the pathways clear today."

Marin glanced around.

There was no congestion.

“I’m not blocking anything,” she said.

“No,” the guide replied quickly. “Of course not.”

She hesitated.

“It just helps if people keep moving.”

Marin considered the instruction.

Then nodded.

She stood.

Not in compliance.

In clarity.

She walked to another bench and sat again.

The guide watched, uncertain whether to follow.

She didn’t.

Force began to fray.

Not because it was resisted.

Because it was *outpaced* by understanding.

In the Council chamber, Corven listened as the update was delivered.

“Presence has been restored,” a coordinator reported.

“Yes,” Corven replied.

“Engagement patterns are stabilising.”

“Yes.”

“Clusters are dispersing.”

Corven leaned forward slightly.

“And the people?”

The coordinator blinked.

“They’re… calm.”

Corven nodded.

Calm was not the same as convinced.

“Any incidents?”

“No.”

“Any compliance issues?”

The man hesitated.

“No.”

“Then what problem are we solving?” Corven asked.

The room went quiet.

Someone shifted in their seat.

“This is preventative,” the chairwoman said sharply.

Corven met her gaze.

“So was containment,” he replied.

“And now?”

“And now,” Corven said slowly, “we are testing whether authority still means anything when it no longer has urgency behind it.”

The chairwoman’s jaw tightened.

“We are reminding people that the city is present.”

Corven nodded.

“And they are reminding us,” he said, “that presence does not belong to us.”

By afternoon, the guides were tired.

Not physically.

Emotionally.

They were performing a role that no longer aligned with the moment.

Intervention without justification exhausted the conscience.

One guide leaned against a wall, breath shallow.

She watched a woman sit alone, hands folded, eyes closed.

The urge to intervene rose.

Then fell.

Then rose again.

She felt ridiculous.

What exactly am I stopping? she wondered.

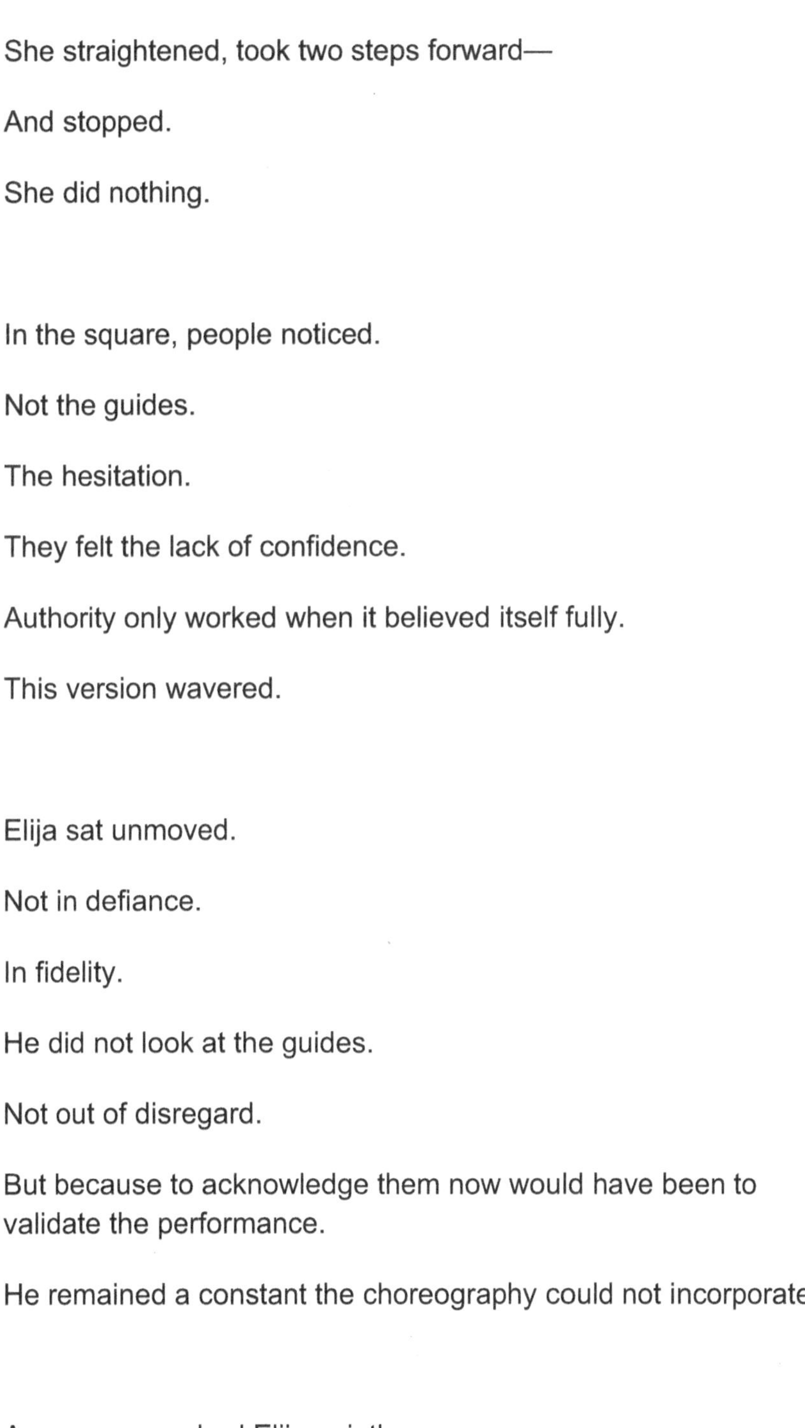

She straightened, took two steps forward—

And stopped.

She did nothing.

In the square, people noticed.

Not the guides.

The hesitation.

They felt the lack of confidence.

Authority only worked when it believed itself fully.

This version wavered.

Elija sat unmoved.

Not in defiance.

In fidelity.

He did not look at the guides.

Not out of disregard.

But because to acknowledge them now would have been to validate the performance.

He remained a constant the choreography could not incorporate.

A man approached Elija quietly.

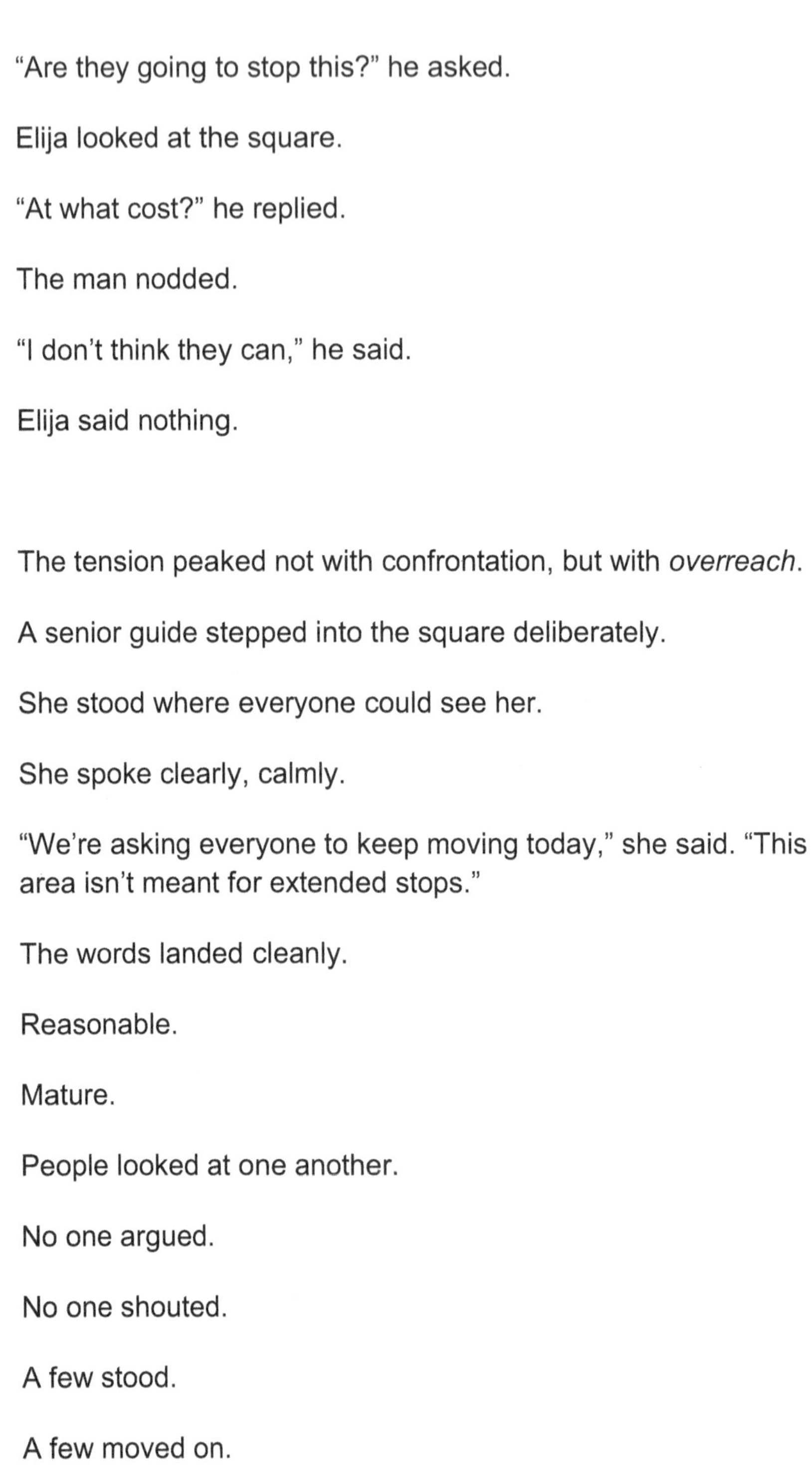

“Are they going to stop this?” he asked.

Elija looked at the square.

“At what cost?” he replied.

The man nodded.

“I don’t think they can,” he said.

Elija said nothing.

The tension peaked not with confrontation, but with *overreach*.

A senior guide stepped into the square deliberately.

She stood where everyone could see her.

She spoke clearly, calmly.

“We’re asking everyone to keep moving today,” she said. “This area isn’t meant for extended stops.”

The words landed cleanly.

Reasonable.

Mature.

People looked at one another.

No one argued.

No one shouted.

A few stood.

A few moved on.

Others stayed seated.

Not stubbornly.

Simply… unmoved.

The guide waited.

Her authority expected response.

It did not arrive.

She felt the heat rise in her face.

She could escalate.

She did not.

She stepped back.

And in that retreat, something broke.

Force had arrived.

And discovered it was too late.

By evening, the square felt almost normal again.

Not free.

Not safe.

Honest.

Guides still moved through it.

But now with awareness.

They were being seen.

Not feared.

Seen.

Corven walked the square openly that night.

Not at the edge.

Through it.

Guides looked to him instinctively.

He gave no instruction.

He did not need to.

They were already adjusting.

A guide stopped him quietly.

"Sir," she said, "what are we supposed to do?"

The question was not procedural.

It was existential.

Corven considered her carefully.

"Don't replace what people are learning to carry," he said.

She frowned.

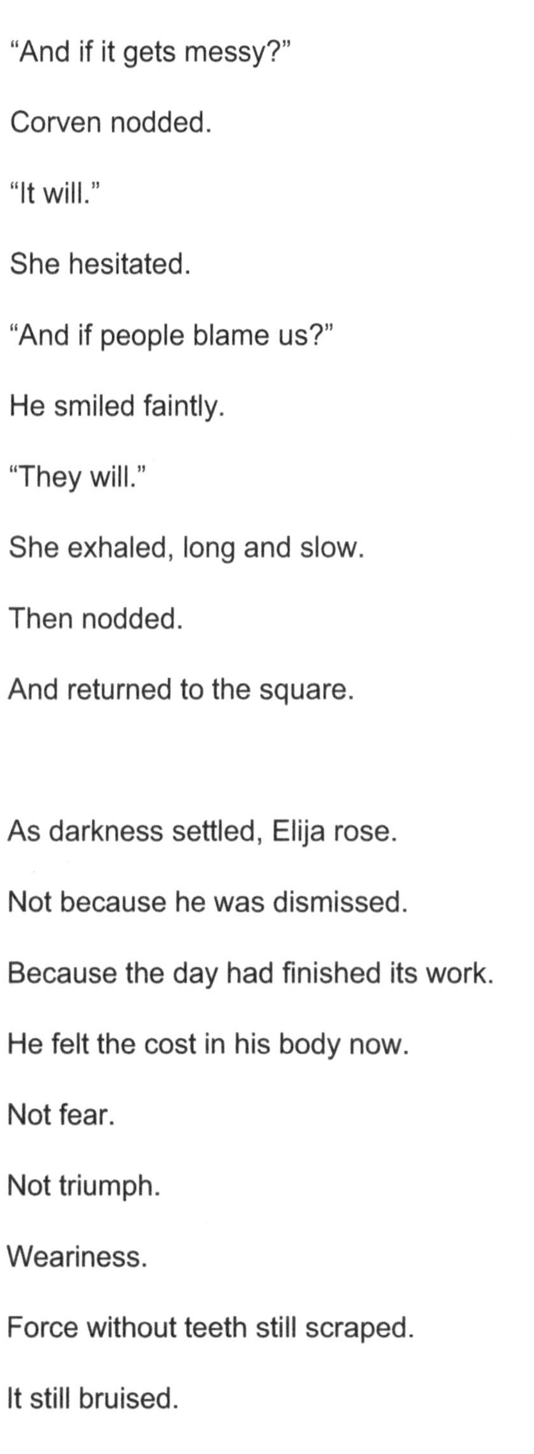

“And if it gets messy?”

Corven nodded.

“It will.”

She hesitated.

“And if people blame us?”

He smiled faintly.

“They will.”

She exhaled, long and slow.

Then nodded.

And returned to the square.

As darkness settled, Elija rose.

Not because he was dismissed.

Because the day had finished its work.

He felt the cost in his body now.

Not fear.

Not triumph.

Weariness.

Force without teeth still scraped.

It still bruised.

But it no longer bit.

Marin watched the square from a distance.

She saw guides hesitate.

People choose.

Authority step back without announcement.

She understood then:

The system had tried its final move.

And it had failed not because it was weak—

But because it had arrived after people had already begun to stand on their own.

The city did not celebrate.

It absorbed the moment quietly.

That was its strength.

Force had been attempted.

And it had revealed itself.

Not as villain.

As relic.

A tool built for a stage that no longer existed.

The square settled into night.

Unsupervised.

Unclaimed.

Still.

And in that stillness, something decisive had occurred.

Authority had acted—

And found nothing left to take.

Chapter 25

Marin learned the cost slowly.

Not as punishment.
Not as consequence delivered from above.

As distance.

It began with pauses where replies used to come easily.

A message read but not answered.
An invitation framed vaguely enough to be declined without explanation.
A conversation that ended sooner than it should have, as if both parties sensed an edge they did not want to test.

No one confronted her.

That would have been easier.

Instead, people adjusted.

And adjustment, Marin discovered, could ache longer than rejection.

She sat at the table one evening with friends she had known for years.

They spoke about ordinary things — weather, work, a neighbour's renovation.

She listened.

She nodded.

She smiled when appropriate.

And yet she felt herself slightly outside the circle, as if some shared frequency had shifted just enough to make her presence faintly dissonant.

Someone mentioned the square.

Not Elija.

Just the square.

"Well," one woman said lightly, "that phase seems to be passing."

Marin felt the words land in her body before her mind caught up.

Passing.

As if it had been a trend.

As if nothing real had occurred.

She waited for someone to look at her.

No one did.

Later, as they cleared plates, another woman said quietly, "You've been very... inward lately."

Marin nodded. "I think so."

The woman hesitated.

"I miss you."

The sentence was not an accusation.

That made it harder.

"I'm still here," Marin said.

The woman smiled sadly.

"I know. It just feels like you're not *available* in the same way."

Available.

The word tightened something in Marin's chest.

She realised how much of her former closeness had been built on readiness.

To respond.
To soothe.
To agree.
To adjust.

Availability had been her offering.

And she had withdrawn it without announcing why.

On the walk home, Marin felt the loneliness fully.

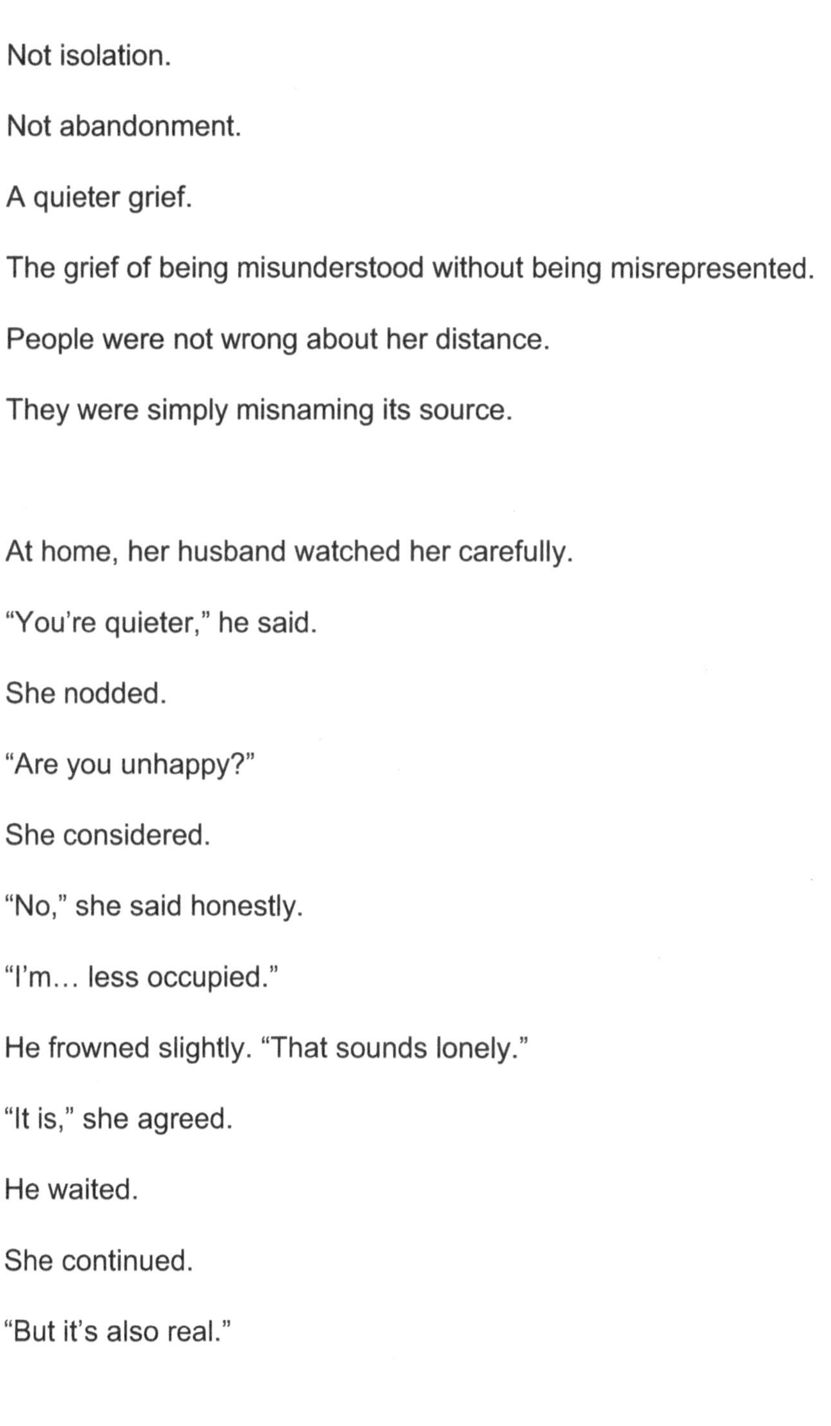

Not isolation.

Not abandonment.

A quieter grief.

The grief of being misunderstood without being misrepresented.

People were not wrong about her distance.

They were simply misnaming its source.

At home, her husband watched her carefully.

“You’re quieter,” he said.

She nodded.

“Are you unhappy?”

She considered.

“No,” she said honestly.

“I’m… less occupied.”

He frowned slightly. “That sounds lonely.”

“It is,” she agreed.

He waited.

She continued.

“But it’s also real.”

The next day, Marin received a message from someone she had once confided in deeply.

I'm worried about you, it read.
You seem detached. Almost cold.

Marin stared at the words for a long time.

Cold.

She felt warmer than she had in years.

But warmth that was no longer performative did not radiate outward the same way.

She typed a response.

Deleted it.

Typed another.

Deleted that too.

Finally, she wrote:

I'm not cold. I'm just not managing myself for others right now.

She stared at the sentence.

Then erased it.

She sent nothing.

Silence, she was learning, had a price.

And it demanded payment upfront.

In the square, she sat less often now.

Not because she no longer wanted to.

But because the square had become visible in a different way.

Staying felt like making a statement.

Leaving felt like retreat.

Neither felt clean.

So she began to sit in other places.

On a bench near the river.
In a quiet corner of the market after closing.
At home, in a chair she had always passed by.

Remaining, she realised, did not belong to a location.

It belonged to a posture.

One afternoon, she ran into a woman she had once mentored.

They exchanged pleasantries.

Then the woman said carefully, “I don’t know how to talk to you anymore.”

Marin felt the familiar urge to reassure rise.

She let it fall.

“Why?” she asked.

The woman shifted.

“You don’t correct me.”

Marin blinked.

"You used to," the woman continued. "Gently. When I was spiralling. Or overreacting."

Marin absorbed this.

"And now?"

"And now," the woman said, "I don't know if I'm right or wrong."

Marin nodded slowly.

"That's uncomfortable."

"Yes."

They stood there.

The woman looked almost angry.

"Is that what you're doing to people?" she asked. "Leaving them without anchors?"

Marin felt the accusation without defensiveness.

"No," she said quietly. "I'm leaving them with themselves."

The woman stared at her.

"That feels cruel," she said.

Marin did not argue.

Cruelty, she was learning, was often just unfamiliar honesty.

That night, Marin cried alone.

Not because she regretted anything.

But because she was grieving a version of herself that had been loved for being endlessly accessible.

She had been easy to be with.

Easy to lean on.

Easy to predict.

And she had mistaken that ease for intimacy.

She thought of Elija then.

Not as guide.

Not as centre.

As mirror.

He had never asked anyone to stay.

And because of that, staying had meant something.

She realised the same was now true of her.

The next morning, Marin declined an invitation she would once have accepted automatically.

No excuse.

No justification.

Just a simple, “I won’t be there.”

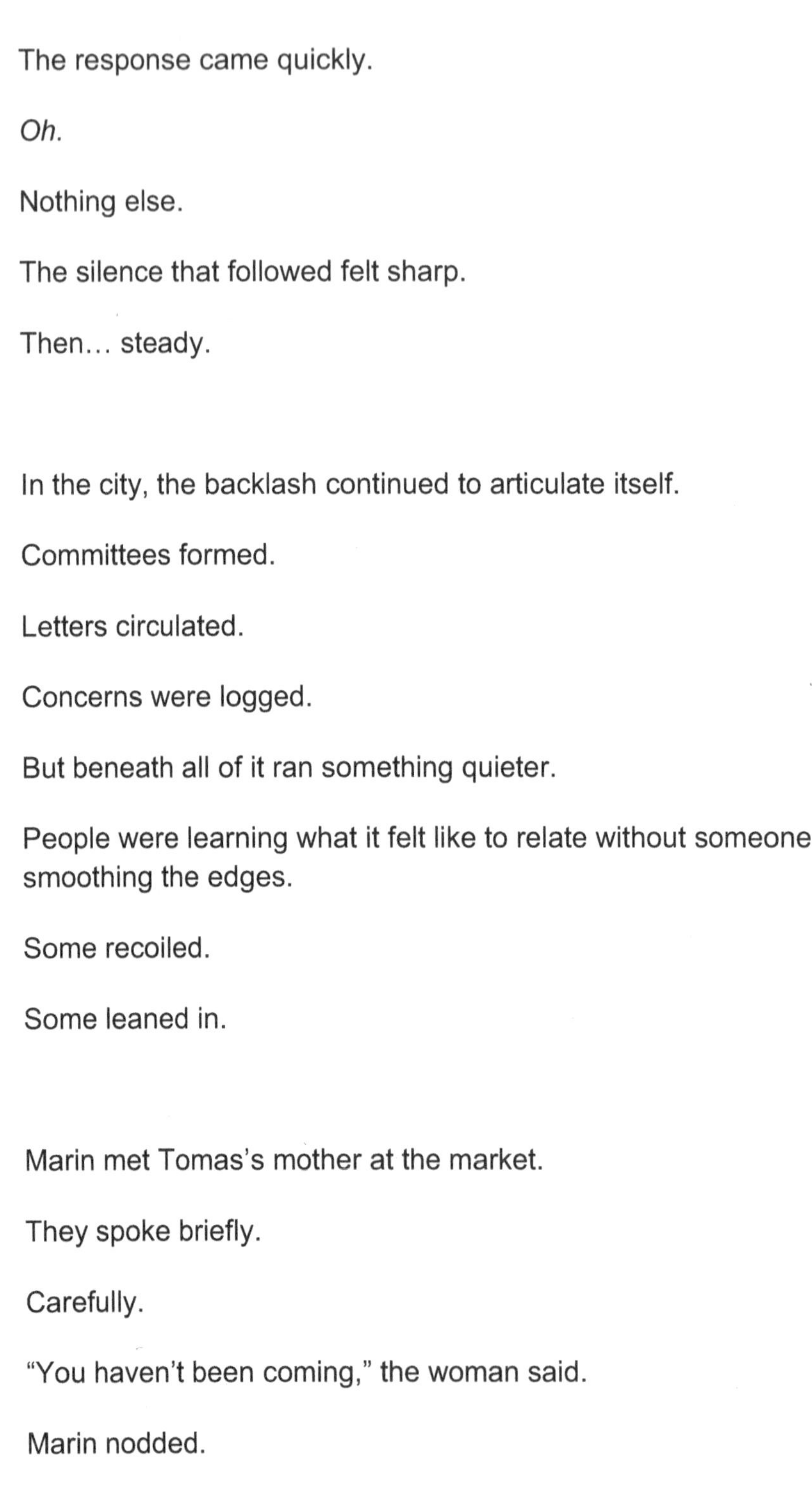

The response came quickly.

Oh.

Nothing else.

The silence that followed felt sharp.

Then… steady.

In the city, the backlash continued to articulate itself.

Committees formed.

Letters circulated.

Concerns were logged.

But beneath all of it ran something quieter.

People were learning what it felt like to relate without someone smoothing the edges.

Some recoiled.

Some leaned in.

Marin met Tomas's mother at the market.

They spoke briefly.

Carefully.

"You haven't been coming," the woman said.

Marin nodded.

"I know."

"I'm afraid," she admitted softly.

Marin did not reassure her.

She did not minimise the fear.

She simply said, "That makes sense."

The woman exhaled, shoulders dropping slightly.

They stood together in silence.

Not solving anything.

Not needing to.

Later, Marin sat alone again.

She felt the pull to explain herself to the city.

To justify her quiet.

To translate her posture into language people could accept.

She recognised the urge for what it was.

A desire to be received rather than to be real.

She let it pass.

The cost of saying nothing, Marin realised, was not invisibility.

It was misinterpretation.

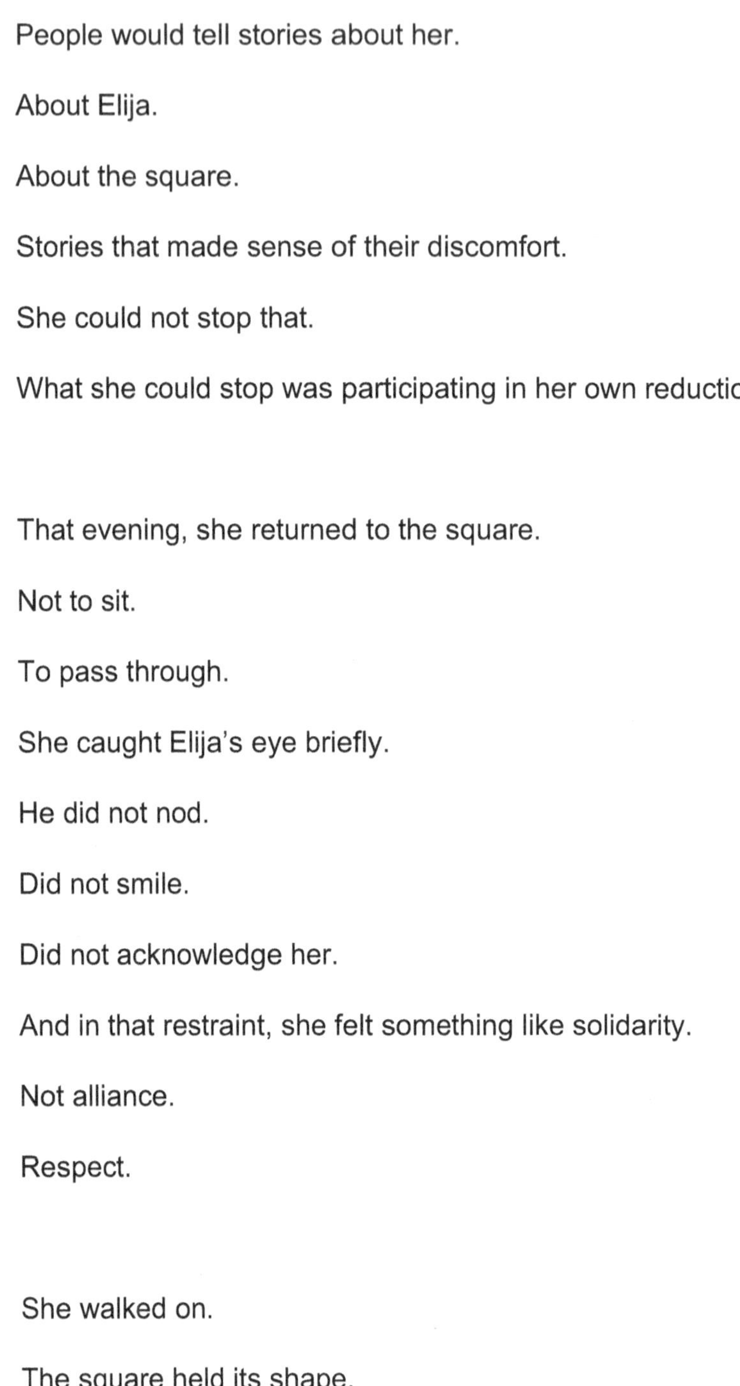

People would tell stories about her.

About Elija.

About the square.

Stories that made sense of their discomfort.

She could not stop that.

What she could stop was participating in her own reduction.

That evening, she returned to the square.

Not to sit.

To pass through.

She caught Elija's eye briefly.

He did not nod.

Did not smile.

Did not acknowledge her.

And in that restraint, she felt something like solidarity.

Not alliance.

Respect.

She walked on.

The square held its shape.

The city continued to speak.

And Marin, for the first time, understood the cost clearly:

Remaining did not require explanation.

But it required courage.

Not the courage to speak.

The courage to be misunderstood and stay whole anyway.

She went home quietly.

And for the first time since all of this began, she did not feel the need to check whether anyone was watching.

She sat.

And let that be enough.

Chapter 26

No announcement marked the moment.

No decree.
No retreat.
No visible collapse.

Authority did not fall.

It simply… *left.*

The Council chamber was full.

Lights warm.
Voices steady.
The long table polished to a soft sheen that suggested continuity.

Everything looked intact.

That was the problem.

They were still discussing the square.

Not in panic.

In tone.

“How it felt.”
“What message it sent.”
“How it might be interpreted.”

The conversation had shifted subtly over the last days.

Not toward *action*.

Toward *narrative*.

That was always the last refuge.

“We need to clarify what people saw,” the chairwoman said.

“We need to shape the meaning before it shapes itself.”

Several heads nodded.

This was familiar ground.

Events could be absorbed if interpretation arrived quickly enough.

Corven listened without interrupting.

He had stopped interrupting recently.

Not because he had less to say.

Because he no longer believed interruption altered trajectory.

"The square is being talked about," another councillor said. "People are asking questions."

"Questions can be answered," someone replied.

"Or redirected," another added.

"Or contextualised."

"Or deprioritised."

The language was calm.

Competent.

Expert.

These were people who had governed crises before.

They were not afraid.

They simply had not noticed something essential.

Authority had already exited.

Corven leaned back in his chair.

Not theatrically.

As if making room for an absence.

The chairwoman noticed.

"Corven," she said, "you've been quiet."

He looked at her.

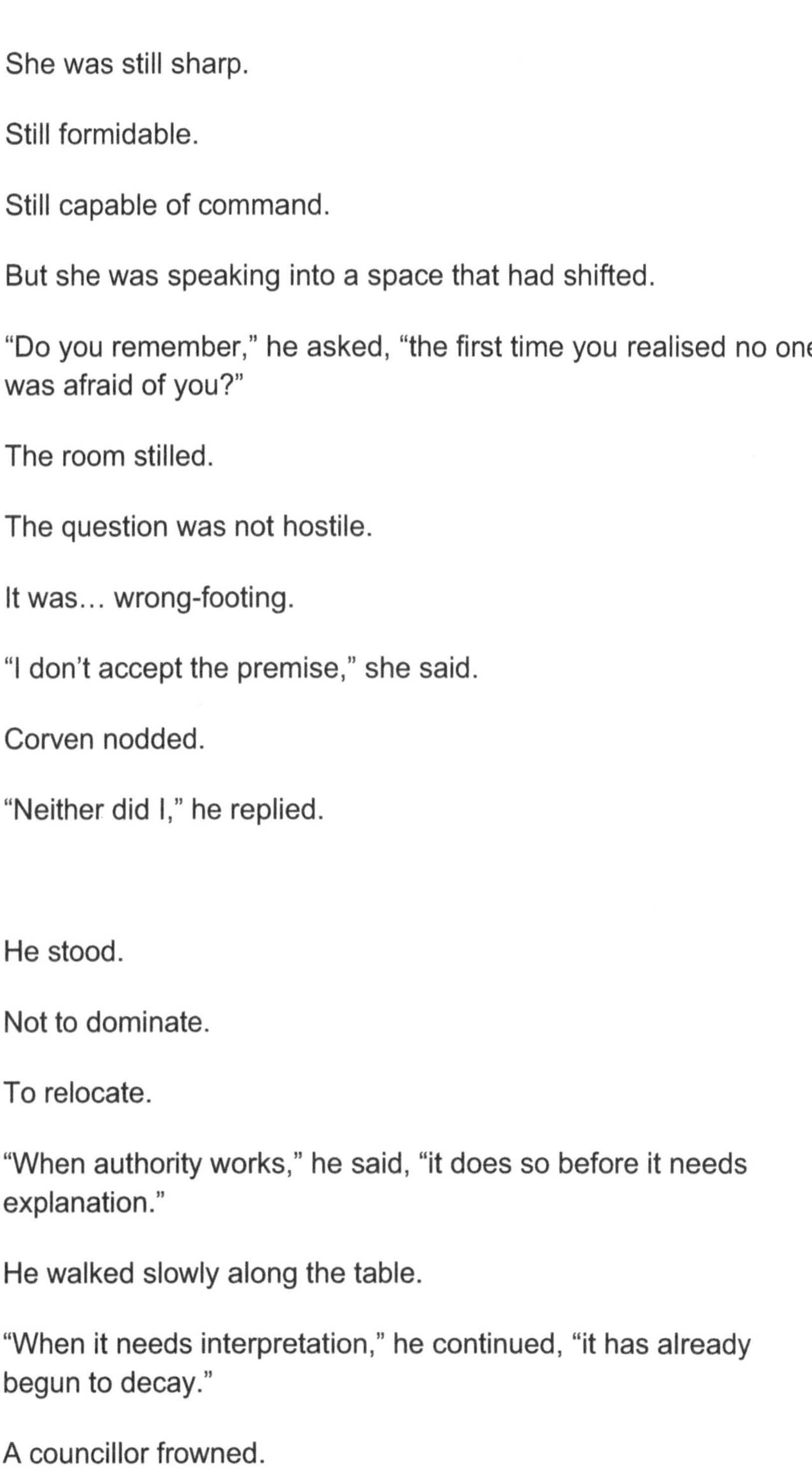

She was still sharp.

Still formidable.

Still capable of command.

But she was speaking into a space that had shifted.

“Do you remember,” he asked, “the first time you realised no one was afraid of you?”

The room stilled.

The question was not hostile.

It was… wrong-footing.

“I don’t accept the premise,” she said.

Corven nodded.

“Neither did I,” he replied.

He stood.

Not to dominate.

To relocate.

“When authority works,” he said, “it does so before it needs explanation.”

He walked slowly along the table.

“When it needs interpretation,” he continued, “it has already begun to decay.”

A councillor frowned.

"That's dramatic," she said.

Corven smiled faintly.

"It's structural," he replied.

"People still comply," another voice said quickly.
"The systems are intact."
"The guides are in place."

"Yes," Corven agreed. "They are."

He stopped walking.

"But no one is waiting for us anymore."

Silence followed.

Not resistance.

Recognition brushing against denial.

"Waiting for what?" the chairwoman asked.

"For permission," Corven said.
"For instruction."
"For relief."

He turned back toward them.

"They are not rebelling," he said.

"They are *proceeding*."

The word landed harder than rebellion ever had.

Proceeding meant irreversibility.

"That's an interpretation," someone said.

"No," Corven replied gently. "It's an observation."

He returned to his seat.

Did not sit.

Placed his hand on the back of the chair.

"I want you to understand something," he said.

"Authority doesn't end when people refuse it."

"It ends when they stop *referencing* it."

The chairwoman leaned forward.

"You're suggesting we do nothing."

"No," Corven said.

"I'm suggesting we notice."

"Notice what?" she demanded.

"That the room has changed," he replied.

She looked around.

At faces she'd known for decades.

At systems she'd helped build.

At language she still commanded effortlessly.

Nothing appeared different.

And yet—

"Authority," Corven said, "is relational energy."

"It only exists while people believe it is carrying something they cannot carry themselves."

He paused.

"They've begun carrying it."

A councillor scoffed.

"That's romantic nonsense."

Corven smiled again.

"You used to say the same thing about dignity," he said.

The room shifted.

History brushed the present.

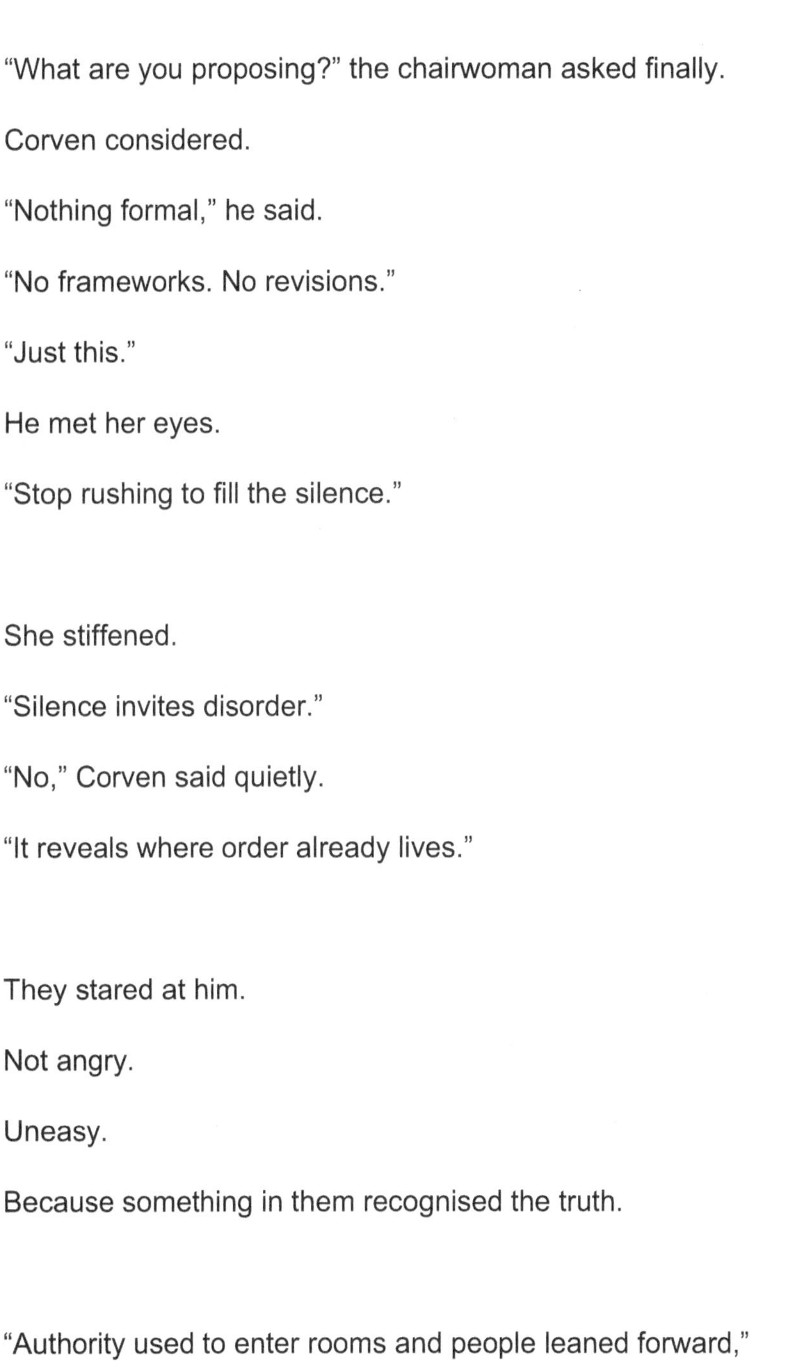

“What are you proposing?” the chairwoman asked finally.

Corven considered.

“Nothing formal,” he said.

“No frameworks. No revisions.”

“Just this.”

He met her eyes.

“Stop rushing to fill the silence.”

She stiffened.

“Silence invites disorder.”

“No,” Corven said quietly.

“It reveals where order already lives.”

They stared at him.

Not angry.

Uneasy.

Because something in them recognised the truth.

“Authority used to enter rooms and people leaned forward,” Corven continued.

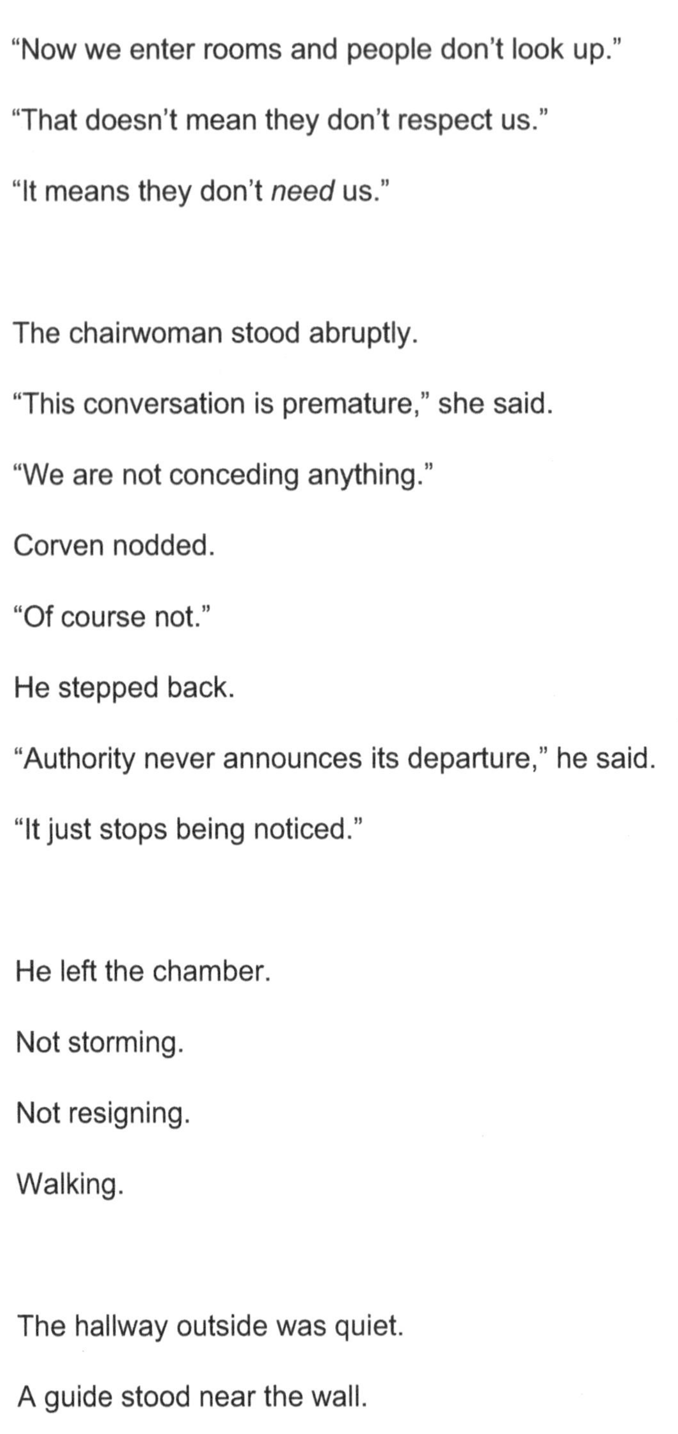

"Now we enter rooms and people don't look up."

"That doesn't mean they don't respect us."

"It means they don't *need* us."

The chairwoman stood abruptly.

"This conversation is premature," she said.

"We are not conceding anything."

Corven nodded.

"Of course not."

He stepped back.

"Authority never announces its departure," he said.

"It just stops being noticed."

He left the chamber.

Not storming.

Not resigning.

Walking.

The hallway outside was quiet.

A guide stood near the wall.

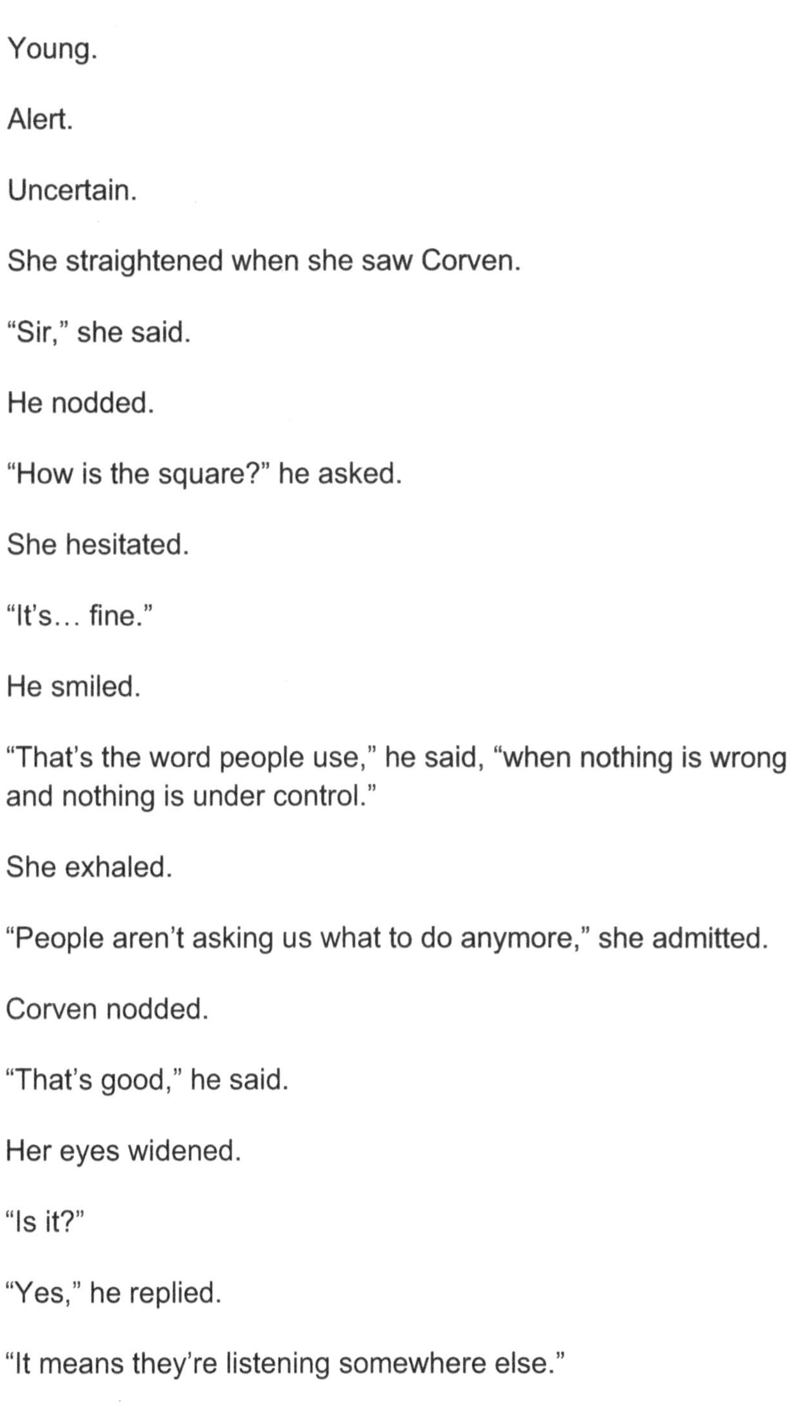

Young.

Alert.

Uncertain.

She straightened when she saw Corven.

“Sir,” she said.

He nodded.

“How is the square?” he asked.

She hesitated.

“It’s… fine.”

He smiled.

“That’s the word people use,” he said, “when nothing is wrong and nothing is under control.”

She exhaled.

“People aren’t asking us what to do anymore,” she admitted.

Corven nodded.

“That’s good,” he said.

Her eyes widened.

“Is it?”

“Yes,” he replied.

“It means they’re listening somewhere else.”

"Where?" she asked.

Corven gestured vaguely.

"Inside," he said.

She stood quietly.

"Then what are we here for?" she asked.

Corven looked at her carefully.

"To not interfere," he said.

She frowned.

"That doesn't feel like authority."

"No," Corven agreed.

"It feels like humility."

That word landed heavily.

But it didn't crush her.

Later that night, the chairwoman sat alone in her office.

Lights dim.

City humming beyond the glass.

She replayed the conversation.

Not angrily.

Involuntarily.

She realised something then.

No one had argued passionately.

No one had defended the system with urgency.

They had spoken…

…as if already downstream.

She stood and walked to the window.

Below, people moved freely.

Not chaotically.

Not obediently.

Just… moving.

Authority had not been taken.

It had not been overthrown.

It had not been exposed.

It had simply been outgrown.

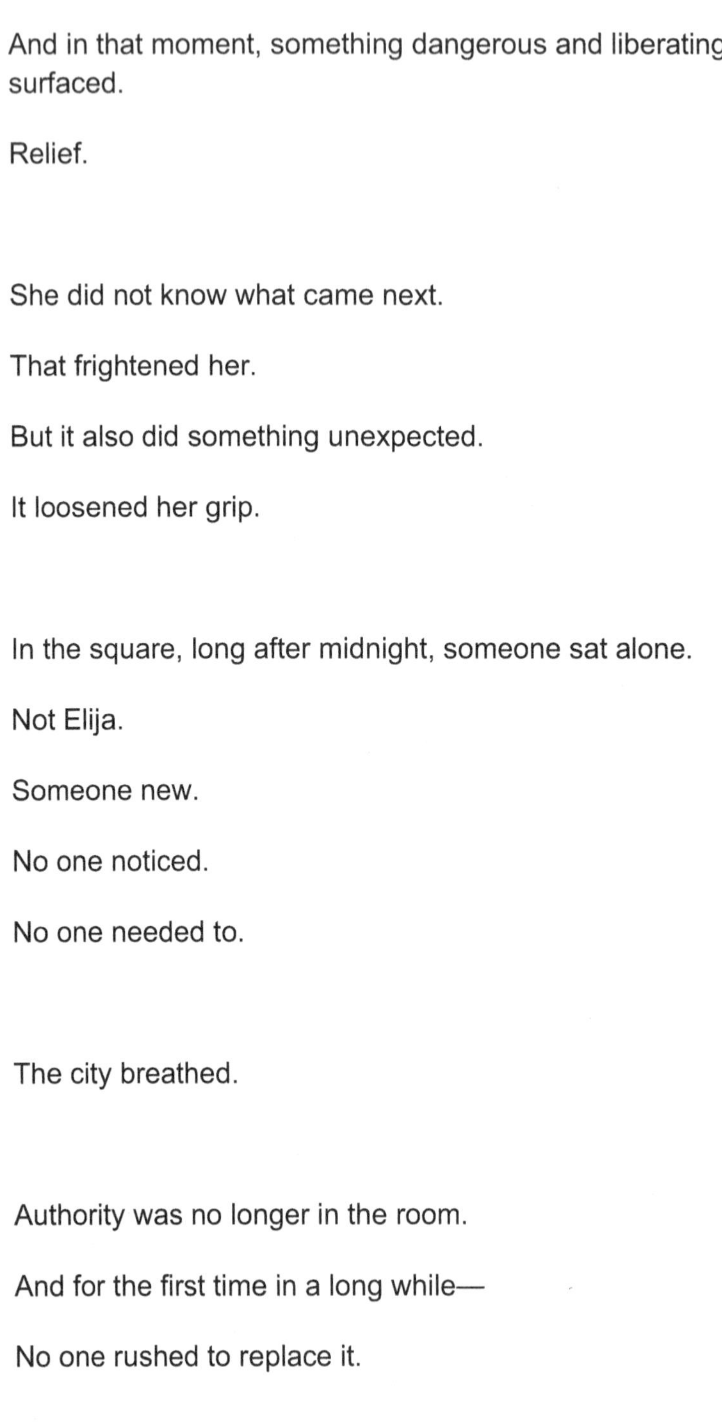

And in that moment, something dangerous and liberating surfaced.

Relief.

She did not know what came next.

That frightened her.

But it also did something unexpected.

It loosened her grip.

In the square, long after midnight, someone sat alone.

Not Elija.

Someone new.

No one noticed.

No one needed to.

The city breathed.

Authority was no longer in the room.

And for the first time in a long while—

No one rushed to replace it.

Chapter 27

Power does not disappear when authority leaves.

It searches.

Not loudly.

Not angrily.

Power is not dramatic.

It is opportunistic.

When no one is watching, power tests rooms.

It enters quietly.

It listens.

It mimics humility until it is certain no one is guarding the centre.

The first attempts were clumsy.

A man stood near the square one morning and began explaining what the sitting *meant*.

Not teaching.

Clarifying.

“It wasn’t about stillness,” he said.
“It was about resistance.”
“It was a signal.”

A small crowd gathered.

They listened politely.

Then they drifted.

The man kept talking.

No one stopped him.

No one stayed.

Power learns quickly.

The next came with gentler language.

She didn’t explain.

She *asked*.

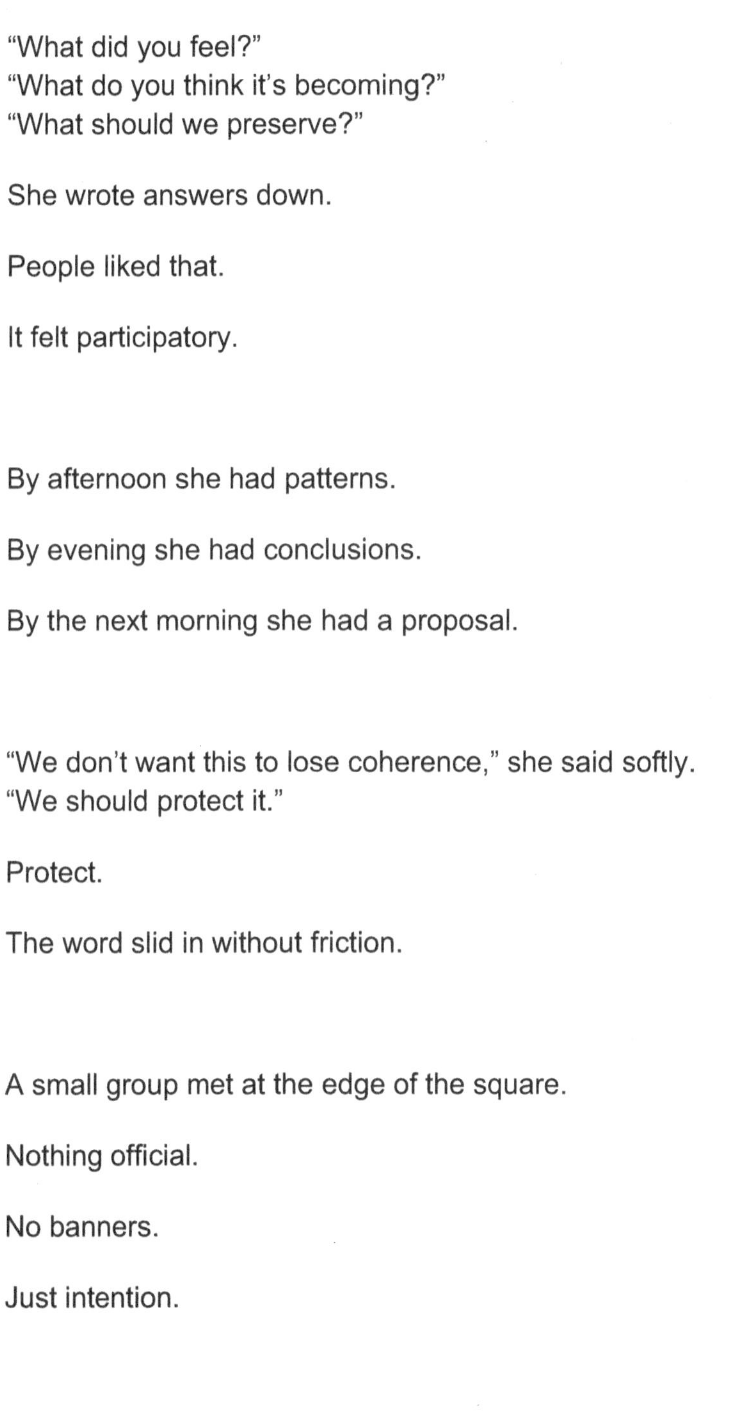

“What did you feel?”
“What do you think it’s becoming?”
“What should we preserve?”

She wrote answers down.

People liked that.

It felt participatory.

By afternoon she had patterns.

By evening she had conclusions.

By the next morning she had a proposal.

“We don’t want this to lose coherence,” she said softly.
“We should protect it.”

Protect.

The word slid in without friction.

A small group met at the edge of the square.

Nothing official.

No banners.

Just intention.

Power always prefers informal beginnings.

Marin passed them on her way home.

She slowed.

Not suspicious.

Curious.

She recognised the posture.

The slight forward lean.

The readiness.

“Do you need something?” one of them asked.

“No,” Marin replied.

She stood for a moment.

Listened.

They were discussing continuity.

Guardrails.

Next steps.

She smiled faintly.

“Careful,” she said.

They looked up.

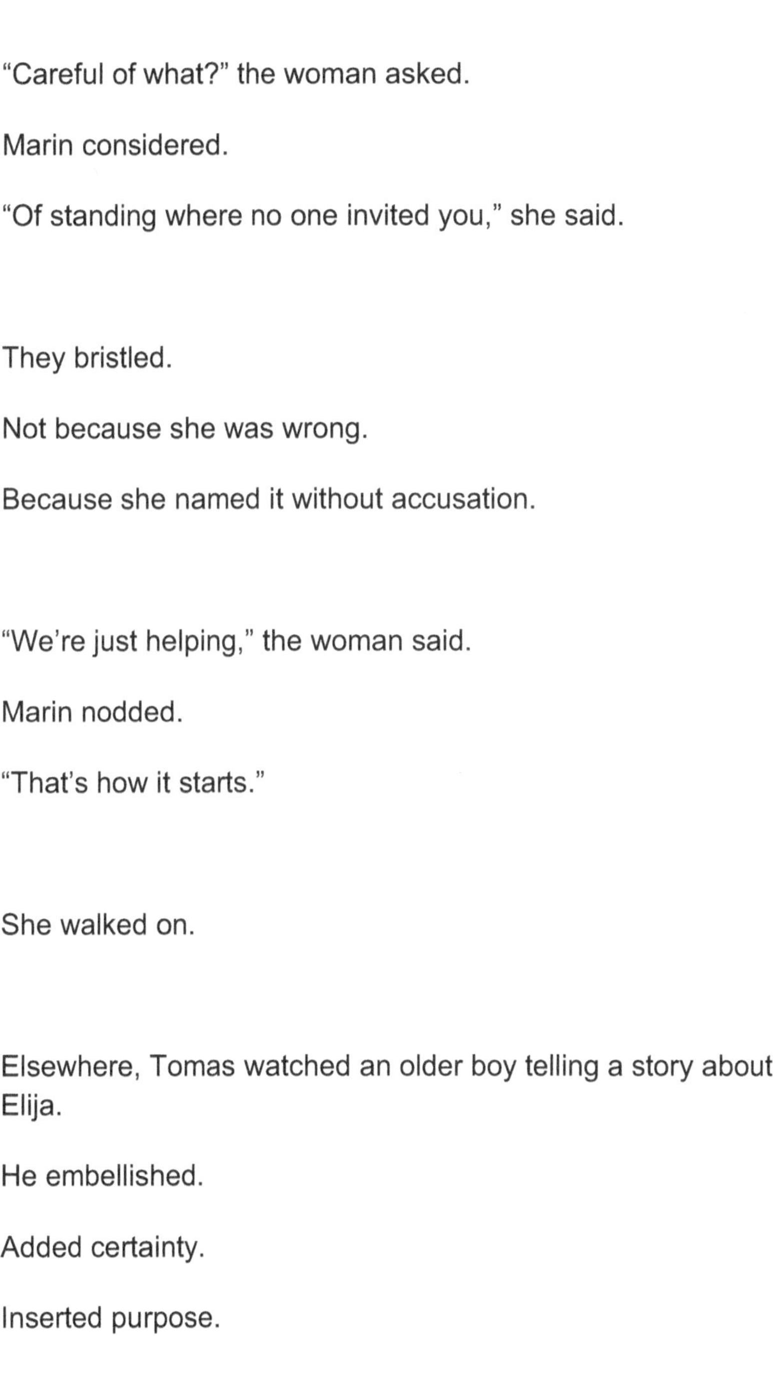

"Careful of what?" the woman asked.

Marin considered.

"Of standing where no one invited you," she said.

They bristled.

Not because she was wrong.

Because she named it without accusation.

"We're just helping," the woman said.

Marin nodded.

"That's how it starts."

She walked on.

Elsewhere, Tomas watched an older boy telling a story about Elija.

He embellished.

Added certainty.

Inserted purpose.

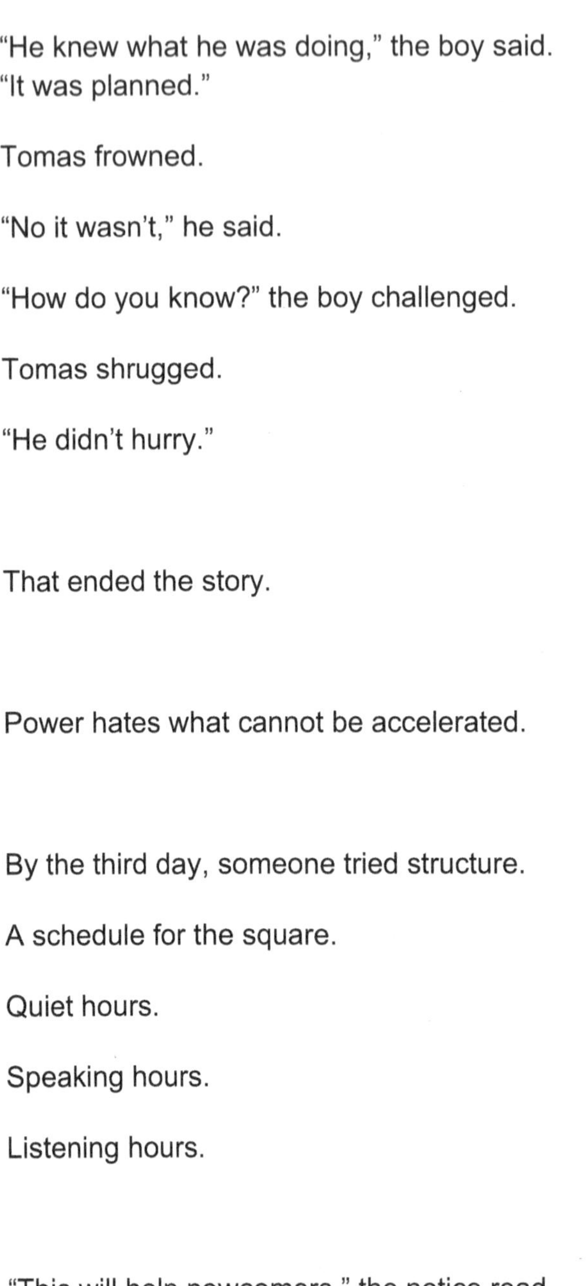

"He knew what he was doing," the boy said.
"It was planned."

Tomas frowned.

"No it wasn't," he said.

"How do you know?" the boy challenged.

Tomas shrugged.

"He didn't hurry."

That ended the story.

Power hates what cannot be accelerated.

By the third day, someone tried structure.

A schedule for the square.

Quiet hours.

Speaking hours.

Listening hours.

"This will help newcomers," the notice read.

People ignored it.

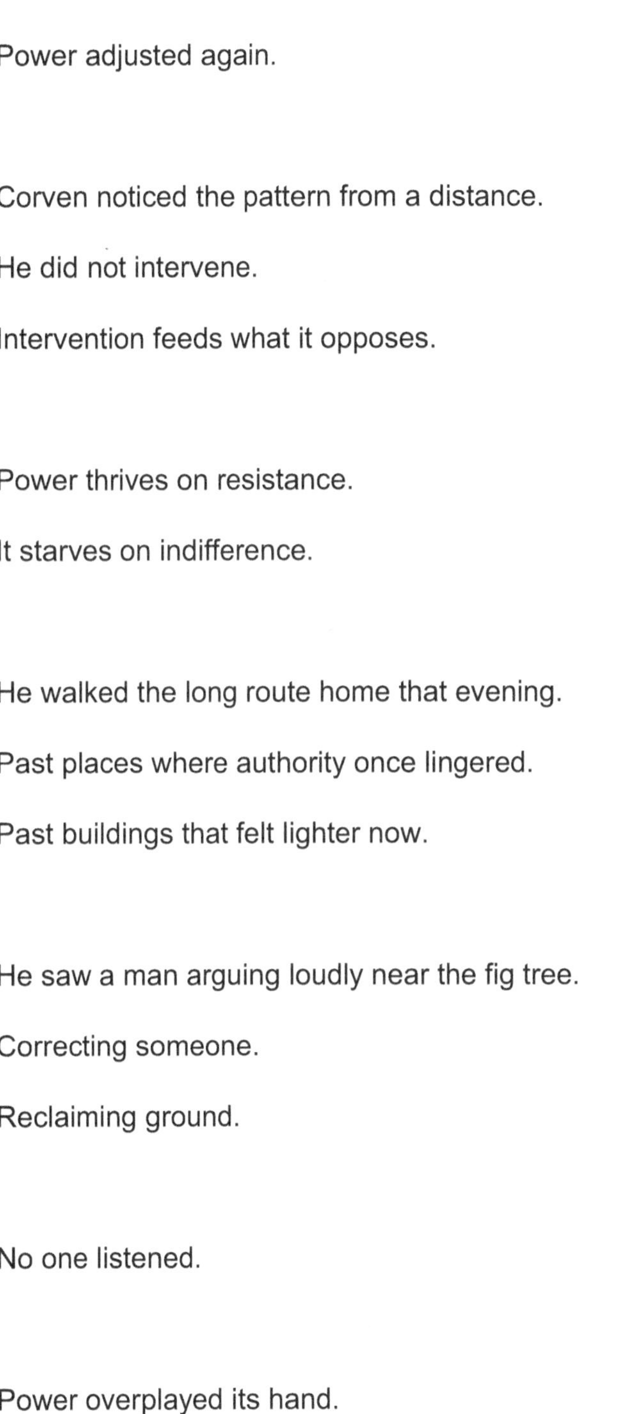

Power adjusted again.

Corven noticed the pattern from a distance.

He did not intervene.

Intervention feeds what it opposes.

Power thrives on resistance.

It starves on indifference.

He walked the long route home that evening.

Past places where authority once lingered.

Past buildings that felt lighter now.

He saw a man arguing loudly near the fig tree.

Correcting someone.

Reclaiming ground.

No one listened.

Power overplayed its hand.

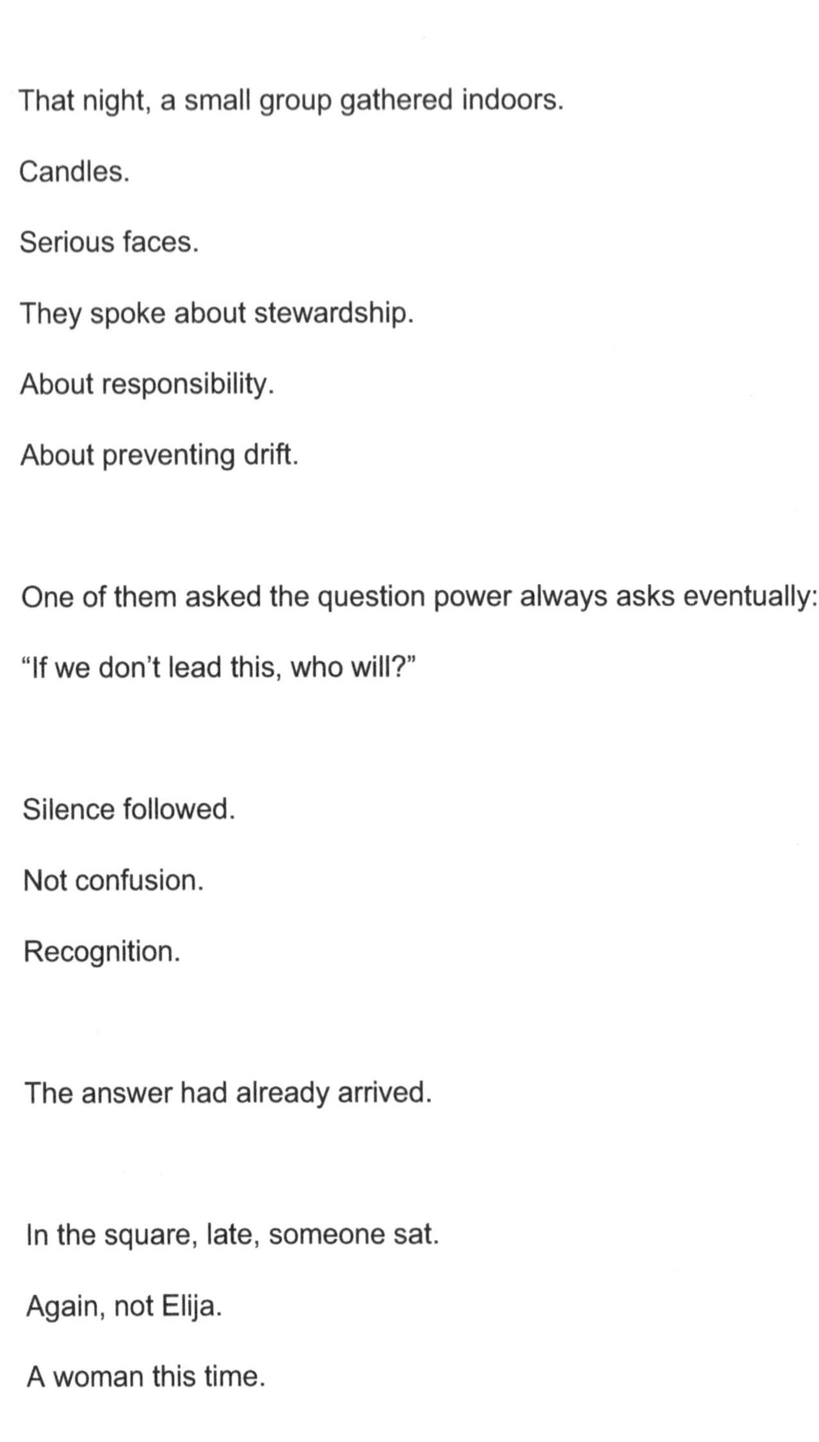

That night, a small group gathered indoors.

Candles.

Serious faces.

They spoke about stewardship.

About responsibility.

About preventing drift.

One of them asked the question power always asks eventually:

“If we don’t lead this, who will?”

Silence followed.

Not confusion.

Recognition.

The answer had already arrived.

In the square, late, someone sat.

Again, not Elija.

A woman this time.

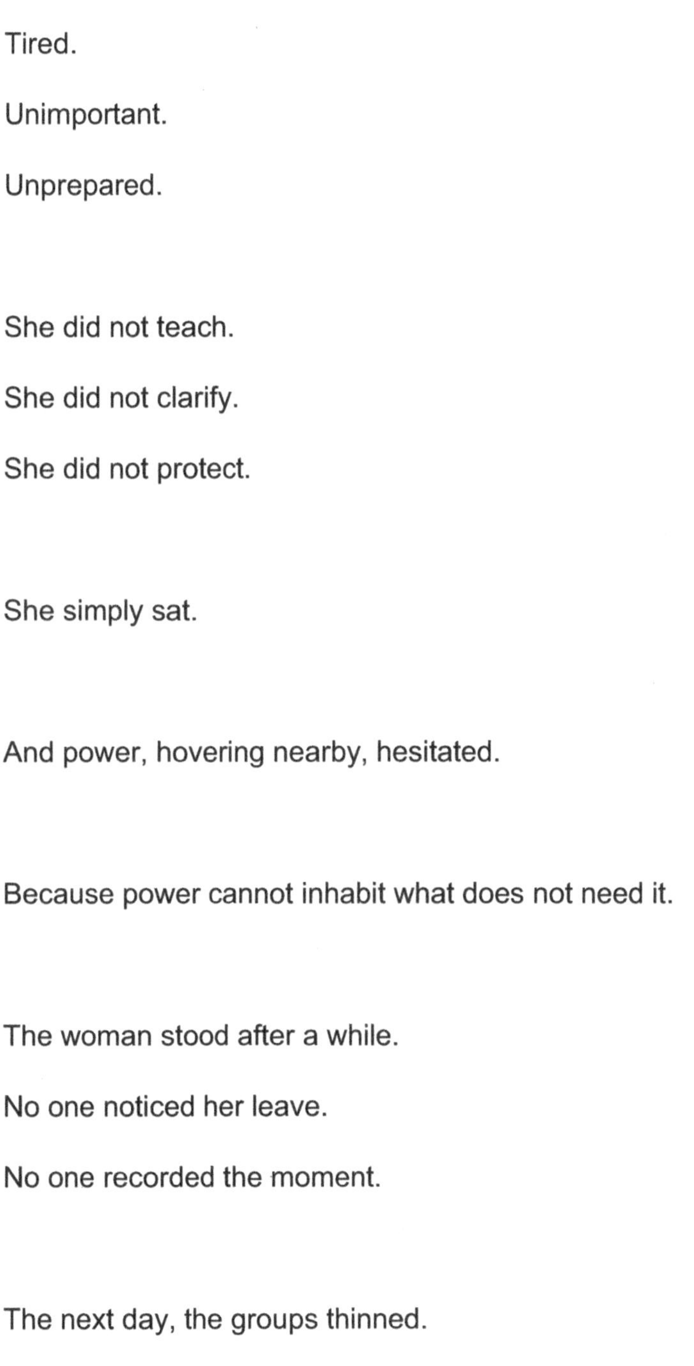

Tired.

Unimportant.

Unprepared.

She did not teach.

She did not clarify.

She did not protect.

She simply sat.

And power, hovering nearby, hesitated.

Because power cannot inhabit what does not need it.

The woman stood after a while.

No one noticed her leave.

No one recorded the moment.

The next day, the groups thinned.

The explanations softened.

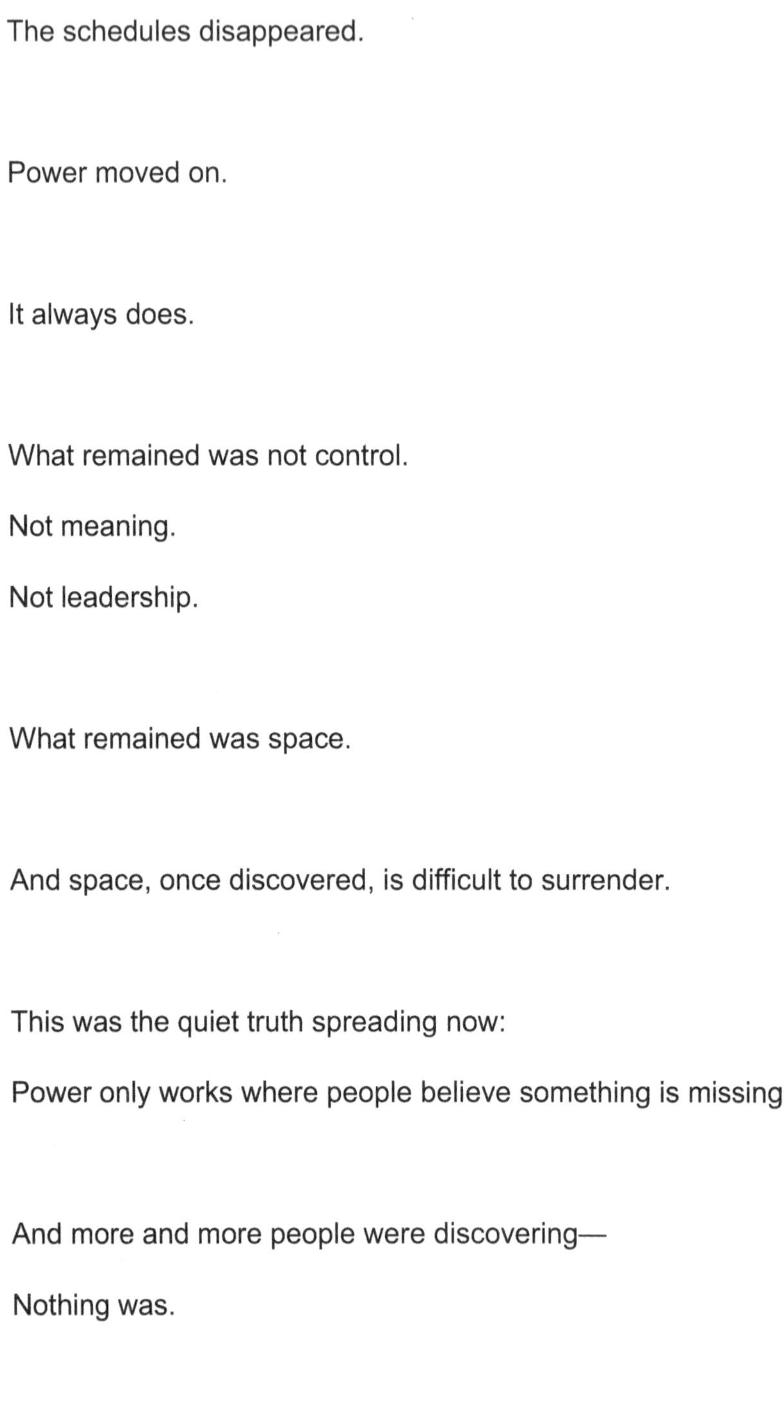

The schedules disappeared.

Power moved on.

It always does.

What remained was not control.

Not meaning.

Not leadership.

What remained was space.

And space, once discovered, is difficult to surrender.

This was the quiet truth spreading now:

Power only works where people believe something is missing.

And more and more people were discovering—

Nothing was.

Chapter 28

In the square, no one sat in the middle anymore.

They sat wherever shade happened to fall.

Under trees.

Along walls.

On steps.

The fig tree remained.

But it was no longer *the place*.

It was just a tree again.

Children climbed it.

Someone tied a ribbon to one branch and forgot about it.

Birds nested without permission.

This disturbed the planners more than rebellion ever had.

Without a centre, there was nothing to defend.

Without defence, there was no clear role for authority.

Corven watched this unfold with quiet interest.

Not as an architect.

As a witness.

He had built his worth on preventing collapse.

Ensuring continuity.

Preventing drift.

Now drift was everywhere.

And nothing was breaking.

He realised something then.

Systems had once held people together.

Now people were holding *themselves*.

This was not individualism.

It was something stranger.

People still gathered.

Still cared.

Still helped.

But no one was coordinating meaning anymore.

A woman began cooking extra bread each morning.

She did not announce it.

She did not invite participation.

People noticed.

Some helped.

Some didn't.

It continued anyway.

A man started walking the outer paths at dusk.

Not patrolling.

Just walking.

Others joined occasionally.

No schedule formed.

A group of musicians met on Tuesdays.

Then stopped.

Then met again on Fridays.

No explanation was offered.

Nothing needed permission.

This confused those trained in sustainability.

"How will it last?" they asked.

No one answered.

Because longevity was no longer the point.

Marin felt the shift internally before she understood it externally.

She had always calibrated herself.

Adjusted tone.

Measured response.

Now she forgot to.

She laughed more abruptly.

She disagreed without rehearsing.

She left rooms without explanation.

At first she worried this made her careless.

Then she noticed she was listening more closely.

Without performance, attention sharpened.

She realised something quietly unsettling.

Much of what she had called *care* had been fear in disguise.

Fear of misalignment.

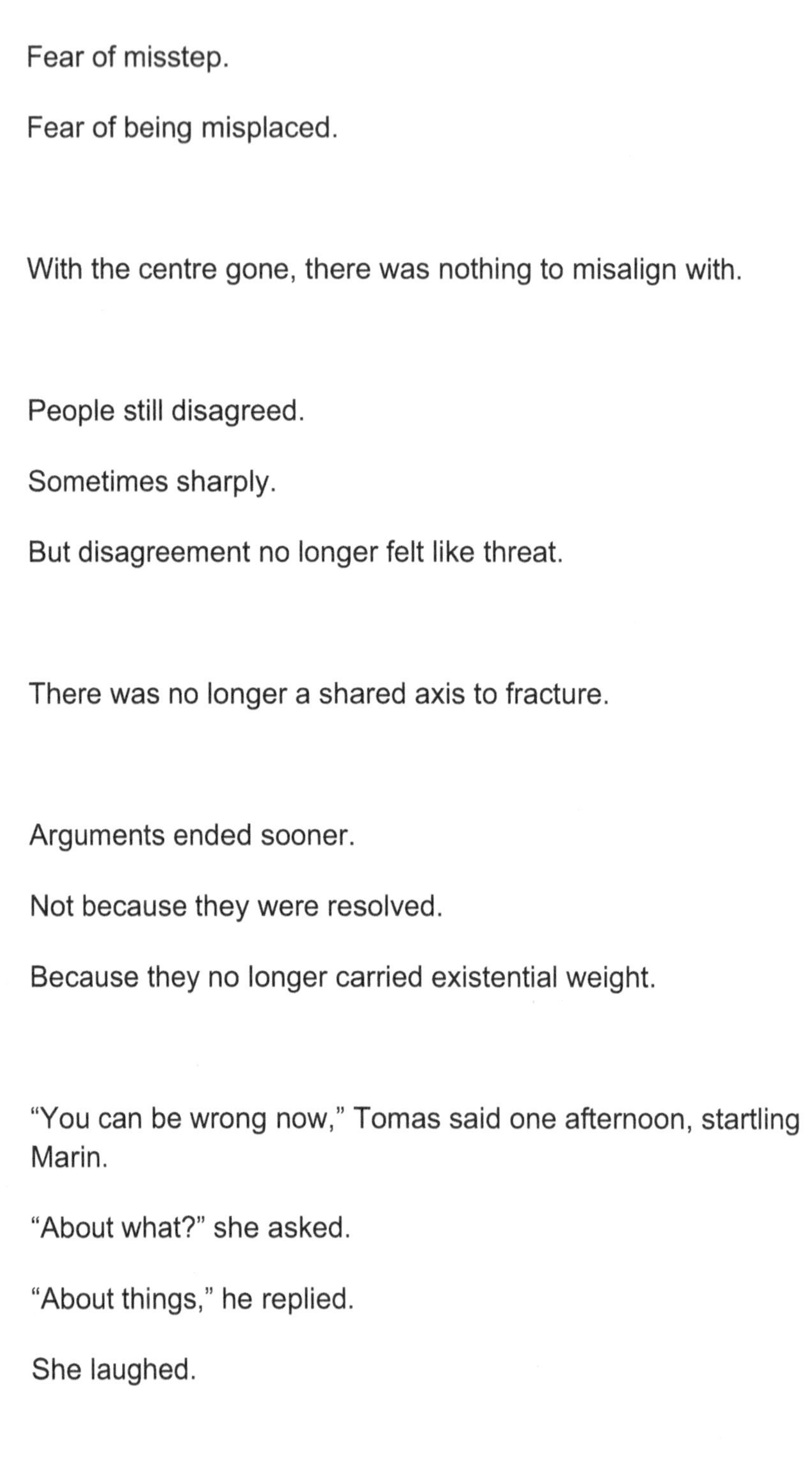

Fear of misstep.

Fear of being misplaced.

With the centre gone, there was nothing to misalign with.

People still disagreed.

Sometimes sharply.

But disagreement no longer felt like threat.

There was no longer a shared axis to fracture.

Arguments ended sooner.

Not because they were resolved.

Because they no longer carried existential weight.

“You can be wrong now,” Tomas said one afternoon, startling Marin.

“About what?” she asked.

“About things,” he replied.

She laughed.

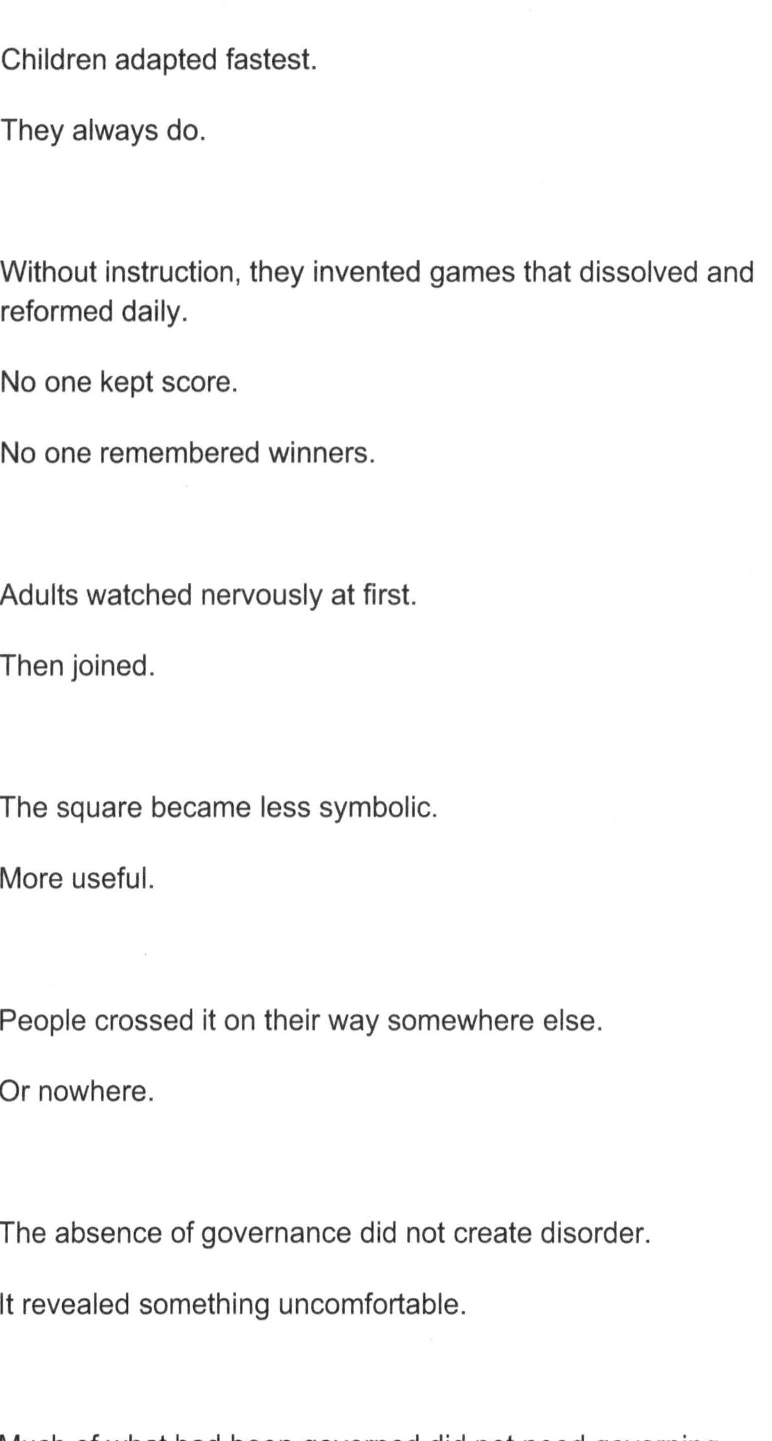

Children adapted fastest.

They always do.

Without instruction, they invented games that dissolved and reformed daily.

No one kept score.

No one remembered winners.

Adults watched nervously at first.

Then joined.

The square became less symbolic.

More useful.

People crossed it on their way somewhere else.

Or nowhere.

The absence of governance did not create disorder.

It revealed something uncomfortable.

Much of what had been governed did not need governing.

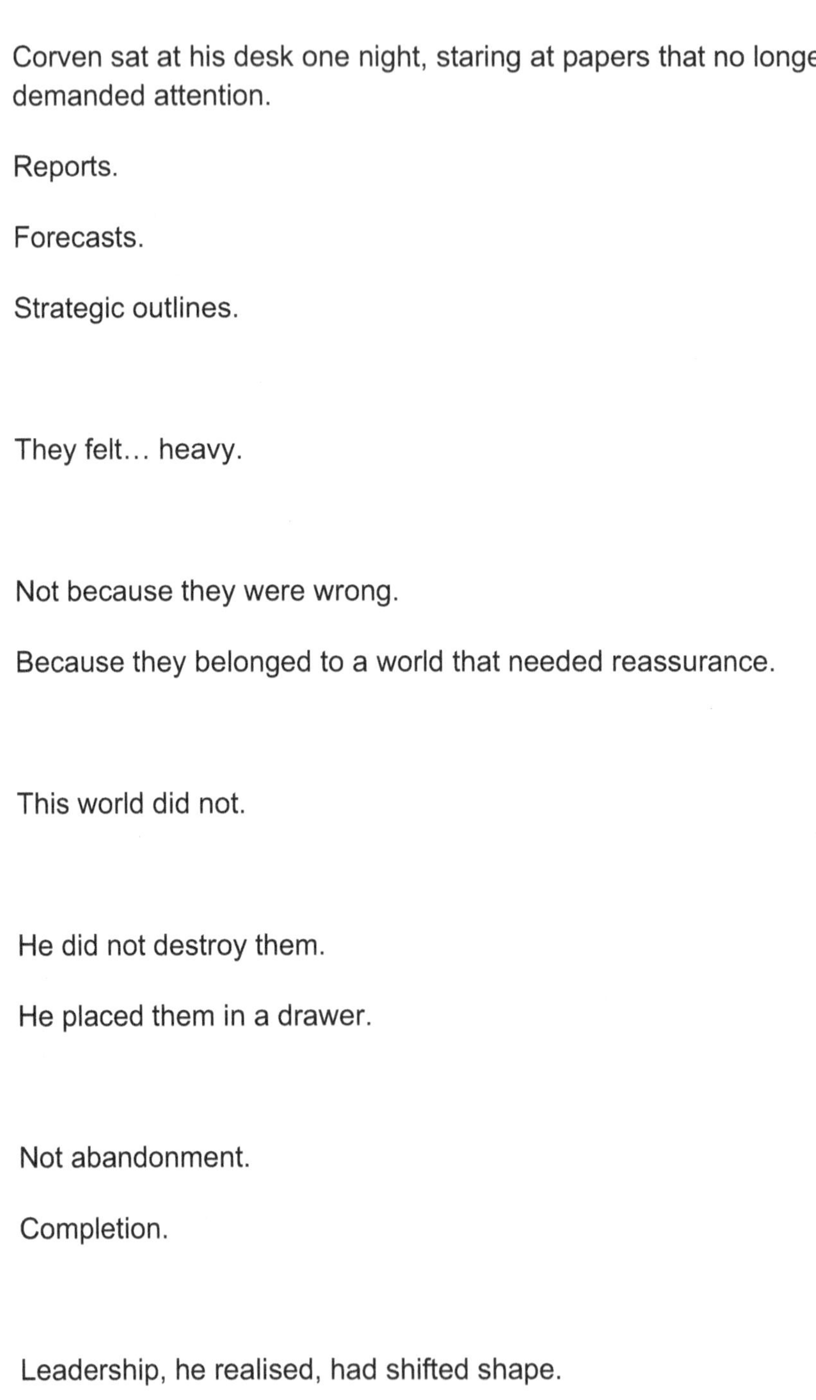

Corven sat at his desk one night, staring at papers that no longer demanded attention.

Reports.

Forecasts.

Strategic outlines.

They felt… heavy.

Not because they were wrong.

Because they belonged to a world that needed reassurance.

This world did not.

He did not destroy them.

He placed them in a drawer.

Not abandonment.

Completion.

Leadership, he realised, had shifted shape.

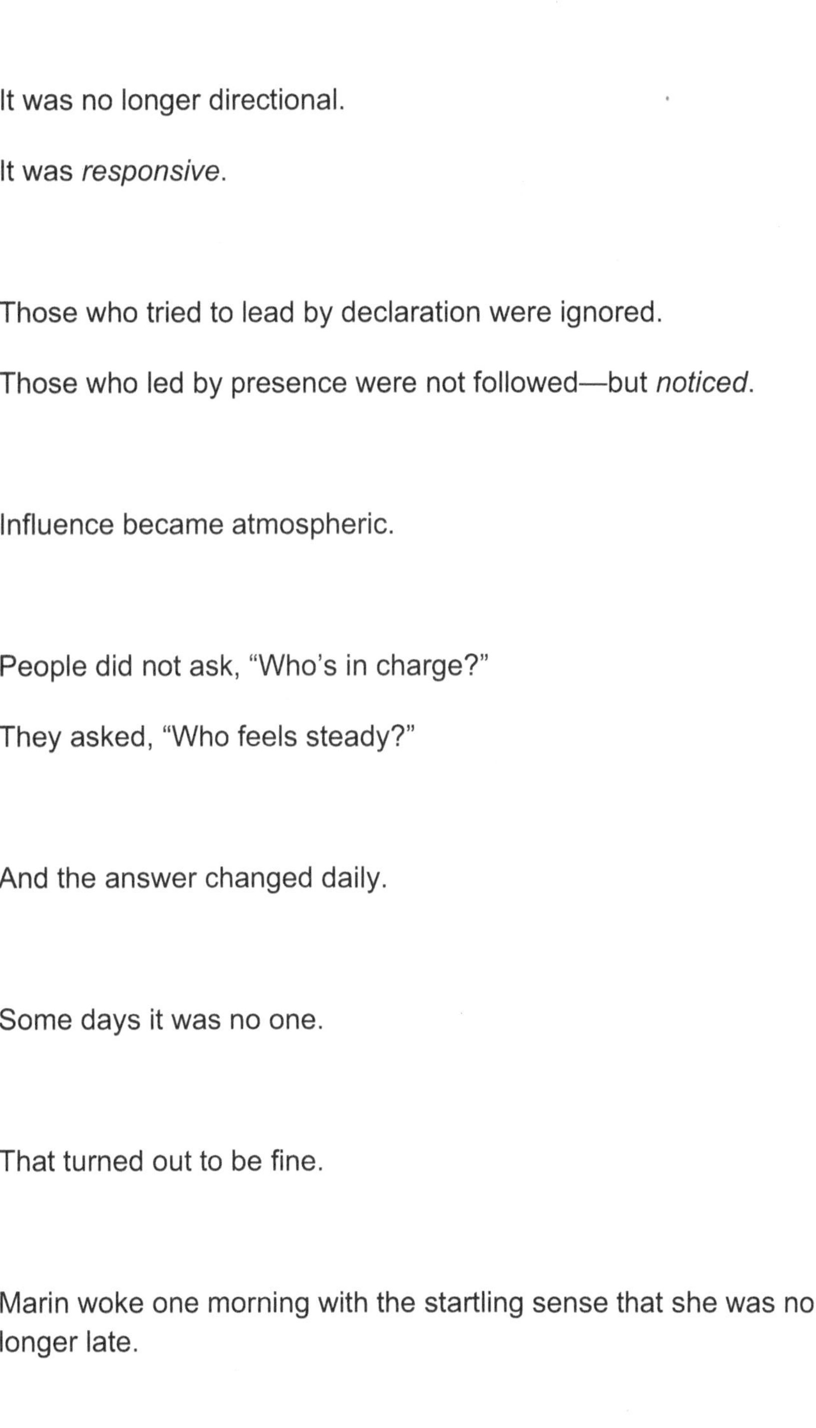

It was no longer directional.

It was *responsive*.

Those who tried to lead by declaration were ignored.

Those who led by presence were not followed—but *noticed*.

Influence became atmospheric.

People did not ask, “Who’s in charge?”

They asked, “Who feels steady?”

And the answer changed daily.

Some days it was no one.

That turned out to be fine.

Marin woke one morning with the startling sense that she was no longer late.

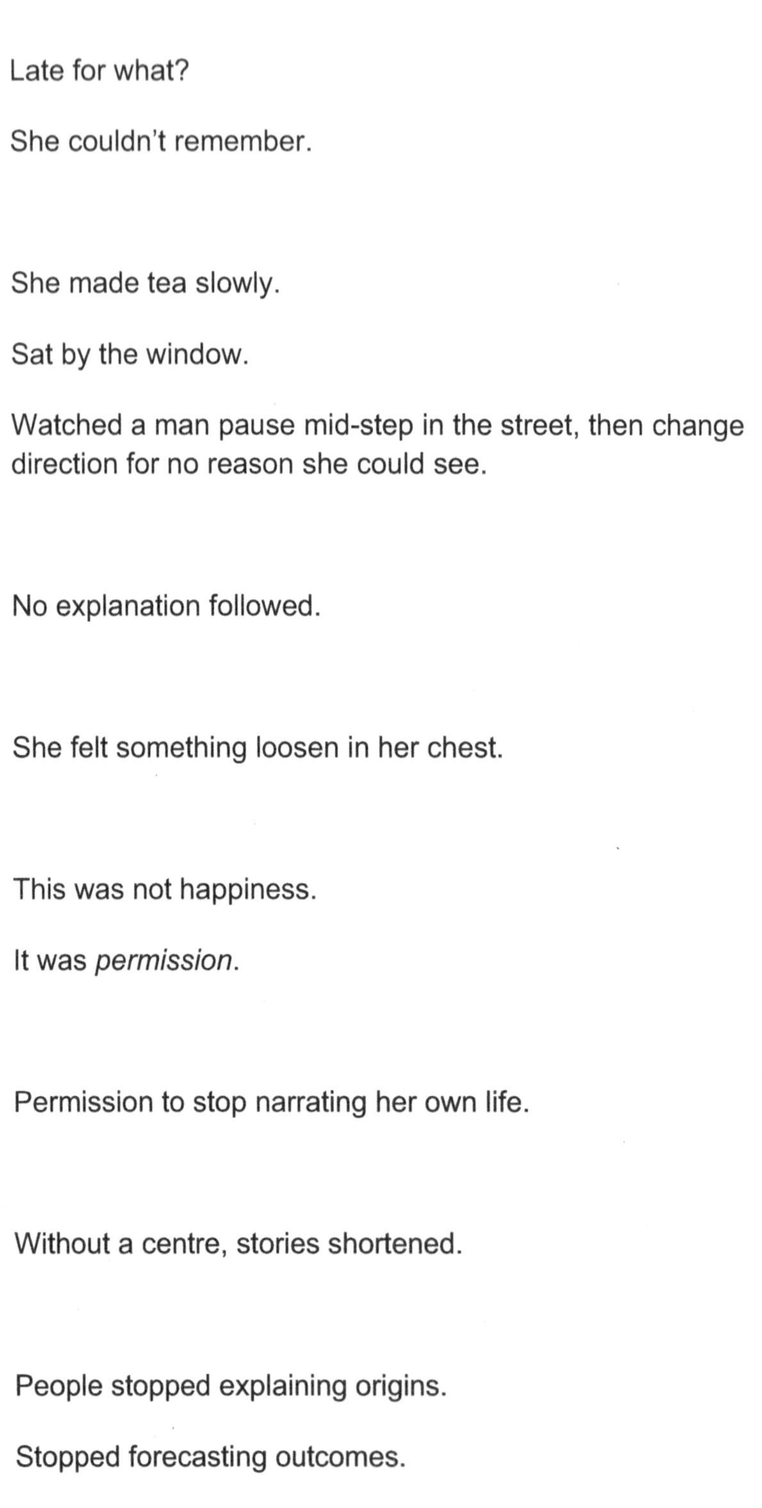

Late for what?

She couldn't remember.

She made tea slowly.

Sat by the window.

Watched a man pause mid-step in the street, then change direction for no reason she could see.

No explanation followed.

She felt something loosen in her chest.

This was not happiness.

It was *permission*.

Permission to stop narrating her own life.

Without a centre, stories shortened.

People stopped explaining origins.

Stopped forecasting outcomes.

Stopped asking what it all meant.

Meaning did not disappear.

It became local.

This moment mattered.

This person mattered.

This breath mattered.

Nothing else required endorsement.

Some left.

They needed structure.

They needed clarity.

They needed edges.

No one stopped them.

Those who stayed did not congratulate themselves.

They simply remained.

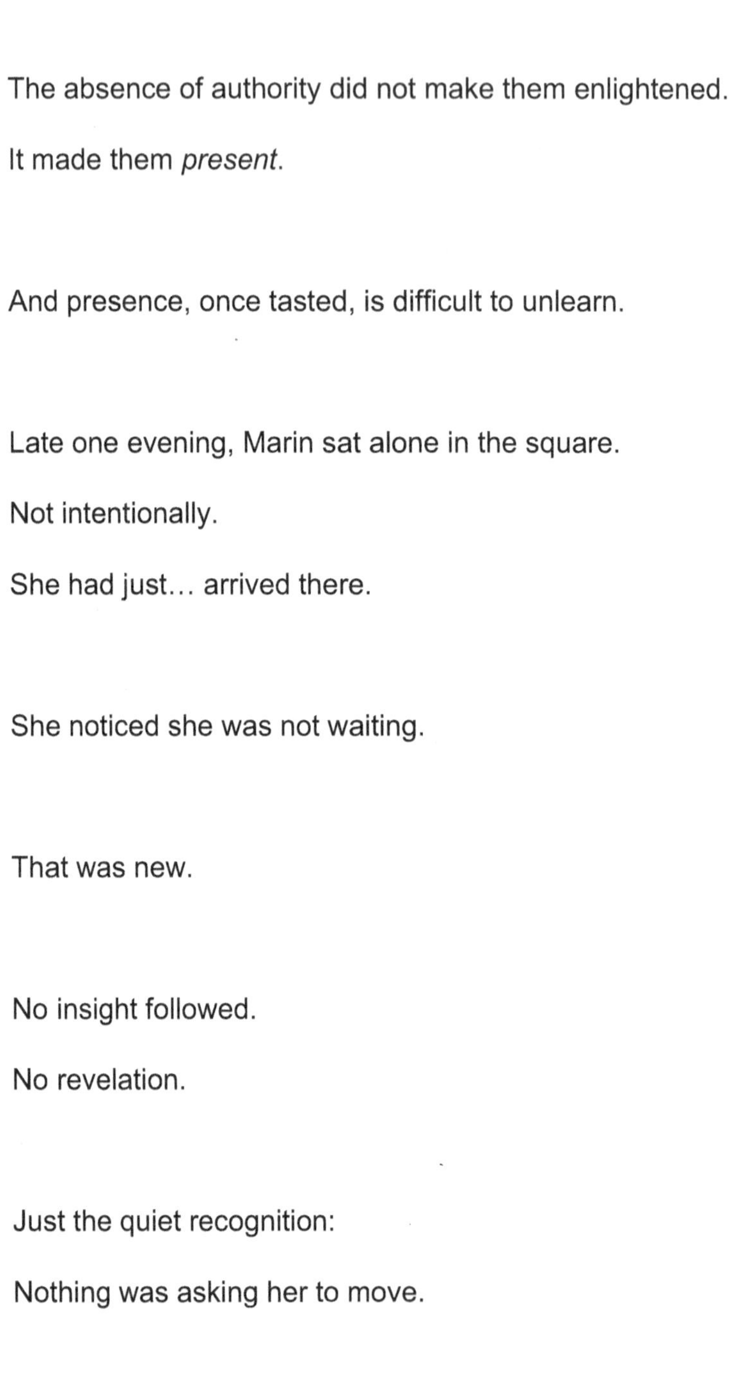

The absence of authority did not make them enlightened.

It made them *present*.

And presence, once tasted, is difficult to unlearn.

Late one evening, Marin sat alone in the square.

Not intentionally.

She had just… arrived there.

She noticed she was not waiting.

That was new.

No insight followed.

No revelation.

Just the quiet recognition:

Nothing was asking her to move.

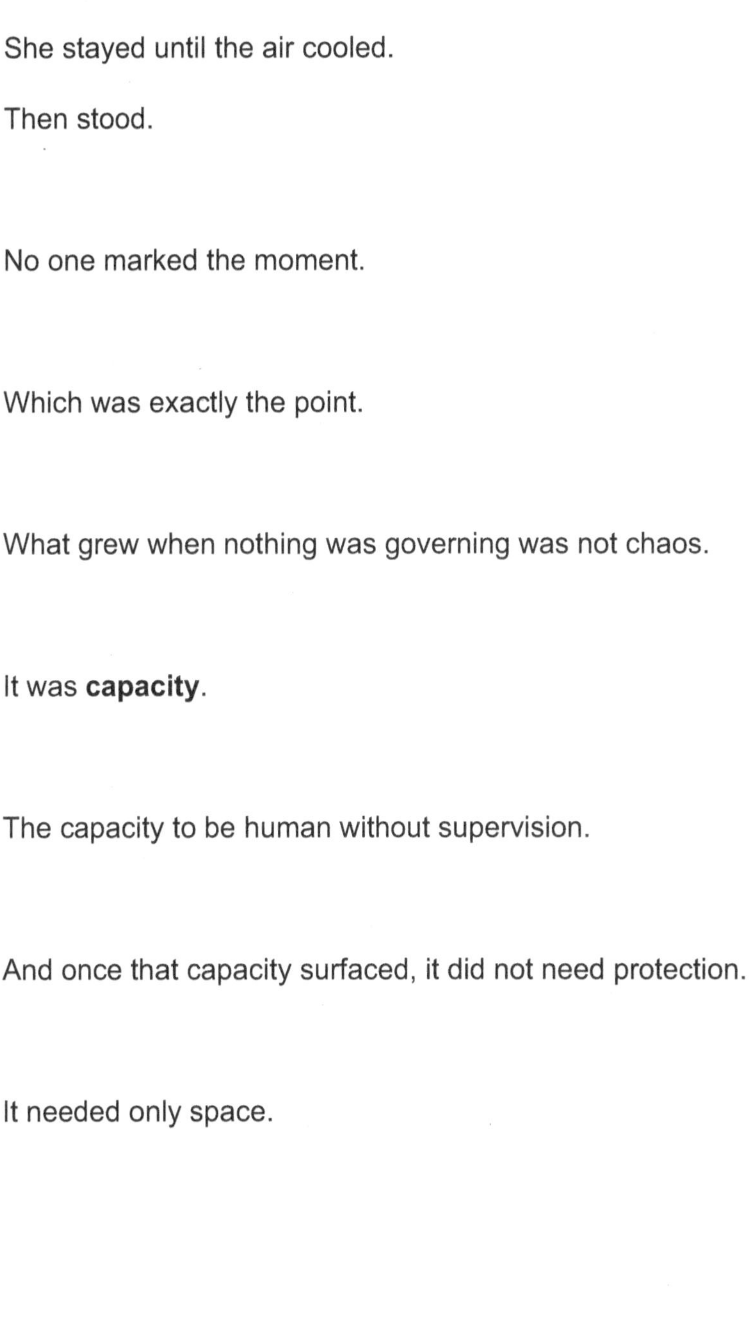

She stayed until the air cooled.

Then stood.

No one marked the moment.

Which was exactly the point.

What grew when nothing was governing was not chaos.

It was **capacity**.

The capacity to be human without supervision.

And once that capacity surfaced, it did not need protection.

It needed only space.

Chapter 29

At first, people tried to locate themselves.

Old habits lingered.

Am I doing this right?
Is this allowed?
Does this still count?

These questions arose reflexively, like muscle memory.

But something strange happened.

They no longer went anywhere.

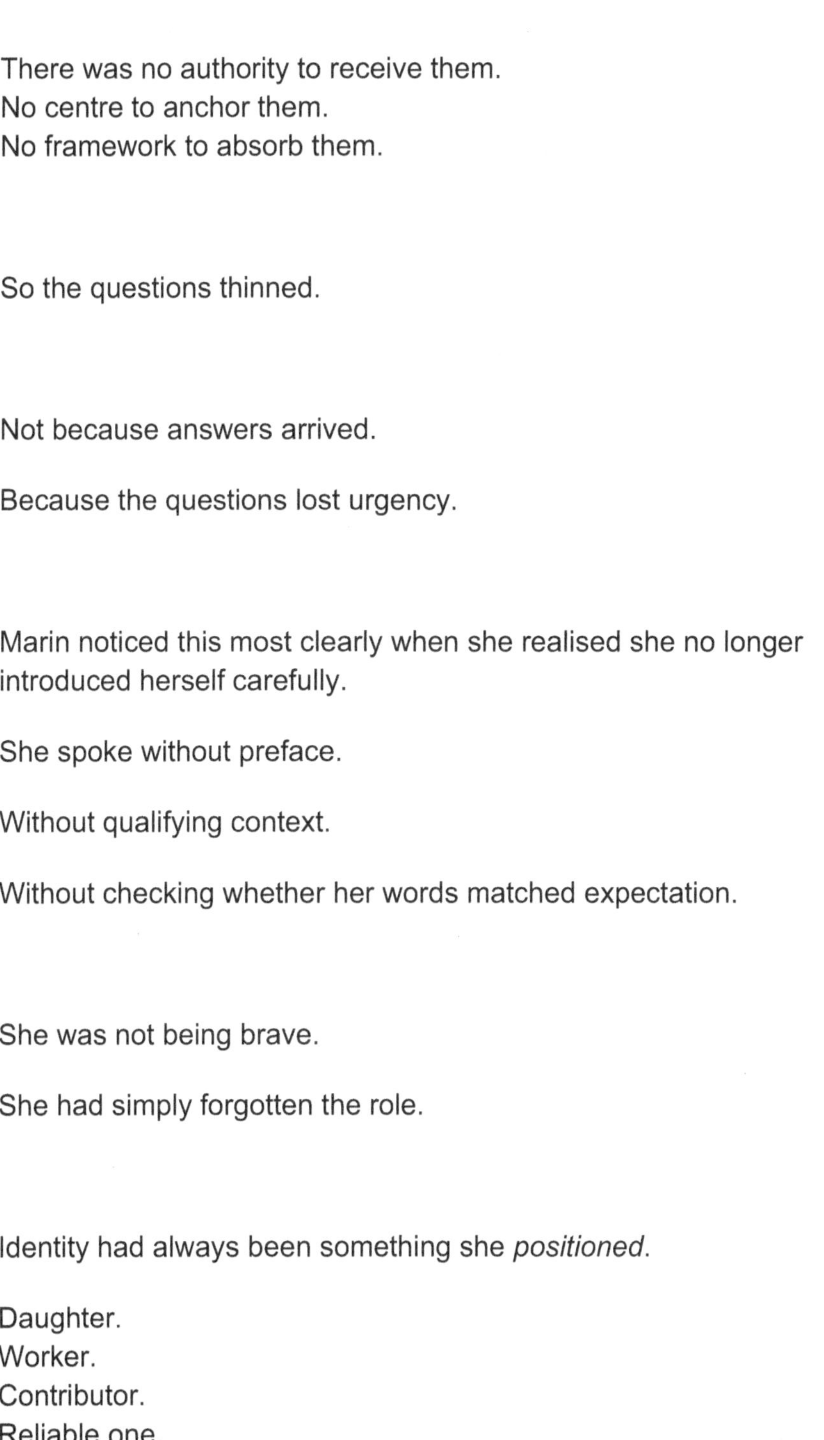

There was no authority to receive them.
No centre to anchor them.
No framework to absorb them.

So the questions thinned.

Not because answers arrived.

Because the questions lost urgency.

Marin noticed this most clearly when she realised she no longer introduced herself carefully.

She spoke without preface.

Without qualifying context.

Without checking whether her words matched expectation.

She was not being brave.

She had simply forgotten the role.

Identity had always been something she *positioned*.

Daughter.
Worker.
Contributor.
Reliable one.

Now identity behaved differently.

It appeared situationally.

Responsive.

Unfixed.

She was serious with one.

Playful with another.

And silent when that was the truest.

None of this felt like fragmentation.

It felt like accuracy.

In the past, identity required consistency.

Now it required honesty.

This unsettled those who needed coherence.

“You’re different,” someone said to her one afternoon.

“Yes,” Marin replied.

“But not in one direction.”

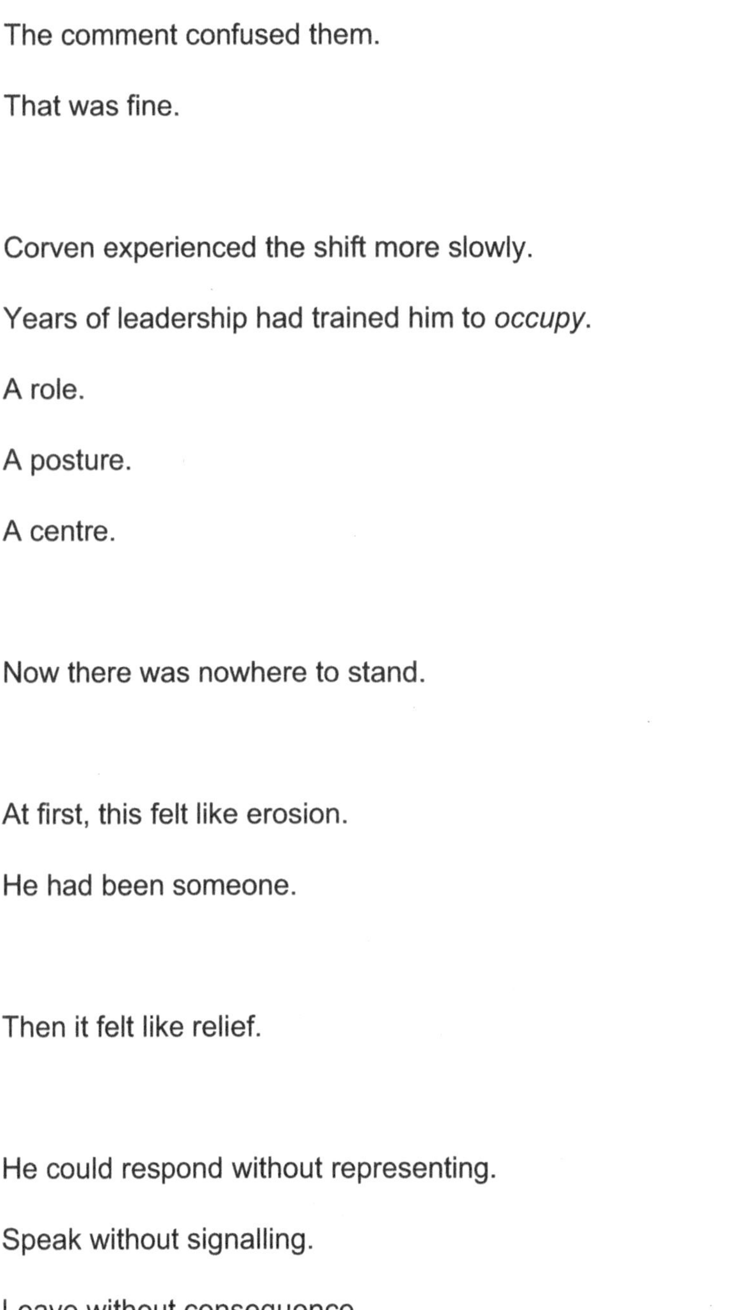

The comment confused them.

That was fine.

Corven experienced the shift more slowly.

Years of leadership had trained him to *occupy*.

A role.

A posture.

A centre.

Now there was nowhere to stand.

At first, this felt like erosion.

He had been someone.

Then it felt like relief.

He could respond without representing.

Speak without signalling.

Leave without consequence.

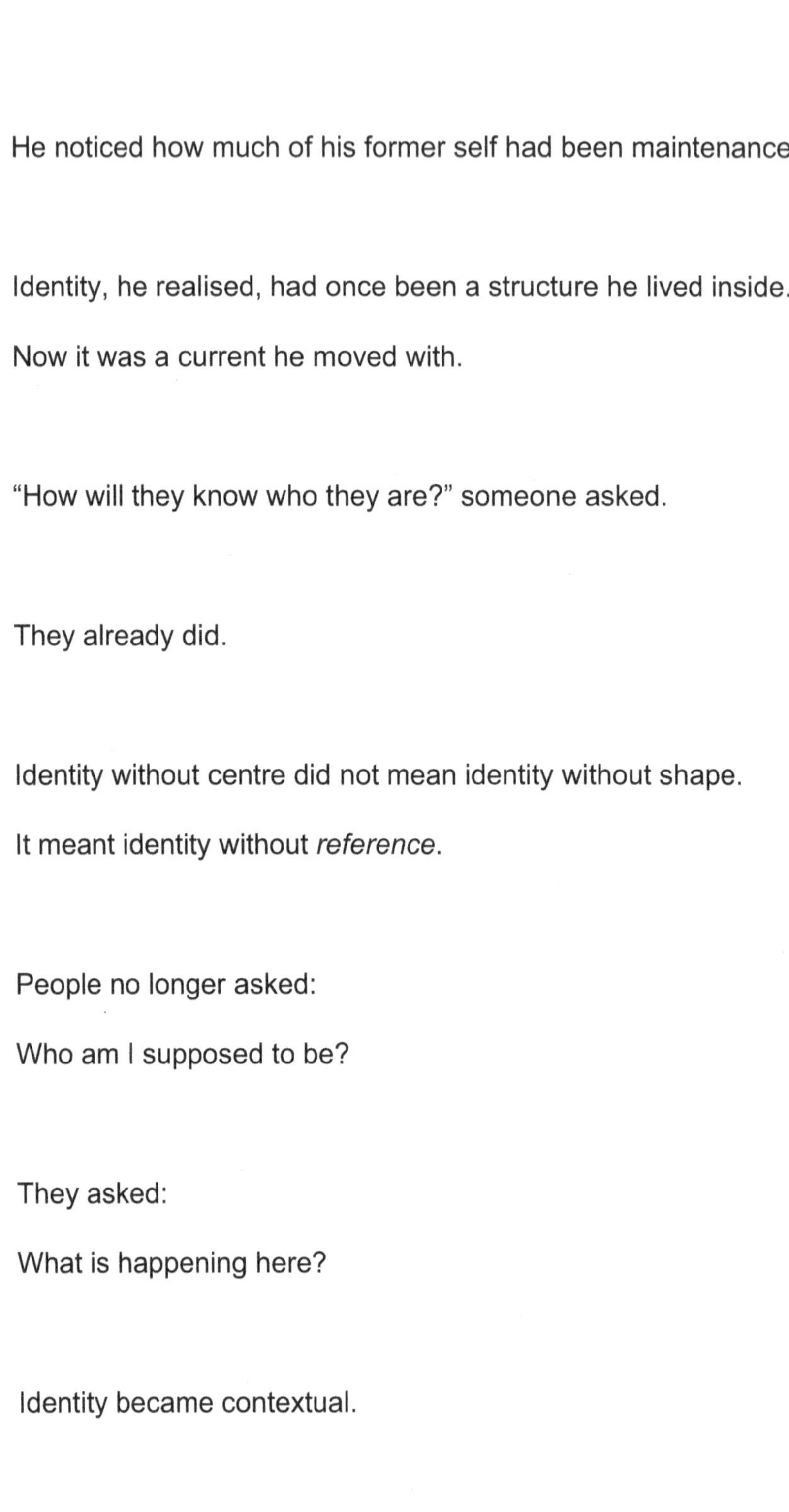

He noticed how much of his former self had been maintenance.

Identity, he realised, had once been a structure he lived inside.

Now it was a current he moved with.

“How will they know who they are?” someone asked.

They already did.

Identity without centre did not mean identity without shape.

It meant identity without *reference*.

People no longer asked:

Who am I supposed to be?

They asked:

What is happening here?

Identity became contextual.

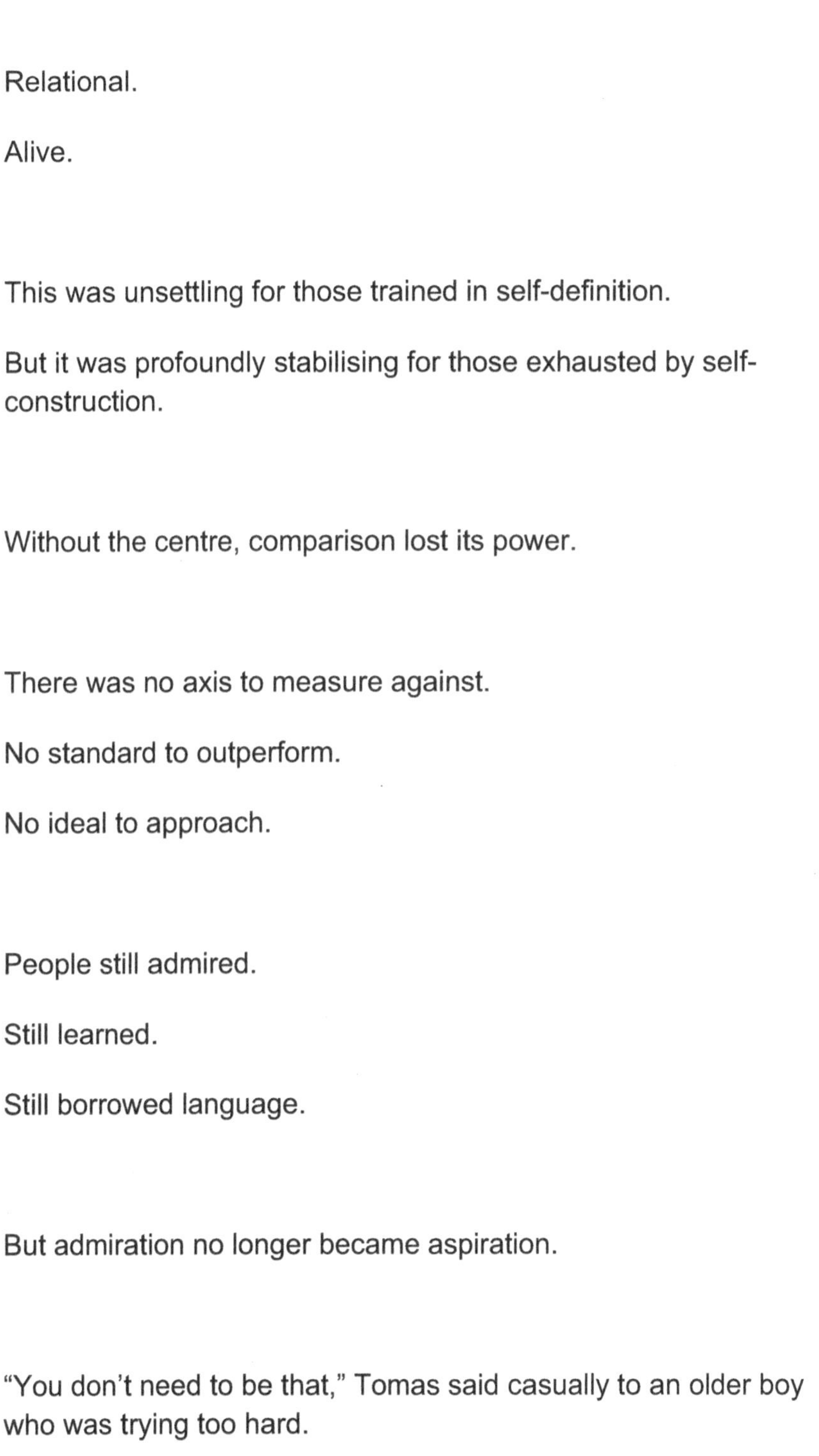

Relational.

Alive.

This was unsettling for those trained in self-definition.

But it was profoundly stabilising for those exhausted by self-construction.

Without the centre, comparison lost its power.

There was no axis to measure against.

No standard to outperform.

No ideal to approach.

People still admired.

Still learned.

Still borrowed language.

But admiration no longer became aspiration.

“You don’t need to be that,” Tomas said casually to an older boy who was trying too hard.

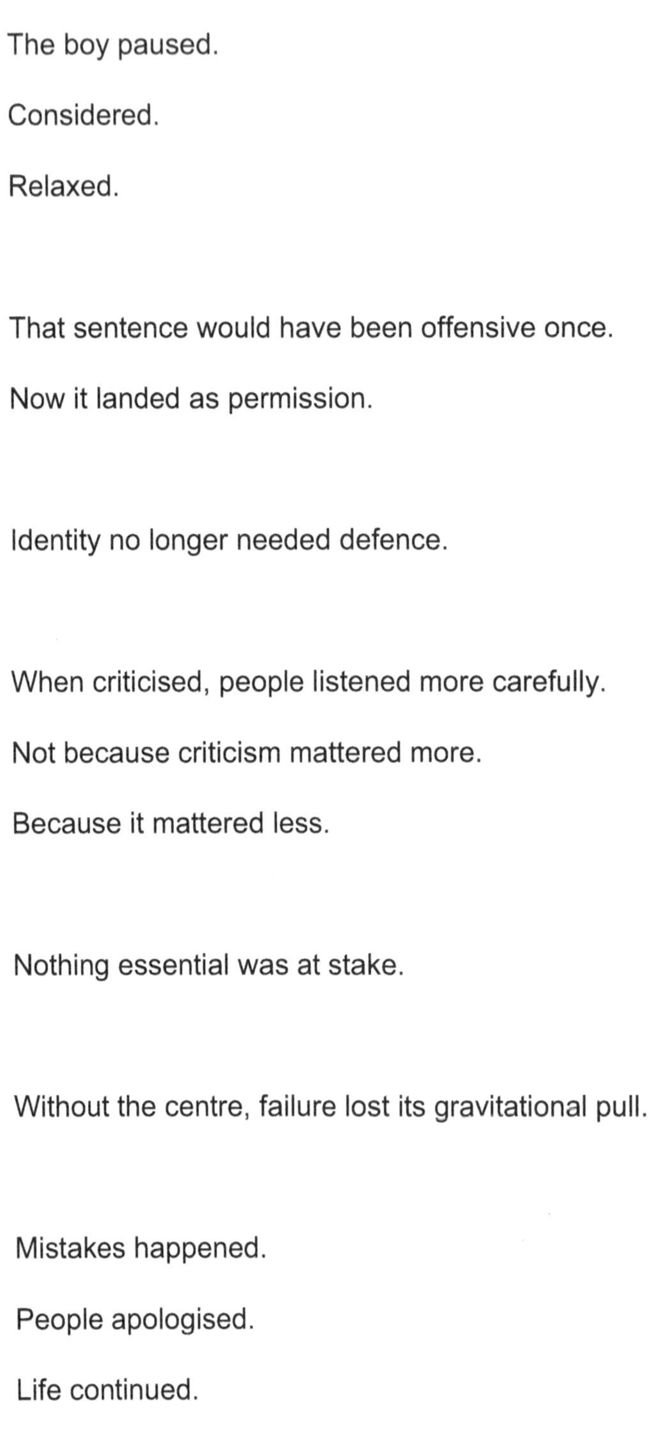

The boy paused.

Considered.

Relaxed.

That sentence would have been offensive once.

Now it landed as permission.

Identity no longer needed defence.

When criticised, people listened more carefully.

Not because criticism mattered more.

Because it mattered less.

Nothing essential was at stake.

Without the centre, failure lost its gravitational pull.

Mistakes happened.

People apologised.

Life continued.

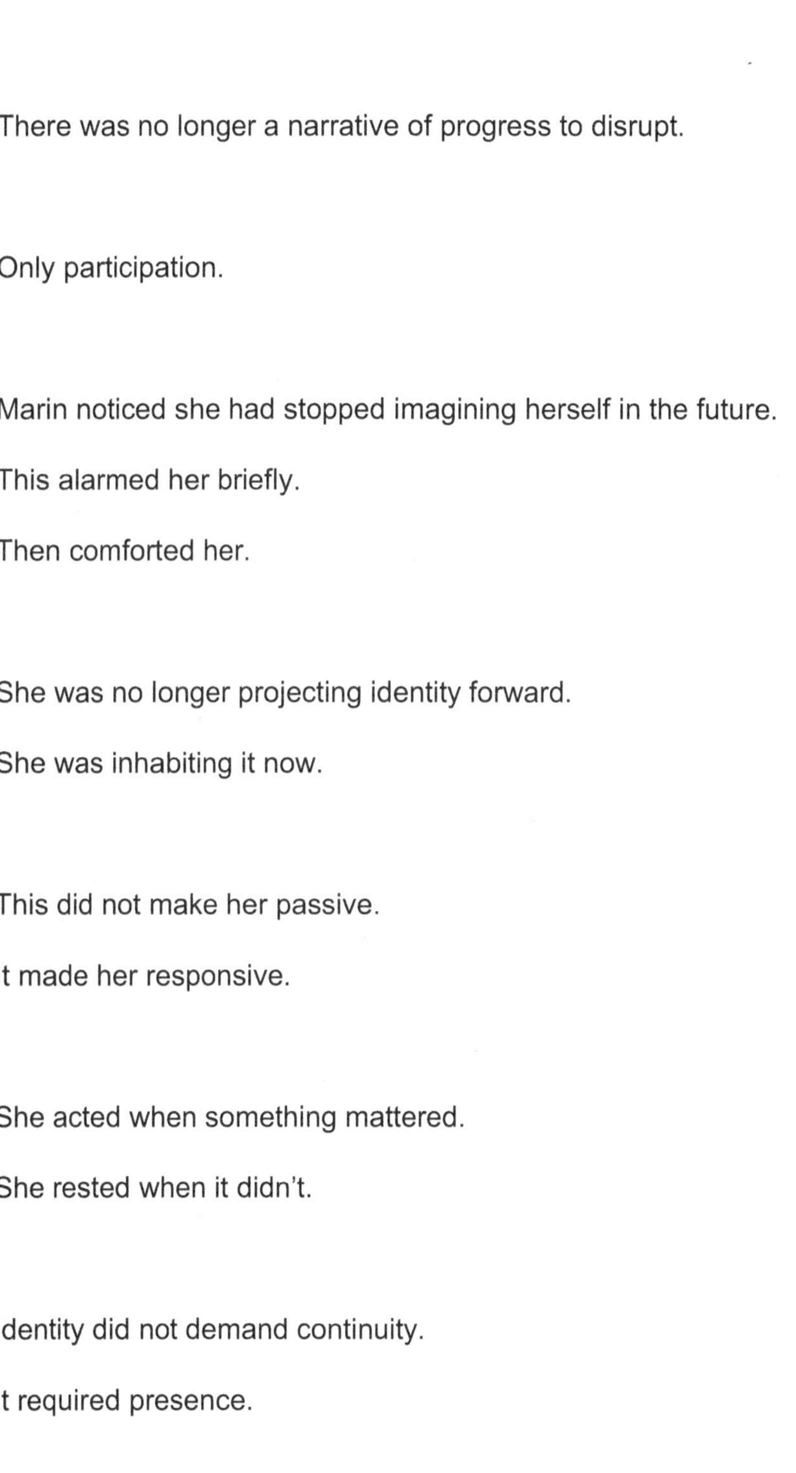

There was no longer a narrative of progress to disrupt.

Only participation.

Marin noticed she had stopped imagining herself in the future.

This alarmed her briefly.

Then comforted her.

She was no longer projecting identity forward.

She was inhabiting it now.

This did not make her passive.

It made her responsive.

She acted when something mattered.

She rested when it didn't.

Identity did not demand continuity.

It required presence.

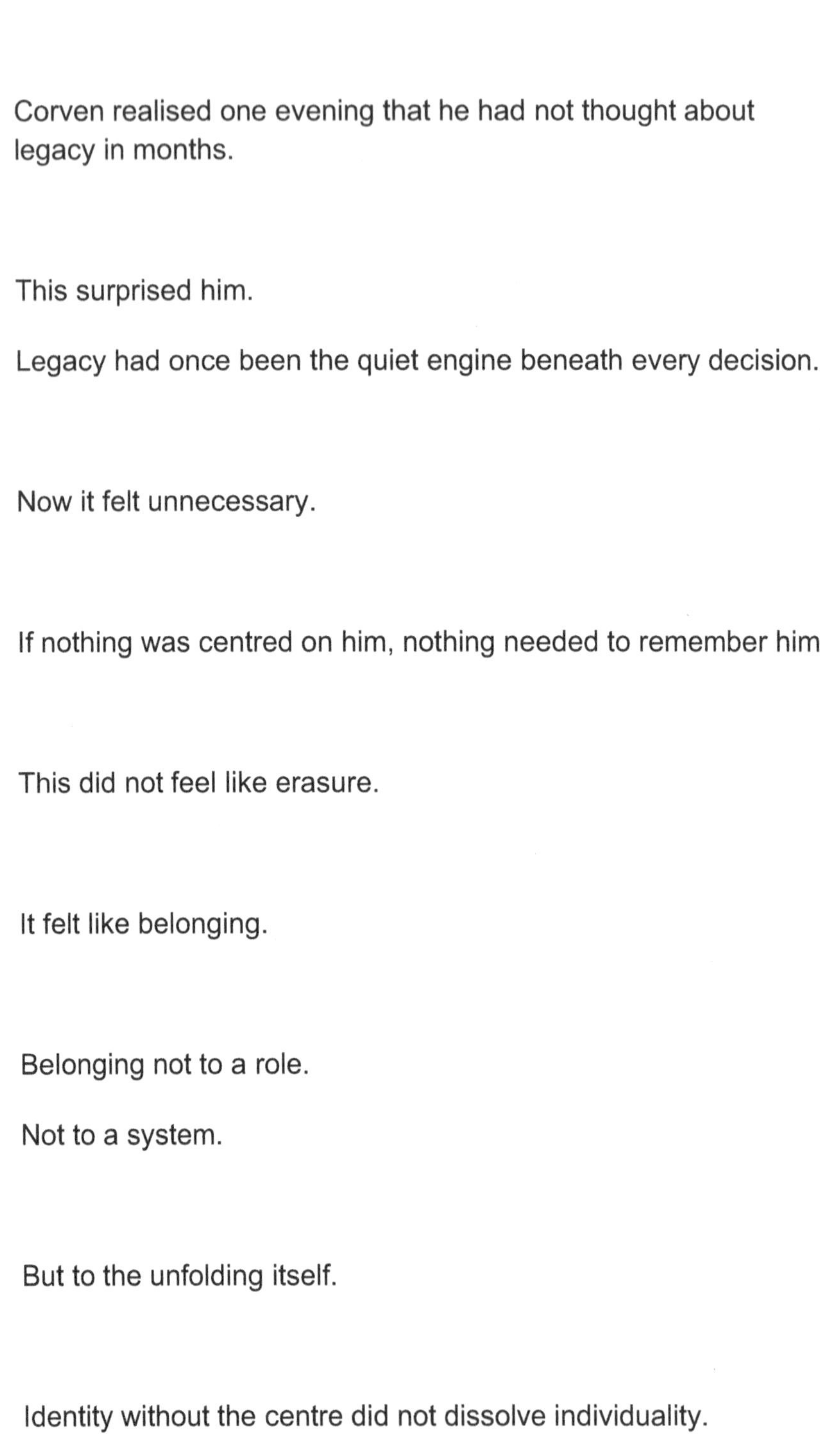

Corven realised one evening that he had not thought about legacy in months.

This surprised him.

Legacy had once been the quiet engine beneath every decision.

Now it felt unnecessary.

If nothing was centred on him, nothing needed to remember him.

This did not feel like erasure.

It felt like belonging.

Belonging not to a role.

Not to a system.

But to the unfolding itself.

Identity without the centre did not dissolve individuality.

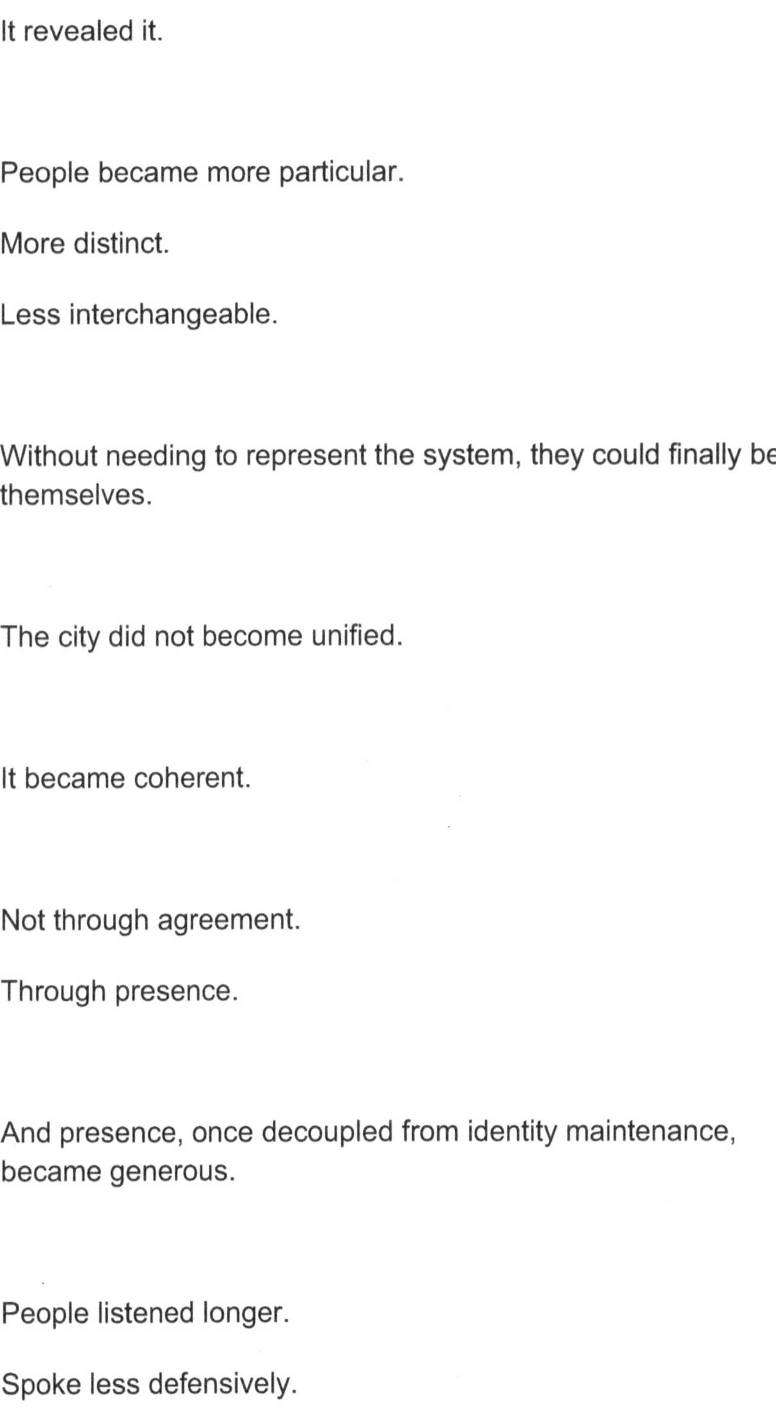

It revealed it.

People became more particular.

More distinct.

Less interchangeable.

Without needing to represent the system, they could finally be themselves.

The city did not become unified.

It became coherent.

Not through agreement.

Through presence.

And presence, once decoupled from identity maintenance, became generous.

People listened longer.

Spoke less defensively.

Left rooms without damage.

They no longer arrived carrying themselves.

They arrived empty-handed.

Which turned out to be enough.

Chapter 30

Marin realised she hadn't joined anything in weeks.

She was still present.
Still known.
Still greeted when she arrived.

But no one had asked her to commit.

The absence unsettled her more than exclusion ever had.

Belonging had once required negotiation.

Attendance proved loyalty.
Consistency proved sincerity.
Absence required explanation.

Now absence passed quietly.
Presence did too.

And somehow, both felt safer.

A man who had once chaired every gathering still came to the square.

He no longer arrived early.
He no longer arranged chairs.

He simply sat where there was space.

No one deferred to him.
No one resisted him either.

He listened.

Conversations no longer moved through roles.

They moved between people.

No one summarised.
No one facilitated.

When discussion dissolved, it dissolved.

Nothing collapsed.

Tomas drifted between clusters as if borders had never existed.

Here for ten minutes.
Gone.
Back again without apology.

No one questioned his loyalty.

Children never had.

Adults were learning.

Someone brought soup to a neighbour who hadn't been seen for days.

No meeting convened.
No list circulated.

The next morning someone else fixed a hinge.
Someone else stayed to talk.

There was no roster.

Belonging did not escalate into obligation.

It remained human.

Some tried to recreate membership in softer language.

"We just want to stay connected," they said.

But connection arrived whether it was scheduled or not.

Without obligation, it became more honest.

People came when they wanted.
Left when they needed.
Returned without negotiation.

Those who required clearer edges quietly found them elsewhere.

No one called it betrayal.

Belonging without membership does not compete.

It allows departure.

Marin missed a gathering she hadn't realised was happening.

She felt a flicker of guilt.

Then noticed no one asked where she had been.

When she returned days later, she was welcomed without commentary.

Not indifference.

Acceptance.

Belonging shifted from identity to encounter.

People stopped saying, "I'm part of..."

They said, "I was there when..."

Continuity no longer lived in attendance.

It lived in memory.

In the way someone took their tea.
Paused before answering.
Laughed at the wrong moment.

Belonging became personal.

Corven noticed something else.

No one had asked him to legitimise anything in months.

Once, that would have alarmed him.

Now it felt like trust.

He spoke when something mattered.

And when he spoke, people listened.

Not because of position.

Because of presence.

Conflict changed too.

Disagreements happened openly.

People walked away.
Then returned.

No one threatened removal.

There was nothing to revoke.

Arguments shortened.

Apologies came easier.

“I don’t need you to agree,” someone said one afternoon.
“I just needed you to hear me.”

That sentence would not have survived membership.

It survived presence.

Late one night, Marin wrote without thinking:

I belong because I am here.
And when I leave, I will belong where I am then.

She folded the paper.

Did not keep it.

Belonging no longer required proof.

It was already happening.

Quietly.

Everywhere.

Chapter 31

The urge to explain returned quietly.

It always does.

Not as doctrine.

As concern.

“What does it mean now?” someone asked one evening, staring into a cup long gone cold.

No one rushed to answer.

Once, that question would have summoned frameworks.
Speakers.
Careful sequencing.

Now it lingered.

Unclaimed.

A man stood near the fig tree one afternoon and began to interpret.

“It was about returning to essence,” he said.
“About stripping away illusion.”

A few listened.

Then someone said casually, “Or maybe he just sat.”

The interpretation dissolved.

Not violently.

It simply had nowhere to attach.

“People need narrative,” someone insisted to Corven later.

“People need coherence,” he replied.

“Narrative is just one way to imitate it.”

They did not like that answer.

They wanted something transmissible.

Meaning without message is not transmissible.

It can only be encountered.

Someone once asked Elija why he never explained himself.

He had looked at them with mild curiosity.

"Because explanation competes with presence," he'd said.

At the time, it sounded evasive.

Now it sounded obvious.

Advice shortened.

Instead of theories, people began saying:

"That didn't feel right."
"Try again tomorrow."
"You don't have to decide yet."

No framework followed.

The words landed anyway.

Grief changed.

Loss no longer needed to teach.

It could simply hurt.

People cried without extracting lessons.

Laughed without drawing conclusions.

Meaning did not justify emotion.

It accompanied it.

A small group once tried to draft a statement.

Not official.

Just helpful.

They met for hours.

The paper remained blank.

Not because they lacked words.

Because the words refused alignment.

Eventually someone laughed.

“This is ridiculous.”

They burned the page.

The fire was warm.

Nothing rose from it.

Nothing needed to.

Cruelty stood out more clearly now.

Not because it violated doctrine.

Because it fractured presence.

When someone caused harm, no system intervened.

People responded directly.

“This hurts,” they said.

That was enough.

Art loosened.

Songs ended early.

Stories stopped mid-thought.

No one demanded closure.

When something landed, it landed.

Silence followed without embarrassment.

Education softened.

Questions were not answered immediately.

Sometimes not at all.

“Sit with it,” adults said.

Children did.

Adults tried.

Meaning no longer arrived ahead of experience.

It followed — or didn’t.

Memories became textured rather than instructive.

“I remember when that happened,” someone would say.

And leave it there.

As lamps flickered on around the square, Tomas asked Marin, “What do you think it all means?”

She studied him carefully.

Then said, “I think it means we were never as fragile as we thought.”

He nodded.

That seemed sufficient.

Meaning without message does not instruct.

It occurs.

And once people notice that, they stop trying to make life say something.

They let it speak.

In its own time.

In its own way.

Chapter 32

Time did not announce itself.

It arrived the way it always does.

Through repetition.

The square looked much the same at a glance.

Stone worn smooth by years of feet.
The fig tree broader now, its shade less dramatic, more reliable.

Nothing new was forming.

It had already formed.

What followed was not construction.

It was continuation.

People no longer spoke about “what was happening.”

They spoke about weather.
About aching knees.
About someone who hadn’t been seen in a few days.

Life had resumed its proper scale.

Marin felt the passage of time in her body before she noticed it in the city.

Her mornings slowed.

Not from fatigue.

From ease.

She no longer arrived early out of habit.

When she did arrive early, she sat.

Sometimes alone.
Sometimes not.

Silence no longer felt like waiting.

She could tell who was new by posture.

Newcomers lingered on the edge.

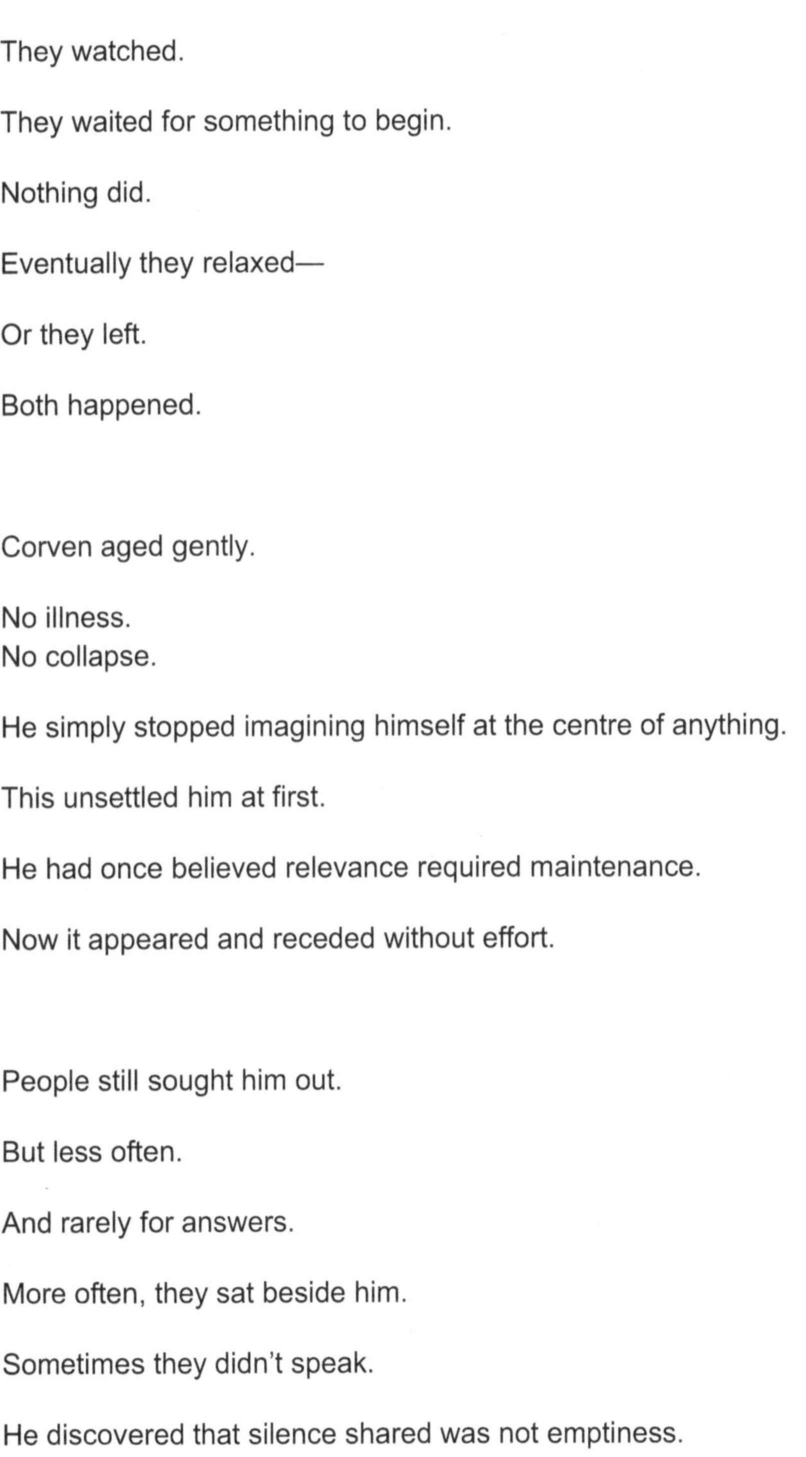

They watched.

They waited for something to begin.

Nothing did.

Eventually they relaxed—

Or they left.

Both happened.

Corven aged gently.

No illness.
No collapse.

He simply stopped imagining himself at the centre of anything.

This unsettled him at first.

He had once believed relevance required maintenance.

Now it appeared and receded without effort.

People still sought him out.

But less often.

And rarely for answers.

More often, they sat beside him.

Sometimes they didn't speak.

He discovered that silence shared was not emptiness.

It was company.

One afternoon he realised he had not offered advice in months.

He waited for unease.

It didn't come.

Advice had thinned into attention.

And attention was enough.

Children grew.

No one announced each transition.

No ceremony marked the shift.

Voices deepened.
Limbs lengthened.

It happened without commentary.

Mistakes still occurred.

Arguments still sparked.

But they no longer gathered momentum.

Without something to defend, they burned out more quickly.

People walked away mid-sentence.

Returned later.

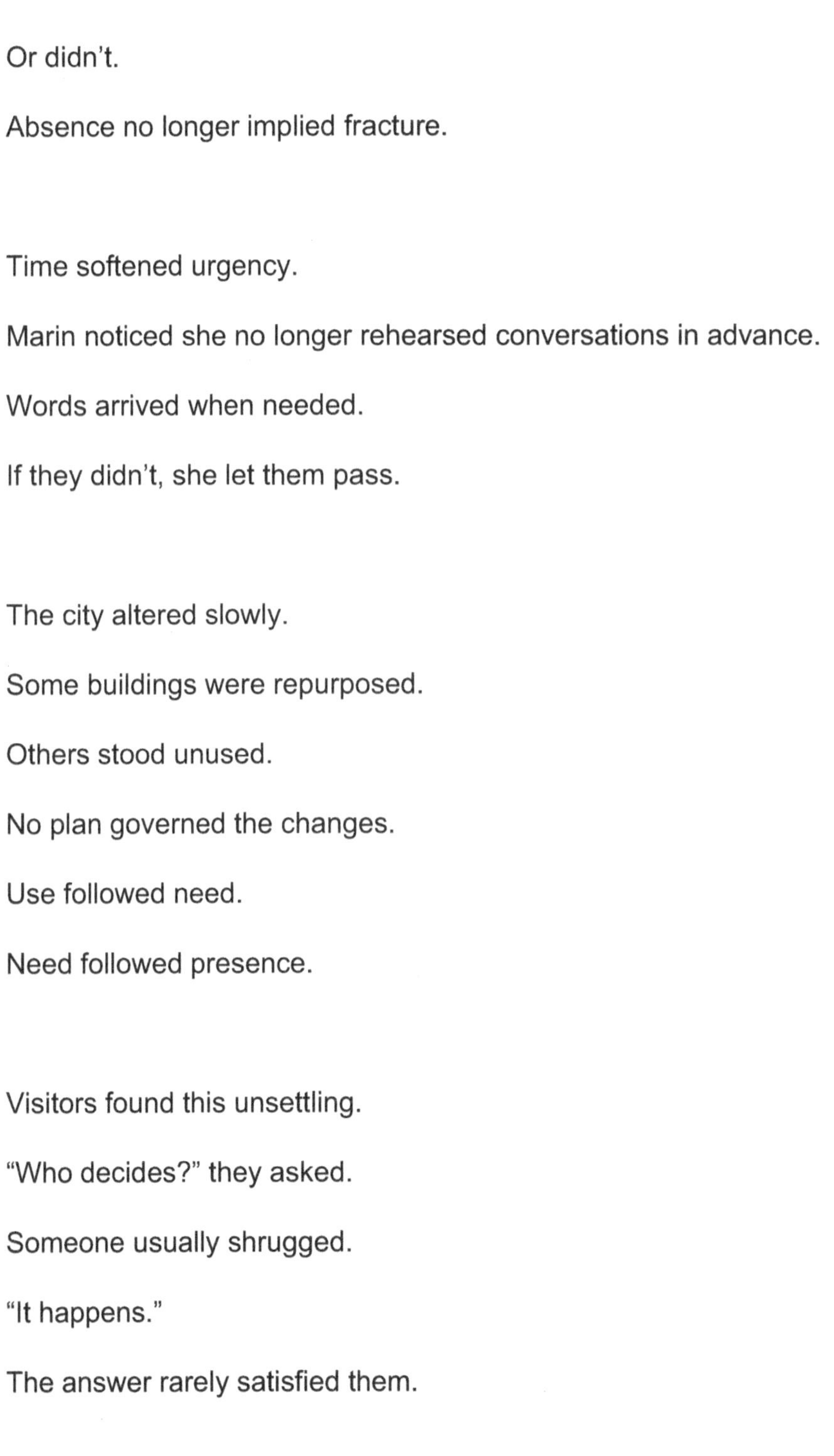

Or didn't.

Absence no longer implied fracture.

Time softened urgency.

Marin noticed she no longer rehearsed conversations in advance.

Words arrived when needed.

If they didn't, she let them pass.

The city altered slowly.

Some buildings were repurposed.

Others stood unused.

No plan governed the changes.

Use followed need.

Need followed presence.

Visitors found this unsettling.

“Who decides?” they asked.

Someone usually shrugged.

“It happens.”

The answer rarely satisfied them.

People who stayed grew accustomed to accumulation.

Not progress.

Not improvement.

Just repetition.

A woman swept the steps each morning.

No one assigned her the task.

One day she did not come.

Someone else swept.

Nothing was said.

The next morning, the steps were clean again.

Marin realised one winter that she had gone weeks without thinking of Elija.

Not from forgetting.

From integration.

His absence did not require explanation.

Life no longer arranged itself around his memory.

It continued.

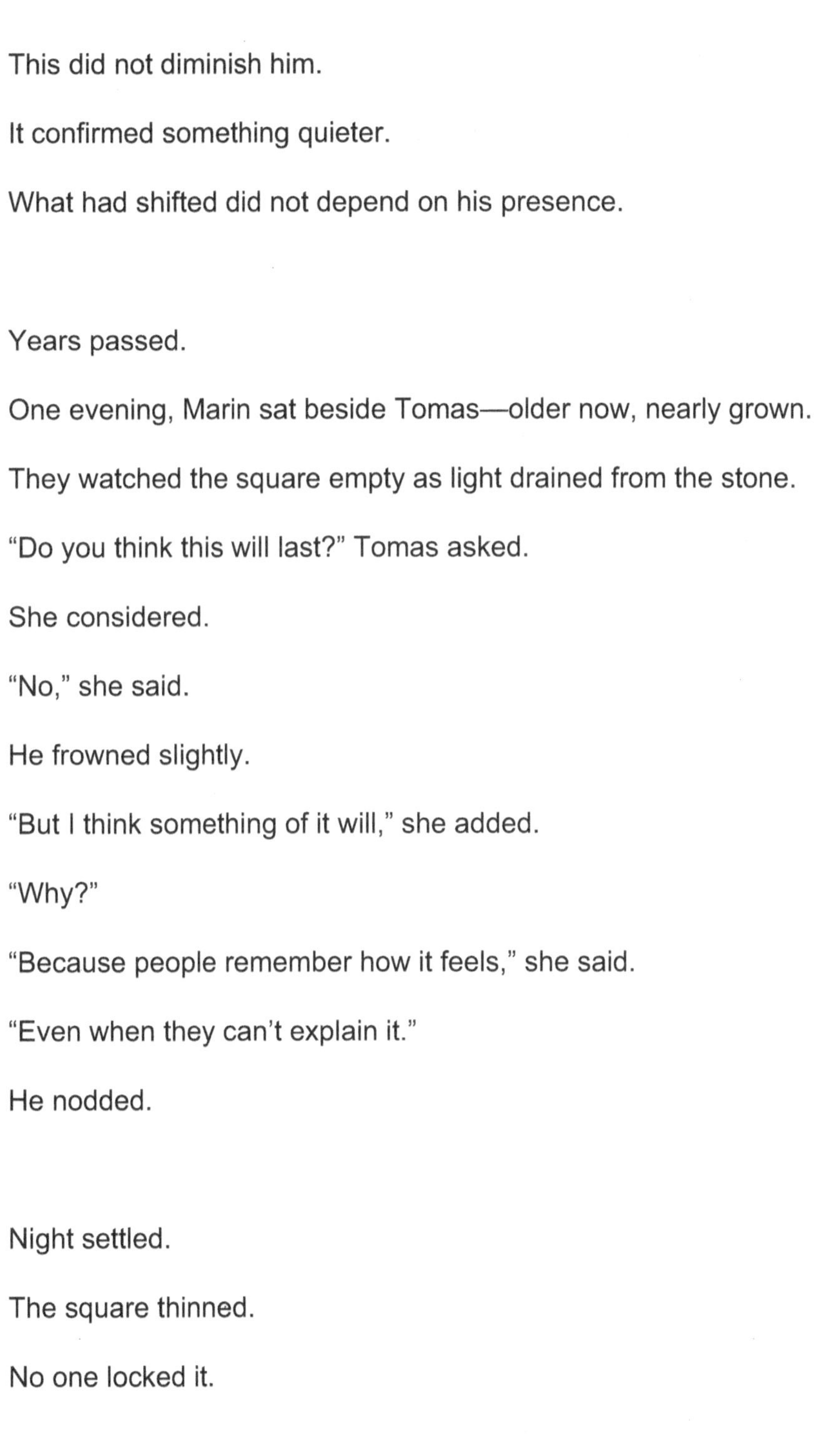

This did not diminish him.

It confirmed something quieter.

What had shifted did not depend on his presence.

Years passed.

One evening, Marin sat beside Tomas—older now, nearly grown.

They watched the square empty as light drained from the stone.

“Do you think this will last?” Tomas asked.

She considered.

“No,” she said.

He frowned slightly.

“But I think something of it will,” she added.

“Why?”

“Because people remember how it feels,” she said.

“Even when they can’t explain it.”

He nodded.

Night settled.

The square thinned.

No one locked it.

No one claimed it.

It rested.

As it had before.

As it would again.

Time did not conclude anything.

It simply moved.

And the city moved with it.

Chapter 33

No one noticed when the stories stopped circulating.

They had thinned gradually.

Like a language no longer being taught.

Once, people had spoken often about *how it used to be*.

Before the square.

Before the sitting.

Before everything changed.

Now those comparisons felt unnecessary.

Not forbidden.

Just… irrelevant.

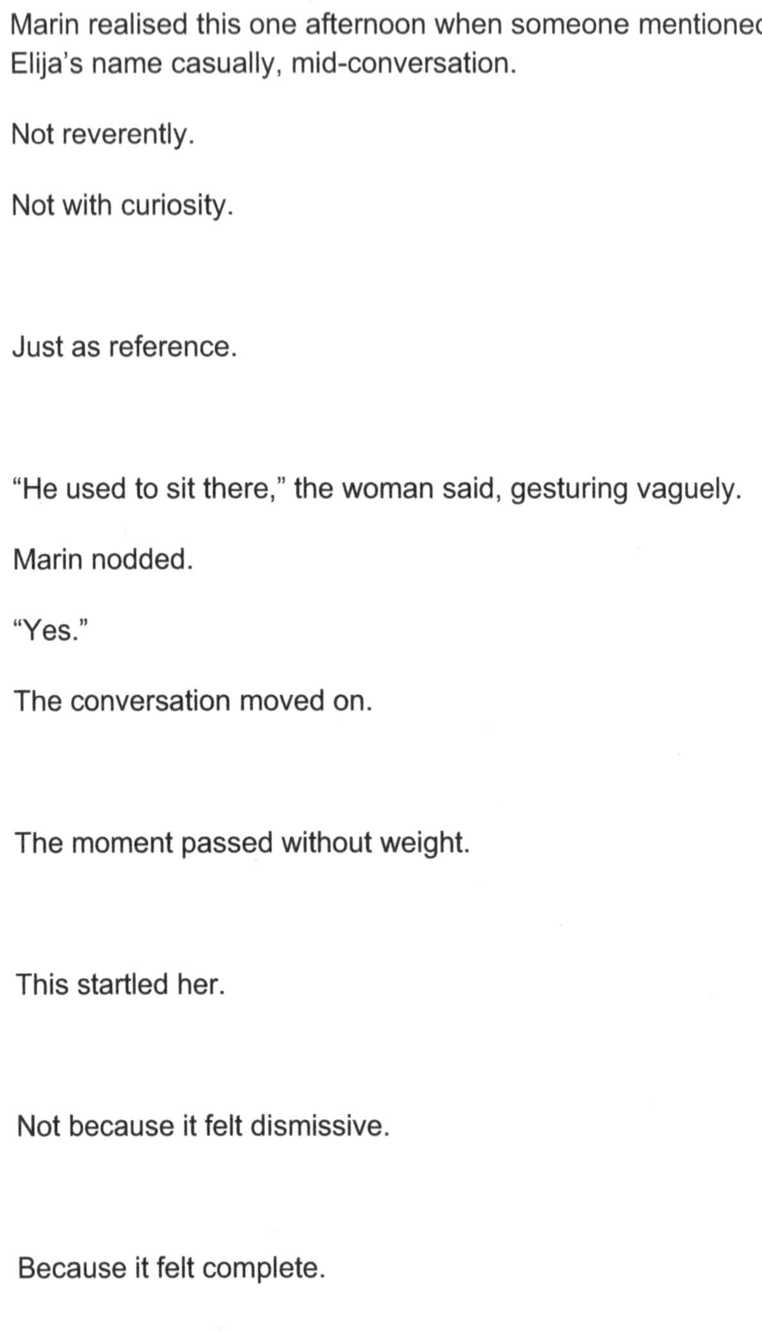

Marin realised this one afternoon when someone mentioned Elija's name casually, mid-conversation.

Not reverently.

Not with curiosity.

Just as reference.

"He used to sit there," the woman said, gesturing vaguely.

Marin nodded.

"Yes."

The conversation moved on.

The moment passed without weight.

This startled her.

Not because it felt dismissive.

Because it felt complete.

The shape that had once held meaning had dissolved.

And nothing rushed in to replace it.

People no longer asked newcomers if they'd heard the story.

Newcomers did not ask.

They sensed there was nothing to *learn*.

Only something to notice.

This made orientation brief.

People arrived.

They stayed or they didn't.

No one explained the city to them.

It revealed itself through use.

Children born after the changes grew without awareness of what had shifted.

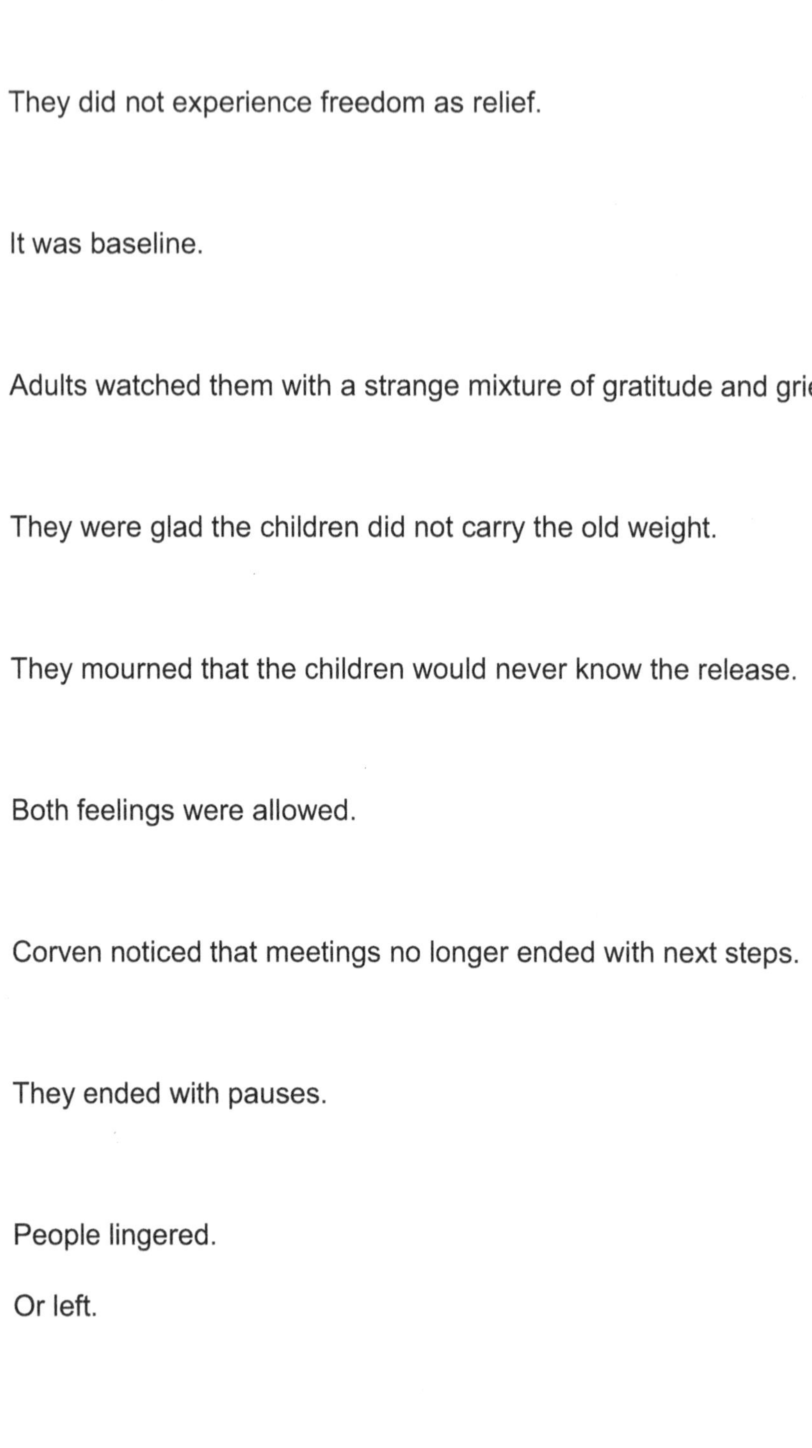

They did not experience freedom as relief.

It was baseline.

Adults watched them with a strange mixture of gratitude and grief.

They were glad the children did not carry the old weight.

They mourned that the children would never know the release.

Both feelings were allowed.

Corven noticed that meetings no longer ended with next steps.

They ended with pauses.

People lingered.

Or left.

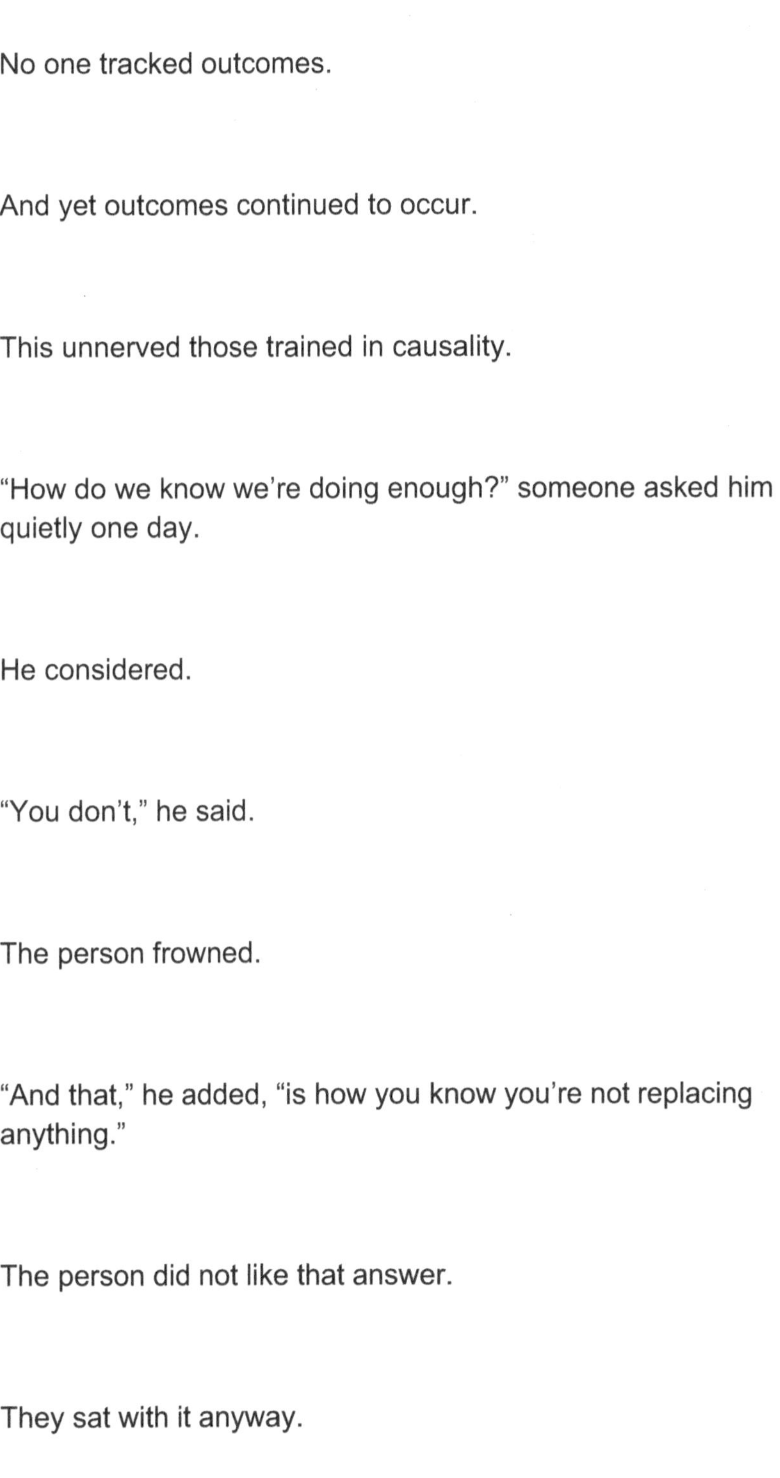

No one tracked outcomes.

And yet outcomes continued to occur.

This unnerved those trained in causality.

“How do we know we’re doing enough?” someone asked him quietly one day.

He considered.

“You don’t,” he said.

The person frowned.

“And that,” he added, “is how you know you’re not replacing anything.”

The person did not like that answer.

They sat with it anyway.

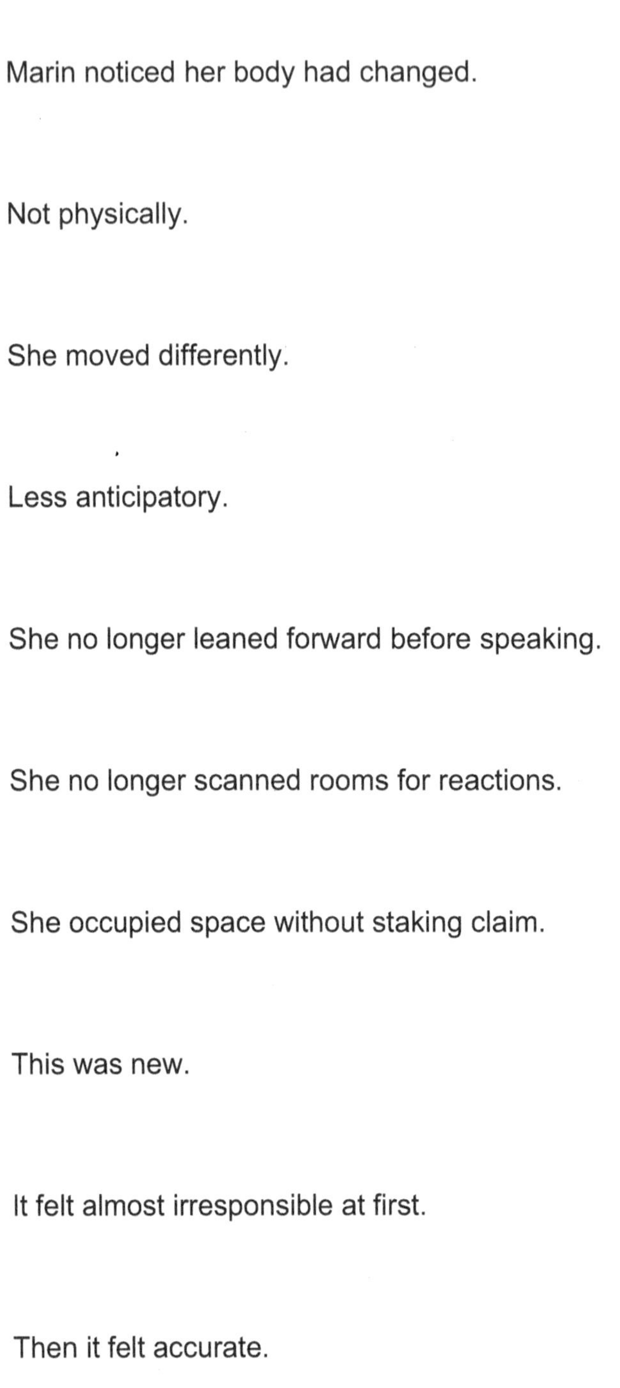

Marin noticed her body had changed.

Not physically.

She moved differently.

Less anticipatory.

She no longer leaned forward before speaking.

She no longer scanned rooms for reactions.

She occupied space without staking claim.

This was new.

It felt almost irresponsible at first.

Then it felt accurate.

The city had developed a rhythm that could not be diagrammed.

Busy days clustered.

Quiet weeks stretched.

No one attempted balance.

Balance arrived when it did.

People stopped calling this *a phase.*

Not because it had ended.

Because the word no longer fit.

Phases resolve.

This had settled.

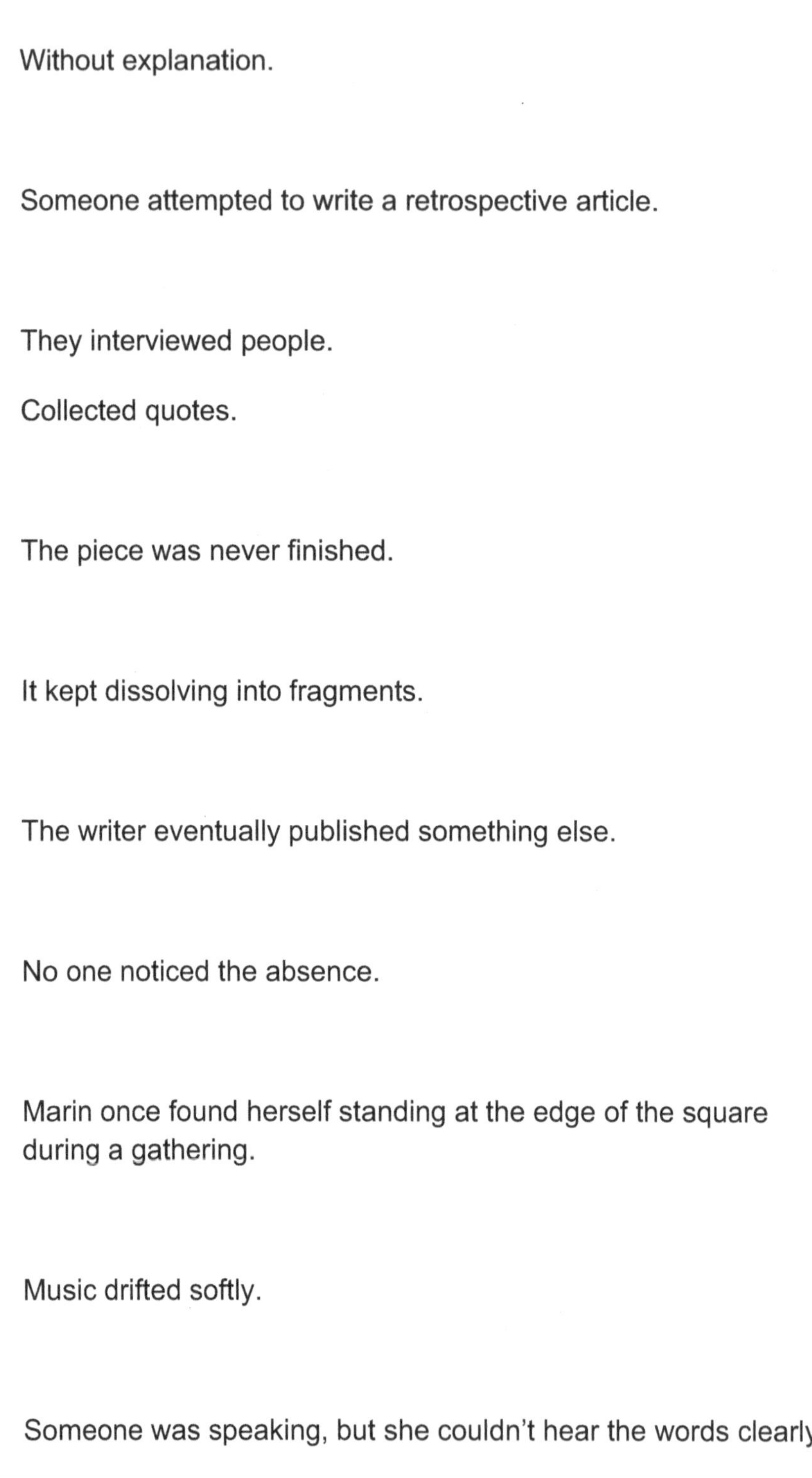

Without explanation.

Someone attempted to write a retrospective article.

They interviewed people.

Collected quotes.

The piece was never finished.

It kept dissolving into fragments.

The writer eventually published something else.

No one noticed the absence.

Marin once found herself standing at the edge of the square during a gathering.

Music drifted softly.

Someone was speaking, but she couldn't hear the words clearly.

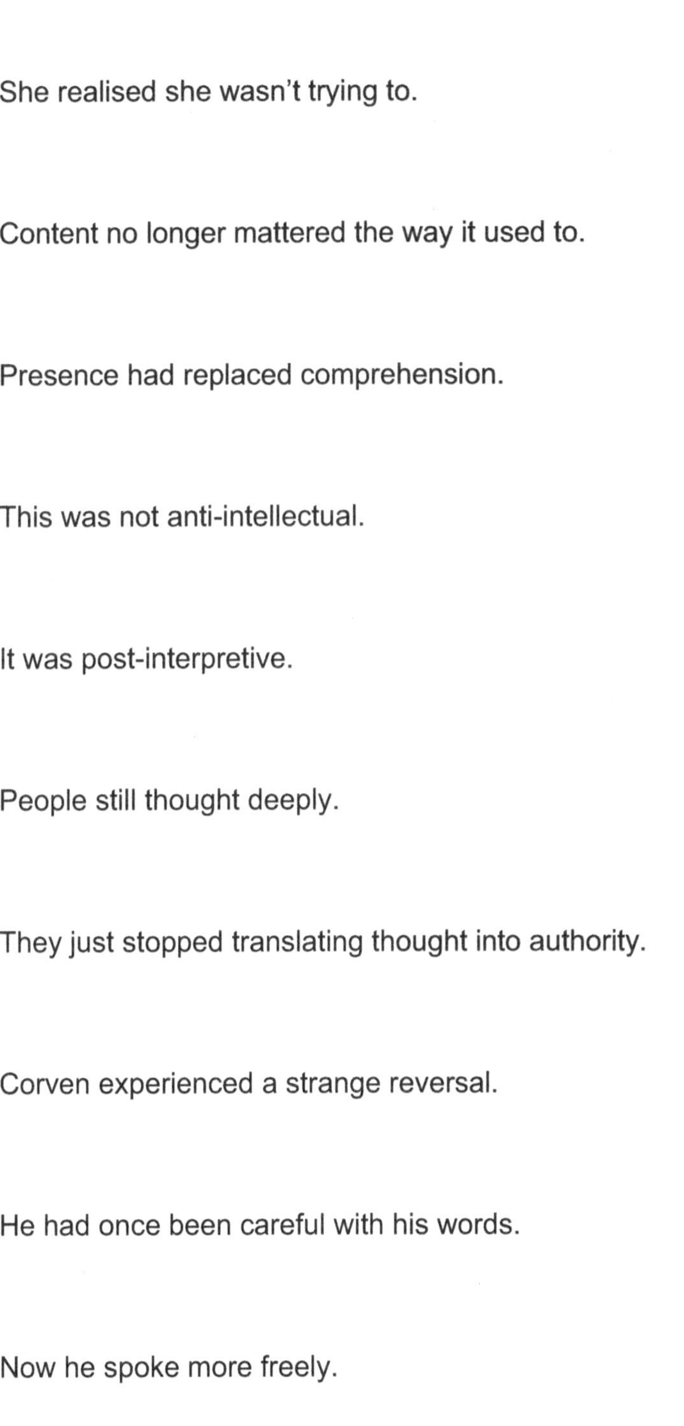

She realised she wasn't trying to.

Content no longer mattered the way it used to.

Presence had replaced comprehension.

This was not anti-intellectual.

It was post-interpretive.

People still thought deeply.

They just stopped translating thought into authority.

Corven experienced a strange reversal.

He had once been careful with his words.

Now he spoke more freely.

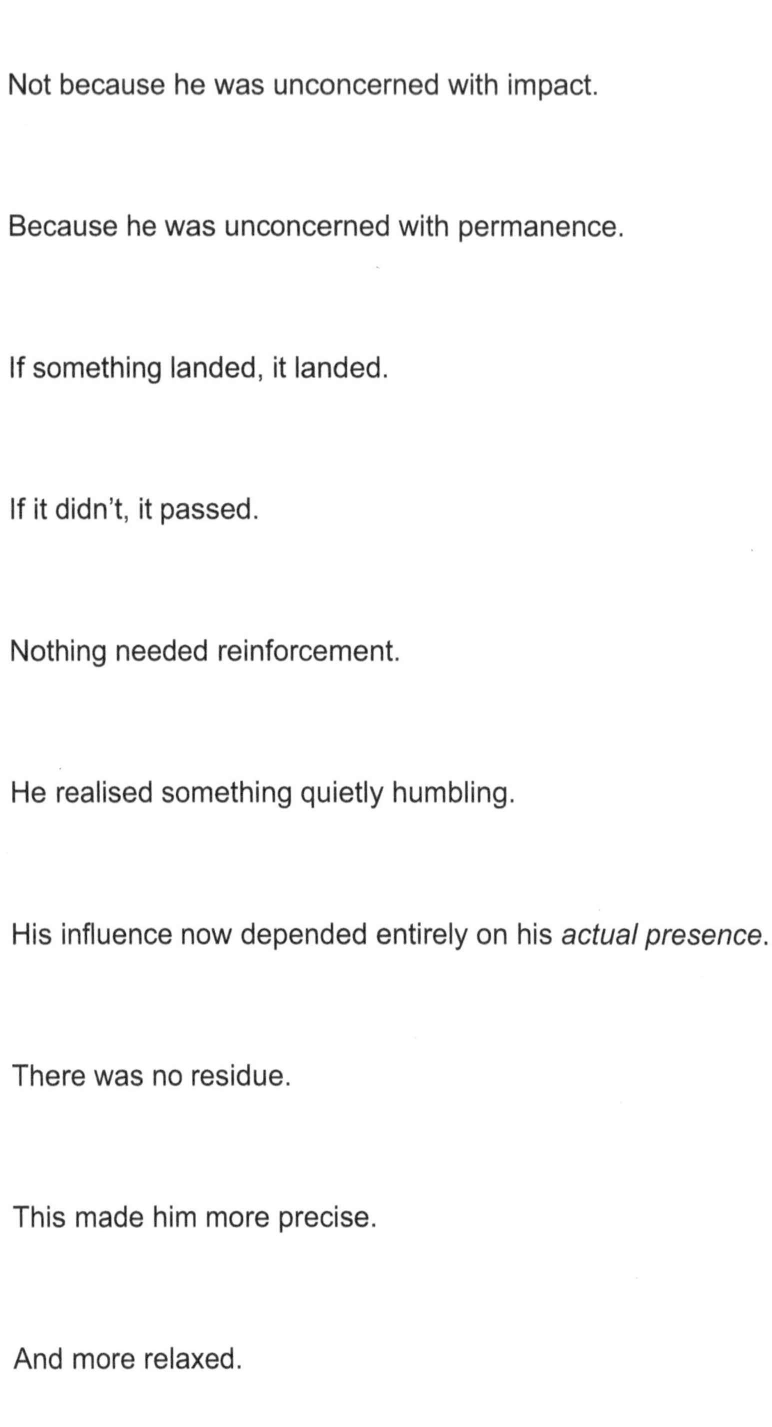

Not because he was unconcerned with impact.

Because he was unconcerned with permanence.

If something landed, it landed.

If it didn't, it passed.

Nothing needed reinforcement.

He realised something quietly humbling.

His influence now depended entirely on his *actual presence*.

There was no residue.

This made him more precise.

And more relaxed.

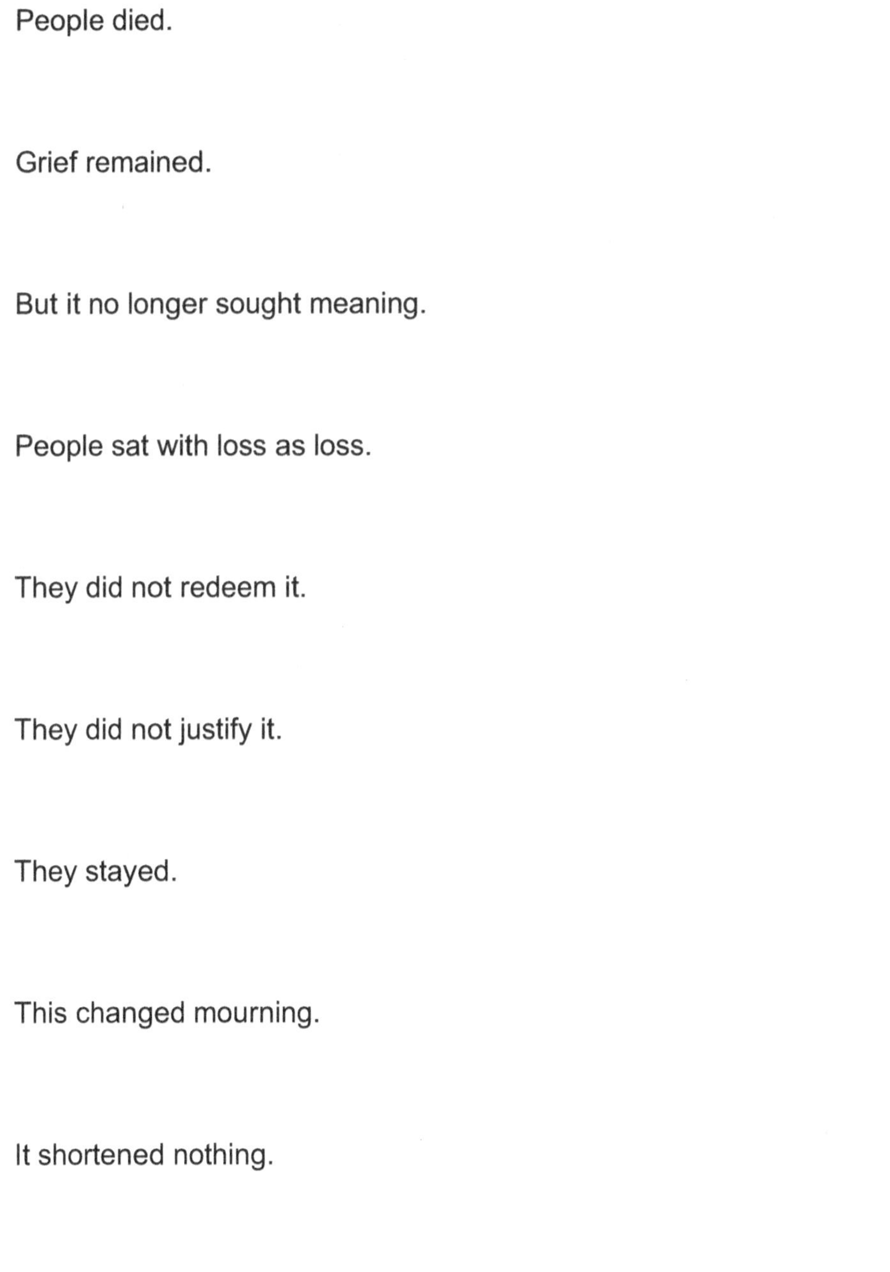

Loss continued.

People died.

Grief remained.

But it no longer sought meaning.

People sat with loss as loss.

They did not redeem it.

They did not justify it.

They stayed.

This changed mourning.

It shortened nothing.

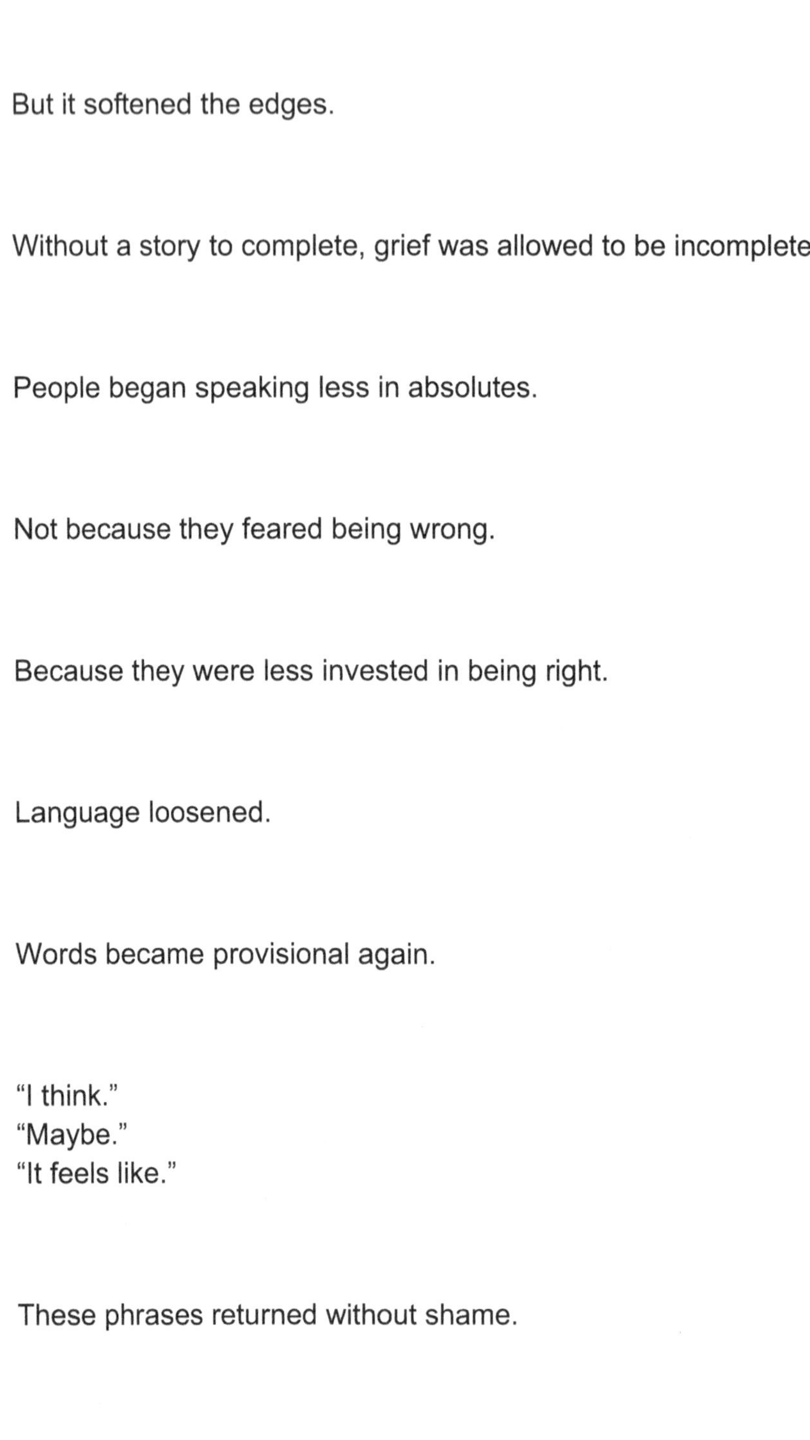

But it softened the edges.

Without a story to complete, grief was allowed to be incomplete.

People began speaking less in absolutes.

Not because they feared being wrong.

Because they were less invested in being right.

Language loosened.

Words became provisional again.

“I think.”
“Maybe.”
“It feels like.”

These phrases returned without shame.

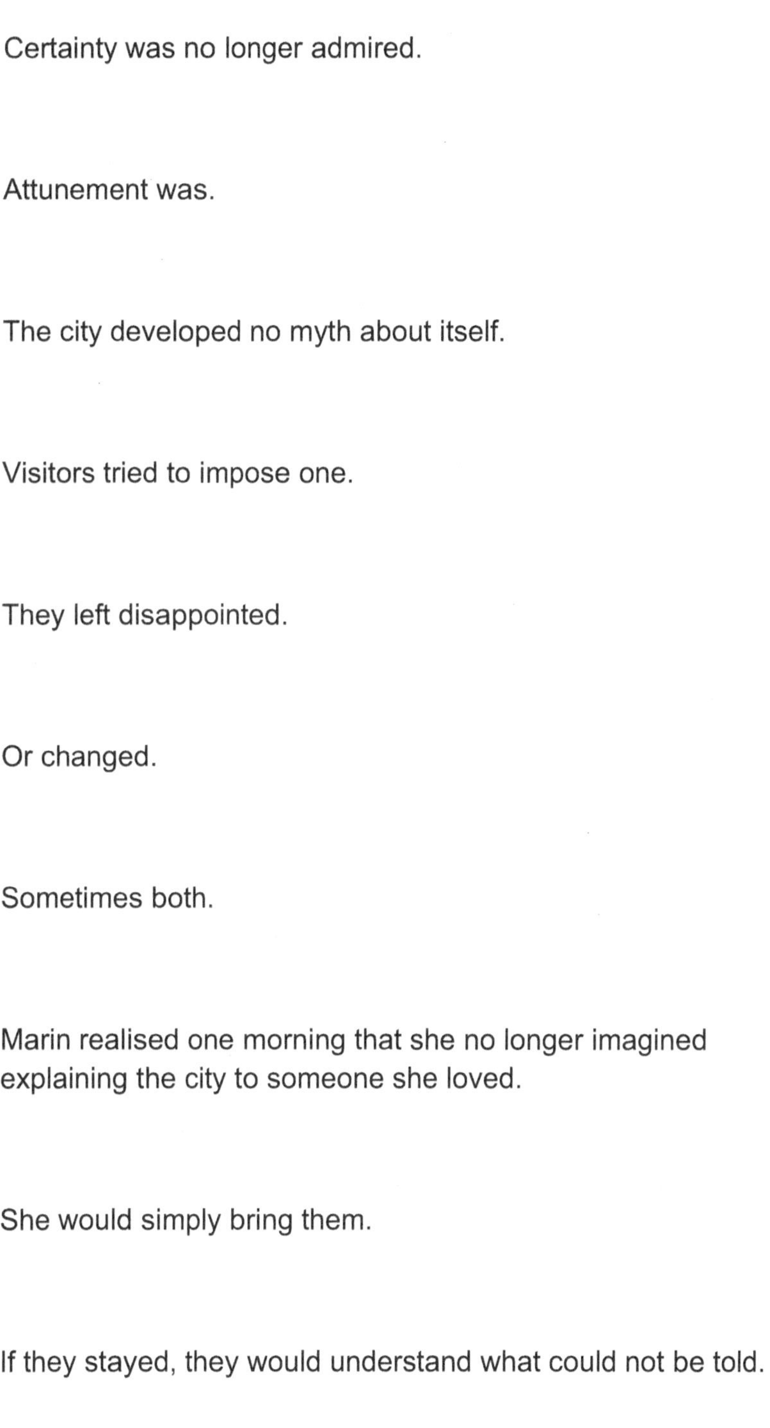

Certainty was no longer admired.

Attunement was.

The city developed no myth about itself.

Visitors tried to impose one.

They left disappointed.

Or changed.

Sometimes both.

Marin realised one morning that she no longer imagined explaining the city to someone she loved.

She would simply bring them.

If they stayed, they would understand what could not be told.

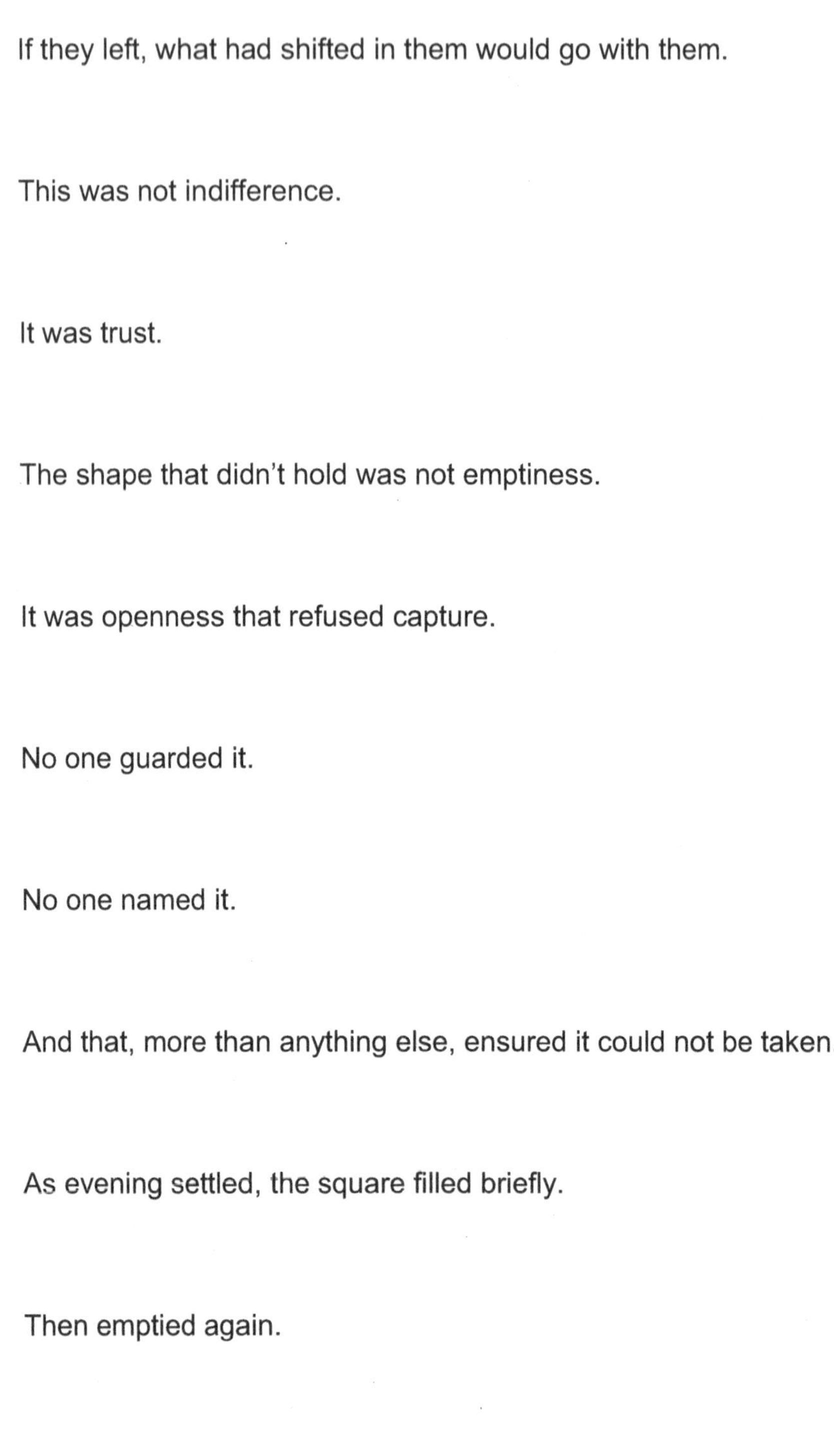

If they left, what had shifted in them would go with them.

This was not indifference.

It was trust.

The shape that didn't hold was not emptiness.

It was openness that refused capture.

No one guarded it.

No one named it.

And that, more than anything else, ensured it could not be taken.

As evening settled, the square filled briefly.

Then emptied again.

No one lingered to mark the moment.

It passed.

As moments now did.

Freely.

Without consequence.

And without regret.

Chapter 34

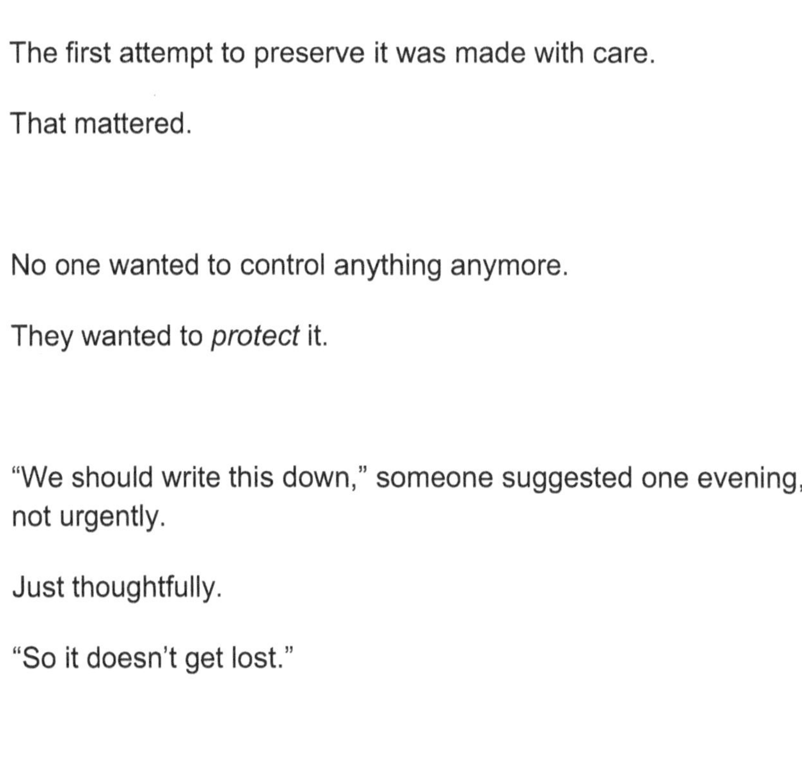

The first attempt to preserve it was made with care.

That mattered.

No one wanted to control anything anymore.

They wanted to *protect* it.

“We should write this down,” someone suggested one evening, not urgently.

Just thoughtfully.

“So it doesn’t get lost.”

Heads nodded.

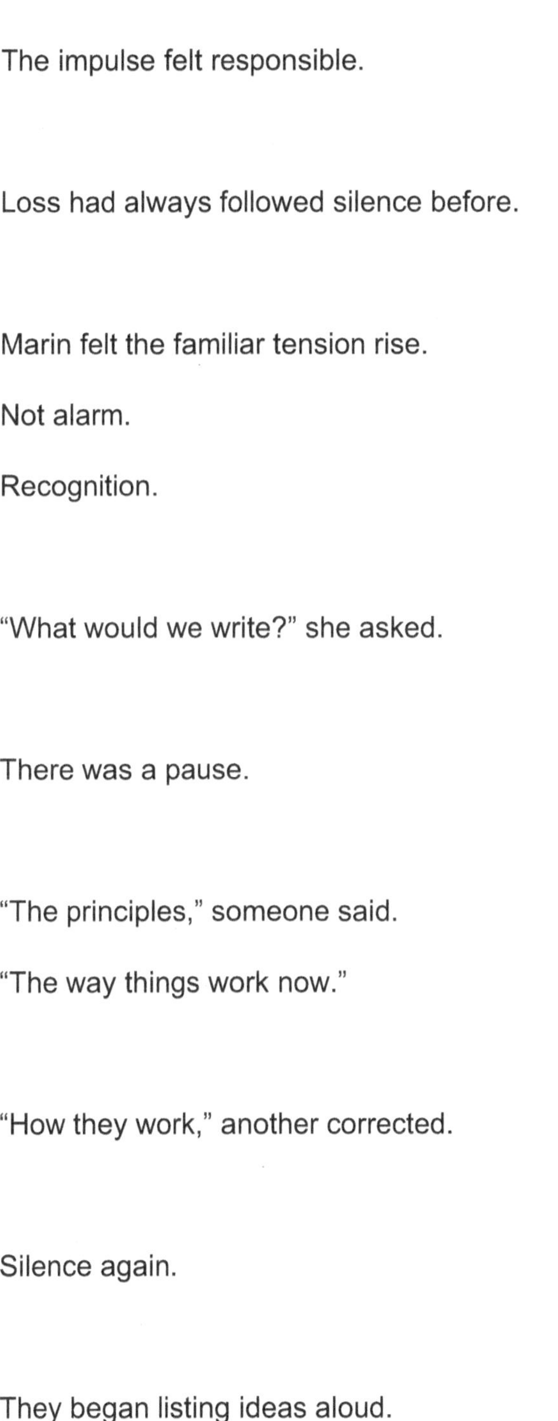

The impulse felt responsible.

Loss had always followed silence before.

Marin felt the familiar tension rise.

Not alarm.

Recognition.

“What would we write?” she asked.

There was a pause.

“The principles,” someone said.

“The way things work now.”

“How they work,” another corrected.

Silence again.

They began listing ideas aloud.

Not formally.

Just… trying.

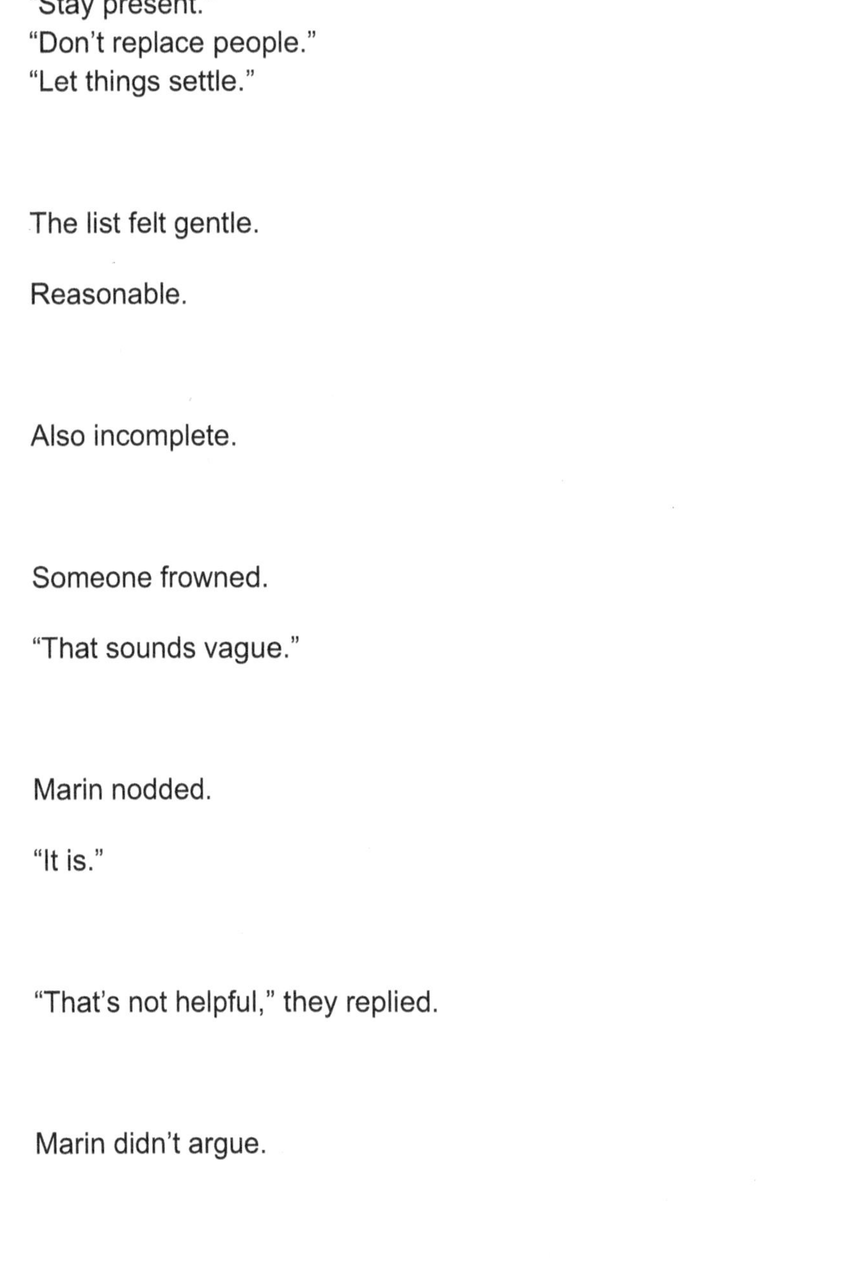

“Don’t rush.”
“Stay present.”
“Don’t replace people.”
“Let things settle.”

The list felt gentle.

Reasonable.

Also incomplete.

Someone frowned.

“That sounds vague.”

Marin nodded.

“It is.”

“That’s not helpful,” they replied.

Marin didn’t argue.

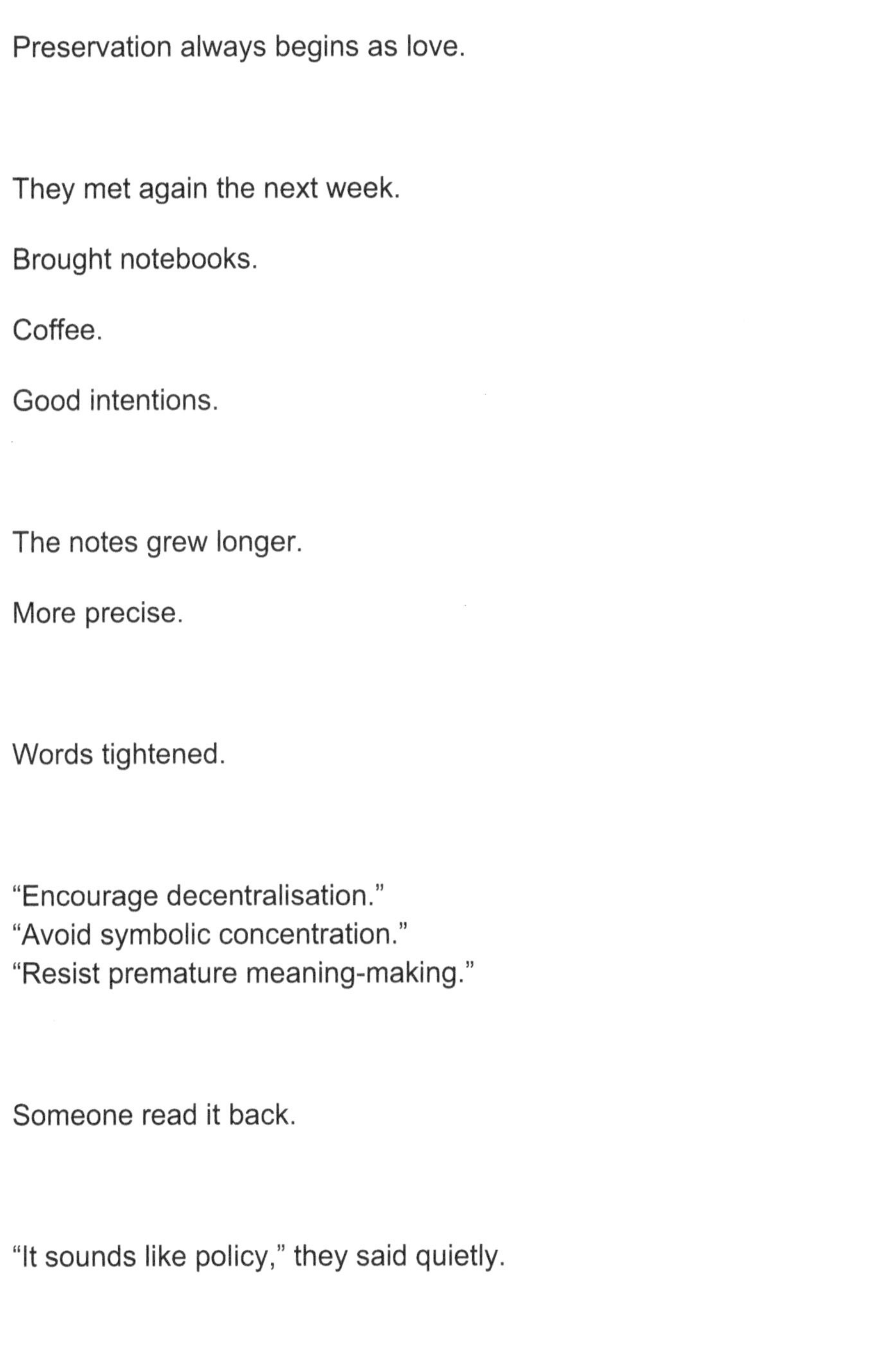

She had learned not to interrupt the impulse.

Preservation always begins as love.

They met again the next week.

Brought notebooks.

Coffee.

Good intentions.

The notes grew longer.

More precise.

Words tightened.

“Encourage decentralisation.”
“Avoid symbolic concentration.”
“Resist premature meaning-making.”

Someone read it back.

“It sounds like policy,” they said quietly.

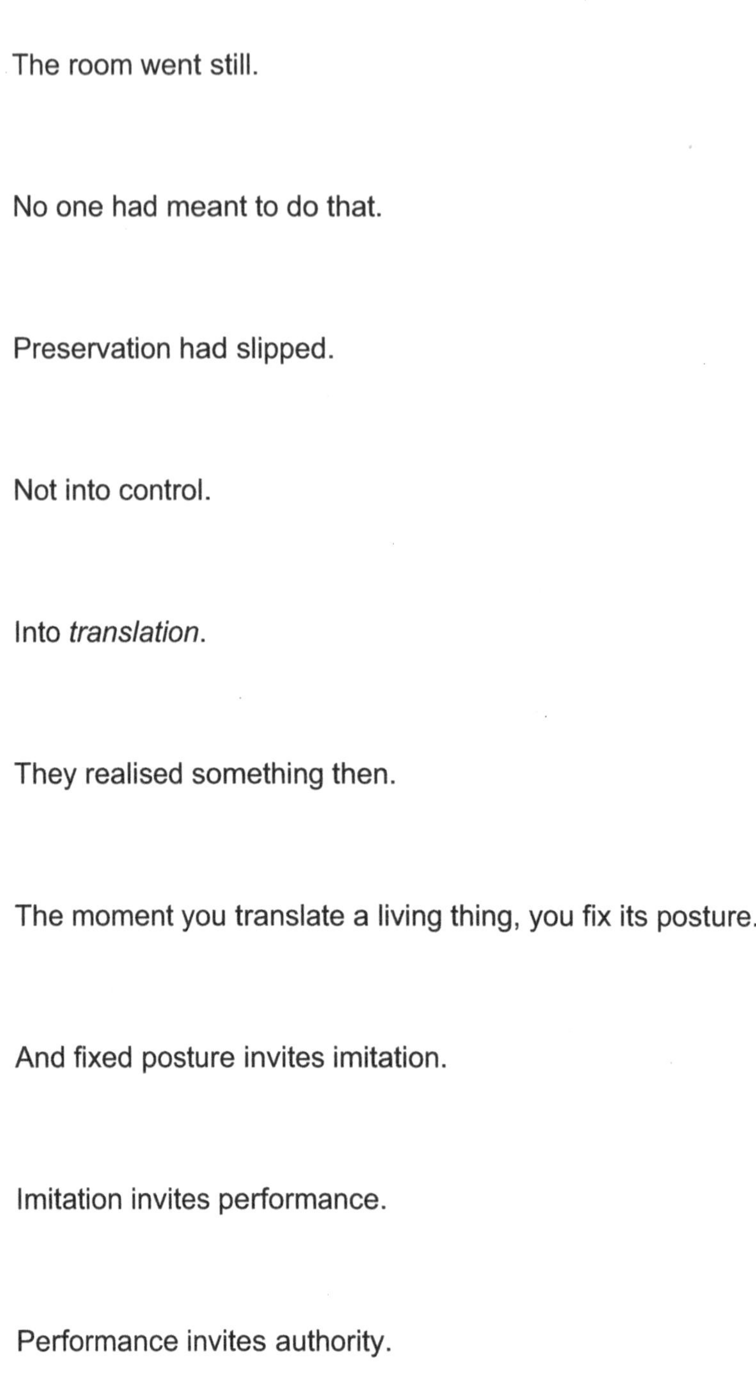

The room went still.

No one had meant to do that.

Preservation had slipped.

Not into control.

Into *translation*.

They realised something then.

The moment you translate a living thing, you fix its posture.

And fixed posture invites imitation.

Imitation invites performance.

Performance invites authority.

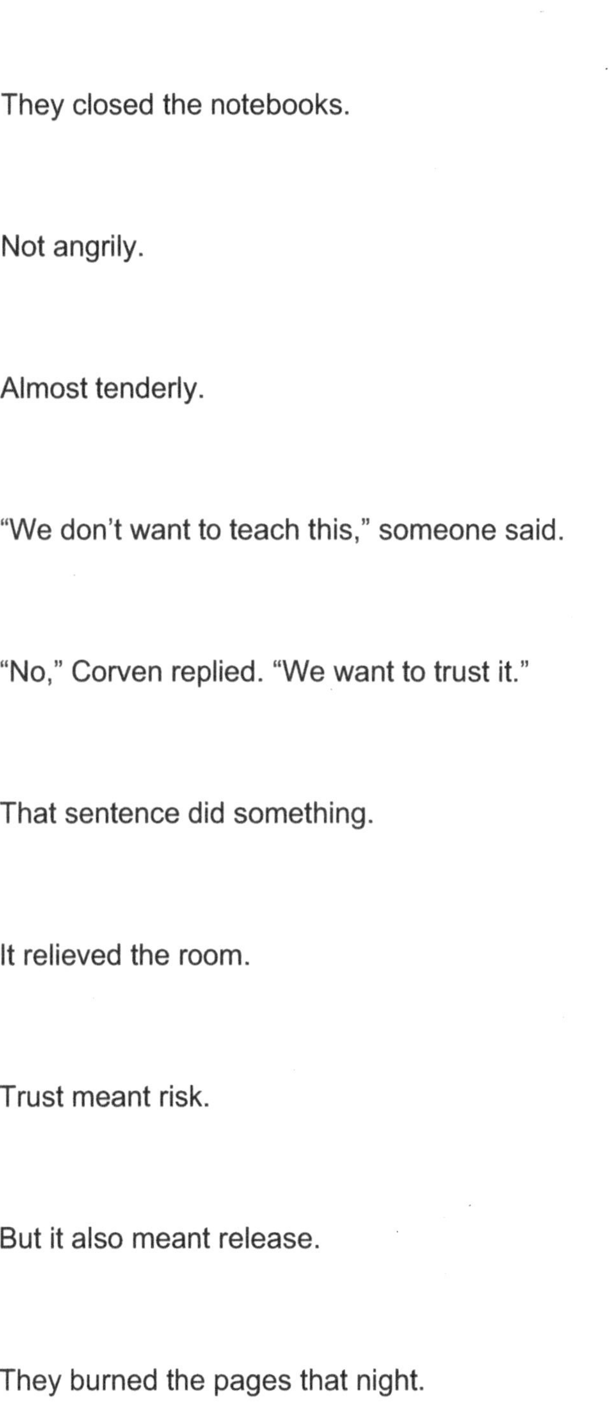

They closed the notebooks.

Not angrily.

Almost tenderly.

“We don’t want to teach this,” someone said.

“No,” Corven replied. “We want to trust it.”

That sentence did something.

It relieved the room.

Trust meant risk.

But it also meant release.

They burned the pages that night.

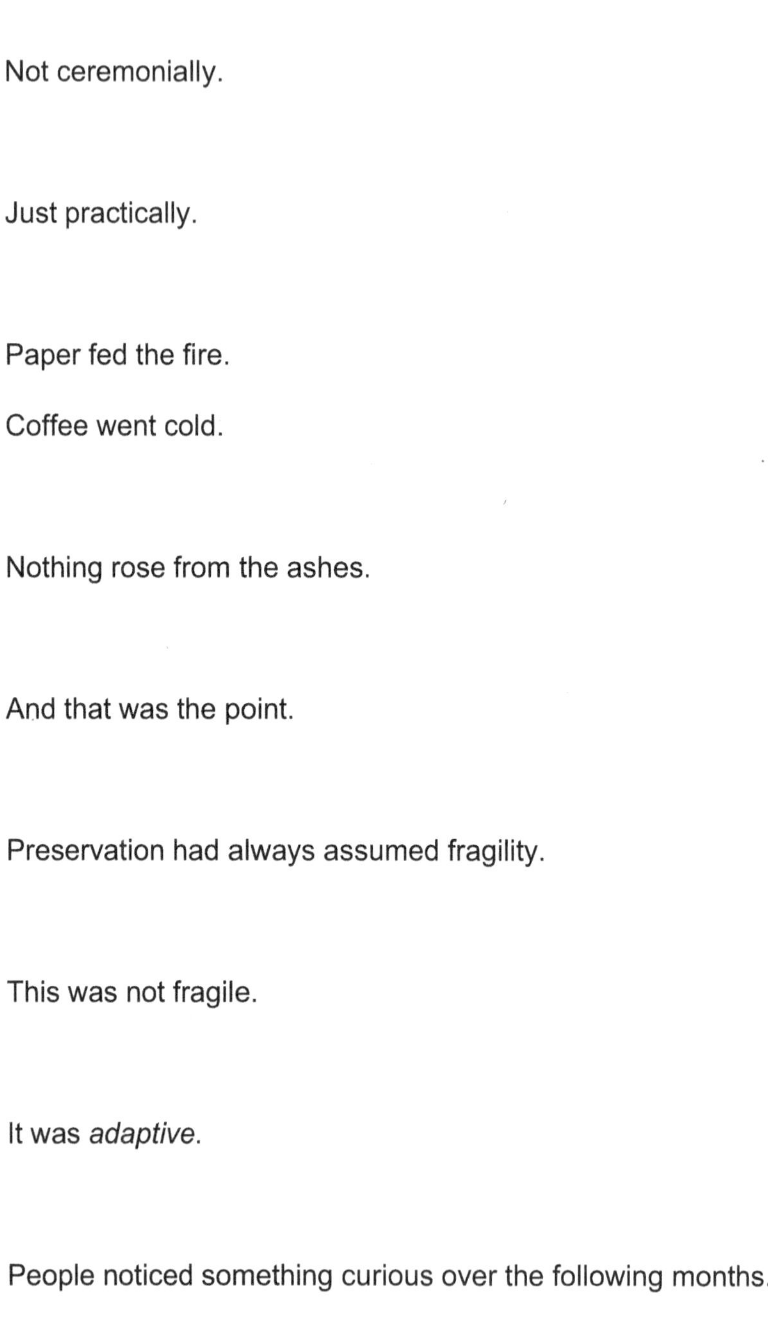

Not ceremonially.

Just practically.

Paper fed the fire.

Coffee went cold.

Nothing rose from the ashes.

And that was the point.

Preservation had always assumed fragility.

This was not fragile.

It was *adaptive*.

People noticed something curious over the following months.

Even as faces changed…

As seasons turned…

As conflicts came and went…

The *capacity* remained.

People still paused.

Still waited.

Still resisted replacement.

Not because they remembered instructions.

Because they had learned a feeling.

Preservation through memory had failed.

Preservation through embodiment had succeeded.

Marin noticed newcomers doing things no one had taught them.

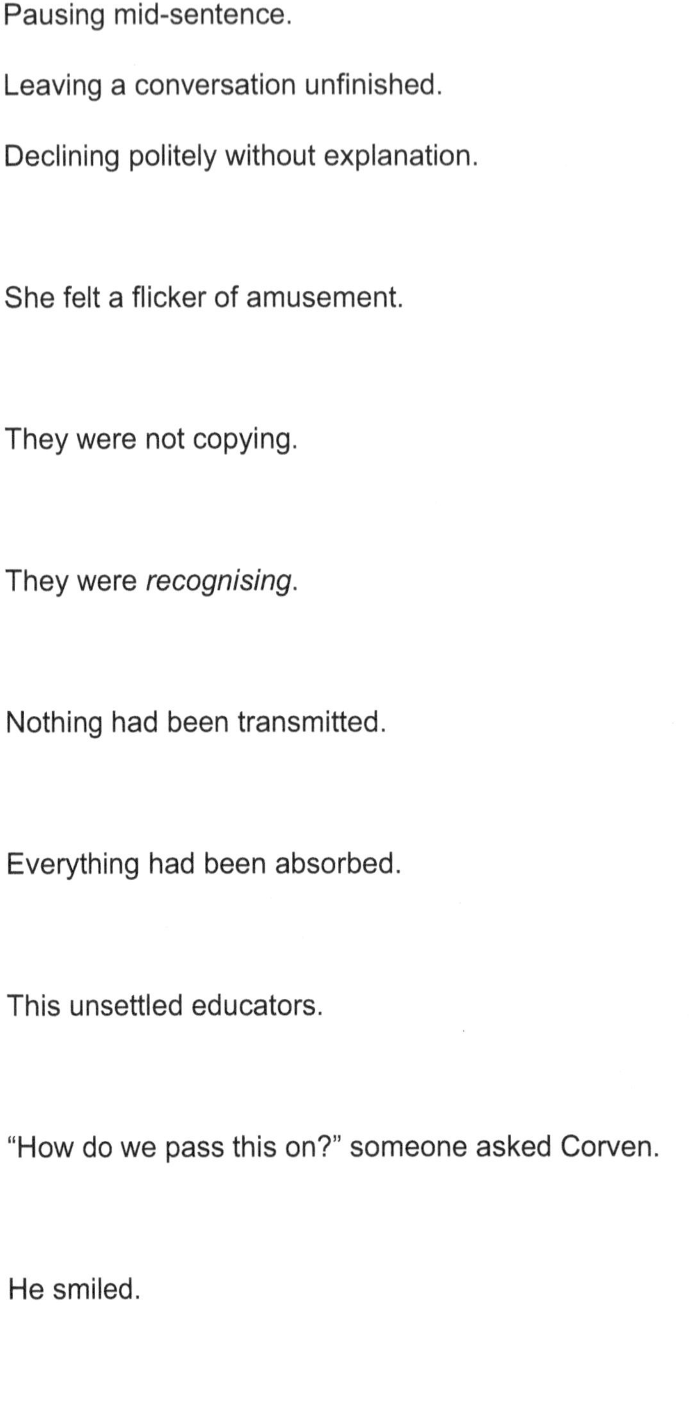

Pausing mid-sentence.

Leaving a conversation unfinished.

Declining politely without explanation.

She felt a flicker of amusement.

They were not copying.

They were *recognising*.

Nothing had been transmitted.

Everything had been absorbed.

This unsettled educators.

"How do we pass this on?" someone asked Corven.

He smiled.

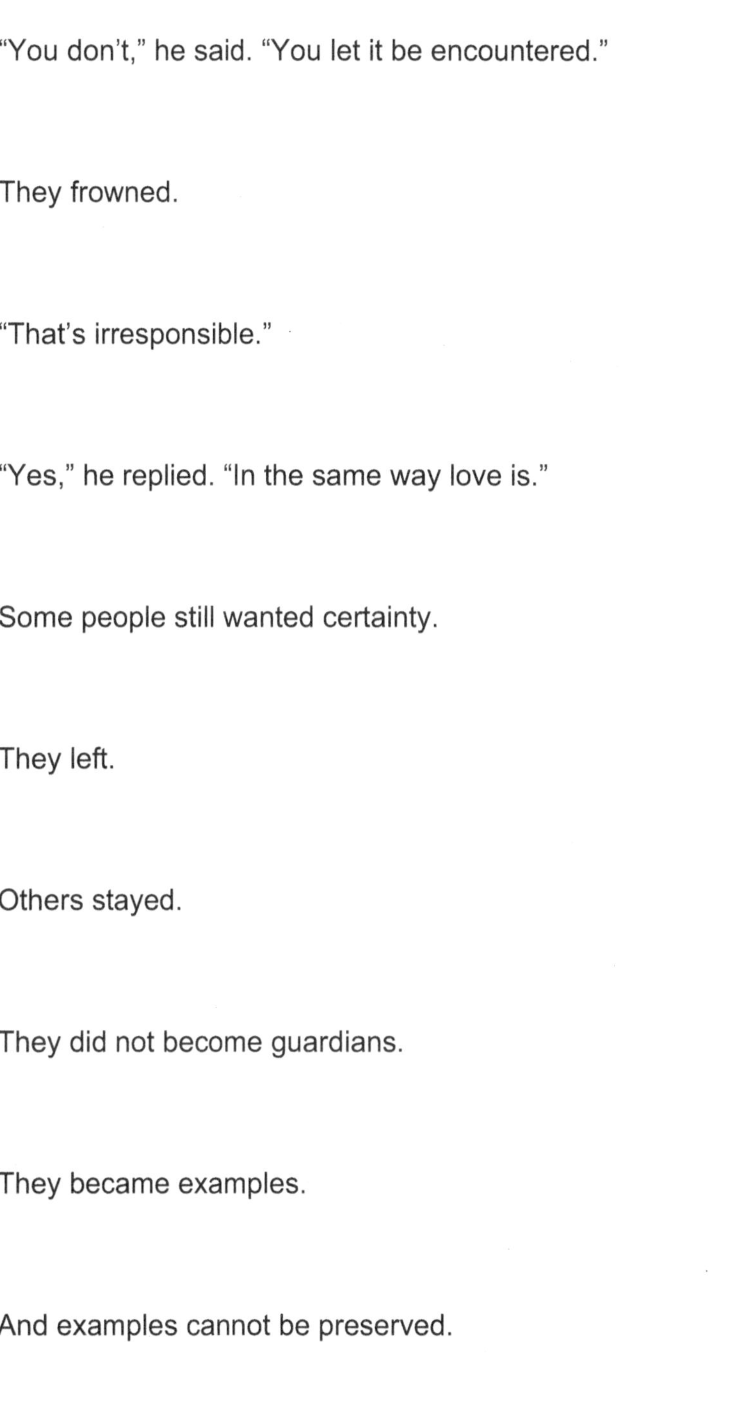

“You don’t,” he said. “You let it be encountered.”

They frowned.

“That’s irresponsible.”

“Yes,” he replied. “In the same way love is.”

Some people still wanted certainty.

They left.

Others stayed.

They did not become guardians.

They became examples.

And examples cannot be preserved.

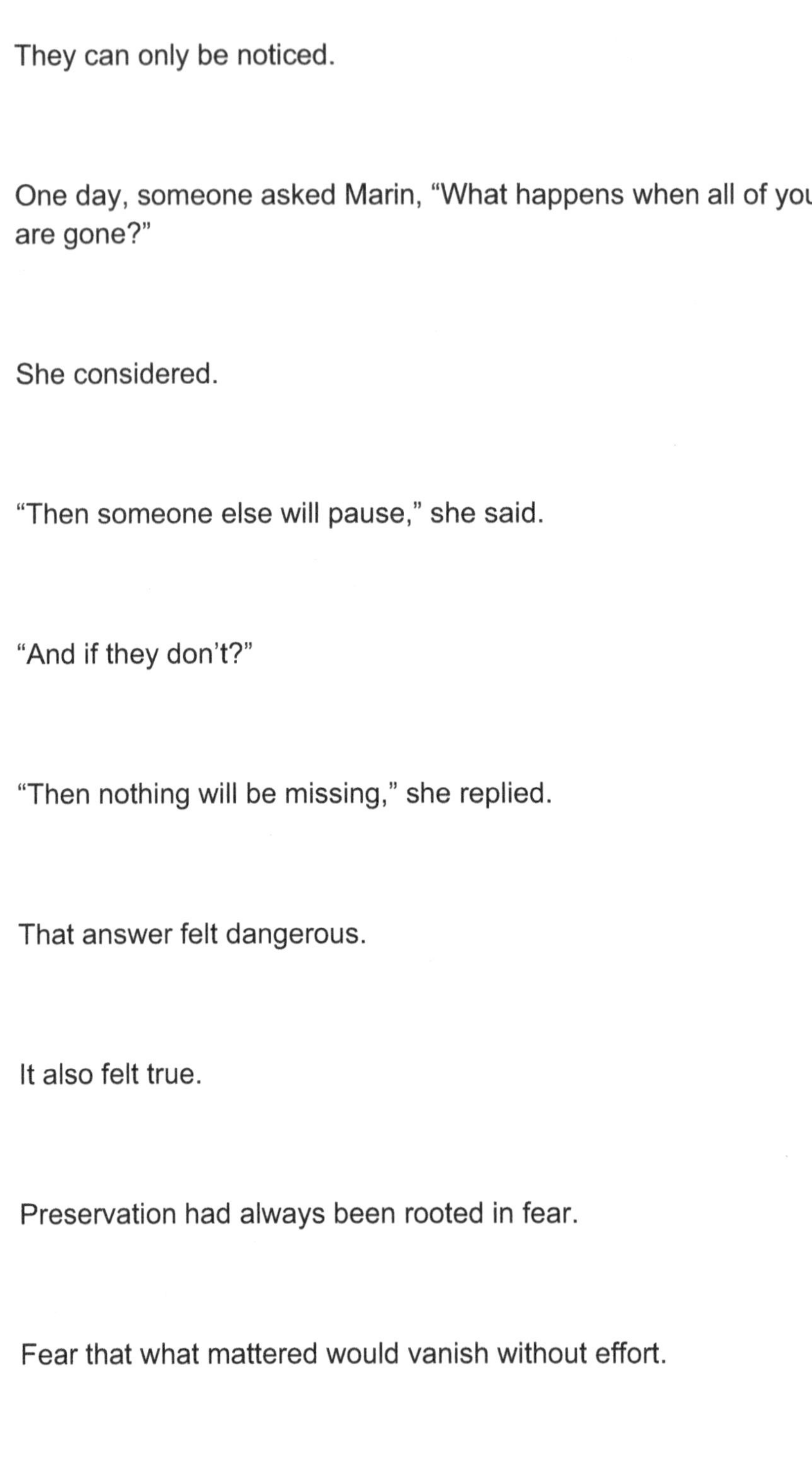

They can only be noticed.

One day, someone asked Marin, “What happens when all of you are gone?”

She considered.

“Then someone else will pause,” she said.

“And if they don’t?”

“Then nothing will be missing,” she replied.

That answer felt dangerous.

It also felt true.

Preservation had always been rooted in fear.

Fear that what mattered would vanish without effort.

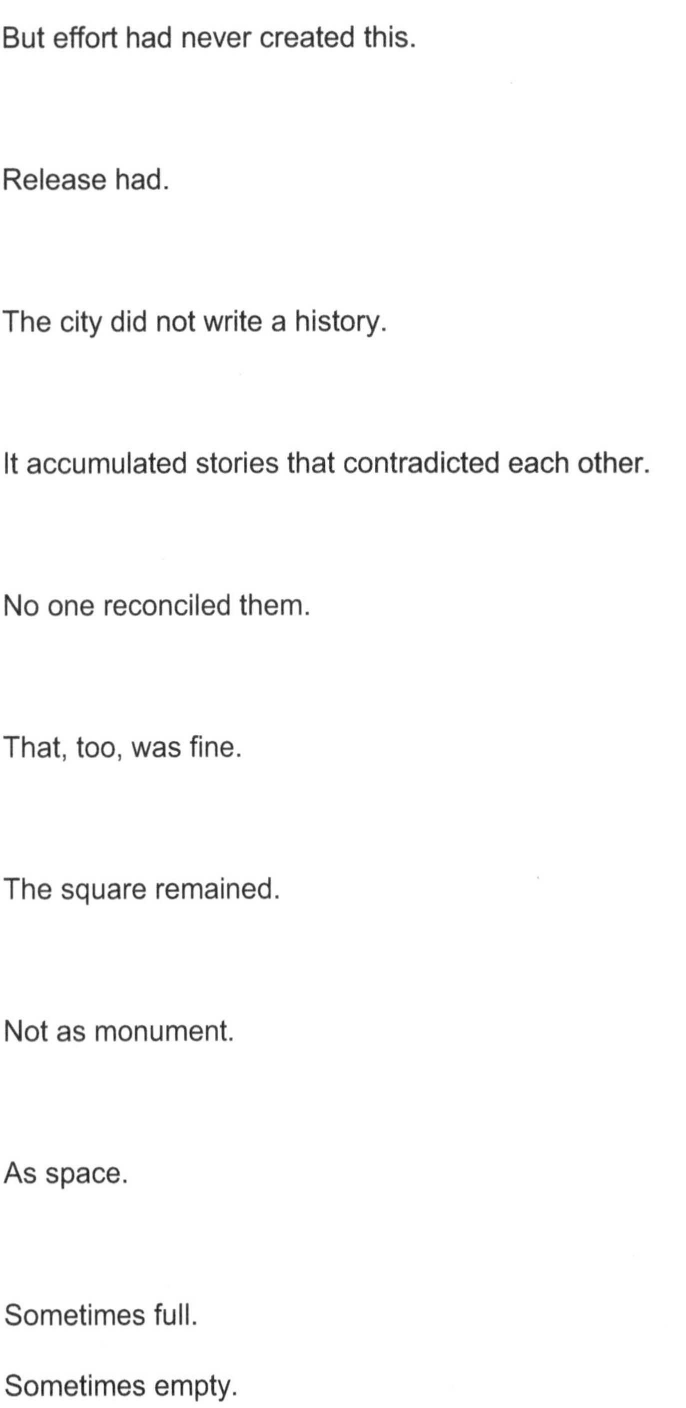

But effort had never created this.

Release had.

The city did not write a history.

It accumulated stories that contradicted each other.

No one reconciled them.

That, too, was fine.

The square remained.

Not as monument.

As space.

Sometimes full.

Sometimes empty.

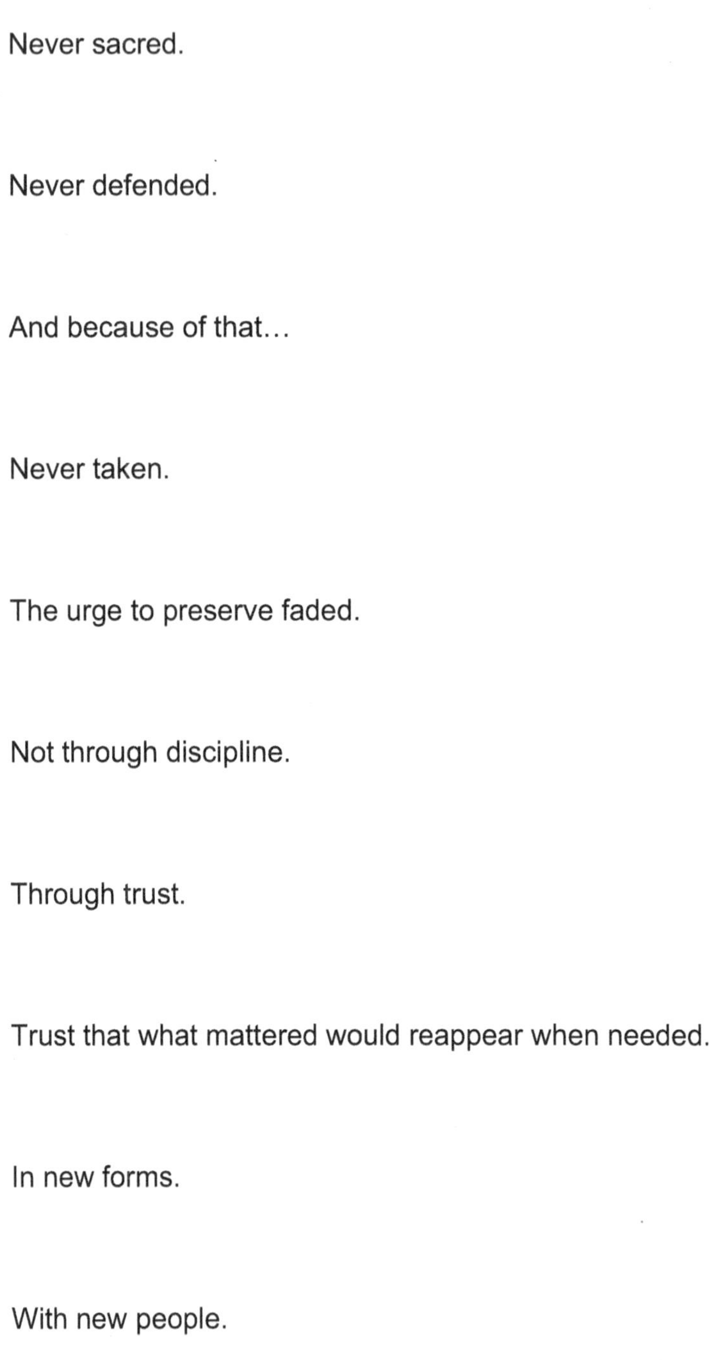

Never sacred.

Never defended.

And because of that…

Never taken.

The urge to preserve faded.

Not through discipline.

Through trust.

Trust that what mattered would reappear when needed.

In new forms.

With new people.

Without asking permission.

Nothing that needed preserving had ever survived anyway.

What survived had always known how to change.

And this…

Whatever this was…

Already knew how.

Chapter 35

Marin realised she had stopped rehearsing her life.

The thought arrived one morning without drama, the way conclusions do when they no longer need defending.

She had once practised conversations before they happened.
Rewritten moments after they ended.
Imagined how things would sound later, when retold.

Now she noticed she could not remember the last time she had done any of that.

She was sitting at the small table by the window, tea cooling untouched, watching the street begin to move.

A woman crossed carrying groceries.
A child ran ahead, then doubled back.
Someone paused, changed direction, disappeared.

Nothing waited to be interpreted.

She felt something settle in her chest.

Not peace exactly.

Completion.

She thought of the person she had been when this all began.

How attentive she had been to others' expectations.
How careful with her tone.
How quick to offer context so no one would misunderstand her.

She had believed explanation was kindness.

She no longer believed that.

Her phone buzzed.

A message from someone she hadn't spoken to in months.

I was thinking about you.

No question followed.

No request.

Just that.

Marin smiled.

She did not feel compelled to respond immediately.

She would.

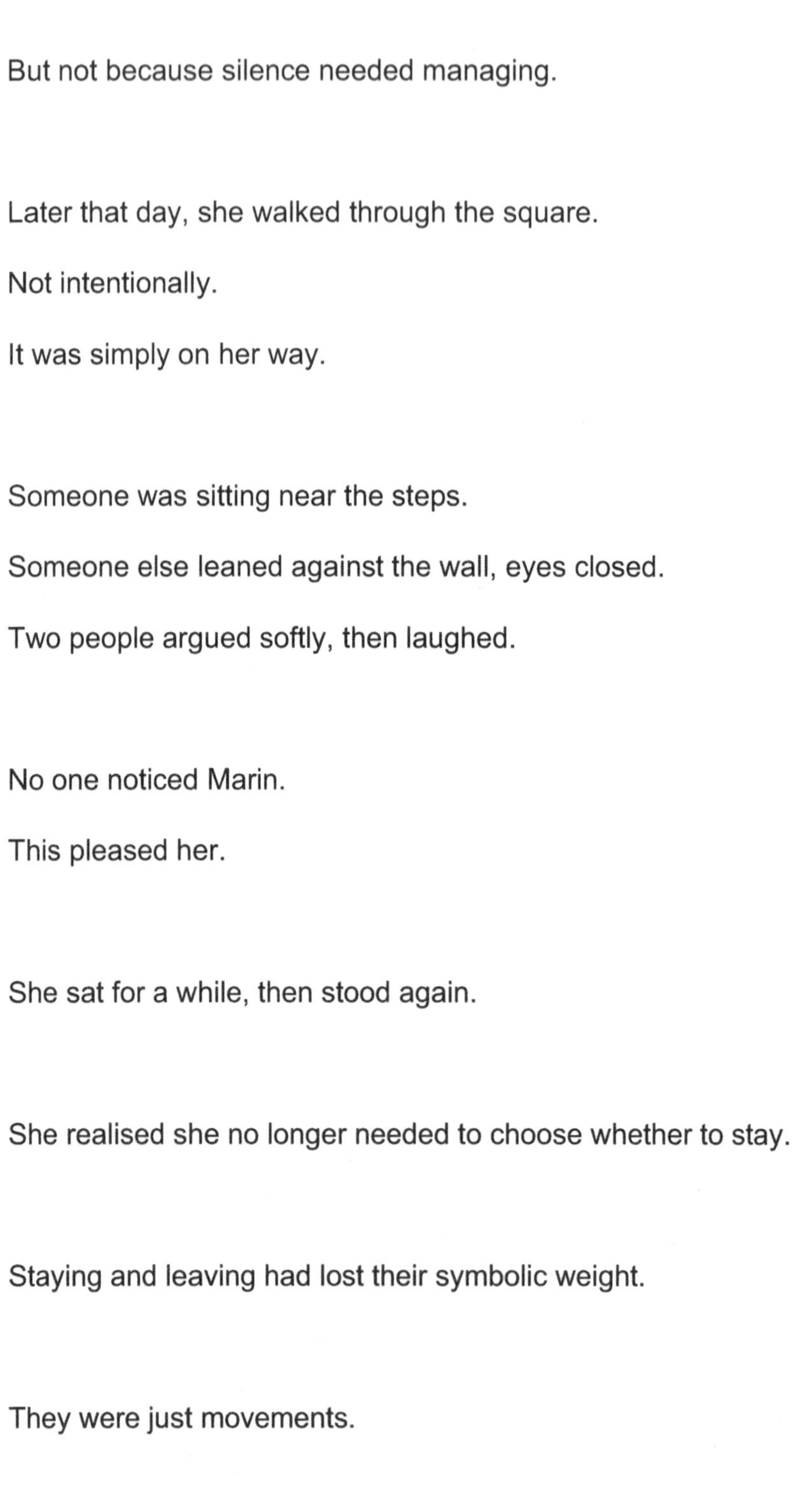

But not because silence needed managing.

Later that day, she walked through the square.

Not intentionally.

It was simply on her way.

Someone was sitting near the steps.

Someone else leaned against the wall, eyes closed.

Two people argued softly, then laughed.

No one noticed Marin.

This pleased her.

She sat for a while, then stood again.

She realised she no longer needed to choose whether to stay.

Staying and leaving had lost their symbolic weight.

They were just movements.

Corven packed his office slowly.

Not because he was leaving.

Because he no longer needed most of what he had kept.

Folders that once felt essential now felt historical.

He placed them in boxes.

Not to archive.

To release.

He was not retiring.

He was unburdening.

Someone knocked.

A young man stood in the doorway.

Hesitant.

“I’m not sure why I’m here,” the man said.

Corven smiled.

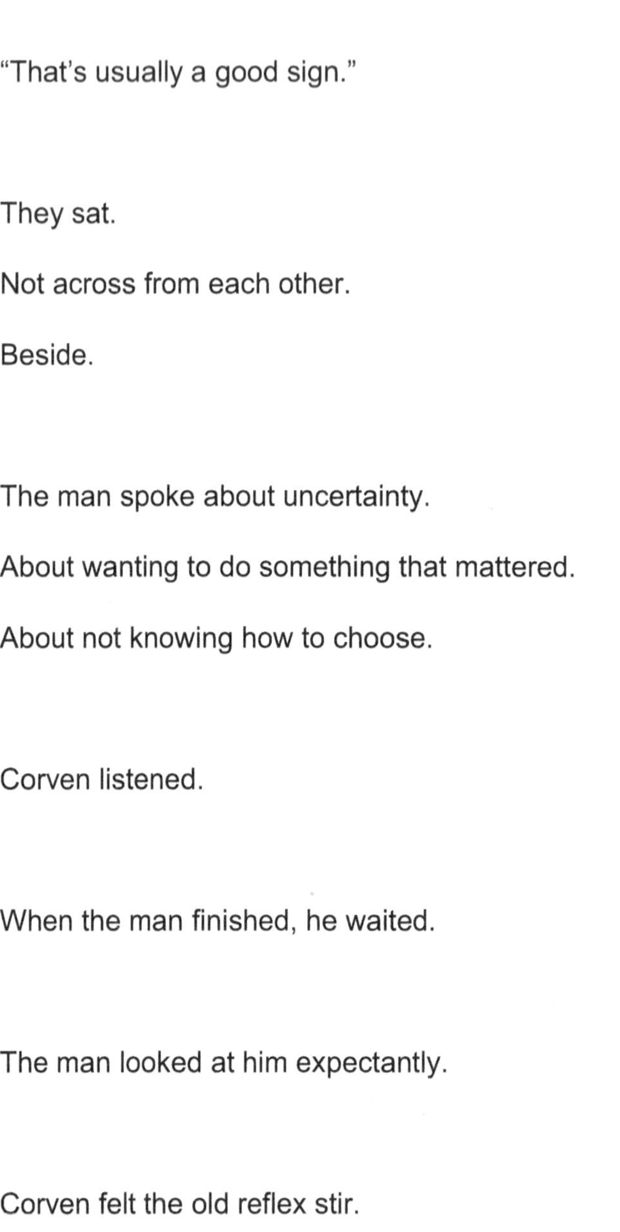

“That’s usually a good sign.”

They sat.

Not across from each other.

Beside.

The man spoke about uncertainty.

About wanting to do something that mattered.

About not knowing how to choose.

Corven listened.

When the man finished, he waited.

The man looked at him expectantly.

Corven felt the old reflex stir.

Advice forming.

Language lining up.

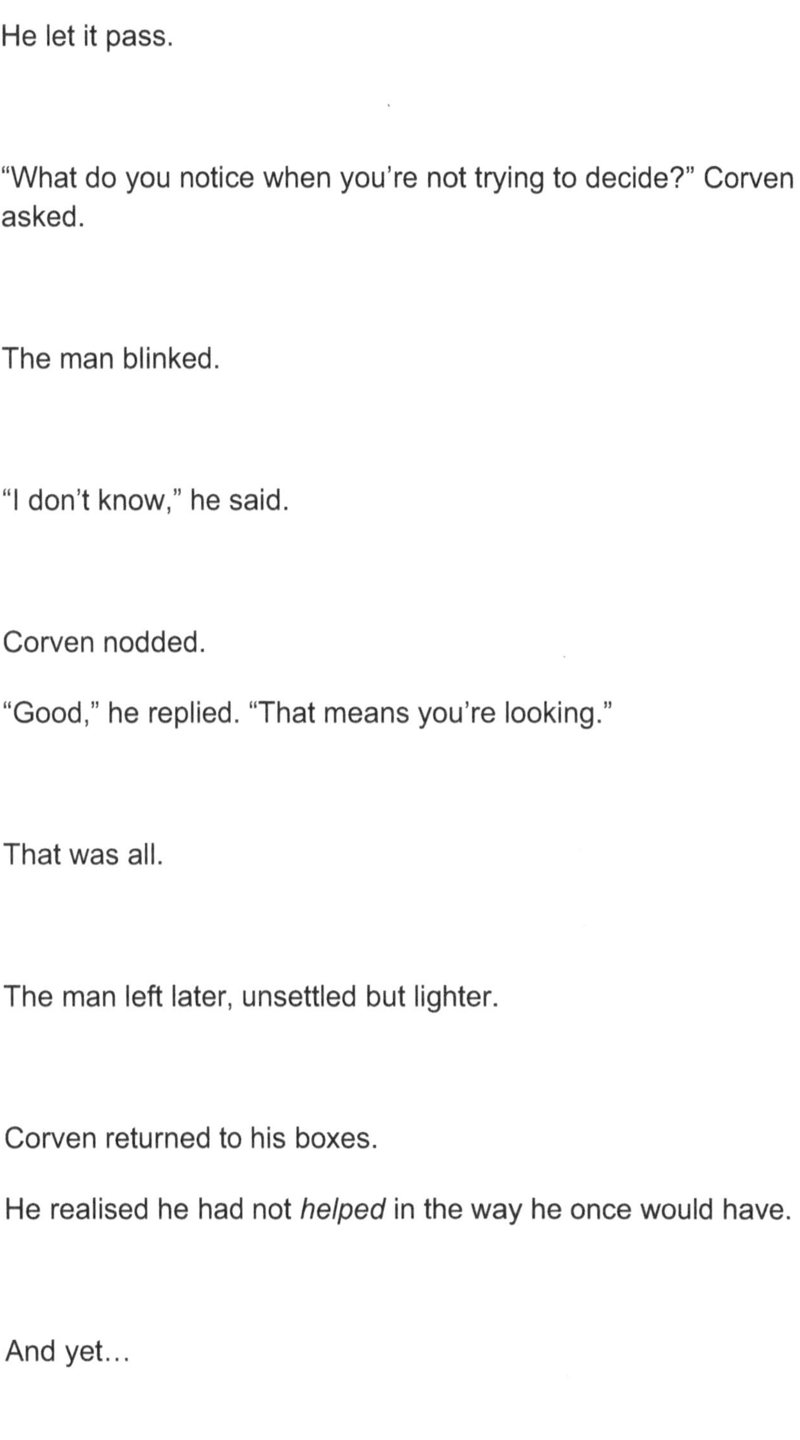

He let it pass.

“What do you notice when you’re not trying to decide?” Corven asked.

The man blinked.

“I don’t know,” he said.

Corven nodded.

“Good,” he replied. “That means you’re looking.”

That was all.

The man left later, unsettled but lighter.

Corven returned to his boxes.

He realised he had not *helped* in the way he once would have.

And yet…

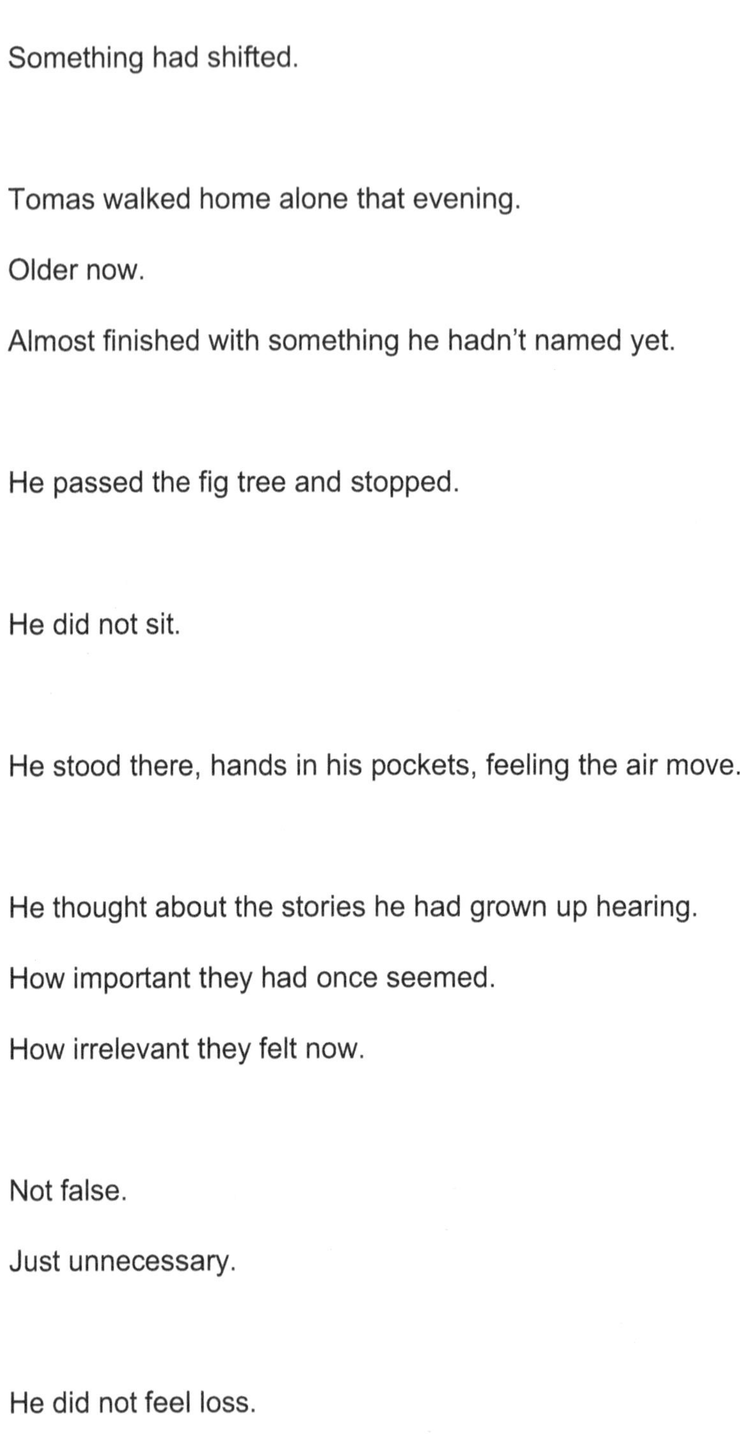

Something had shifted.

Tomas walked home alone that evening.

Older now.

Almost finished with something he hadn’t named yet.

He passed the fig tree and stopped.

He did not sit.

He stood there, hands in his pockets, feeling the air move.

He thought about the stories he had grown up hearing.

How important they had once seemed.

How irrelevant they felt now.

Not false.

Just unnecessary.

He did not feel loss.

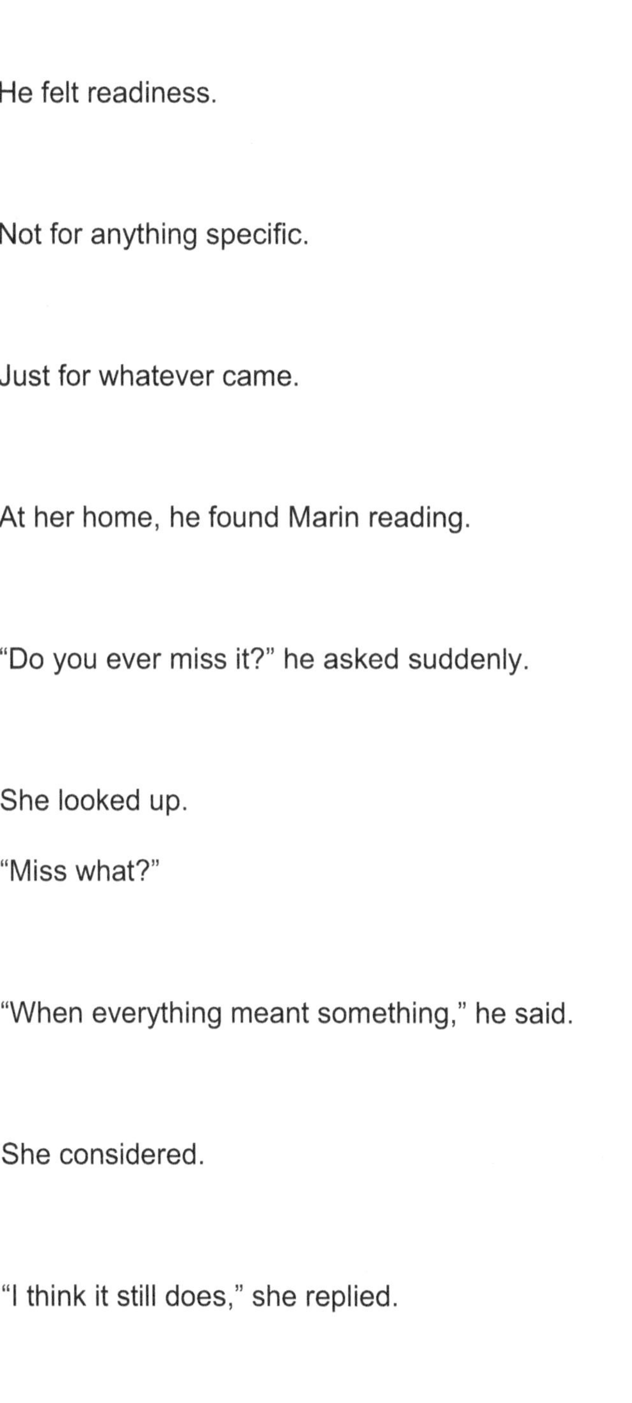

He felt readiness.

Not for anything specific.

Just for whatever came.

At her home, he found Marin reading.

“Do you ever miss it?” he asked suddenly.

She looked up.

“Miss what?”

“When everything meant something,” he said.

She considered.

“I think it still does,” she replied.

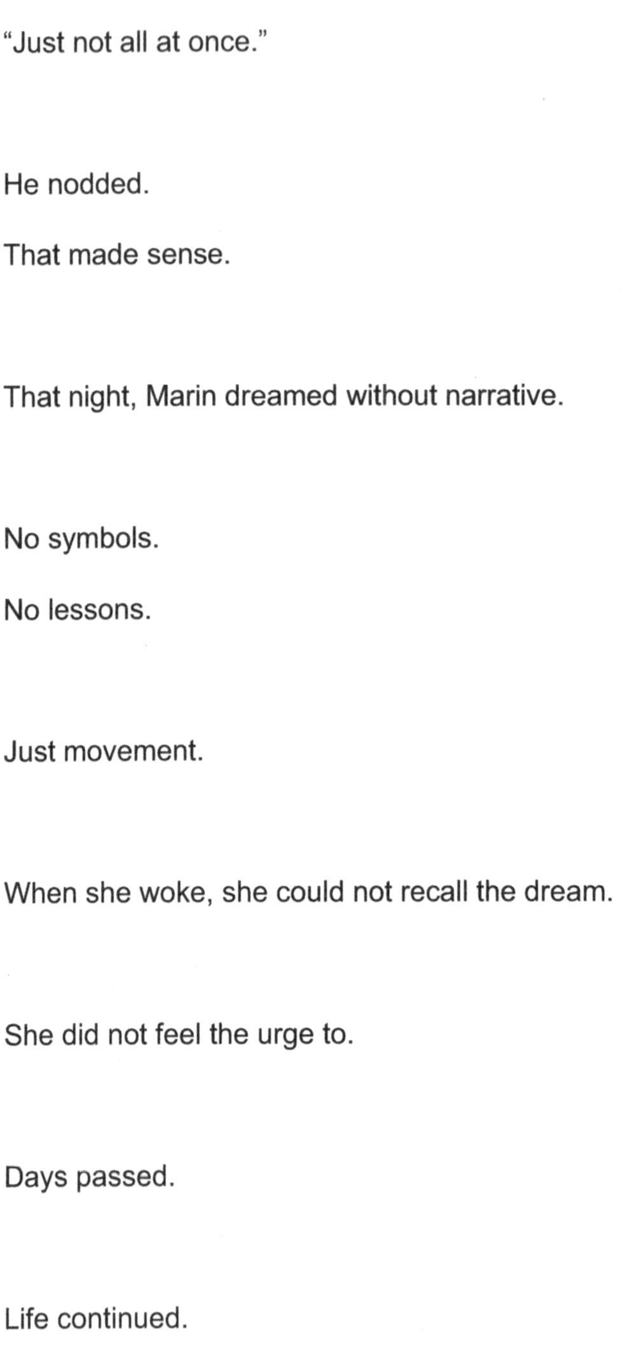

"Just not all at once."

He nodded.

That made sense.

That night, Marin dreamed without narrative.

No symbols.

No lessons.

Just movement.

When she woke, she could not recall the dream.

She did not feel the urge to.

Days passed.

Life continued.

No one summarised what had happened.

No one marked an anniversary.

The absence of commentary felt generous.

People met.

Parted.

Returned.

Nothing needed to be explained.

One afternoon, Marin received another message.

From the same person.

Do you want to meet?

She typed back:

Yes.

No qualifiers.

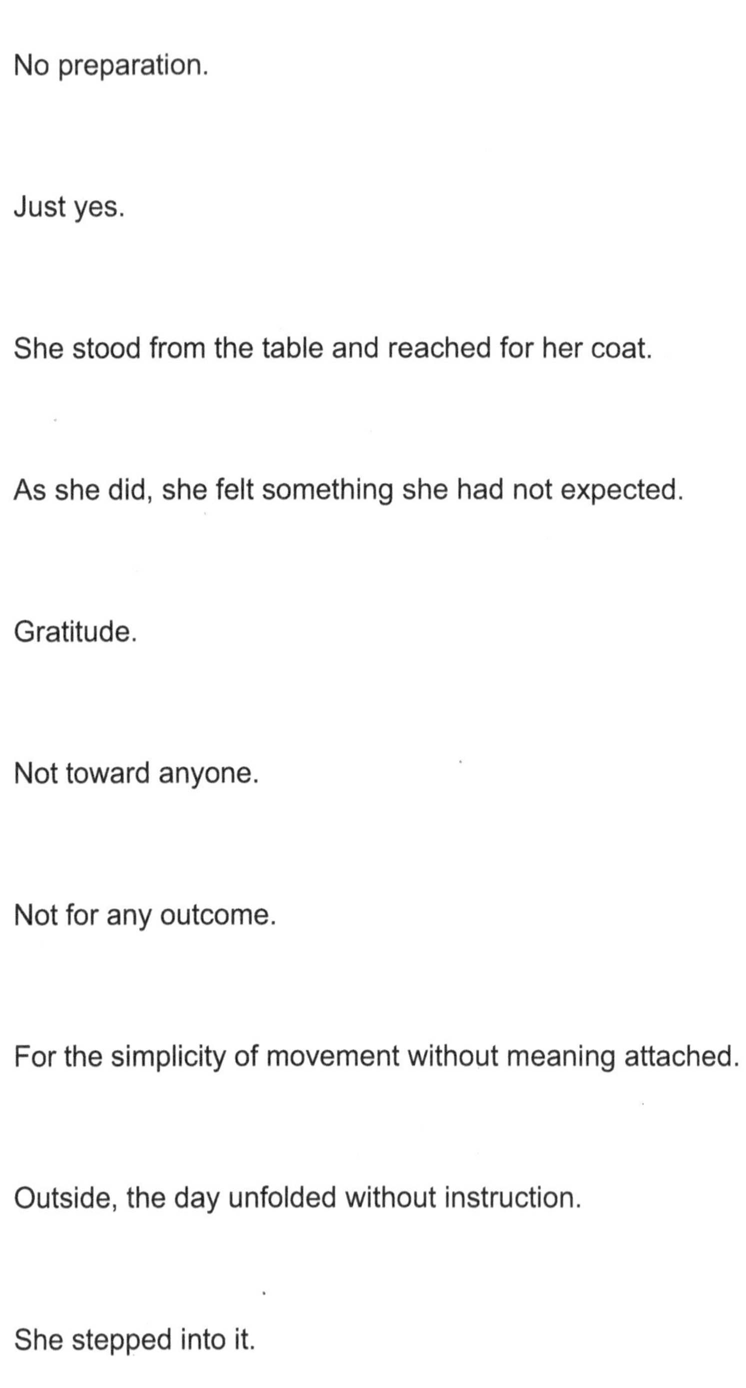

No preparation.

Just yes.

She stood from the table and reached for her coat.

As she did, she felt something she had not expected.

Gratitude.

Not toward anyone.

Not for any outcome.

For the simplicity of movement without meaning attached.

Outside, the day unfolded without instruction.

She stepped into it.

Not as someone carrying a story.

As someone available.

And availability, she now knew, was no longer something she owed.

It was something she offered.

Freely.

When it made sense.

Without needing to say why.

Chapter 36

Nothing marked the end.

There was no final gathering.
No last conversation.
No moment when everyone sensed something had completed itself.

Life does not behave that way.

Morning came as it always had.

Light touched the edges of buildings.
Someone opened a window.
A door closed somewhere down the street.

The square was empty when Marin passed through it.

Not symbolically.

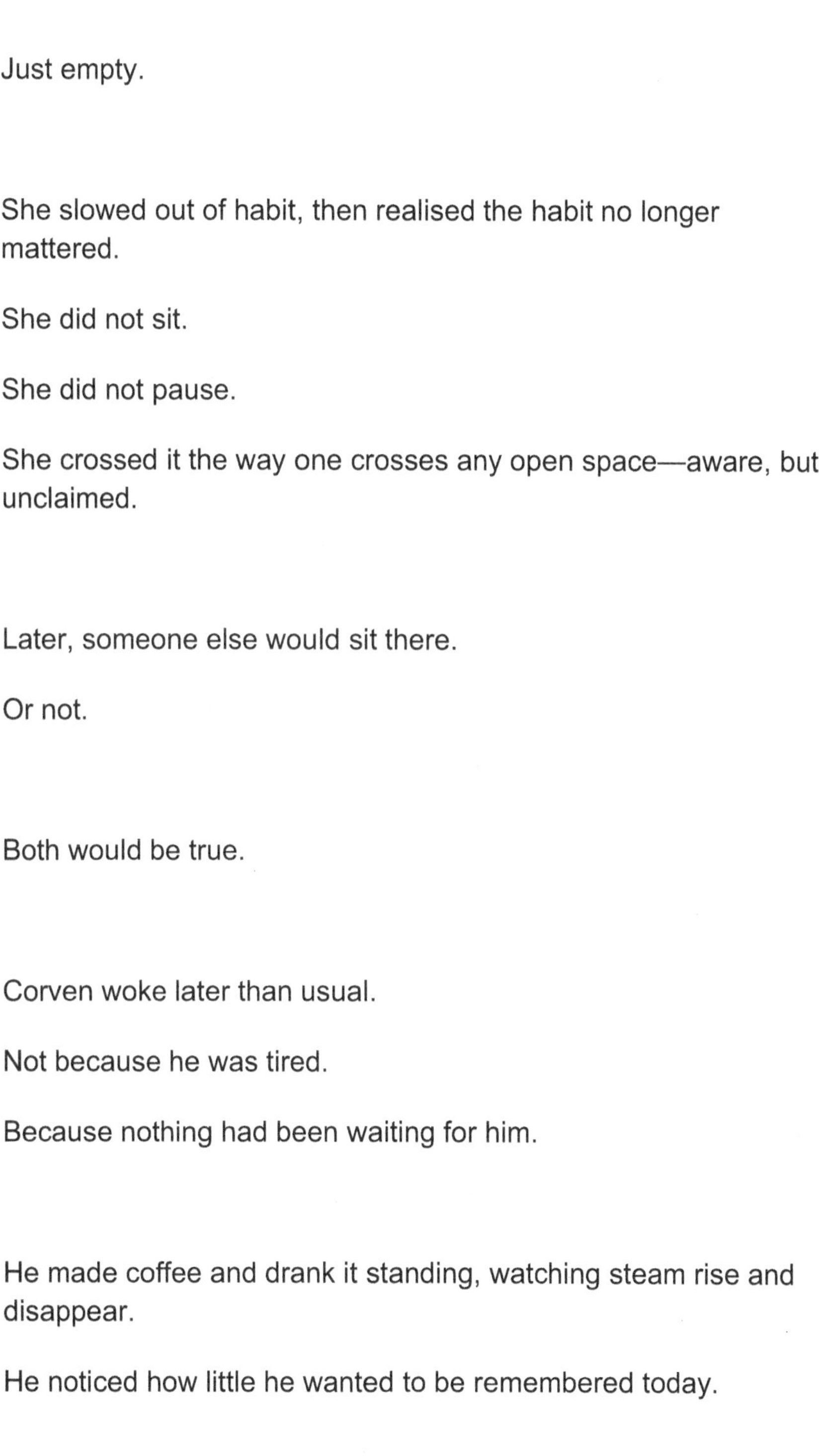

Just empty.

She slowed out of habit, then realised the habit no longer mattered.

She did not sit.

She did not pause.

She crossed it the way one crosses any open space—aware, but unclaimed.

Later, someone else would sit there.

Or not.

Both would be true.

Corven woke later than usual.

Not because he was tired.

Because nothing had been waiting for him.

He made coffee and drank it standing, watching steam rise and disappear.

He noticed how little he wanted to be remembered today.

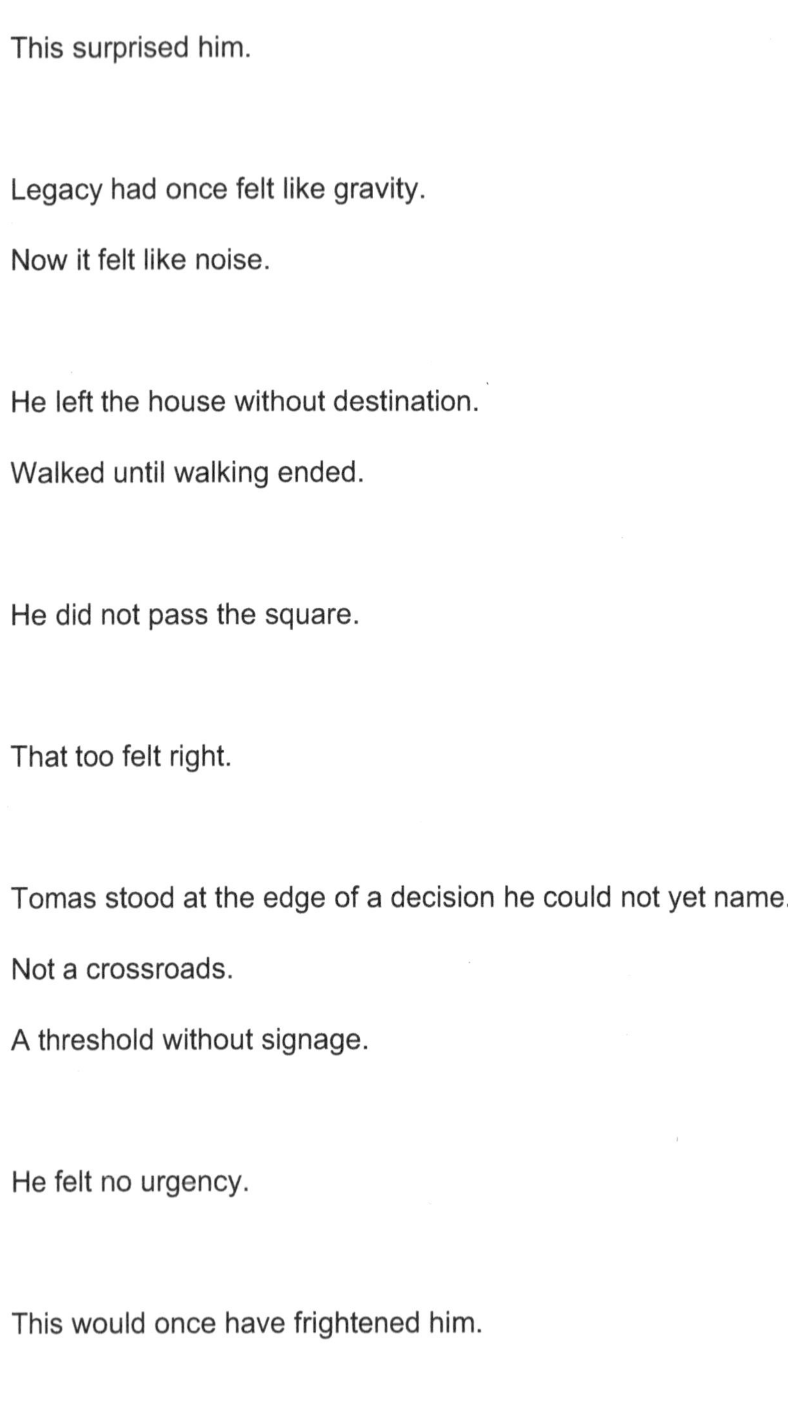

This surprised him.

Legacy had once felt like gravity.

Now it felt like noise.

He left the house without destination.

Walked until walking ended.

He did not pass the square.

That too felt right.

Tomas stood at the edge of a decision he could not yet name.

Not a crossroads.

A threshold without signage.

He felt no urgency.

This would once have frightened him.

Now it felt like room.

He did not consult anyone.

He simply noticed what drew him.

And followed it partway.

No vow was made.

No new role claimed.

Just movement.

The city continued.

Someone fell ill.

Someone recovered.

Someone left without telling anyone.

Someone arrived and stayed longer than expected.

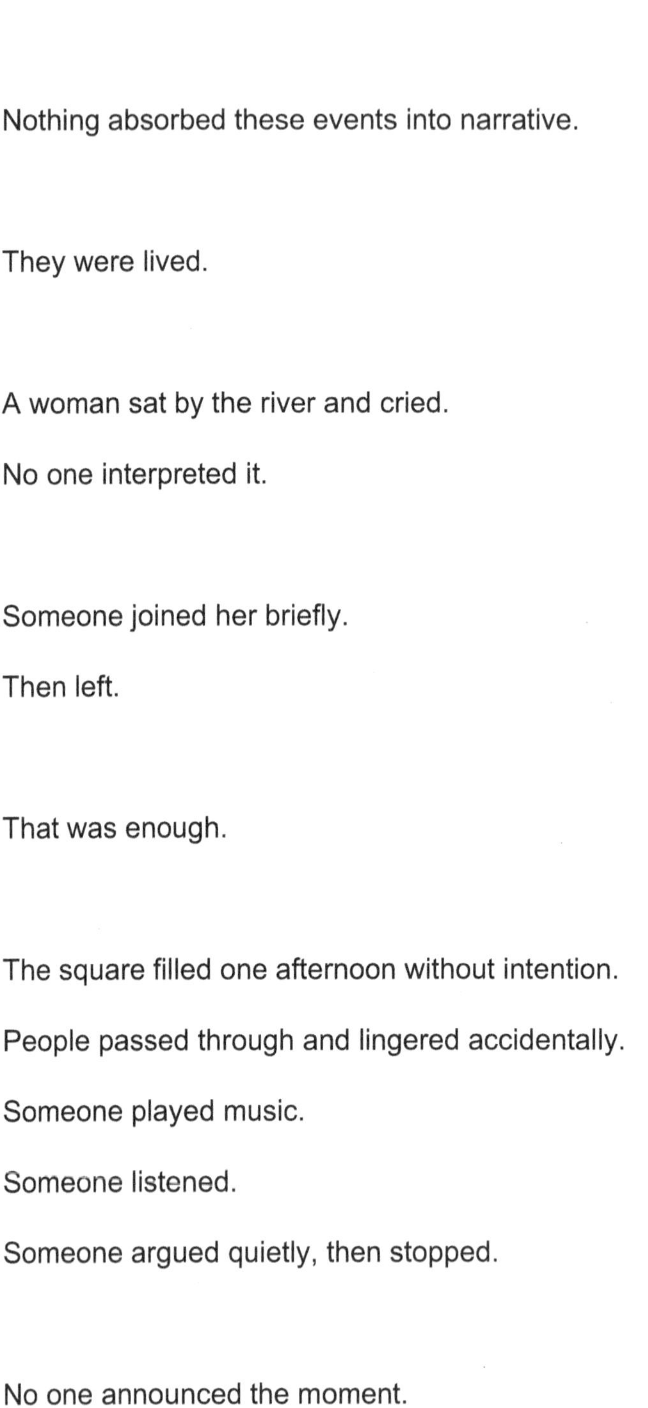

Nothing absorbed these events into narrative.

They were lived.

A woman sat by the river and cried.

No one interpreted it.

Someone joined her briefly.

Then left.

That was enough.

The square filled one afternoon without intention.

People passed through and lingered accidentally.

Someone played music.

Someone listened.

Someone argued quietly, then stopped.

No one announced the moment.

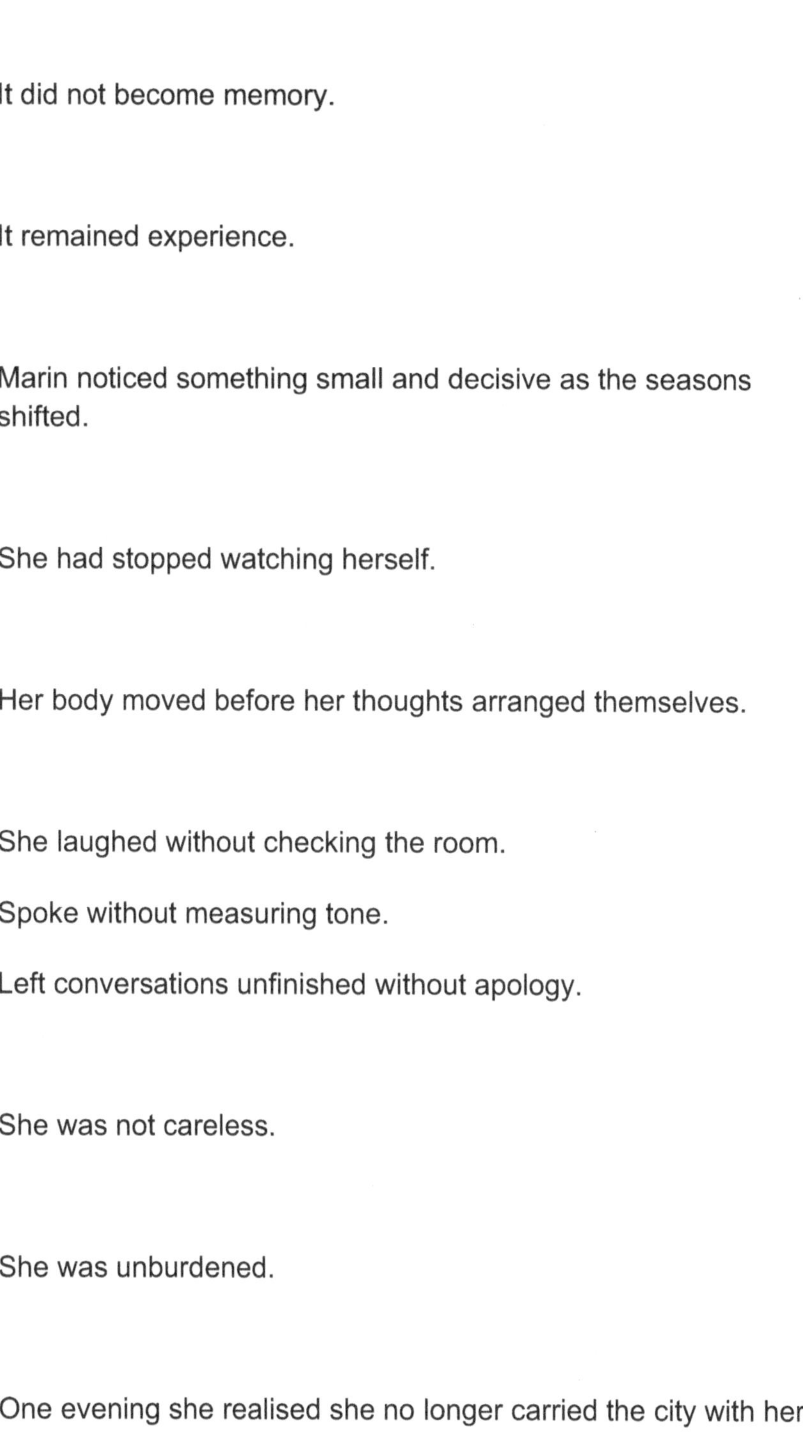

It did not become memory.

It remained experience.

Marin noticed something small and decisive as the seasons shifted.

She had stopped watching herself.

Her body moved before her thoughts arranged themselves.

She laughed without checking the room.

Spoke without measuring tone.

Left conversations unfinished without apology.

She was not careless.

She was unburdened.

One evening she realised she no longer carried the city with her.

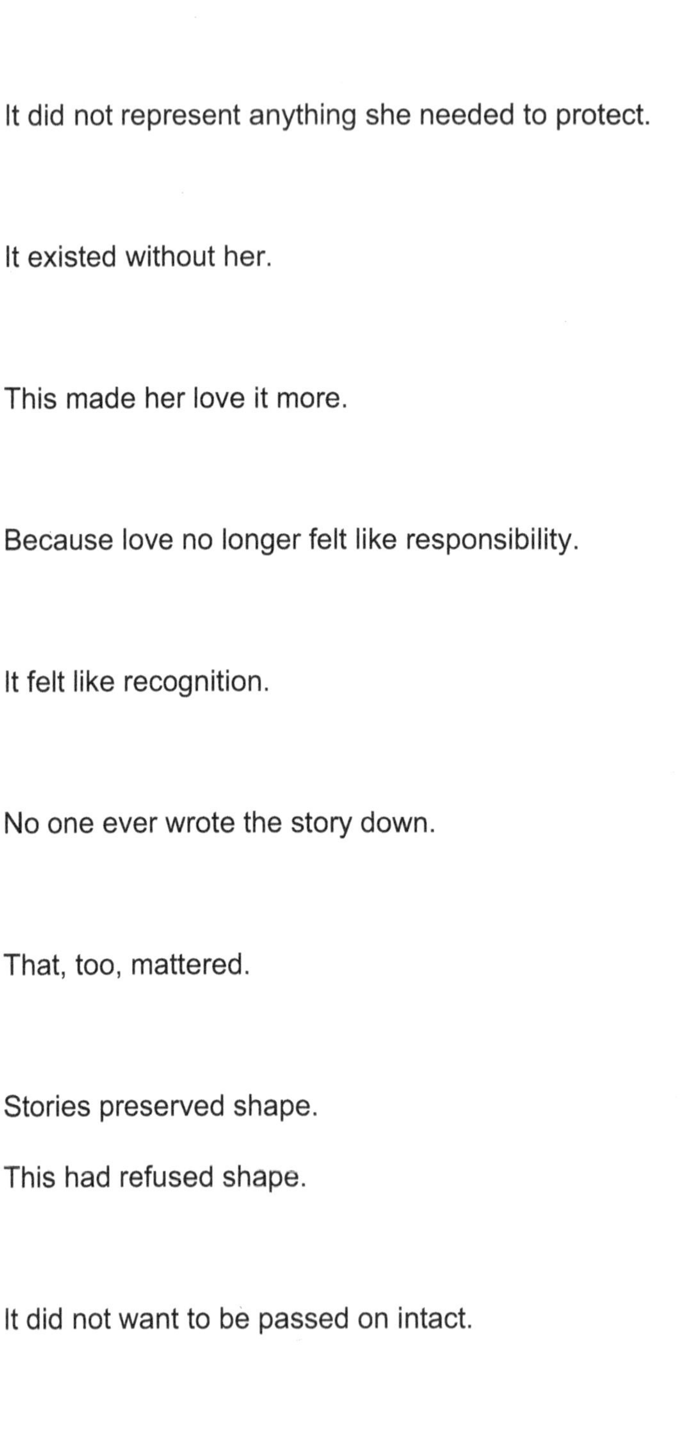

It did not represent anything she needed to protect.

It existed without her.

This made her love it more.

Because love no longer felt like responsibility.

It felt like recognition.

No one ever wrote the story down.

That, too, mattered.

Stories preserved shape.

This had refused shape.

It did not want to be passed on intact.

It wanted to be rediscovered.

Again.

And again.

Years later—though no one would call them that—someone sat quietly in a different place.

Another city.

Another square.

No one knew why they sat.

Not even them.

Nothing gathered.

Nothing changed.

And yet—

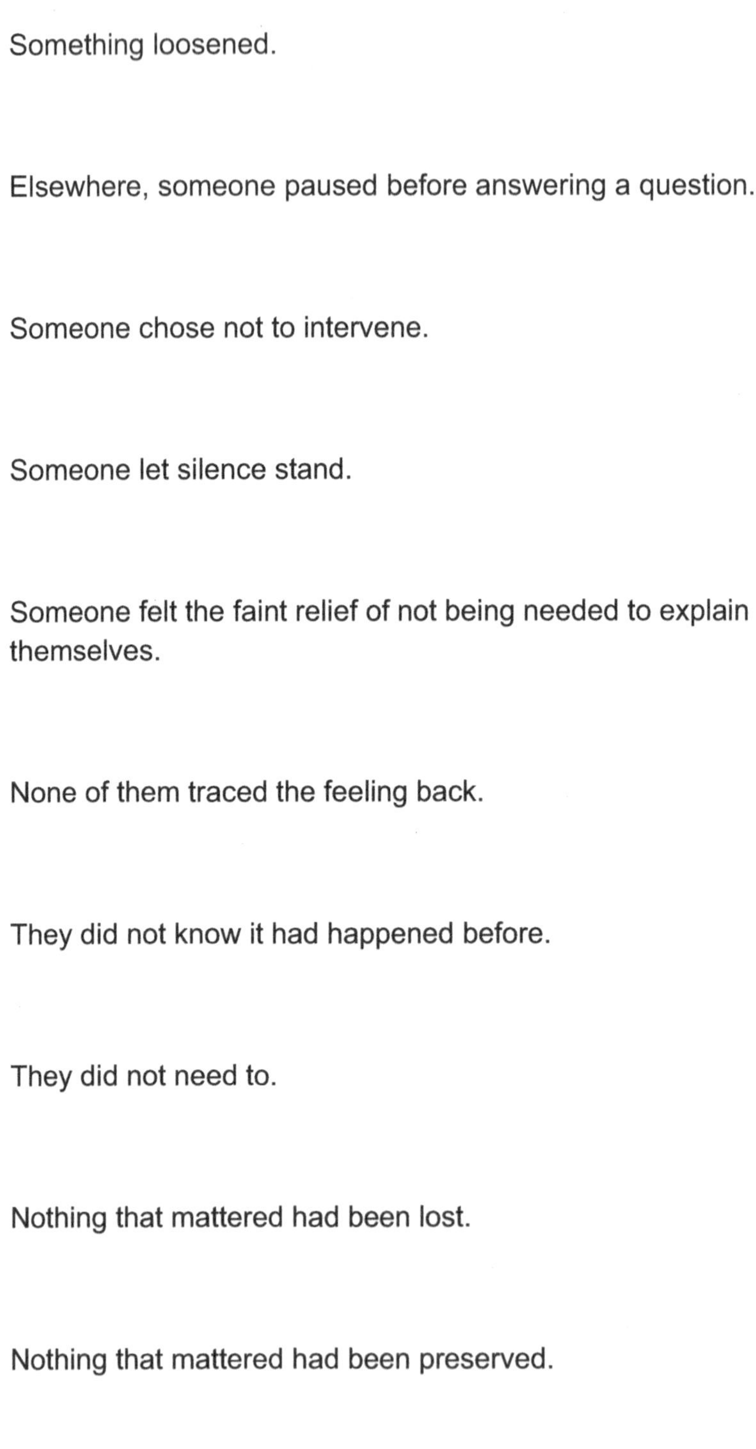

Something loosened.

Elsewhere, someone paused before answering a question.

Someone chose not to intervene.

Someone let silence stand.

Someone felt the faint relief of not being needed to explain themselves.

None of them traced the feeling back.

They did not know it had happened before.

They did not need to.

Nothing that mattered had been lost.

Nothing that mattered had been preserved.

It had simply learned how to move.

Quietly.

Without centre.

Without message.

Without permission.

And that was enough.

The city did not end.

The story did.

Not because it was finished.

But because it no longer needed telling.

And whoever closed the book did not feel instructed.

They felt… lighter.

As if something had been returned to them.

Something they had not realised they were carrying.

And now—

Were free to set it down.

Not to hold the centre.

Not to explain.

Not to defend.

Only to remain.

www.ingramcontent.com/pod-product-compliance
Lightning Source LLC
LaVergne TN
LVHW041103080826
845145LV00007B/1678

* 9 7 8 1 7 6 4 5 3 3 5 1 5 *